CALGARY PUBLIC LIBRARY

DEC 2018

OF MEN AND ANGELS

BY THE SAME AUTHOR

The Celibate
Pagan and her Parents
Easter
Unity
Good Clean Fun
A Sea Change
The Enemy of the Good
Jubilate
The Breath of Night
Widows and Orphans

OF MEN AND ANGELS

Michael Arditti

A

Arcadia Books Ltd
139 Highlever Road
London W10 6PH

www.arcadiabooks.co.uk

First published in the United Kingdom 2018
Copyright © Michael Arditti 2018

Michael Arditti has asserted his moral right to be identified as the author of this work in accordance with the Copyright, Designs and Patents Act, 1988.

All Rights Reserved. No part of this publication may be reproduced in any form or by any means without the written permission of the publishers.

A catalogue record for this book is available from the British Library.

ISBN 978-1-911350-26-2

Typeset in Minion by MacGuru Ltd
Printed and bound by TJ International, Padstow PL28 8RW

ARCADIA BOOKS DISTRIBUTORS ARE AS FOLLOWS:

in the UK and elsewhere in Europe:
BookSource
50 Cambuslang Road
Cambuslang
Glasgow G32 8NB

in Australia/New Zealand:
NewSouth Books
University of New South Wales
Sydney NSW 2052

For Philippe Bertrand

Then the LORD rained upon Sodom and upon Gomorrah
brimstone and fire from the LORD out of heaven;
And he overthrew those cities, and all the
plain, and all the inhabitants of the cities,
and that which grew upon the ground.

Genesis 19: 24–25

ONE

By the Rivers of Babylon

How do ye say, We are wise, and the law of the
Lord is with us? Lo, certainly in vain made
he it; the pen of the scribes is in vain.

Jeremiah 8: 8

It pleases you to picture me with wings. My natural element is air and humans have literal imaginations. But if you study the myths that have become your scriptures, you will struggle to find a single feather. Whatever the elaborations of later writers, the poets who first brought me to life in Canaan some three or four thousand years ago perceived me as unexceptional. Why else would they have shown Abraham and Lot offering me food, shelter and water to wash my dusty feet? Why else would they have made Sarah doubt my news that she was to bear a child?

It is not just my appearance that has been embellished over time. Having constructed an intricate Creation myth, you then agonised over the angels' place in it. Were we formed on the first day with the light, on the second with the sky, or on the fifth with the other flying creatures? Furthermore, what part did we play on the sixth day when God created you? That question at least I can answer. It was not we who helped to create you but you who created us. You wanted to bridge the gulf that had opened between heaven and earth. In your oldest stories, you have God walking with Adam, wrangling with Abraham and even wrestling with Jacob. But the more mindful that you grew of the majesty and mystery of God, the harder it was to envisage His approaching you in person. You needed intermediaries and came up with us.

I have the distinction of being the first angel named in your Bible: Gabriel. It may surprise you to learn that only three of us are identified in its pages, the others being Michael and Raphael – and even Raphael's place is contentious, since Protestants regard the Book of Tobit, in which he features, as apocryphal. In all, I make four undisputed appearances: two to Daniel explaining his visions; one to Zechariah announcing the birth of his son, John; and, of course, one to Mary, heralding the birth of Jesus. Meanwhile, tradition – or rather traditions, since there is no agreement even among adherents of the same faith – credits me with being the anonymous angel mentioned in several other episodes. So, to the Jews, it was I who averted the sacrifice of Isaac and rescued Shadrach, Meshach and Abednego from the fiery furnace. It was I who, according to Ezekiel, was sent to destroy Jerusalem (although, by then, as you shall see, I had experience of civic destruction). To the Christians, it was I who warned Joseph to flee from Herod, I who appeared to Jesus in Gethsemane and who rolled the stone away from His tomb. Nor does my role end with the Bible. Muslims believe that I dictated the Qur'an to Muhammad, accompanied him on his night journey to Jerusalem and was present at his death. Mormons believe that I am the spiritual incarnation of Noah and restored the priesthood keys to Joseph Smith.

My immediate concern is the very first story with which I am associated: that of Abraham and his extended family. Having encouraged the Egyptian slave, Hagar, to return to her mistress, Sarah, and apprised her of the imminent birth of her son, Ishmael, I visited Abraham in his tent, together with Michael and Raphael. Even here, however, there is no consensus about our respective roles. Christian tradition, no doubt anticipating my part in that far more momentous annunciation, depicts me announcing the birth of Isaac to Abraham and Sarah, while Jewish tradition affords that honour to Michael, leaving me with the less edifying task of annihilating Sodom. The ease with which I effect it – shattering the rock on which the sinful city stands with a single finger – is in inverse proportion to the devastation caused, the repercussions of which are still being felt by those trapped beneath the rubble.

It is not for me to question my allotted role. I am no more of a free agent in the human narrative than in the divine plan that it seeks to elucidate. Yet just as I cannot but admire your ability to turn timeworn myths into a subtle and enduring theology, so I cannot but deplore the consequences. And looking back at the earliest account of events in Sodom, I am amazed at the difference from the story that later became canonical. Indeed, my fellow angels and I barely appear at all.

THE ACTS OF ABRAHAM AND LOT, HIS BROTHER'S SON, AND THEIR GOD, YAHWEH, WRITTEN ACCORDING TO THE ANCIENT ROLL BY JARED, SON OF MICAIAH, IN THE THIRTY-FIRST YEAR OF NEBUCHADREZZAR, KING OF BABYLON

A certain man dwelt in Ur in the land of the twin rivers, whose name was Terah. And Terah begat three sons and one daughter: Nahor and Abraham, these two did Yona bear unto him; and Haran and Sarah, these two did Tehevita bear unto him.

And Haran took a wife in those days and the wife of Haran conceived and bore him a son and he called his name Lot, and she conceived and bore him a daughter and he called her name Milcah.

And Nahor and Abraham also took unto them wives; the name of Nahor's wife was Milcah, the daughter of his brother, Haran; the name of Abraham's wife was Sarah, the daughter of his father, Terah.

But Sarah was barren; she bare no child.

And it came to pass that Kindattu, King of Elam, looked upon the plenteousness of Ur: the palaces and the temples and the treasure-houses of silver and gold and precious stones. And he made league with the Kassites that dwelt in the heights of the Zagros, and he gathered together all his armies and his horses and his chariots and they descended upon the city, like as wolves greedy of their prey.

They broke down the walls of the city and they burnt all the houses with fire: the palace of the king's house, and the temples, and every great man's house and all that was therein burnt they with fire; only the silver and the gold and the precious stones and the vessels of brass and of iron they took with them out of the city.

Then Haran, son of Terah, entered into the burning temple to deliver the image of the moon god, Sin, which Terah and his sons and his sons' wives and his kinsmen and his bondmen were wont to worship every Sabbath, that is the Festival of the New Moon. But the flames consumed his body like the meat offering that was laid upon the altar.

And Terah and his sons, and his son's son, Lot, all did grieve sorely for Haran that was slain.

But the Lord came unto Abraham in the visions of the night, saying, Why grievest thou for thy brother Haran, who cleaved unto a false god? It is I, Yahweh, who alone can save thee from the wrath of Elam and the vengeance of the Kassites. It is I, Yahweh, son of the great El, king of the gods and ruler over all the earth, whom alone thou shouldst worship.

And Abraham was troubled, even in his sleep, and he answered him, saying, Tell me, Lord, what wouldst thou have me do?

And the Lord answered, Get thee out of thy country, and from thy kindred and from thy father's house, unto a land that I will show thee. And I will bless thee and make thy name great among all nations and thou shalt prosper in all that thou dost.

So Abraham departed as the Lord had told him and he took with him Terah his father, and Sarah his wife, she that was barren and bare no child, and Lot, the son of his brother Haran, with his herdmen and his bondmen and his flocks and his cattle. And they journeyed north across the hills and high places and entered into Canaan.

Now Terah waxed exceeding old and gave up the ghost in the wilderness, far from the land of his fathers. Abraham and Lot did honour him in his death, making baldness upon their heads and cutting off the extremities of their beards. They made doleful lamentations over him like the cries of the ostrich and they buried him in the valley of the mountains.

They removed from thence unto a mountain east of Bethel and they pitched their tents thereupon. And Abraham did look about him and, behold, he saw that the land was most fruitful. There grew the vine, the hazel, the cypress and the myrtle; the cedar, the olive tree, the incense tree and all the trees of the wilderness.

And there was water upon the mountain.

And Abraham blessed the Lord that had brought him out of Ur and led him into Canaan. He built an altar unto Yahweh and unto Asherah, his wife, upon the mountain. He took him a goat, a ram, a turtle-dove and a pigeon to the altar. He cleaved them in twain and sprinkled the blood upon the altar and he made a meat offering to Yahweh upon the altar that he would be with him and that he would not abandon him all his life.

Now all that the Lord did promise was performed. Abraham gained dominion over the highways and the byways, the rivers and the springs of the plains and the watering places of the wilderness, and he did exact tribute from all the companies that journeyed thereon.

And Abraham increased abundantly and Lot, his brother's son, increased abundantly alongside him. And Lot took for a wife Idrith from the daughters of Canaan.

And Abraham rejoiced exceedingly for all that was his, save for his wife Sarah that was barren. And Abraham and Sarah cried towards Yahweh and Asherah. And Abraham made them meat offerings of the firstlings of his flocks and herds and drink offerings of the blood of grapes. But they had shut up Sarah's womb.

Now there was a drought upon the land, that dried up the springs, and Abraham went down into Egypt with Sarah his wife to sojourn there; for the famine was grievous in the land.

And when he was come near to enter into Egypt, he said unto Sarah his wife, Behold now I know that thou art a fair woman to look upon and thine eyes are like to kindle the lusts of the Egyptians. Therefore say not that thou art my wife, lest they will kill me but they will save thee alive. Say, I pray thee, that thou art my sister, that it may be well with me for thy sake, and my soul shall live because of thee.

And it came to pass that the woman was brought unto Pharaoh and she found favour in his eyes and for her sake he entreated Abraham well. And that night Pharaoh took her into his house and he did defile her.

And the Lord plagued Pharaoh and all which were of his house, his menservants and his maidservants and his eunuchs, with great plagues because of Sarah, Abraham's wife. He smote them with the scab and with the itch, and with the emerods and with the burning ague, and with the botch from the soles of their feet unto the tops of their heads.

And Pharaoh called all the physicians of Egypt and all the wise men and the sorcerers thereof, but they were as broken reeds for they could not restore him to health.

Then the Lord appeared to Pharaoh in a dream, saying, It is I, Yahweh, that hath done these things unto thee for that thou hast committed whoredoms with Sarah, the wife of my servant Abraham. Send her away that these afflictions might be lifted from thee.

When Pharaoh heard these words, his soul was vexed and he called Abraham and said to him, What is this that thou hast done to me? How saidst thou to me, She is my sister, when behold of a surety she is thy wife? And Abraham said unto him, Because I feared I should die for her.

And yet indeed she is my sister; she is the daughter of my father, but not the daughter of my mother; and she became my wife.

Then Pharaoh returned Sarah to Abraham. And he gave her silver and gold and clothing of fine linen and purple, and bondservants that were of his house and also Hagar, that was the daughter of his concubine, to be her handmaid.

And he gave Abraham silver and gold and oxen and sheep

and he asses and she asses and menservants and maidservants for the sake of Sarah his wife.

And Pharaoh said unto Abraham, Let us make peace between your god and my gods, for we have seen the great and terrible things thy god hath done.

And Abraham took a blade of flint, and for a token of his covenant with Pharaoh he did circumcise the flesh of his foreskin, after the manner of the Egyptians. And he did circumcise the flesh of the foreskins of all his bondmen, they that were born of his house and they that were bought with money of the stranger.

And Abraham gave thanks to Yahweh, his god, for the covenant that he had cut with Pharaoh.

And Abraham departed out of Egypt, and with him Sarah and all that he had. He journeyed from the south through Negeb, even unto Bethel where he had first pitched his tent. There he found Lot, who marvelled to see how great Abraham was grown.

So Abraham ascended up to the mountain and to the altar that he had built there unto the Lord. He put off his shoes from his feet, and he covered his face, and he knelt upon his knees, and he spread forth his hands toward heaven. He made a meat offering and a drink offering and he praised the name of Yahweh for all the flocks and the treasures that he had bestowed on him and that he had brought him safe out of Egypt.

But Sarah his wife was no longer pleasing in his sight, for that she bore the stain of Pharaoh. And he bade her that she should purify herself of her uncleanness. And the woman said to him, My Lord, turn not away thy face from me, for did I not hearken unto thy words in all that thou commandest me and say that thou wert my brother?

But the heart of Abraham was hardened against Sarah his wife and, when she came unto him at night, he was as a withered sapling.

Then again the Lord appeared unto Abraham, saying, I am Yahweh that brought thee from Ur of Sumer to give possession of this land to thee and to thy seed forever.

And Abraham answered and said, How shalt this be, for behold thou hast given me no seed? Thou hast shrivelled the womb of Sarah my wife like a wineskin in the smoke. I have no heir of my blood but Lot, the son of my brother which is dead. To him and his seed hast thou given this land.

And the Lord said unto him, This shall not be thine heir; but he that shall come forth out of thine own bowels shall be thine heir.

And Abraham wondered at the words of the Lord and he hastened into the tent unto Sarah, though she was grown cold to his touch since they had passed out of Egypt.

And every Sabbath, when the new moon was come, he took an heifer and a she goat and an ewe lamb to be an offering unto Yahweh and Asherah, and did sprinkle the blood round about upon the altar that he had built. But the fountain of Sarah's blood still flowed.

Now Sarah was fearful and afraid lest her lord put her away. So she brought Hagar her maid the Egyptian before him, saying, Behold now the Lord hath restrained me from bearing. I pray thee, go in unto my maid Hagar; and she shall bear children upon my knees, that I may also have children by her.

And Abraham hearkened to the voice of Sarah. And he went in unto Hagar, and she conceived and bare him a son: and Abraham called the name of his son which Hagar bare him, Ishmael.

And Abraham called Lot unto him and said, Now that I have a son of my bone and flesh, thou shalt no longer be mine heir and do me honour at my death. And Lot was in bitterness of soul that he must humble himself before the issue of a concubine.

And it came to pass that Abraham looked upon the sheep

and the goats of Lot that swallowed up the increase of the earth and he was full of wrath and did require of him the firstlings of his flocks and his herds for a tithe.

And Lot said to him, Did I not put the portion of Haran my father with thy portion? Did not my bondmen dig the wells of water with thy bondmen? Why shouldst thou now require of me the firstlings of my flocks for a tithe?

Then Abraham was ashamed and said unto him, Let there be no strife between thee and me and between my bondmen and thy bondmen; for we be brethren. Behold is not the whole land before thee? Separate thyself, I pray thee, from me.

And let there now be an oath betwixt us, even between me and thee, and let us distribute the land for an inheritance. And Lot put his hand under the thigh of Abraham and they divided the land.

And Abraham took for his portion all the land from the plains of Mamre to Beersheba, from the east side to the west side, and Lot took for his portion all the land from the springs of Jericho to the south of the salt sea.

But the land that Abraham had appointed to Lot was lean and barren. Neither in the high hills in summer neither in the valleys in winter found he pasture for his flocks. And he came unto Sodom and he made league with the king of Sodom to pay him tribute.

And Lot increased exceedingly in Sodom. He fed his flocks in the fallow ground without the city; he sent forth his companies to and fro throughout the land; he spake wise counsel unto the king of Sodom. But the men of Sodom trusted him not, for that he was a stranger.

And when his daughters were come to years and it was with them after the manner of women, he brought them unto the priests of the temple and they did give the first issue of their bodies to the moon god that he might drop down dew upon the fields in summer. But still the men of Sodom trusted him not.

Now Hagar, Abraham's concubine, grew slothful in her work and ate the bread of idleness. She looked not unto the hand of Sarah her mistress.

And Sarah rebuked and chastised her, but Hagar answered her and said, The gods have endued me with a good dowry, for I have borne my lord a son of his loins. Thy breasts are dry as the wilderness of Sinai but mine are fat and full as the plains of Jezreel.

Then Sarah went in secret up to the mountain and made a drink offering unto Asherah. She fell before the image on her face, and bowed herself to the ground, and wept sore, and prayed to the queen of heaven that she would be mindful of her tears and open the doors of her womb.

And she sunk down with a deep sleep, but having her eyes open, and she saw a light above the brightness of the stars, and she heard a voice speaking unto her and she was dismayed.

And the voice like as the pleasant harp said unto her, Prepare a pottage of the seeds of lotus, with fat meat, eggs and the milk from a young she goat, and serve it unto thy lord and he shall once more be as the stalk of the lotus plant in thy bed.

And the woman did according to all that the voice had bidden her, and she fed Abraham her lord with the pottage, and he went in unto her and she conceived. And when she saw that she did conceive, she sent word to her brother's son, Lot, saying, Rejoice with me for my reproach hath been lifted from me.

And Lot rejoiced that the days of Sarah were turned from wormwood to honey. But Idrith his wife was troubled and said unto him, Take heed, for if the babe be a boy, then he must be heir to all the lands and goods whereof thine uncle is possessed. Therefore give not thine elder daughter to the son of his concubine but take husbands for the elder and the younger alike from the men of the city.

And Lot hearkened to her words and betrothed the damsels to those that were about him. And when Abraham heard these things, anger burned within him and he sent Eliezer his steward unto Sodom to require that Lot should turn and repent.

And Eliezer entered into the city. Lot seeing him rose up to meet him and brought him unto his house and bade him rest. And he sent forth his daughters to fetch water from the cistern that he might wash his feet. And he set before him meat, and cakes of bread, and pomegranates, and nuts and almonds, and they did eat.

At even he spread out skins upon the housetop whereupon the man might lie, for it was the drought of summer. And Eliezer laid himself down and slept.

But he was raised from his sleep by a great bruit, for the men of Sodom did riot in the street. And he called unto Lot and asked him straitly, saying, What manner of mischief is this?

And Lot answered and said, It is the men of the city, both old and young, retiring from the fields where they danced with all their might before Baal. They set up his image under the green bay tree and spilled their seed of copulation to the god.

Then Eliezer was astonished and wagged his head and cried out with a loud voice that it was a detestable thing and an abomination before Yahweh. But Lot besought him to refrain his mouth for he was a stranger and a gazing stock in the city.

And Eliezer returned to Abraham his master and said to him, The men of Sodom shall be an execration unto all the earth. They defile the land with their witchcrafts and their wickedness. They whore after Baal in the night, spilling their seed to gain his favour.

When Abraham heard the voice of his words, his anger waxed hot and he sware, saying, The men of Sodom are like untimely figs, which cannot be eaten they are so vile. Even as Yahweh slew all the sons of El to rule over the heavens and the earth, so will I smite all those that do worship strange gods.

But when Sarah his wife heard this, she was affrighted for her kindred in Sodom. She adjured Abraham, saying, Cause not the fierceness of thy wroth to fall upon the city, but spare it for the sake of the child that quickens in my belly. But Abraham heeded her not.

So she went again up to the mountain and she offered a meat offering and a drink offering unto Yahweh and called upon the Lord that he would melt the heart of Abraham.

And the Lord appeared unto her, saying, Sarah thou art weak as is the way with women. Thou must walk in the statutes of Abraham thy lord and ever esteem his precepts. Yet will I send forth my messengers unto the city that they mark and see what manner of men they are. For I know not the reins and hearts of the men of Sodom.

And I swear unto thee this oath that, if they find even ten that honour me within the city, I will stay Abraham's hand.

And there came two angels of Yahweh to Sodom at even; and Lot sat in the gate of Sodom where he trafficked among the merchantmen. And Lot seeing them rose up to meet them; and he bowed himself with his face bowed toward the ground.

And he said, Behold now, my lords, come in, I pray you, into your servant's house, and tarry all night, and wash your feet, and ye shall rise up early, and go on your ways. And he pressed upon them greatly; and they turned in unto him, and entered into his house.

And Lot reverenced them and prepared great provision for them and set before them salted kid and barley cakes and clusters of raisins. And they did eat and were satisfied.

And he brought them up upon the housetop and spread out coverings of skins. But before they lay down, the men of the city beheld them and compassed the house round, both old and young, all the people from every quarter:

And they called unto Lot, and said unto him, What are these that came in to thee this night? Bring them out unto us, that we may know them. Shew them to us that we may see whether they be true men or spies.

And Lot went out at the door unto them, and shut the door after him, and said, I pray you brethren, let me not be put to shame. These men are in my safeguard. They did sit at meat with me. I am charged to preserve them until the salt has quit their bellies.

Behold, here are my daughters, maidens that have known no men. Yea, I had rather that you took by force these virgins than that you turn your hands upon these men.

And they that heard him were astonished and had him in derision. And Idrith his wife said unto him, These are my daughters that I have given suck. Dost thou forsake thine own seed for strangers? But Lot understood what appertained unto all them that came under the shadow of his roof.

And the men of Sodom pressed sore upon him, even upon Lot, and came near to break down the door. But the angels put forth their hand, and pulled Lot into the house to them, and shut the door.

And they smote the men that were at the door of the house, both small and great, with blindness: so that they wearied themselves to find the door.

And the angels said unto Lot, Hast thou here any besides thy wife and thy daughters and thy sons in law? Make haste and bring them forth from this place: for thou, even thou only, in this city art righteous in the eyes of the Lord. The Lord Yahweh is a jealous god. He will strengthen thy kinsman Abraham and stretch out his sword upon all those who profane his name.

And Lot went out and spake to his sons in law, which were betrothed to his daughters, and said, Up, get you out of this place: for the Lord Yahweh will destroy this city. But they hissed at him, saying, Are not the walls of Sodom six cubits thick? Is not the thunderbolt of Baal mightier than the sword of Yahweh?

And when the morning arose, Idrith lingered in her chamber. She spake unto Lot, saying, Shall I leave the sweetness of the city and dwell once more in a tent of goat hair? Shall I no longer guide mine own house but bear the yoke of Abraham?

While she did yet beseech him, the angels laid hold upon her hand, and upon the hand of Lot, and upon the hand of his two daughters; the Lord being merciful unto them: and they brought them forth, and set them without the city.

And the angels said unto them, Escape for your lives lest the men of the city do take you in hostage. Look not behind ye lest you should see the city laid waste and desolate, and fall into despair.

And it came to pass that Abraham rose up and marched upon Sodom. He built a fort against it and set engines of war round about it. He broke down the towers with his axes and with ladders mounted its walls.

And the men of Abraham fell upon the city and they smote all the men thereof with the edge of the sword, and the women and the children, and every beast, and all that came to hand, utterly destroying them: there was not any left to breathe. And a great flame of smoke rose up from out of the city.

And the heart of Abraham was lifted up and he gave thanks unto Yahweh his lord that did rule over all the nations and did drive out his enemies like dust before the east wind.

But when Sarah his wife, that was big with child, lifted up her eyes afar off, she was still and exulted not in the punishment of the city.

And the angels of Yahweh led Lot and his wife and his daughters over the plain even unto the salt sea. And when evening was come, they were weary and laid themselves down to rest.

But Idrith looked behind her toward the ruinous city. And her heart was full of heaviness and she found no consolation. She gathered up stones from the edge of the sea and bound them in the border of her robe. And she cast herself into the sea and was drowned.

And when Lot rose up early on the morrow, he found her laid on the shore like a meat offering seasoned with salt.

Then Lot and his daughters took Idrith up into the mountains to bury her in a cave, after their manner. And Lot laid off his mantle and rent his garment. He covered his head in earth and he sat in ashes. He lamented her and howled like as the jackal in the wilderness.

And Lot took his daughters in his arms to comfort them, one upon his right breast and one upon his left.

1

Jared, son of Micaiah, harboured a shameful secret. Unlike his fellow exiles, he did not dream of returning to Jerusalem and rebuilding the temple but, rather, of remaining in Babylon, enjoying the adventure, and becoming a trusted advisor to the king.

In truth, he had few happy memories of Jerusalem. He had been four years old when the enemy forces laid siege to the city, and six when they finally destroyed its defences. He could still recall his excitement at his first sight of the earthworks encircling the walls, swiftly followed by guilt in the face of his family's fear. But his abiding memory was of boredom – intense, interminable boredom – when his mother forbade him to leave the house in case he were hit by one of the stones or arrows, which, according to her, the wicked King Nebuchadrezzar was aiming directly at him. Her vigilance was mocked by months of inertia, until a sudden spate of missiles led her to look wretchedly at his father and triumphantly at him.

He remembered the hunger that made an echoing well of his stomach and the soups prepared from weeds that grew in the paving and which tasted like puddles, although he knew better than to grumble since both Asaph and Shimron explained that the soups were far more repugnant to their mother, whose cooking had once been renowned. He remembered the dispute between Seraiah, the high priest, who insisted that the last remaining goat in the Temple precinct be sacrificed to the Lord and the officials who declared that He had abandoned them and they should use it to feed themselves.

He remembered too the predatory looks on the gaunt faces of people in the street, which lent credence to Asaph's claim that in the poorer districts they were eating corpses, gnawing at their bones like the wild beasts that Asaph had previously invoked to scare him. But this time, when he repeated the story to his mother, she made no attempt to reassure him and simply muttered a prayer.

So, as he admitted to his pillow, it was almost a relief when the enemy finally breached the walls. Soldiers in glinting helmets clambered through the cracks and clattered through the streets. Some of the young men fought back, but they were ill-equipped, half-starved and exhausted. Jubilant shouts, barked commands and chilling screams rent the air, mingling with the measured lamentations of the Levites in the Temple. Later, on the gruelling trek to Babylonia, he heard talk of how the soldiers rampaged through the city, cutting throats as casually as pomegranates. At this, the men would curse – long, cold curses that seemed to come from somewhere way beyond anger – and the women would spit, even though their mouths were dry. They called the Babylonians monsters, which worried him since, try as he might, he could not forget the story of King David massacring 22,000 Arameans in a single battle. There were only 12,000 people living in the whole of Jerusalem and the soldiers had barely killed half of them. So if the Babylonians were wicked, that must make the Judeans even worse.

After the initial carnage, the soldiers scoured the city, rounding up all the men. His father, having forbidden Asaph and Shimron to resist in a voice that seemed to echo from Mount Sinai, now ordered the entire family to await its fate with *dignity*: a new word to Jared, which he took to mean *silence* since no one spoke, not even his garrulous aunt. When the soldiers came, his mother forgot her dignity and, in a moment as thrilling as it was frightening, she screamed and leapt on the man who had hold of Asaph, until she in turn was restrained by his aunt. 'What's to become of us?' she cried, as the soldiers dragged off their three captives, which was a double waste of a question when the officer had already told them in plain, if heavily accented, Hebrew to prepare to leave for Babylonia and she might have asked something useful like 'When will you give us some food?'

For the next three days nobody entered or left the house, but the voices wafting up from the Temple courtyard kept them abreast of the news. King Zedekiah and his sons had escaped through a secret passage in the palace gardens, only to be recaptured near Jericho and led before King Nebuchadrezzar at Riblah, where the princes were beheaded in full view of their father. Then, as if determined that nothing should displace that image, King Nebuchadrezzar had gouged out King Zedekiah's eyes with his own hands, which was the cruellest torture Jared could imagine. He tentatively pressed the spongy flesh above his eyelids, until his mother asked him what he thought he was doing, her tone suggesting that she knew.

Her repeated insistence that life was meaningless without her husband and sons, which Jared could not help but find hurtful, was confounded by their sudden reappearance. Screeching as if she had stood on something wriggly, she clasped them to her, all three at once, refusing to let go for an instant. She pressed her head to his father's chest and stroked Asaph and Shimron's cheeks, before sinking to her knees and weeping even more fiercely than when she had thought them dead. His father helped her to her feet and hugged her, while his aunt, who was grateful for everything, moved to his brothers, laughing and crying and kissing their hands. Jared held back, his genuine relief at their return tempered by his renewed subordination. Then his father swept him up in his arms; Shimron ruffled his hair; and Asaph gave him a punch that, for once, was not intended to hurt.

His father described their escape, drawing it out as if it were a sacred story. They too had been taken to Riblah, along with the priests, doorkeepers, temple officials and fellow scribes. They were all sentenced to death since King Nebuchadrezzar blamed them for encouraging King Zedekiah to break his oath of allegiance. Their own sentence was revoked after the intervention of Jeremiah, whom King Nebuchadrezzar favoured for his staunch support of the Babylonian cause, which was what had made him hated in Jerusalem. On one occasion, Jared's father and grandfather, Gemariah, had saved him from an angry mob who were threatening to stone him for treason. Jeremiah now pleaded for Micaiah and his sons to the king, who spared their lives. For this, Jared was prepared to forgive the prophet his scratchy voice and mouldy smell and even his way of resting his hand on a boy's head without asking.

With his father and brothers' return, Jared was impatient to set off for Babylonia, although he knew better than to say so out loud. This was the second mass deportation of the Judeans, and his parents and Shimron and even Asaph, who claimed – unconvincingly to Jared's mind – to remember the first one ten years earlier, failed to understand why the order to leave was delayed. The reason soon became clear. This time King Nebuchadrezzar was not content merely to break the city's resistance; he aimed to destroy its soul. Day after day, people watched in horror as the soldiers set about systematically demolishing the Temple. First, they pulled down the gilded bronze pillars that stood on either side of the porch and were so huge that they had been given names – Jachin and Boaz – like mountains. Next, they ripped the carvings off the walls and melted down the incense burners and candelabras on the very altar that had served for sacrifice. Then, they committed the worst of all crimes by entering the Holiest Place, which was forbidden to everyone but the high priest since it housed the Ark of the Covenant. This, in a way that Jared did not fully comprehend, was Yahweh's throne in Jerusalem.

He knew that something terrible must be happening when

the group of women who stood in the Temple courtyard from morning to night, weeping and wailing and beating their breasts at each fresh desecration, fell silent, their silence more penetrating than any scream. His father, who was standing beside him at their upper window, ordered him to close his eyes. He tried to obey but curiosity overcame him and he peeped at the dozen men staggering down the steps beneath a massive statue of a lion with an eagle's wings and a man's face. He took this to be the Ark until, after loading it precariously on a cart and driving away, they brought out an identical creature. Finally, four men emerged shouldering a large golden chest, which looked wide enough but too unstable to be a throne. From his father's strangled sobs, Jared knew that this must be the Ark.

'Where will the Lord sit now that they've stolen the Ark?' he asked.

'Nowhere. He has abandoned us forever,' Micaiah said through tears he made no attempt to hide. Jared clasped his hand, feeling at once grown-up and alone.

The day of departure dawned at last. By bribing one of the sentinels, Shimron had procured a donkey and cart, which Jared's mother filled with jars, pots and bedding, his father's writing tablets and seals, while insisting that anything inessential – in which she included Jared's hoop and jump-rope and even the three minuscule mouse skulls that she would never have noticed had he not mentioned them – be left behind. They joined the long line of people gathered at the Fish Gate: a few like themselves with carts; the majority weighed down with baggage. Jared blushed to see his two best friends, Hushim and Calev, both sons of executed priests, who would have to make the journey on foot while he sat in state with his mother and aunt. He wondered whether to clutch his ankle in a phantom sprain, but he was afraid that Asaph and Shimron, who were walking on either side of the cart while his father led the donkey, would taunt him.

The soldiers marked their exit with music: banging drums; blowing trumpets; shaking timbrels; and plucking some sort of stringed instrument that Jared had never heard before. The sound was so stirring that he would have been happy to listen to it all the way to Babylonia, until he glanced at the downcast faces of his family and wondered if it were because he was still a boy that he felt things differently from everyone else.

They trundled down the rocky path into the Kidron Valley, but he knew better than to wince for, however painful it might be for him, it was far worse for his aunt, who was so delicate that she had never married. There was no respite when they reached the plain where, having goaded them on all morning, the soldiers made them wait in the scorching sun with no protection but their sodden kerchiefs. The delay was explained when a second squad of soldiers arrived with King Zedekiah, his ankles fettered and crusts grown over his eye sockets like freshly filled graves. He shuffled and stumbled, dragging himself along in the face of Babylonian mockery and Judean blame. Suddenly a cry rent the air, as clear as one voice and as compelling as a thousand, and Jared turned to catch sight of Jerusalem in flames, a thick pall of smoke drifting across a premature sunset, as though the entire city were a sacrifice to an implacable god.

'A second Sodom,' his aunt said quietly.

'What's Sodom?' Jared asked.

'A town that the Lord destroyed in the time of Abraham,' his mother replied, giving his aunt one of her remember-he's-only-six looks.

'Why?' asked Jared, who could never forgive Abraham for his readiness to slay his son.

'Because the children asked too many questions,' his mother replied crisply.

Despite the heat and the dust and the gnats and the jolts, the start of the journey exhilarated Jared, who had only been out of the city twice since his fourth birthday, during the brief interlude when the enemy raised its siege to fight the Egyptians. He was almost sick with excitement on arriving at Tyre, where he had his first sight of the sea: the real sea, not just the Sea of Bronze where the priests washed their hands and feet in the Temple courtyard. But after two … three … four weeks on the move, the excitement waned. They passed great cities with magical names – Damascus, Riblah, Hamath – without once stopping. He was hungrier than he had been during the siege, although his mother told him that he had a short memory. Every day the soldiers gave them two bowls of porridge, which tasted like mud, and a gourd of water. He was always thirsty. The skin around his mouth was cracked, and his body was covered in scabs, but they were not the sort that were fun to pick. When they finally reached the Euphrates, they were jeered at and even stoned by farmers in the fields. One of them threw a root, which landed in the cart. Jared immediately began to chew it, but Asaph grabbed it from him and threw it back.

'Is it poisoned?' Jared asked.

'Will you let them humiliate you?'

Jared felt that the noises his stomach was making were humiliating enough.

Not all their party survived the journey. The first to die was the donkey, who kicked up his hind legs in a kind of dance and pitched forward, his mouth flecked with foam, leaving Asaph and Shimron to pull the cart between them. The second was his aunt, who grew increasingly withdrawn, not even flicking the flies from her face, until one morning they found her curled up in a corner of the cart, as inert as the bedding. Jared refused to ride beside the corpse, so for the rest of the day he walked with his father until his knees felt like knotted rope. When they stopped for the night, the soldiers gave them permission to take the body into a field, where his father said prayers and Jared thought about the donkey to make himself cry. With no burial place, they had to leave the body in the field, although his mother seemed more distressed that it was so far from their ancestors than that it might be eaten by lions.

Finally, four months after leaving home, they caught their first glimpse of Babylon. The city was so vast that its walls were visible when they were still three days' march away. But Jared's relief was short-lived since, far from entering the city, as he had expected, they continued their journey. He feared that they would never stop until they reached the edge of the world and the soldiers pushed them into the Chaos.

'How much longer will it be?' he asked, as the city vanished like an Egyptian promise.

'I swear to the Lord, if he asks that one more time, I'll strangle him,' Asaph said.

'Don't torment your brother,' their mother said, more mildly than Jared might have wished.

That had been eleven years ago, although the memory remained vivid. Jared's worst fears had been allayed when they stopped at Tel-Abib, a settlement a few days south of Babylon, which was home to thousands of Judeans from the previous deportation. Every night in Jerusalem, he had said a prayer for their safe return, even when there was too little food for those trapped inside the city. Their welcome now was so muted that he longed to retract his prayers. They made it clear that they blamed the new arrivals for a rebellion that had destroyed the trust they had painstakingly built up with their overlords. Jared's family was singled out for censure since Gedaliah, whom King Nebuchadrezzar had appointed as governor of Judah, was their cousin. Among his first decrees had been to redistribute estates from the exiles to their former labourers. It made sense to Jared that the land should be cultivated rather than left lying idle but, to the ousted owners, it was a double dispossession and signalled the permanence of their fate.

At first, each of the incoming families was lodged with an established one. Then they were allotted a house on a small plot of land belonging to the king. Jared was thrilled at the prospect of becoming a farmer, but his father, who had long extolled the simple lives of their ancestors, was less enthusiastic now that he had to follow suit. Moreover, as part of their tribute to the crown, Shimron was conscripted into the army. Orpah, their mother, was distraught and kept repeating a phrase from the prophet Isaiah about the righteous being doomed to perish, which Jared thought tactless. He was sorry for Shimron and felt that, if anyone had to perish, it should be Asaph, who would now be free to persecute him at will. But soon after Shimron's departure, Asaph was assigned to a team repairing the network of canals ravaged during the long war with Assyria. He left home every day before dawn and returned after dark, his hands raw from pulling out reeds and back strained from dredging silt, too tired to give Jared more than a token cuff.

Just as Micaiah was mortified that the grandson of the great Shaphan, the man who had promulgated the newly discovered Book of Law in the reign of King Josiah, should be reduced to manual labour, so Orpah deemed it humiliating for the granddaughter of the court chamberlain, Asaiah, to be living in a house with a dirt floor. She reserved her deepest rancour for the primitive sanitation. Neatly forgetting the years under siege when they had cleansed their skin with vinegar and the months on the road when they had defecated in fields, she railed against the water shortage that forced them to bathe in the irrigation canals and squat over a rough stone latrine.

Jared was bemused that his parents, who had instilled in him the duty of gratitude, should display so little of it themselves. But, since they had also instilled in him the duty to honour his father and mother, he kept his bemusement to himself.

In time, the tension between the two waves of exiles eased and Micaiah was elected as one of the community's elders. Beyond their day-to-day role in certifying contracts, judging disputes and negotiating with the authorities, their principal function was to ensure that the people upheld the Law and remained faithful to Yahweh. Since the Law decreed that Yahweh should be worshipped in the Temple and the Temple was many weeks' journey away and in ruins, they introduced a new form of service, gathering in the fields every rest day to pray and read the sacred stories. Jared had looked forward to the Temple services: not just the once-a-year ones such as Firstfruits and Tabernacles but the once-a-month ones on the Sabbath. He had thrilled to the Levites singing psalms, their voices seeming to rise from the depths of the Temple Mount, and the procession of priests, swathed in white from their tunics to their turbans. He had watched in a mixture of fascination and dread as the trussed-up beasts were led to the slaughter, some writhing and squealing and some preternaturally still, as though sensing the sanctity, before their throats were slit, their bodies dismembered, their blood sprinkled and flesh laid upon the altar. But now there were no priests and no sacrifices, just protracted recitations of rules and prayers and rules about prayers, such as turning in the direction of Jerusalem even in the glare of the sun or the middle of a dust storm.

The most boring services were the ones led by Ezekiel. He held forth at such length that Asaph swore that listening to him was as exhausting as digging a canal. He had the same piercing voice, curt manner and sour smell as Jeremiah, but, unlike Jeremiah, he claimed not merely to have been called by Yahweh but to have seen Him. While everyone else in Tel-Abib was ready to take him at his word, the discrepancies in his account – sometimes he described Yahweh as made of fire and sometimes of bronze and sometimes of both, even though the fire would have melted the bronze – fuelled Jared's suspicions. But when he suggested that Ezekiel might have made it up or else, he added quickly at the sight of his father's frown, that what Ezekiel called a vision might simply have been a dream, Micaiah whipped him for impiety, which made him resent the prophet all the more. He was convinced that, however much Ezekiel called on people to repent, he would be disappointed if they did since he would have no further cause to admonish them.

Ezekiel's wife had died, so Orpah sometimes invited him for a meal on an evening when Asaph had brought back a fish from work. Jared dreaded these occasions, when his mother apologised repeatedly for the food as if to remind their guest that they had known better days, and Ezekiel replied that he never noticed what he ate, which sounded rude but must have been true since, prior to their arrival in Tel-Abib, he had lain on his mat for over a year eating bread made of cow dung. During these visits, Jared was under strict instructions not to speak out of turn, in other words not to speak at all, which wasn't hard since Ezekiel scarcely drew breath. Asaph, who regarded Ezekiel as a Babylonian lackey, maintained that he was in love with his own voice. Micaiah, more generously, said that he considered it his duty to disseminate knowledge imparted to him by the Lord.

Ezekiel, who as a young priest had been present on the momentous day when Shaphan first read the Book of Law to King Josiah, retained a deep respect for members of Shaphan's family, with one exception: the scribe's youngest son, Jared's great-uncle, Jaazaniah. He too had been exiled with King Jehoiachin but, as royal recorder, he had been confined in King Nebuchadrezzar's palace before being released to serve as Judean representative at court.

'He abandoned his birthright and married a Babylonian whore,' Ezekiel said, with the particular animus he reserved for female failings.

'What's a whore?' Jared asked, eager for Ezekiel to explain his favourite word.

'A woman who worships foreign gods,' his father said quickly.

'A woman who sells herself to men,' his brother said with a smirk.

'Like a slave?' Jared asked.

'That's right,' his father said, scowling at Asaph.

'So we're all whores?' Jared asked. 'Ow!' he cried, as his father slapped his head. 'You said that we're all slaves in Tel-Abib.'

As the years went by, with the people still in servitude, it was clear that the Sabbath services were not enough to restore them to Yahweh's favour. With no Temple in which to sacrifice, the only way that they could approach the Lord was through His sacred stories and the only way that they could atone for their sins was through rigorous observance of His laws. Urged on by Ezekiel, the elders proposed to make a definitive copy of their scriptures. With the sacred scrolls abandoned – and in all likelihood burnt – in Jerusalem, they would have to rely on the memories of the scribes who had copied the texts and of the priests who had recited them at court. The problem was that, apart from the psalms of King David, which the Levites had sung daily in the Temple and of which those in exile had perfect recall, even the priests and scribes remembered the stories differently.

Jared acknowledged the extent of this during a gloom-ridden service on the Day of the Dead, when they prayed for their ancestors who had perished in the Great Flood and every subsequent disaster. A former priest recited the story of the Flood but, even allowing for his thick northern accent, it was obvious that it was quite unlike the version that Micaiah had taught his sons. Rather than ordering Noah to take seven pairs of the good animals and two of the bad into the Ark, Yahweh ordered him to take two pairs of them all; rather than the flood waters abating after forty days and forty nights, they persisted for a year; rather than Noah's sending out a dove in search of dry land, he sent a raven. Jared, who at thirteen stood beside his father on the men's side of the field, struggled to reconcile the inconsistencies. But when he asked whether Noah might have sent out a dove after forty days and then a raven after a year, Micaiah told him not to torment himself. The yearlong Flood was an ancient Samarian doctrine, which their priests had brought to Jerusalem when King Josiah destroyed their temples. It would be imprudent to question it now.

Further contradictions emerged on the Feast of the Trumpets, when the priest who recited the Creation story described Yahweh first making man, then plants, then birds and animals and, finally woman, because the animals alone were not sufficient companions for him. But, as any boy who had attended the Temple school or even heard the scripture readings could have told him, the sequence was first plants, then fish and birds, then animals, and finally man and woman. Micaiah's 'separate doctrines' explanation did not hold up since, while it was possible that the Flood had lasted longer in cold, low-lying regions, the world itself was created only once. Moreover, some people put forward different narratives altogether. Their neighbour, Hadassah, who, to Micaiah's annoyance, claimed descent from Seth, Adam's youngest son, told Orpah of the family legend that Adam had been created from a heap of dust and a drop of Asherah's monthly blood.

'Who's Asherah? What's monthly blood?' Jared asked.

The two women glowered at him as if he had been spying on them, even though he was across the courtyard shelling chickpeas.

'Nothing that need concern you,' his mother said. 'You must promise never to speak of it, especially to your father.'

Jared promised. He had no wish to disturb his father, who had been charged by the elders with compiling the scriptures. With Shimron and Asaph away, he had taken Jared as his assistant, impressing on him his place in a long and noble family tradition. It was a formidable task. In Jerusalem, the scribes had used specially treated goatskins: here, they made do with whatever skin was to hand. In Jerusalem, they had crushed sea snails to dye the ink a luminous blue that put them in mind of heaven; here, they mixed gum with soot and the ink was black. But, if the materials were inferior, the principles were the same. First and foremost, the scribe was required to be pure in both body and spirit. Not only must he scrub himself from head to toe before starting work but he must wash his hands every time that he wrote the name of Yahweh. When writing the name of Yahweh, he must never look up, even if the king himself entered the room. And if there were the slightest mistake in any scroll that contained the sacred name, it was to be placed in a designated chest which, once full, would be buried.

Jared feared that he would fill the chest in the first few days, his anxiety exacerbated by his father's reproachful reminders about the scarcity of skins. Gradually, he grew more practised and even came to relish the restraints. Washing was so much more rewarding when the object was to be pure rather than clean. Progress was slow. Although neither voiced it, Jared shared his father's resentment of his mother's refusal to let him bring a single scroll from the Temple, even one that did not describe any Judean victories, for fear that the Babylonians would read it and charge him with sedition. With no written records, they were forced to rely on peoples' memories. And, while there was a reassuring unanimity about the laws on diet and dress and marriage and sacrifice, there was none about the lives of their ancestors. After listening to widely differing accounts of Cain's conversation with Abel prior to killing him, Micaiah thought it best not to include it, dismissing Jared's protests that the murder now felt like an unprovoked attack. Lacking a consensus on either Seth's invention of the alphabet or Methuselah's prophecies, he likewise omitted them. On the other hand, the adherents of the alternative Creation and Flood stories were so jealous of their favoured versions that he chose to combine them, claiming that the Lord would forgive the incongruities if they served to unite His people.

Father and son transcribed the stories for over a year, but their enterprise was brought to a halt by the murder in

Judah of the governor, Gedaliah, and several of his Babylonian officials, by Ishmael, son of Nethaniah, a cousin of King Jehoiachin's mother. The Tel-Abib community girded itself for reprisals, although Micaiah trusted that his family would be exempt on account of its kinship with Gedaliah. He was cruelly disabused when a squad of soldiers stormed into their compound in search of Asaph. Jared had never been so grateful for his small stature and smooth chin than when they pushed him aside and seized his father, who, refusing to be cowed, explained that Asaph was at work on an outlying canal and might not return for several weeks. The captain replied, using his fists for emphasis, that Asaph and his three confederates had fled after the interception of their letters to Ishmael. They would be found and punished. In the meantime, he knew that Micaiah was in contact with them and demanded to be told their whereabouts. Rejecting both Micaiah's denials and Orpah's pleas, he instructed his men to drag the prisoner into the house. Jared put his arms around his mother, part in protection, part in restraint, only to be startled by a stinging slap across his face.

'You! Why didn't you stop them?' she asked, ignoring both the insuperable odds and her own orders, before breaking into frenzied howls.

Wishing that he had not lately copied out the blinding of Samson, Jared strove to stifle all thoughts of the tortures that the soldiers might be inflicting on his father. His mother fell to her knees, emitting a long, low wail, which seemed to express not only her own grief but that of every Judean woman since the bondage in Egypt. The sun's slow crawl across the sky mocked the eternity of their wait, until at last the soldiers came out and sauntered back through the courtyard, paying no more heed to Jared than to the lizards basking on the wall. After assuring himself of their departure, Jared ran up to the house, terrified of what he might find. But no sooner had he braced himself to enter than his father staggered out, naked, the familiar darkness of his chest merging with the forbidden darkness of his loins. His eyes were unscathed, but his violent shudders, together with the blood seeping down his legs, showed that he had been beaten. Jared longed to comfort him, but he was deterred by his bare skin. He searched desperately for something to cover it and, catching sight of his scroll, grabbed it from his writing board and proffered it to his father, who gazed at it blankly. So Jared wrapped it around his hips, putting one end in his hand to hold it in place. Suddenly Micaiah stirred, looked down at the scroll and flung it off. 'Sacrilege!' he cried. 'You stain the word of the Lord.' At the sound of his voice, Orpah rallied, clasped him to her breast and gathered her robe around his calves as if they were what was private. Then without loosening her grip, she led him shuffling back into the house.

Alone and bewildered, Jared felt like Ham cursed by Noah for seeing his nakedness. Eager to make amends as much for his own weakness as for the soldiers' savagery, he set about tidying the courtyard, collecting the grain that had been spilt, grateful for the tedium of the task.

For two weeks Micaiah barely moved from his mat, while Orpah tended to him as if he were a sick child. Jared worked alone on the scriptures, certain that a perfect scroll would raise his father's spirits. But without the strict master at his side, he found his thoughts straying and pen slipping even when writing the sacred name. He was grateful for any distraction, such as their neighbours' enquiries after his father's health, although he was confused by their tight-lipped allusions to his ordeal since he was far from the first Judean in Tel-Abib to have been beaten. He longed for Asaph to return and take charge, but there was no word from him or his companions. Despite his mother's angry denials, Jared was convinced that he was dead. Even when Micaiah recovered, the house was as sombre as a house of mourning, although whether this were for Asaph or Gedaliah or Micaiah himself, Jared was unable to say. He took every opportunity to escape into the fields, no matter how punishing the toil. Then, one afternoon when he was drenched in sweat and his hands on the harrow felt as leathery as the scrolls, his mother called him indoors to meet the man who would change his life, his father's uncle Jaazaniah.

2

As they made the sluggish journey upriver, Jared turned his face away from the boat for fear that, by betraying his excitement, he would revive his father's doubts and prompt him to turn back to Tel-Abib. He still found it hard to believe that Micaiah had accepted Jaazaniah's invitation to move to Babylon. It turned out that he had asked them once before, but Micaiah had declined on account of his uncle's impious marriage. Fortunately, Jaazaniah had been more amused than offended by such bigotry, which he described to Jared as a family failing. So, having heard from palace sources of Asaph's disappearance (although, from the looks passing between them, Jared suspected that the primary source had been his mother), he had sought official permission to repeat the offer. Even Ezekiel, whom Jared had been convinced would raise objections, urged the virtues of the move. But it was Orpah who put forward the conclusive argument that they would be showing little faith in themselves, let alone in the Lord, if they felt threatened by the presence of pagan gods.

Jared, who had been fired by his uncle's description of the city, was enthralled as he followed him from the docks through the warren of windowless streets. While knowing that the stark walls were designed to absorb the heat, he could not shake off the suspicion that they also served to protect the residents' secrets: a suspicion strengthened by the ropes tied across several doorways.

'Wouldn't it be easier to use bars?' he asked his uncle.

'You'll see that it's a custom here, when a man leaves his

house, he fastens a cord around the doorposts and stamps it with his seal.'

'So no one can break in?'

'Maybe. But also so he can see if anyone visited while he was out.'

'What if his wife's still at home?'

'Precisely.'

Although he could only guess at his meaning, Jared felt hot.

They arrived at Jaazaniah's house to find that it too was secured with a seal, which he broke with a knowing smile at Jared. He led them into a spacious courtyard, telling them to make themselves comfortable while he fetched his wife. Perching on the edge of a bench, Micaiah and Orpah seemed intent on ignoring the instruction. Jared, however, eager to mark his territory, sprawled in a strange kind of chair with a back and ledges for his arms. Studying his surroundings, his attention was drawn to a niche containing a small statue of a woman's torso with the largest breasts and widest hips he had ever seen, tapering to a part of her body he had never seen. Feeling his mother's eyes boring into him, he squirmed and was about to excuse himself when his uncle returned with his aunt.

Even if Jared had been less tutored in politeness, he would have leapt to his feet, since his aunt was without doubt the most beautiful woman he had ever encountered. Jaazaniah had been married before to Dinah, whom Orpah had forbidden Jared either to mention or to forget. She had been exiled along with Jaazaniah and their two sons, only to die a few months after their arrival. The boys were sent to settlements in Casiphia, where they had married and fathered children. On his appointment as Judean representative, Jaazaniah proposed to bring them to the city, but they had refused to meet his new wife. Micaiah, ever ready to ascribe his own cynicism to others, maintained that Jaazaniah's concern for their family sprang from his rejection by his own. All that mattered to Jared, however, was that he had rescued them from Tel-Abib.

Jaazaniah's wife was called Beletsarrausur, which translated as 'Oh Lady Ishtar protect the king'. Its length, sibilance and invocation to the goddess were thrilling to Jared, whose own name was short and blunt and who was not permitted to speak the name of his god out loud. She was gratifyingly slight, with pitch-black hair that fell loosely over her shoulders; full, moist lips; a dusting of white powder on her cheeks; and, most enchanting of all, lustrous green paint around her eyes. She bowed to Micaiah, sending the tassels on her chest gently swaying, lifted Orpah's hands to her mouth, and kissed Jared on the forehead, her skin exuding a spicy fragrance that recalled the incense offerings in the Temple.

'What a handsome boy!' she said, ruffling his hair.

'He's seventeen,' Orpah said, in case his small size and downy cheeks had misled her.

'And so manly,' his aunt continued, as if his mother had interrupted rather than corrected her. 'I expect he's already won many hearts.'

Jared felt his cheeks flush, although he was unsure whether it were due to her compliment or her presence. He doubted that he had won a single heart since he had scarcely spoken to a girl his own age. While echoing his friends' complaints about the strict segregation in the settlement, he had secretly welcomed it. Now, for the first time, he found himself susceptible to female charms. Beletsarrausur was exactly the sort of Babylonian woman whom his mother had warned him against, which made him all the more determined to befriend her.

'I hope that you'll be very happy in Babylon,' she said.

'I'm sure I will, if all the Babylonians are as kind as you, and as beautiful,' he replied defiantly.

'Why didn't you tell me that you had such an adorable nephew, Jaazaniah?'

'I didn't know myself until a week ago.'

'But I must put you right; I'm not Babylonian.'

'Isn't your name—?'

'My parents gave me a local name because they wanted me to fit in, but by birth I'm a Hittite.'

'You'll find, as you come to know the place, that it's a mongrel city,' Jaazaniah said. 'That's what happens when you conquer the world. There are Hurrians and Kassites and Hittites and Elamites and Assyrians and Chaldeans and even the odd Egyptian. Many came as slaves and stayed on as free men and women, marrying one another and the Babylonians.'

'The Judeans have always been a pure-blooded race,' Micaiah said, dealing his words like a blow.

'Times change, my nephew,' Jaazaniah said, quietly emphasising his seniority. 'I see that you're admiring the goddess, Jared.'

Jared flinched, as though the roughly hewn stone had been living flesh. 'What goddess?' he stuttered.

'Ishtar. As in your aunt's name. You'll find her in shrines across the city.'

'Why doesn't she have a face?'

'Oh she does. Many. But her divine power lies in her body.'

'The Most High God has no body,' Micaiah said, as if to remind Jaazaniah of his heritage.

'He must do sometimes,' Jared said, surprised at his father's lapse. 'Think of all the people who've seen Him: Moses and Aaron and Adam and Abraham, even Ezekiel.'

Far from acknowledging his help, Micaiah glared as if to condemn his treachery. Beletsarrausur, whom Jared was already crediting with tact to match her beauty, came to the rescue, insisting that they must be hungry after their journey and inviting them to eat. Jared gaped as two servants brought in olives and pistachios; quinces, grapes and pomegranates; a sweet soup and a salty soup; cheese cakes and date cakes; and, best of all, mutton, baked in a rich liquorice and carob sauce, which his aunt assured him was not in honour of their arrival but everyday fare. Moreover, when his mother, ever wary of foreign food, scolded him for dipping his fingers in the bowls too often, his aunt countered that he was 'a growing boy' and, on her lips, it did not sound like a gibe.

The meal over, she led them upstairs. For the first time in ten years, they were to sleep on an upper floor. She stopped to show them the washroom, adding that the servants were always on hand to scrub and shower them, whereupon Orpah looked homesick for the canal. Then, without a hint of embarrassment, she pointed out a small stone privy and two water jugs to wash away the waste. Orpah, who in Tel-Abib had regularly complained that she felt like a cow fertilising the field, gazed coldly at the opulent sanitation, but Jared was delighted.

He was less taken with the sleeping arrangements. Lack of space, for which Beletsarrausur apologised profusely, forced him to share a room with his parents. For years he had been subject to dreams that left him drained in both body and spirit. When, in fear of his life, he had told his father of the terrifying emissions, Micaiah had explained that they were induced by Lilith, who used the fluid to create her company of demons. He made Jared promise to banish any impure thought the instant that it occurred but, despite repeated pleas to Yahweh, the dreams persisted, as pleasurable to experience as they were painful to recollect. For once, however, it was not his own body that he was afraid would shame him. While transcribing the Law, he had been perturbed to discover that Moses had imposed a duty on husbands to lie with their wives, which the priests had subsequently codified. So in Tel-Abib, where his father laboured on the land, he was required to lie with his mother twice a week but, in Babylon, where he had no work, he was required to do so nightly. Horrified by the thought of witnessing their coupling, Jared passed the first night racked by every rustle but, to his relief, there was no sign of movement between the beds.

The next morning, red-eyed but elated, Jared accompanied his uncle on a tour of the city. Despite the stench, to which

Jaazaniah assured him he would soon grow accustomed, he was entranced by the curiously featureless streets, so different from those he remembered in Jerusalem. With nothing to distinguish them but the roadside shrines and patterned brickwork, he was fearful of losing his way, but even that was less daunting in an unfamiliar city than in one in which he was supposed to feel at home.

They reached the riverbank, which teemed with people. Most of the men carried long staffs like his uncle's but, where Jaazaniah's was crowned with a miniature bull, theirs displayed all manner of animals, birds and flowers. The women wore tasselled tunics, like his aunt's, along with ribbons in their hair and jewels on their chests, which in Jerusalem would have been reserved for the priests. Slaves in loincloths hauled crates and jars on their sinewy backs, some so black that they looked painted. Jared followed Jaazaniah over the five-arched bridge to the opposite bank and the heart of a bustling market. The rough cries of bakers and brewers, farmers and fishermen, perfumers and jewellers, traders in leopard skins and slaves, mingled with the nasal chant of a street musician and the muffled cries of an elderly woman whose teeth were being pulled.

Leaving the market, Jared found that the streets on this side of the river were wider, lined with palm trees, and dotted with temples. He struggled to memorise the names and functions of their various gods but there were too many for a single walk. Everywhere he looked he saw scaffolding, which his uncle explained was a sign of King Nebuchadrezzar's plan to rebuild the city. His most ambitious project had been the restoration of Etemenanki, the great tower in the temple of Marduk. Dashing Jared's hopes of climbing it, Jaazaniah steered him through the turreted gateway into the temple courtyard where, craning his neck, Jared glimpsed all seven of its tiers, in a vivid sequence of white, black, red, white again, orange, silver and gold. He was amazed to learn that his uncle had attended the dedication ceremony in King Jehoiachin's retinue. He listened open-mouthed to his account of the procession of more than a dozen kings, some like Jehoiachin imprisoned in the palace, others equally subjugated but allowed to retain their thrones. The more glittering their crowns and resplendent their robes, the greater the glory of their conqueror.

Jared's admiration for the Babylonians' achievements made him all the more conscious of his own aimlessness. After several weeks of inertia, he even found himself hankering for Tel-Abib. Then one evening Jaazaniah came home, bursting with news. The king had decreed that six young Judeans of superior intellect, appearance and lineage should be brought to the palace and instructed in Babylonian history and culture in order that they might be sent back to Judah as provincial administrators. With five already chosen, Jaazaniah had proposed Jared as the sixth and, although Asaph's rebellion was a black mark against him, he had used all his influence with Ashpenaz, high steward of the palace, to have it erased.

'So I'm to live at the palace?' Jared asked, incredulously.

'Why else have I told the servants to bring out the best beer?'

Jared tried to weigh his response between gratitude for Jaazaniah's good offices and recognition of his parents' misgivings, but gratitude prevailed. He could scarcely contain his excitement when, three days later, his uncle escorted him to the palace. Built by King Nebuchadrezzar's father, its brickwork was of the same brownish yellow as the rest of the city, although far more elaborately decorated. Jared gazed at the glazed frieze of winged lions and bulls, looking suspiciously like the cherubim in Ezekiel's vision, until Jaazaniah hurried him away, promising that he would have time enough to study it later. They presented themselves at the main gate where, after a cursory interrogation, two guards opened a heavy bronze door leading into a large courtyard. As they walked across it,

Jaazaniah explained that the buildings were strictly divided, with those to the east and west housing the palace guards and servants, and those to the north and south housing members of the four royal families held captive: Ashkelon, Ekron, Tyre, and Judah.

'King Jehoiachin lives over there?' Jared asked, with a shiver.

'Not just the king. Both his wives, his children, his mother and the Great Lady, King Josiah's widow.'

'Are they chained to the walls?' Jared pricked up his ears to detect the groans.

'Not at all,' Jaazaniah replied, smiling. 'This isn't one of those old stories your father made you copy. They're at liberty to move around the courtyard – except Zedekiah, of course.'

'The king?'

'It's best not to call him that here. The rest of his family shun him. He's kept in a dungeon below the ground. King Nebuchadrezzar gave him his life, purely in order that he'd regret it.'

Jared recalled the shuffling, stumbling figure on the road to Babylonia and shared that regret.

They passed through a second gateway, its blue stone ceiling flecked with gold, and entered an even larger courtyard.

'This is where the king's officials govern the entire country – and, indeed, much of the world,' Jaazaniah said, ushering Jared up an outer staircase to the first floor and then up an inner one to the second, where they walked down an airless corridor into a small room, dimly lit by a single candle, with a low stone table at the centre and bone-like carvings on the wall.

At Jaazaniah's command, Jared fell to his knees. With his head pressed to the floor, he wondered whether he had been brought unawares into the presence of the king but, looking up, he found himself opposite a mountainous man with a face at once infantile and ancient. His uncle introduced him as

Ashpenaz, the high steward, to whom he would be accountable for the next three years. The two men exchanged pleasantries, after which Jaazaniah took his leave, instructing Jared to work hard, obey orders and bring honour to the family, the last of which Jared presumed to be more for Ashpenaz's benefit than his own.

No sooner had Jaazaniah left than Ashpenaz moved to Jared and, without a word, grabbed his head, thrust his fingers into his mouth and tugged his front teeth. He was still reeling when Ashpenaz twisted the hair in his armpits, pinched his upper arms, punched his chest, pressed his thumb into his stomach, and, finally, lifted his robe and squeezed his testicles. He bit his tongue as Ashpenaz pronounced him 'small but satisfactory'. Then speaking at speed as if to trap him, Ashpenaz explained that, while living in the palace, he would be confined to the two outer courtyards. He must never enter the third, which housed the state rooms, let alone the fourth, which housed the king's private apartments, or the fifth, which housed the harem. He smiled grimly on naming the last as if its lure would prove irresistible to any young man, warning that he would take a whip to him himself should there be any infringement. From the gleam in his eye, he appeared to relish the prospect.

After studying him keenly, Ashpenaz gave him his Babylonian name, Muranu, which meant *little lion*, a considerable relief after Jaazaniah's disclosure that his own name, Nergal, meant *dunghill cock*. He then took him to the classroom to meet his companions. It was clear at a glance that all five fulfilled the king's stipulation of good looks, and the steward's introductions confirmed their noble birth. Although Ashpenaz used their Babylonian names, he had no sooner left the room than they replaced them with their Judean ones, all except Prince Sheshbazaar, King Jehoiachin's eldest son, who had been born in Babylon and named at the behest of King Nebuchadrezzar himself. At twenty-two, he was the senior in age as well as rank; next came twenty-one-year-old Hushai of Levite descent; then Neriah and Omri, both twenty and sons of King Jehoiakim's generals; and finally nineteen-year-old Jehozadak, son of Seraiah, the high priest who had been executed at Riblah on the same day that Micaiah and his sons were spared.

Sensitive that at seventeen he was the youngest of the group, Jared struggled to conceal his appreciation of privileges that they regarded as rights. No one was more pained by his subservience than Sheshbazaar, whose regal airs were the last link to his ancestral throne. 'We're no better than the palace acrobats,' he said, 'summoned to perform whenever the king needs distraction.'

While the others practised archery with the guards, Jared took his bundle and followed Hushai to the dormitory, where the joy of having escaped from his parents' bedroom vanished in the fear that the presence of his five companions would leave him more vulnerable than ever to Lilith's attacks. In the event, she chose to target Neriah, whose shamefaced attempts to scrub his polluted robe provoked ribaldry every morning. His own challenge came in the classroom, where he struggled to keep pace with his fellows, all of whom had been at their lessons for several months and two of whom, Sheshbazaar and Jehozadak, made no secret of deeming him an interloper. He was, however, a quick study, soon matching them in calculations and surpassing them in astronomy, a subject alien to the Judeans, who saw the stars as a reflection of Yahweh's glory rather than a celestial portent. His weak point was writing. He had learnt Aramaic in Tel-Abib, speaking it more fluently than either his parents, who were set in their ways, or Asaph, who was slow on principle. So he had been astonished to find that the Babylonians wrote in a different language from the one that they spoke and, moreover, used signs instead of letters. Not only were there too many signs for his brain to master, but some signs stood for more than one word and some words used more than one sign.

They spent weeks copying the names of cities, countries, stars and gods, while learning to hold their pens flat on the clay and form the signs with a series of short jabs. Fortunately, it was easy to rub the clay clean and there was no incriminating chest for any spoilt tablet that contained the names of Marduk, Ishtar or Enlil. He felt a deep sense of satisfaction when his first tablet was baked, even though it was no more than a list of weights and measures. After that, the chief scribe put him to work on the story of Gilgamesh and the Great Flood, which bore a disconcerting resemblance to that of Noah.

For all Jaazaniah's counsel of discretion, Jared could not resist extolling palace life when he returned to visit his parents. Frustrated by their refusal to admit the virtues of any city but Jerusalem, he urged them to explore Babylon and see its marvels for themselves.

'And while you blithely wander the streets,' Micaiah said, 'your people are toiling beneath them, repairing the canals in pits as black as Sheol.'

Although reluctant to defy his father, Jared refused to be bound by his prejudice. Living in Babylon, he felt a kinship with the whole world, not just his own nation. 'Step outside,' he said. 'Walk down to the river. Visit the market. No one will force you to enter a temple.'

'They don't need to. I come across their idols on every corner: statues with eyes that don't see, ears that don't hear, flesh that doesn't feel.'

'Oh, but they do,' Beletsarrausur interposed. 'The gods inhabit the statues on our behalf. They let the wood and the stone and the silver and gold become part of themselves.'

'Forgive me,' Micaiah said. 'I've no right to impugn your beliefs in your own home.'

Jared was astounded to hear his father apologise, let alone to a woman. 'Are the scribes happy with you, Jared?' his mother asked, although it was clear that she was more concerned to extricate his father than to know the answer.

'Yes,' Jared said. 'I've caught up with the others in transcription. I've finished compiling lists and begun work on the Great Flood.'

'They teach you the story of Noah?' Micaiah asked.

'No, Gilgamesh,' Jared replied.

'Who?'

'He's their hero, a man even bigger than Goliath.'

'That's no surprise,' Orpah said bitterly. 'Everything here has to be bigger.'

'He searches for one of his ancestors, Utnapishtim, who's the only human being ever to have been granted immortality by the gods – their gods, that is. He was king of the ancient city of Shuruppak when Enlil, the leader of the gods, decided to destroy mankind with a flood.'

'To punish their wickedness?' Micaiah asked.

'No, because there were too many of them and their clamour was causing him to lose sleep.'

'You're causing us to lose sleep,' Orpah said. 'Should we destroy you?'

'Mother, please! The plan was supposed to be a secret but Ea, another god, not as powerful as Enlil but well respected for his wisdom, realised that a world without mankind would be a disaster for the gods, who would have no one to work for them. He told Utnapishtim to build an ark – actually, a boat, though it's just like Noah's, only round. It had six decks and nine parts, so Ea was more concerned with the interior than the Lord was. Utnapishtim went aboard with his wife and his family and his possessions and his furniture and his workmen and every kind of animal. The flood lasted seven days.'

'Is that all?'

'And when the waters died down, the boat was stranded on the top of Mount Nisir.'

'You mean Mount Ararat?'

'No. Utnapishtim sent out first a dove, then a swallow and

then a raven,' Jared said, hoping for the first time that his father would interrupt so that he might remind him of the differing birds in their own Flood story, but he kept silent. 'The first two came back, but the raven didn't. So Utnapishtim opened the ship's doors and let out all the animals and made sacrifices to the gods.'

'And that's it?' Micaiah asked. 'It's clear that the Babylonians stole the story from us just as they stole our land. They've replaced the Lord with their own false gods.' He turned to Beletsarrausur. 'Forgive me.'

'I'm a Hittite.'

'But wouldn't it be the other way round?' Jared asked. 'After all, Abraham was Noah's descendant and he came from here. Remember "Ur in the land of the twin rivers." Surely he must have brought the story with him?'

'Is this what you call education?' Micaiah asked Jaazaniah. 'I have three sons. One is fighting with the army in Lydia. One is an outlaw with no chance of reprieve. But I fear that this one is more lost to me than both his brothers.'

Despite Jaazaniah's assurance that Micaiah's words sprang from concern for his two elder sons rather than disappointment in his youngest, Jared felt that his father was right. He might live closer to his parents than either Shimron or Asaph – assuming that they remained alive – but he had moved further away in spirit. This was confirmed on his return to the palace, where a series of good reports had persuaded Ashpenaz to admit the young Judeans to the third courtyard, from which they might watch the passage of emissaries and officials and even catch sight of the king himself. While still forbidden to venture further (unless, Ashpenaz informed them mordantly, they were willing to sacrifice their manhoods), they caught tantalising glimpses of the trees in the harem garden, their branches hanging as if from the clouds. They heard the rush of the streams and the plash of the fountains and, on the rare days when there was a wind, they breathed the heavy, honeyed fragrance that emanated either from the flowers or the women who lolled among them.

The women were the subject of fevered speculation in the Judean dormitory. The ever-effusive Hushai claimed that castration would be a small price to pay for access to the harem. Sheshbazaar, pulling rank, declared that it would be too great for someone with a duty to perpetuate the royal line. Omri remarked that it would be too great for anyone since what they gained in proximity they would lose in performance, to which Neriah replied that many eunuchs remained perfectly able to perform. After much scurrilous conjecture about his evidence, they turned as one to Jared, who had hoped to pass unnoticed. Feeling the sweat beading on his brow and his throat constricting, he mumbled a few vapid phrases, which they attributed to youth and inexperience. The truth was that he was more excited by his friends' talk about the women than by the women themselves.

Among the palace rooms to which the Judeans gained admittance were the library and the gallery. Labynetus, the chief scribe, took them on a tour on the day that Omri, the laggard of the group, completed his last exercise tablet. Even he could not fail to be impressed by the rows of ancient tablets on the library shelves: government records and accounts; maps of the world and the heavens; royal correspondence; recipes and remedies; and, above all, sacred stories. As reverently as a priest raising the slaughter-knife, Labynetus picked up a thousand-year-old tablet from the reign of King Hammurabi. Jared was amazed to discover that it was yet another version of the Great Flood, with a hero named Atrahasis. But when, to the unconcealed horror of his companions, he asked if they might copy it, Labynetus replied that the script was no longer in use.

While Labynetus tried to interest them in other rare tablets, the Judeans found themselves drawn to two frayed wicker baskets full of scrolls and a plain wooden chest with Hebrew lettering, which the scribe explained had been salvaged from the Jerusalem Temple before it was reduced to ashes. As his auditors gazed with wonder, gratitude and, in Jehozadak's case, tears, at sacred texts that they had supposed lost forever, Labynetus added that it was the king's practice to translate the writings of all his tributary states, the better to understand the people.

Like the library, the gallery was filled with treasures from Babylonia's own history and that of the many countries it had conquered. Dominating the first room was a cluster of ancient Sumerian gods, men with long square beards and women with protuberant breasts and bellies. To one side of them was a trio of Assyrian governors, all with identical heads despite a three-hundred-year age gap; to the other was a large stone lion with a weathered mane, trampling on a slave. Shepherding them into a second room, Labynetus promised a display of antique weaponry to stir any young man's heart. But as they entered, all six of them were transfixed, not by the axes, spears and shields but by two golden beasts, at least fifteen-foot tall, each with a man's head, eagle's wings and lion's body. Tucked between them, barely visible, was an intricately decorated golden chest.

At last Sheshbazaar broke the silence. 'Did these also come from Jerusalem?'

'Yes,' Labynetus replied impatiently. 'But take a look at this magnificent Assyrian sword! It belonged to King Ashurbanipal.'

The Judeans ignored him, staring at the Ark and the Cherubim plundered from the Holiest Place in the Temple.

'And the Ark – the chest – did you find … is there anything inside it?' Jehozadak asked.

'Nothing of interest,' Labynetus replied. 'There's an ancient chariot from Hatti in the next room that you'll find much more exciting. But if you don't believe me …' Before anyone could protest, he moved to the Ark and flung open the lid. 'There, nothing! Now do you want to see the chariot?'

No one replied. Jared stole a glance at his companions, each of them stunned by the scribe's sacrilege and the loss of the Tablets of Law. Chiding their ingratitude and threatening chastisement, Labynetus ushered them out. But no threat of his could compare with the abomination that they had witnessed. Yahweh had been deprived of His throne as surely as King Jehoiachin or, although Jared knew better than to breathe his name, King Zedekiah. Where was He now that He had no earthly resting place? Had He remained in Jerusalem without pomp or priests? Was He living among His people in exile? Or had He abandoned them forever?

Eager to prove to his parents that he had rejected neither his faith nor his roots, Jared used the occasion of his next visit home to tell them what he had seen. But he had not anticipated the intensity of his father's grief. As Micaiah rolled his eyes and fought for breath, tearing at the neck of his robe as if he were choking, Jared feared that the news would kill him. He watched in horror as his mother grabbed his father's shoulders, screaming at him to help and then pushing him away when he tried. Beletsarrausur, meanwhile, ordered a servant to prepare a potion of tamarisk, honey and curd, which she insisted on dispensing to Micaiah herself, even when he dribbled it down her arms. Sip by sip, he recovered his composure.

'The Temple is destroyed and the Ark defiled,' he said, as Beletsarrausur went out to make him a poultice. 'Where are the people to find the Lord?'

'In the sacred stories, Father. Isn't that what you taught me in Tel-Abib?'

'How, when all we have left are memories? We rescued what we could. But so much is lost; so much is forgotten.'

'No,' Jared said, happy that he could give his father hope. 'All the Temple scrolls are here in Babylon. Even some spoilt ones in a chest that hadn't yet been buried.'

'I saw the Temple burning with my own eyes.'

'The king had them removed and brought here to be transcribed – although they're still in baskets.'

'What use are they to him?'

'He thinks that knowing our stories will give him power over us.'

'Doesn't he have enough already?' Orpah interjected.

'Perfect!' Micaiah said, his face brightening. 'If he wants our story, we shall give it to him.'

'You've had a shock, Micaiah,' Orpah said. 'You're not yourself.'

'Nonsense! It's a golden opportunity. We may be conquered now but we were conquerors in the past. Ours is a great story … a proud story. It will show the king that we're far more than the Kassites or the Hurrians.'

'Or the Hittites,' Orpah added with a scowl.

'And Jared is the one who will write it.'

'Me? What do you mean? Why me?'

'Because you're my son, a scribe by both birth and training. This is the Lord's doing. It's why He led you to the palace: why He showed you the scrolls.'

'Maybe so,' Jared said, without conviction. 'But they're not going to let me bring the scrolls here. And I can't take on such a huge responsibility alone.'

'Of course not. You must enlist your fellows. From all you've told us, they'll be proud to help.'

'What's more, I'd have to persuade Ashpenaz, the high steward.'

'That's easy. Tell him that if they want to transcribe our stories, they'll need an authoritative copy. Then offer to write it for them. But in fact you'll write two: one for them and one for us. Do you remember what Jeremiah told King Jehoiakim?'

'No.'

'It was before he was born,' Orpah said.

'Before he was born,' Micaiah echoed. 'He said that we would remain in exile for seventy years. Well, we've already been here for ten – twenty, if you count those who came with King Jehoiachin. You and I are destined to die here, and nothing we do will change that. But you must pave the way home for your children, or rather your children's children.'

'But even if Ashpenaz agrees to our making the copy, who's to say what's authoritative? How are we to decide between the scrolls? Should we combine the different versions the way you did with the Creation of the world?'

'Put your trust in the Lord. He will guide you, just as He did me.'

As Micaiah expounded the plan, Jared feared that, far from proving his fidelity, he had set himself a trap. While he longed both to make his father proud and to comfort his people, he could not stop thinking of the Flood. If that was not all that it seemed, what about the other stories, which, according to his father, Yahweh had dictated to Moses? Buried in the royal library or in libraries elsewhere, might there be Hittite or Elamite or Egyptian variants of Adam and Abraham, Jacob and Joseph, and even Moses himself? How would it serve the Judeans if the stories in which they found the Lord were lies?

3

Jared assumed that Ashpenaz was smiling, although, in the shadowy room, it was impossible to decipher an expression that was inscrutable even in the light. The threat that the steward conveyed in company was heightened when they were alone. He drummed his heavily jewelled fingers on the table as if trying to decide whether he wanted to caress or throttle the suppliant or, in line with his physical indeterminacy, do both. Stuttering, Jared outlined a proposal that had been perfectly cogent on the stairs.

'It would be a token of our gratitude to the king for inviting us into the palace.'

'Don't you suppose we have scribes of our own who can translate the stories?'

'Of course … I mean of course you have. But the scrolls in the library were so jumbled and dusty, it looked as though no one had opened them in years.'

'You Judeans think far too much of yourselves. True, the king wants to translate your stories, but our scribes have more pressing concerns.'

'Which is all the more reason to accept my offer.'

'And why should I trust you, a beardless youth?' Ashpenaz asked, with no apparent irony.

'You know my great-uncle so I'm sure you know of his father, Shaphan, chief scribe to the great King Josiah. I've grown up in the family tradition. I can read the texts – not just the words but the way they were written. I've been taught by my father to resolve any inconsistencies.'

'What if there are inconsistencies you can't resolve?'

'Then the Lord – our god – will guide me.'

'Your god will guide you to give his story to our gods?'

'Yes,' Jared said hesitantly. 'Besides, I won't be working alone. I'll seek help from my friends. Didn't you choose us to be the intermediaries between our two peoples? Together, we can tell you the story of our nation since the Lord gave Canaan to Abraham – and to us – forever.'

'Forever?' Ashpenaz asked, the combination of anger, derision and pity rendering his voice as unfathomable as his face. 'Then why are you and all your great men and soldiers and craftsmen living here, with only the farmers and labourers left behind?'

'We believe that one day we'll defeat our enemies and return,' Jared retorted, thinking of Asaph.

'Is that so?' Ashpenaz stood up and advanced on Jared, who tried not to gag on the cloying mixture of jasmine and sweat. 'I should like to know how you intend to achieve it,' he added, with a smile that brought dangerous definition to his doughy features. 'Very well, you may copy the story of this Abraham in your language fit only for goatskin. Then, with Labynetus's help, you'll transpose it on to tablets and I'll present it to the king. If he deems it worthy, you'll continue with the work.'

'Are you sure you want us to start with Abraham? What about Adam, the first man?'

'Was he given land?'

'Yes, a great garden, though he was exiled from it.'

'Ha! You Judeans are accustomed to exile. No, stick to Abraham. You say that he was given the land of Canaan by your god. That will interest the king.'

Sanctioned by the steward, Jared asked Jehozadak to assist him. Of all his companions, he was the one to whom Jared felt the closest, so much so that at times he wished that he might fall down the well or else be caught stealing into the harem – no, anywhere but the harem! – triggering his banishment from the palace and relieving the strange intensity of elation and pain that his presence provoked in him. He hoped that the work would consolidate their friendship, but Jehozadak, disturbed by the discrepancies in the scrolls, grew increasingly aloof. The stories were at odds not just with one another but with Temple teaching. Far from worshipping the one true god, Abraham and Sarah were as profligate with their prayers as pagans, making offerings to Asherah as well as Yahweh. Meanwhile, circumcision was not a sign of the unique covenant between the Judeans and the Lord but an Egyptian practice adopted by Abraham to seal his alliance with Pharaoh.

Berating Jared for filling his head with lies, Jehozadak insisted that the scrolls were fakes, dating from the reign of King Ahab. He abandoned the transcription and Jared replaced him with Hushai. Together, they sought to establish which of the scrolls were authentic. Language was no help since, unlike the obsolete script on the tablet of Atrahasis, Hebrew had remained constant since the Lord spoke to Adam in Eden.

Jared was eager to draw on his father's experience when he visited his family during the twelve-day holiday that the Judeans, like other palace servants, were given to celebrate the Babylonian New Year. The opportunity arose after dinner when he sat with Micaiah and Jaazaniah in the courtyard, where spring had drawn a veil of modesty over the Ishtar niche.

'You said that we should honour Abraham, Father, but Sarah was his sister. And didn't Ezekiel tell us that men marrying their sisters were the cause of Jerusalem's fall? I'm sorry,' he added to Jaazaniah, recalling the prophet's tirades against his marriage. 'I know he could be wrong but, in this case, he claimed to have heard from the Lord Himself.'

'Sarah was Abraham's half-sister,' Micaiah said coldly.

'Moreover, he was a liar. In Egypt, he denied that she was his wife. Or would that have been a half-lie?'

'Egypt is a land of lies. He was following the custom of the country. If not, they'd have put him to death.'

'Isn't Babylonia a land of lies? Would you deny that Mother is your wife and let the king lock her in his harem to save your life?'

'Jared, you forget yourself,' Jaazaniah said mildly.

'Not to save myself, no, but to save my nation,' Micaiah replied. 'Although I am not its father, which I consider a blessing, given my sons.'

'Is Gerar also a land of lies?' Jared asked.

'Who mentioned Gerar?'

'Another scroll. It records how Abraham and Sarah travelled to Gerar, just as they had to Egypt. The king of Gerar desired Sarah. Once again Abraham said that she was his sister, and the king lay with her.'

'Any land without the Lord is a land of lies.'

'But the second story is so similar to the first that one must be in error.'

'So who do you suppose made it?' Micaiah asked, his voice dripping with irony. 'Moses when he wrote it down, or the Lord Himself when He told it to him?'

'Neither,' Jared replied uncomfortably. 'Maybe one of the scribes?'

'Who? Your great-grandfather, Shapan? Your grandfather, Gemariah?' Micaiah composed himself. 'Sarah was a very beautiful woman. Why shouldn't she have attracted two different kings?'

'Because she was ninety when she went to Gerar! She'd already scoffed at the idea of having a child.'

The thought of lying with a ninety-year-old revolted Jared who had little enough desire to lie with a nineteen-year-old. He had tried to picture himself as Jacob, so in love with Rachel that he was willing to toil for her father for fourteen years, or David, whose unquenchable lust for Bathsheba led him to contrive her husband's death, only to find himself more drawn to the act of imagining than to its goal.

'Some women's beauty is ageless,' Micaiah replied. 'Besides,

Sarah hadn't yet been worn down by the pains of childbirth and ungrateful children.'

'So should we include both of Abraham and Sarah's journeys in the scroll we compile for the king? You wanted the stories to strengthen people. I'm afraid they'll confuse them.'

'You've been given a sacred trust. You must pray to the Lord for guidance.'

Micaiah went inside, leaving Jared with Jaazaniah.

'It's not fair. He always walks away when he can't think what else to say.'

'He's your father. He doesn't have to be fair.'

'But there's much more we need to discuss. From everything I've read, I don't see how Moses can have written the story of Abraham.'

'Please,' Jaazaniah said, putting his hands over his face as though Jared's words were darts. 'I'm not the man to ask.'

'You're a Shaphan.'

'By birth.'

'It's so full of contradictions, not to say mistakes.'

'That's nothing. Wait till you reach the Book of Law, where Moses describes his own death.'

'Did he see it in a vision?'

'Not to my knowledge.'

'Then how?'

'It's late. We have a busy day ahead of us at the festival. And I don't want to offend your father. It's not for me to challenge what he's taught you.'

'Why not, if you think it's wrong? You brought me here. You introduced me to the palace. You have a responsibility to tell me the truth!'

'You don't give up, do you? Very well. So long as you promise not to use it against your father.' Jared nodded. 'That's not enough. I want to hear the words.'

'I promise.'

'I'm sure you know how the Book of Law came to light.'

'King Josiah ordered the Temple to be purged of all the idols and when they knocked through a wall, the high priest chanced upon the scroll, which contained Moses's last words.'

'Strange to think that it wasn't quite fifty years ago. I must have been the age that you are now. It was my father – your great-grandfather – who had the honour of reading the scroll to the king, who used it to support a programme of religious reforms: demolishing rival temples in the north, slaughtering hundreds of cultic priests and exhuming the bodies of dead ones—'

'He exhumed dead priests?'

'I doubt that they suffered as much as the living. Everything was designed to boost his authority. It was rumoured – of course I can't vouch for the accuracy – that the book wasn't written by Moses at all but by a certain family of scribes and faithful royal servants.'

'You mean ours?'

'I do indeed. Your grandfather; your great-grandfather; your great-uncles, Ahikam and Elasah. I, needless to say, was not part of this conspiracy (if conspiracy it were) on account of my youth and varied misdemeanours. Had I been, I might have pointed out the folly of attributing to Moses passages that could only have been dictated from beyond the grave. Although, to be fair, that didn't seem to cause much concern at the time.'

'So our family was at the heart of a widespread deception?'

'I merely raise the possibility. Now I suggest that you stop brooding and go to bed.'

The following evening, Jared accompanied Jaazaniah and Beletsarrausur to Marduk's temple of Esagila to watch the re-enactment of the Creation story. He had hoped to attend all the ceremonies of the festival, but Jaazaniah explained that the first three days were exclusive to the priests, who gathered in the temple to offer laments for the uncertainty of life and pray for Marduk's blessing on his city. The Creation re-enactment, however, took place in the courtyard and Jaazaniah had secured them seats in the central stand. Jared confessed to being confused by the concept of *re-enactment*, failing to see how something that had happened once could happen again, except in a dream. But, as Jaazaniah had promised, everything became clear at sundown when scores of priests filed on to Etemenanki's two lower tiers and began to recite in flat, uninflected tones. Further excitement was sparked by two masked figures who entered the torchlit arena in front of them and danced in time to the speech. Both were fearsome, their masks a composite of lions' manes and eagles' beaks, their robes a patchwork of fur and feathers, their gauntlets and boots shaped like dragons' claws. Jaazaniah, well-versed in the story, told Jared that they were the gods, Apsu and Tiamit. But, unlike the statues in which the gods chose to present themselves to the people, here the priests chose to represent the gods.

Jared nodded, less to signal that he grasped the distinction than to prevent Jaazaniah's distracting him from the spectacle. Apsu and Tiamit, the sweet and bitter waters who had merged at the beginning of time, were joined by a host of other divinities and, finally, by Marduk himself, whose primacy was marked by the ringing applause. Even as a boy, Marduk towered above the lesser gods, being represented by two priests, one sitting on the other's shoulders, his feet protruding from under the voluminous robes. He wore a giant mask with a flame-like tongue, which he shot out sporadically to the delight of the crowd, and he sported two pairs of eyes and ears, 'so that he can see and hear everything that happens,' Jaazaniah informed Jared, who had already worked it out for himself. He was, however, grateful for Jaazaniah's identification of the four blue-clad acolytes, who leapt into the arena banging cymbals, as the four winds given to Marduk by his father. Their boisterous games so enraged the older gods that they complained to Tiamit, who installed Kingu at the head of a large army to confront Marduk. Kingu, who was both Tiamit's husband and son, was suitably grotesque, with a mask not just on his face but on his elbows, knees and buttocks, the last of which he thrust out and wiggled, provoking a barrage of jeers.

Before sending him into battle, Tiamit invested Kingu with the Tablet of Destiny, which, although too far away for Jared to see clearly, looked much like the tablets that he had transcribed for Labynetus. Marduk, meanwhile, secured his fellow gods' agreement that, should he defeat Tiamit, they would elect him their chief. For once it was possible to make out the priests' words since, no doubt as a measure of their importance, they repeated them as often as the Judeans did the *Shema*: 'May your utterance be law, your word never be falsified.' Four gods fetched Marduk's golden throne, which, Jaazaniah whispered, was the same one on which his statue would sit during the procession later in the week. As yet, however, he had little use for it, and after having strung a bow, fletched an arrow and made a net, he set off in search of Tiamit. Cheers erupted when two more gods brought Marduk's chariot pulled by four white horses, in which he made several circuits of the arena, even though Tiamit stood in full view at the base of a platform. Descending from the chariot, he challenged her to single combat, which, given his build, was both unequal and unwieldy. After some tentative sword thrusts, for which his torso and legs were poorly coordinated, he trapped her in the net and shot an arrow into her belly, which by some ingenious mechanism gushed out a mixture of water and guts. He gathered it up and, with a series of wild incantations, used it to create the universe, much to Jared's bemusement, since it meant that everything that had happened until then must have happened in a void. He had little time for reflection, however, as Marduk was already seeking out Kingu, whom he swiftly dispatched, taking particular pleasure in stabbing his posterior mask. He unhooked the Tablet of Destiny from

Kingu's chest and placed it on his own, before slitting Kingu's wrist, sending a jet of blood on to the ground, whereupon a naked young man emerged from beneath the platform and bowed to him.

'That's you!' Jaazaniah said to Jared.

'What?'

'Well, all of us. According to the story, Marduk created man from the god's blood that fell on to the dust.'

'Just like the Lord creating Adam from dust, only He blew His own breath into him.'

'I doubt that your father would appreciate the comparison.'

'Which do you think contains more of the divine: breath or blood?'

'I think we should be grateful for whatever we've got.'

The ceremony ended with the gods each laying a brick at the base of the platform to signify the temple and tower that they proposed to build in honour of Marduk.

'But they've already been built,' Jared said to Jaazaniah.

'Exactly.'

The priests then recited the fifty names of Marduk, to each of which the spectators responded with one of his divine attributes. After thanking his uncle and aunt for bringing him, Jared asked when they would return. Jaazaniah explained that the next day's ceremonies centred on the ritual humiliation of the king who, while agreeing to be stripped of his regalia and struck in the face at the altar, was careful to ensure that it took place behind closed doors. There would be more to see the following day when the other Babylonian gods, in the form of their statues, arrived by barge from temples across the land, to be met by the priests and princes and taken to the temple to pay homage to Marduk. While granting that Jared was at liberty to join the parade, Jaazaniah warned that the streets beside the river were narrow, the crowds vast and not everyone showed the appropriate reverence. He advised him, instead, to wait for the ninth day and the grand procession in which Marduk and the entire pantheon would be escorted from Esagila to the Festival House on the outskirts of the city. There, they would celebrate Marduk's marriage to Ishtar, which, after accompanying them back to the temple, the king would re-enact with the high priestess in the sacred chamber at the top of the tower. Although the crowds would be larger than ever, the road was wider and there was less danger of crime.

Jared took his uncle's advice, spending the next four days working on the scrolls. He toyed with accompanying Labynetus and his fellow scribes to the docks to greet Nabu, Marduk's son, who was also the god of writing, but he was reluctant to distance himself still further from his friends. As fearful of pollution as his parents, they refused to leave the palace grounds during the entire festival, passing the time playing Twenty Squares and other board games with junior members of the guard. Jared longed to reassure them that he had watched Marduk's exploits through eyes fixed on Yahweh, but he refused to court derision by describing the exotic ceremony. Instead, he dropped mischievous hints about the women who had danced naked to represent the waters of chaos, eliciting four looks of envy and frustration and Jehozadak's even more satisfying expression of despair.

Scorning his craven companions, Jared left the palace on the appointed day to meet Jaazaniah and Beletsarrausur. Two hours before the ceremony was due to start, the Processional Way was already teeming and Jared was afraid of missing the rendezvous as he wove through the festive crowd, dodging the guards who were pushing bystanders against the walls. He was relieved to see Jaazaniah raise his staff in welcome and even more so to discover that he had procured them a vantage point on the roof of the adjoining tower. He stood, unremarked, among the group of officials who joked with his uncle and paid his aunt a stream of compliments that would have mortified his mother. Beletsarrausur, however, smiled in such a calculating manner that Jared could not help recalling

Ezekiel's diatribes against foreign women. Feeling disloyal, he was grateful when an insistent drumbeat drew everyone's attention towards Esagila.

Grabbing his hand in a palm that was distressingly moist, his aunt apprised him that the procession was setting off, although for several minutes the only evidence was the muffled music (the drums now accompanied by trumpets, flutes and timbrels) from within the temple gates. Finally, the first group of priests emerged, dressed entirely in black and chanting prayers in a language that even the Babylonians could not understand, a language older than any on their tablets, a language said to be that of the gods themselves. They were followed by a golden palanquin garlanded with pink-and-white blossom, carrying the statue of Marduk's wife, Zarpanit, who was barely visible from the tower, except for the glimmer of her jewelled robes. Young priestesses walked by her side, scattering flowers, which, Jaazaniah whispered knowingly to Jared, had been gathered from the harem garden.

'If Zarpanit is Marduk's wife, how can he be celebrating his marriage to Ishtar?' Jared asked, causing Beletsarrausur to chuckle.

'Not all men – and certainly not all gods – are like your father and me, content with a single wife,' Jaazaniah said, winking at Beletsarrausur. 'Besides, Ishtar is the sort of goddess you marry for one night only.'

'What's she the goddess of?' Jared asked, finding the question easier to ask on the tower roof than in the confines of the courtyard.

'Love,' Beletsarrausur replied.

'In its most basic form,' Jaazaniah added.

Feeling for Zarpanit's predicament, even though she was both a pagan and made of wood, Jared watched the remaining gods file past: some carried by priests, others pushed on carts; each, to judge by the response of the crowd, with his or her particular adherents. The greatest enthusiasm, however, greeted Ishtar who, alone of the passing deities, was naked, although her gilded body looked more precious than all their finery. Unlike the statue in his uncle's house, she had a face, but Jared was too far away to discern its expression. Six young women, three on either side of her, scattered blood-red hibiscus petals. Behind them came a line of giantesses, all with black tresses flowing down their backs, rocking to and fro, holding spindles in their left hands and drawn swords in their right, like Deborah leading her troops into battle.

'Are they her priestesses?' Jared asked.

'And her priests,' Jaazaniah replied.

'Don't tease the boy,' Beletsarrausur said, smiling at Jared, who at once welcomed and resented her concern.

'You explain it to him then.'

'Ishtar is both sexes in one, the goddess of love and the goddess of war, like her star, Dilbat, which is male in the morning but female in the evening.'

'I see,' Jared said, profoundly perplexed as he gazed at the voluptuous figure.

'It's said that she can turn men into women, so take care!' Beletsarrausur said, her eyes laughing. 'But these men – her priests – achieve that for themselves. In order to serve her, they sacrifice the part that would give other women pleasure.'

'And then they abuse themselves to give other men pleasure,' Jaazaniah interposed.

'Why must you make it so ugly?' Beletsarrausur asked.

'Because it is! Your aunt, Jared, likes to see the best in everything, which is admirable but also dangerous. These men are no better than the dog-priests who defiled the Temple in Jerusalem. Remember our talk last week about King Josiah's reforms?'

'Of course.'

'Well one of them – by far the most urgent to most minds – was that he purged the Temple of the dog-priests, men who lured other men to the foulest perversions.'

'Did he slaughter them like the priests in the northern temples?'

'Who knows? They weren't considered worthy of record. They lived in the Temple precinct, a stone's throw from us, and flaunted themselves in women's clothing, which is expressly forbidden in the Book of Law.'

'But you said that the Book of Law was a fake, written by your father and brothers.'

'I said that it might have been. In any case, a law doesn't depend on its author for its authority.'

'Not so loud, Jaazaniah!' Beletsarrausur said. 'People are staring.'

'Let them.'

'And you're upsetting Jared.'

'He ought to know the truth.'

Jared lost track of the conversation. He felt as though he were a thousand cubits off the ground, rather than twenty. Jaazaniah's account of the men tempting other men in the temples of Jerusalem and Babylon opened up a world of possibilities. The priests disappearing from view, although not from his imagination, held the key to desires that he had thought would be locked inside him forever. The secret part of him had, if not a name, at least a precedent. He knew that he should be alarmed when even his uncle, who had renounced so many of his forefathers' prohibitions, was vehement in support of this one. Yet he was no longer in Jerusalem, where the dog-priests had been reviled and probably murdered, but in Babylon, where Ishtar's priests were cheered by the crowd. All at once, he felt a stirring in his loins and his member sprang up like the serpent in Eden before the Lord condemned it to crawl in the dust. Ignoring his aunt's warnings, he clung to a turret to steady himself while he was engulfed by a wave of pleasure. Spent, he pondered the unprecedented assault. Was he so feeble that Lilith felt able to target him even in daylight? Or was he in thrall to the more benign Babylonian goddess?

A thunderous roar interrupted his reverie.

'Over here!' Beletsarrausur shouted, 'it's Marduk.' Jared dragged himself towards her. 'You've got a mark on your tunic.'

'What?' Jared looked down in horror. 'It's just brick dust. It'll brush off.' He watched the crowd fall to its knees in homage to Marduk, his golden statue seated on a golden throne beneath a golden canopy on which the heavens were mapped in jewels. In his right hand, he held a golden sword and, in his left, a golden sceptre and, on his head, he wore a red-and-white plumed turban. Beside him, almost incidental to the splendour, walked the king. Foregoing his usual robes of state, he was all in white, apart from a simple purple sash, and bareheaded (from Jared's perspective, balding), having removed his crown in deference to the god whom he believed governed his fate. He would accompany Marduk to the Festival House, waiting outside like the lowliest groom, while he celebrated his marriage to Ishtar.

Jared longed to sneak behind closed doors to learn in which of her persons she would receive him. Would she hold a sword or a spindle? Or was she as changeable as her star, female when they went to bed and male by morning?

4

Jared stood in the sun-dappled arcade, soaking up the atmosphere of the courtyard. Even the pillars that flanked the temple doorway made him blush. Instead of Jachin and Boaz with their clean straight lines crowned with a cluster of lilies, they resembled his member in the hands of Lilith. The very air smelt of desire. Unlike the stench of charred flesh that clung to the Temple in Jerusalem, it exuded the sweet-salty odour of bodies at night. But the greatest difference lay in the worship. Rather than the solemn procession of Yahweh's priests leading a sacrificial beast to the altar, Ishtar's priests danced frenziedly to a pounding drumbeat. Some leapt in the air; others writhed on the ground. From time to time, one ran into the crowd to seize a euphoric spectator, either disappearing with him down a shadowy passage or else dragging him into the melee, where he would tear off his robe, as if throwing off all the trappings of his workaday life, and gyrate in his loincloth. Among them was a soldier, whom Jared half-expected to draw his sword and slit his assailant's throat, but he simply threw down his weapon and launched himself into the fray.

'I've been watching you.'

'What?' Jared swung round to confront one of the priests, his hair as thick and black as the tassels on his shawl, the blue star on his forehead and tiny golden grapes in his ears prominent on his strong, sweat-soaked face.

'It's the third time you've come here,' he said in an incongruously deep voice.

'No, I was just passing. I walked in by mistake.'

'Did you?'

His head swimming, Jared took a moment to realise that the viper, jaws agape, crawling up the man's arm was made of bronze. 'I think I'm going to—'

'Let me.' The man leant over and clasped his arm. His grip was secure, but the heady aroma of his perfume, a blend of cinnamon, juniper and myrtle, increased Jared's dizziness. 'Better now?'

'I'm fine, thank you,' Jared said, marvelling that a eunuch should be so strong. Unlike Ashpenaz, who was all sibilance and softness, this man could have wrestled Asaph to the ground. 'As I told you, I was passing by when I felt faint. So I came in to sit down.'

'If you say so,' the man replied coldly. 'You're a Judean?'

'Is my accent that broad?'

'Not at all. But you're a free man?'

'I'm an advisor to the king,' Jared said, trusting that it was less a lie than a projection.

'I'm surprised you've come. I thought that you Judeans were determined to set yourselves apart.'

'I told you; I was just—'

'So do you want to see inside the temple?'

'With you?'

'Is that so shocking?'

'A little. It's one of our laws that no man with his stones broken is allowed to enter the temple.'

'Stones? How quaint! Do these feel like stones?' The man grabbed Jared's testicles and squeezed them hard.

Jared yelped as he withdrew his hand. 'You hurt me!'

'Don't worry; your pain won't last … Zakir,' he said brusquely, as if to make up for the momentary lapse.

'What?' Jared asked, unfamiliar with the word.

'My name.'

'Oh, Jared.'

'And to reassure you, the only people not allowed in this temple are those with bad breath. So are you coming?'

Zakir led Jared through the courtyard, past a trio of drummers whose beat was so insistent that it seemed to enter his blood. He wondered whether any of the spectators were watching them the way he had done previous pairings, but they were all intent on the dance. He walked up to the door, turning away from the pillars, and stepped into the pleasingly cool vestibule. Zakir escorted him into the echoing sanctuary, where the flickering of a hundred candles, together with the dry, woody scent of frankincense, took him back to the Temple of his childhood. But, as his eyes adjusted to the gloom, he saw that the decoration could not have been more different. Instead of cedar, cypress and olivewood walls inlaid with images of cherubim and foliage, there were statues of Ishtar, cupping her breasts and splaying her legs more brazenly than in Jaazaniah's courtyard. Elsewhere, she fornicated with partners of both sexes, as if to encourage her votaries to follow suit.

Jared dragged his feet as Zakir steered him towards the central shrine, where the statue of Ishtar had been restored after her recent marriage night with Marduk. 'See, the goddess welcomes couples of every kind,' Zakir said, pointing to a statue of two men embracing, one entering the other from behind. Jared shuddered, although he was too confused to know whether it were from excitement or fear.

'Are they asking her blessing on the crops?' Jared asked, afraid of giving himself away.

'What?'

'Are they spilling their seed to ensure a good harvest, as they did in Sodom?'

'What's Sodom?'

'A city in Judah, or at least it was until it was destroyed. I'm copying the story for the king.'

'No, they're spilling their seed, as you put it, to give her pleasure. Ishtar is the goddess of pleasure.'

'I thought she was the goddess of love.'

'No, something far more sacred. Babylonians believe that

our purpose in life is to do the gods' work so that they can rest. And Ishtar's work is to give pleasure.'

'Judeans believe that our purpose in life is to procreate,' Jared said, articulating for the first time what had been intimated to him since childhood. 'To produce children who'll obey the Lord's laws.'

'So does your king have a marriage ceremony with your god's wife?'

'My god doesn't have a wife!' Jared said. But, even as he spoke, his thoughts turned to Asherah, whose name was to be found only on ancient scrolls or whispered among women. He wondered whether Yahweh might have murdered her as Marduk had Tiamit.

'Your god wants to procreate but he doesn't do so himself?'

'I suppose,' Jared replied uneasily.

'Then I suggest you'd do better to devote yourself to pleasure.'

As Zakir pressed his arm, pleasure became the essence of Jared's entire being. He gazed at the statue of the embracing men, thrilled that what had once been an object of obloquy was now one of veneration.

'So will you join me in giving pleasure to Ishtar?'

'Yes,' Jared breathed, as the cool temple air was replaced by a blast of heat. He felt himself reaching a new awareness, in which knowledge became purpose and purpose power.

'I shall take you to the holiest place.'

'No!'

With one phrase, Zakir had broken the spell. A succession of images flashed before his eyes: the high priest; his father; the Ark; the locked golden doors; his father again. The holiest place was somewhere no one must ever enter, except for the high priest and he only once a year. Horrified, he recoiled from both the statue and Zakir.

'I'm sorry,' he said, unclear why he was apologising rather than denouncing him. 'I'm sorry … I must—'

His body more assured than his words, he rushed through the building and into the courtyard, gulping the air as greedily as the water on the road to exile. He shunned the continuing tumult, swearing never to return as he headed for the palace, but, as if to weaken his resolve, the very next morning Labynetus made them transcribe a thousand-year-old hymn to Ishtar. As he traced the complex signs for *beautiful figure, brilliant eyes* and *warrior queen*, his hand less steady than usual, he grew convinced that the goddess herself was leading him back to Zakir.

Immediately the morning's lessons ended, he slipped out of the palace and returned to the temple. To his surprise, the courtyard was deserted apart from a flight of doves, glutted on crumbs from the sacred cakes brought by votaries such as Beletsarrausur, who once a week baked a cake in the shape of the goddess and offered it at the shrine. The thought of his loving, generous aunt emboldened him. When, during the New Year procession, his uncle had expressed repugnance at the emasculated priests, she defended them, in spite of the enjoyment (excessive, if one listened to – or, in his case, overheard – his mother) she derived from the company of men.

'They say that, if a man lies with one of Ishtar's priests, all his cares will vanish.'

'All of them?' Jared asked, both excited and disturbed by the idea.

'Of course not,' Jaazaniah interposed. 'Why fill the boy's head with nonsense? It's a rumour spread by the priests themselves.'

Jared had no intention of lying with Zakir. He had returned solely to apologise for his rudeness in running off the previous day. As a privileged member of an abject race, he had a duty to show it to advantage. It appeared, however, that his mission would be thwarted, since neither Zakir nor any of his fellows were anywhere to be seen. Aching with frustration, he was debating whether to enter the temple alone and, with no hint of a prayer, ask Ishtar for help, when he spotted a priest deep in conversation with an elderly man in the shadows of the arcade. Although too far away to make out his face, something in his bearing convinced him that it was Zakir. Approaching, he found that he was right.

'I'm sorry to intrude,' he said.

'Then don't!' Zakir replied curtly.

'Do you remember me?'

'It was yesterday afternoon!'

'I'm sorry. I wanted ... I was hoping ... I mean that this time we could worship Ishtar together.'

'He's delicious,' said Zakir's companion, a coarse-featured man sweating profusely. 'We could take him with us.'

'No,' Zakir said, voicing Jared's disgust. 'If he wants me, he can wait here. I'll be out in an hour.' He put his hand on the man's shoulder and ushered him into the temple, turning back to Jared and mouthing 'Or less.'

Jared stood in the arcade, wondering how many doves he could count in an hour. He needed some way to curb the panic that gripped him. He felt a surge of fury at the useless birds who spent their lives eating and waddling and fouling the ground. They rarely even flew and were too fat to be decorative. He longed to run around the courtyard, scaring and scattering them, but he was afraid of being apprehended and accused of sacrilege.

With the sun stationary in a cloudless sky and his own perceptions erratic, he lost track of time. In other circumstances, he might have admired Zakir for not abandoning his companion; in these, he could only puzzle over his perversity. The man was old and ugly, with a lump at the end of his nose like a blocked nostril. From the gust that had hit him, Jared felt that his breath alone should have barred him from the temple. What possible use would he be to Ishtar? As her priest, Zakir had a responsibility to bring her the man who would give her the greatest pleasure: a young man full of pleasure that had not yet been tapped – except by Lilith, which didn't count.

He sat like a beggar on the temple steps, staring at the ground. He was roused not by a gift of food but by Zakir's burning hand on his shoulder. 'Don't look so frightened,' he said. 'I told you I wouldn't be long.'

'You've been hours!' Jared replied, more indignantly than he had intended.

'Don't, I'm not allowed to laugh. Come!' He heaved Jared to his feet and led him into the temple. Although it was as dark as ever, Jared felt sure of his step and followed Zakir towards the shrine, where he introduced him, not by name but by nationality, to a beautiful woman with the same black flowing hair as his own and wearing silver-and-gold embroidered robes, through which her breasts were almost as exposed as Ishtar's. Charging him to enjoy himself and promising him that he had made the right choice – although Jared was unclear whether she were referring to Ishtar or Zakir – she moved away to talk to a young man whom Jared had seen at the palace.

'Does she also serve Ishtar?'

'Of course.'

'But she's a woman.'

'So? Ishtar cares only for the gift, not the basket.'

'Will she give Ishtar pleasure with that man?'

'A great deal by the look of him.'

'But isn't there a danger?'

'Of what? That he'll strangle her in the throes of passion?'

'No!' Jared replied, feeling his own throat constrict. 'Babies!'

'Did they teach you nothing in Judah?'

'I was transported here when I was six.'

'Then the blame is ours. There are many safe ways for a woman to give a man pleasure. There's this.' He pouted his lips and sucked his finger in what looked like the parody of a kiss. 'And this.' He slid the same finger slowly down Jared's buttocks, stopping abruptly and poking.

'Ow!'

'Oh dear, if that's how you feel about a finger …'

'I was thinking about the women,' Jared said, fearful of depriving himself of a sensation that he had nonetheless resolved to resist.

'Yes, poor flowers! Still, I assure you that even in Judah—'

'Never!'

'When Mother and Father were anxious to avoid any more Jareds.'

Jared felt more uncomfortable than at any time since his fifth birthday when, the high priest having relaxed the food laws during the siege, his mother cooked him a plate of snails gathered by Asaph and Shimron, which had tasted like something that came out of his nose.

'Here!' Zakir said, grabbing his hand, which was suddenly flaccid. 'Show me that smile again.'

He conducted him through a small door at the side of the shrine, down a flight of sharply angled steps and into a narrow corridor, which smelt so damp that Jared suspected it must once have been part of the network of canals that ran beneath the city. They entered a small room, furnished only with a couch, a smoking lamp and a bronze statue of two male lovers. One of them clasped his own penis, something that Jared had been forbidden to do even as a child making water, his mother preferring to wipe up any mess than to put him in the way of temptation. Gazing at the protuberant organ, he thought for the first time that she might have been right. He wondered whether Zakir would be disappointed on seeing his own more modest member since, although he dared not articulate the feeling to himself, let alone to the priest, he sensed that he had brought him here to emulate the lovers.

'So what gift do you have for Ishtar?'

'Nothing. I didn't realise …'

'Do you want to insult the goddess?' Zakir asked, the warmth spilling out of his voice like water from a sluice.

'I thought we were giving her pleasure.'

'Pleasure has to be paid for. With barley, lentils, perfume, saffron, gold, whatever you have. Look at these!' He pressed his face against Jared's, pointing to the two crescent moons hanging from his ears. 'These were given to me by the man who was here before you: the man I cheated so that I could be with you.' Jared had thought that the gift was intended for Ishtar, but he knew better than to quibble. 'So what do you have?'

'Nothing. You never said. Does that mean I have to leave?'

'What's this?' Zakir pointed to his buckle.

'It's very precious,' Jared said, spontaneously covering it with his hand. 'A lion my uncle gave me to match my Babylonian name, *Muranu*.'

'Is it too precious to give to Ishtar?' Zakir asked, the smile restored to his face.

'No, of course not,' Jared said, gulping as Zakir rubbed his arms and chest with a sensuousness that made resistance futile. 'But my aunt stitched it on especially.'

'Not especially enough,' Zakir said, tearing the buckle from the belt. 'See how easily it fell off. I'm sure your aunt will understand.' To Jared's amazement, he bit the metal and then, as if pleased with the taste, slipped it into his sandal. 'Look! Your tunic's open. Take it off. And your loincloth. You mustn't deprive Ishtar of her due.'

Jared balked both at being ordered to disrobe and at Zakir's tone, which seemed to relish its own insincerity. Nevertheless, he did as he was asked, feeling as bashful as on his first night at the palace. Having shrugged off his tunic, he lingered over the loincloth, fearful of betraying an excitement that would expose him further. Meanwhile, Zakir threw off his shawl and slipped out of his robe, leaving himself totally naked except for his feet. Jared felt ashamed of his scrawny body, with its tufts of hair and patches of discoloured skin, beside Zakir's solid, hairless body, like the glazed brick of the temple walls. Then, with a gesture at once provocative and defiant, Zakir whipped off his wig, revealing that even his head was hairless.

Jared gasped, which, to judge by Zakir's grin, was the desired response. He kept his eyes fixed on Zakir's face and chest, fearful of what might lie lower. For all his show of sophistication among his friends, he was unsure what castration actually entailed. Finally gathering courage, he glanced down and, to his relief, found that, in appearance, Zakir was a complete man. Moreover, his excitement visibly matched his own.

Zakir approached him, unknotted his loincloth and pressed him to his chest. Jared had not been so close to anyone since infancy. Then he had fitted into the crook of his father's arm; now he fitted into Zakir's entire body – no, deeper, into the very core of his being. There was not one speck of him that did not feel sheltered. Like Adam before he ate the forbidden fruit, he was at peace with the whole of creation. His sole fear was that Lilith would make a final attempt to vanquish him, forcing him to spend before he could give Ishtar – and Zakir – the requisite pleasure. But, as if alive to the danger, Zakir held him tight, rubbing his back and nibbling his ear, until he had slowed the rhythm of his breathing and his blood. So far, Zakir had taken control but, adhering to his parents' laws in this, if in nothing else, Jared judged that it was for him to be the man. He slipped out of Zakir's grasp and tried to reverse their positions but, to his consternation, Zakir moved to a small chest, took out a vial of oil and smeared it first on his member and then, without warning, on Jared's buttocks, before thrusting him roughly on to the couch. Flat on his back with Zakir clasping his ankles in the air, he found himself staring straight at the statue of the two entwined men. For a split second, he knew what was happening before he felt it: a pain that pierced his bowels and spread through his body like a burning blade. He tried to escape but Zakir had the advantage of experience, posture and weight.

'You're hurting me,' he cried, outraged.

'No, I'm not,' Zakir said, with a conviction that Jared resented as much as the pain. 'Feel past it! Feel what's truly there.'

To his surprise, Jared found that he was right. The pain was still acute but, in a way that both dismayed and delighted him, it had become an intrinsic part of his pleasure. Every sensation contained its opposite. He was being ground into the earth and tossed into the sky. He was a fish gasping in a net and a lion tearing at its prey. He was hot and cold, strong and weak and, strangest of all, male and female. Was this what his aunt had meant when she warned of Ishtar's transformative powers?

Having tried to push Zakir away, Jared now drew him closer. He longed to taste the honeyed breath that had entitled him not just to enter but to reside in the temple; yet the moment he advanced his lips, Zakir recoiled, leaving him to wonder whether kissing were a unique Judean custom that the Babylonians regarded as unclean. Suddenly, Zakir's thrusts took on a more emphatic rhythm, to which Jared felt himself incidental. With a series of high-pitched yelps that turned him into one of Omri's joke eunuchs, he shook as though he were palsied, slid out of Jared and rolled panting on to the couch.

Jared felt a mixture of gratitude and awe that was swiftly subsumed by frustration. Freed from the urgency of Zakir's longing, he was subject to his own. His member ached so violently that he almost wanted Lilith to ravish him. But relief came from a far gentler hand, as Zakir reached over and caressed him with such fervour that he could no longer hold back. For the first time, he saw the nacreous drops, like desert dew, on his belly and knew that they were not the seed of demons.

Wordlessly, Zakir handed him a cup of pomegranate juice and rose water. Jared longed to lie beside him, savouring the warmth and comfort of his flesh before engaging in another bout of passion, but to suggest it seemed as selfish as asking for a second helping of a meal that his hosts were keeping back for the next day. Zakir, meanwhile, slipped on his robe, dashing any hope of further intimacy.

'Did you enjoy that?' he asked. Jared nodded, not trusting himself to speak. He felt utterly defenceless, lying naked and spent beneath Zakir's appraising gaze. He knew that he too should dress, but his limbs felt so heavy that he could barely move. 'Me too, even though I shouldn't.'

'But aren't you supposed to feel pleasure for Ishtar?'

'We're supposed to be the receptacles of her pleasure, not our own.'

'Will she be angry with you?'

'What strange questions you ask! If anything, she'll be surprised.' He nipped the hair on Jared's groin. 'What about your god? Will he be angry with you?'

'Yes … no … I don't know. I think that perhaps He won't care because it happened here in Ishtar's temple. Another faith,' he replied, his words more confident than his thoughts. Not only had he transgressed by lying with a man but, to his bemusement, he had played the woman's part. He tentatively broached the subject with Zakir.

'I hope you won't be offended—'

'That sounds ominous.'

'It's just that there's a harem at the palace.'

'No, that doesn't offend me.'

'That's not what I meant! The steward said that if we – myself or my friends – wanted to enter, we'd have to be castrated.'

'Why would you want to enter? From what I've seen, you're happier on this side of the wall.'

'That was before. And it wasn't just me; it was all of us,' Jared said awkwardly. 'I thought it was so that we wouldn't be a threat.'

'Nor would you be. If you must know, it depends when and what is removed. If I were in the harem, the women could still be pleasured and the king be in no doubt that any children they bore were his.'

'When did you dedicate yourself to Ishtar?' Jared asked, aware that, by its nature, the priesthood could not be hereditary.

'You're not one for idle chatter, are you?'

'I'm sorry. Have I offended you?'

'Not that again! Don't worry, men like me are hard to offend. If it's any concern of yours, I was brought here by my father – a destitute ropemaker. He was desperate to gain the goddess's favour. But how could he bring her lentils or barley when he had none even for his family? So, instead, he gave her his three children, solving both his problems at once.'

'Three children?'

'My sisters serve at the temple in Nineveh. I was destined to work in the temple fields, but one of the priests took a liking to me. He saw that I had something special.'

'So he had you castrated?' Jared asked, unable to mask his horror.

'Why not?' Zakir asked defiantly. 'He knew there was no higher calling and that I'd enjoy a privileged life. Twice a day, I eat food offered to the goddess – some of the best in the city. I bathe in her sacred baths. I'm allotted a share of her perfumes and robes. Who could ask for more?'

'Someone who wants children,' Jared said, speaking his thoughts aloud.

'And you! What about this?' Zakir asked angrily, pointing to Jared's member. 'A slave's mark. A cut that serves no purpose but to show your subjugation to your father. And to lessen your pleasure. Put on your clothes!'

Relieved to find that his arms and legs were moving again, Jared tied his loincloth and threw on his tunic. 'You may be right about the subjugation,' he said, conscious that, despite Zakir's denial, he had offended him. 'But not about the pleasure. I don't believe that anyone has ever felt as much pleasure as I have today. I was told that, if I lay with you, all my troubles would cease.'

'That's what they say,' Zakir replied, a faint smile forming on his lips.

'Forever?'

'Oh no. Then you'd never come again.'

'So I can come again?'

'I'm going nowhere,' Zakir said indifferently. 'You know the rules. Next time, bring something worthier of Ishtar than a buckle.'

As Zakir led him back down the corridor, Jared felt the damp rising from the ground through his sandals. He made his way across the temple courtyard into the street, where he was greeted by a profusion of smiles that seemed more knowing than they had done two hours before. He felt that everyone he passed could see – and smell – where he had been, but he feared that the goodwill would dissipate once he entered the palace gates. Taking no chances, he headed for the baths, only to be intercepted by Sheshbazaar, Jehozadak and Omri.

'Where have you been?' the Prince asked.

'Wandering round the city,' he replied. 'It's allowed.'

'Again?' the Prince asked.

'You and Cain,' Jehozadak said.

'I'm not a murderer!'

'I didn't say you were.'

'The voice of conscience!' Omri murmured.

'What is it you find so fascinating?' Sheshbazaar asked.

'He's meeting some girl,' Omri said.

Jehozadak snorted.

'I've done nothing wrong,' Jared said, striving to ignore the clammy reproach on his stomach.

'No? What about forgetting this afternoon's contest with the acrobats?' Omri asked. 'How could we mount three teams with only five men? Jehozadak had to pull out.'

'So I'd have been paired with you?' Jared asked Jehozadak.

'Definitely not.'

'The honour of Judah was at stake,' Sheshbazaar said.

'Not that he cares a fig for that,' Jehozadak said. 'He's all "the beauty of Babylon", "the glories of Babylon", even "the gods of Babylon". Have you forgotten that we're pledged to keep ourselves apart?'

'Oh really?' Jared asked, galled by his scorn. 'And how far do you keep yourself apart? You may not go into their temples but you eat their meat.'

'That's a filthy lie!'

'Where do you think the lamb comes from that we dine on every day while our countrymen make do with bowls of lentils and barley?'

'The palace kitchens.'

'Esagila. The food that's offered to Marduk. Piles and piles of it. Whatever the priests don't want is given to the king. Whatever the king doesn't want is given to his ministers. Whatever the ministers don't want is given to the stewards. And on and on until it reaches us. You may not have Marduk in your heart but you have him in your belly.'

Jehozadak vomited, his body instinctively atoning for the unwitting transgression. No punch of Jared's could have dealt his victim such a blow, but his satisfaction was short-lived since he spent the night racked with guilt for the triple betrayal of family, friends and faith. Any hope that his visit to Zakir would purge his longings vanished as he thrashed about from owl-light to cockcrow, the ache in his loins more insistent than ever. Morning brought no relief. For two days he was unable to eat, although his lie to Jehozadak meant that his abstinence passed unnoticed by the Judeans, who themselves shunned the tainted meat. He was unable to work, mangling his transcriptions until his knuckles were rapped more often than Omri's. He was unable to sleep, his senses so confused that the scent in his nose, taste in his mouth and touch on his flesh were all Zakir's, and he felt as if they were lying together, naked, in front of his friends and the scribes, stewards, servants and soldiers of the palace.

His desire for Zakir grew so intense that he longed for his death. He pictured an earthquake or fire destroying Ishtar's temple with all her priests inside it. His willingness to countenance such carnage as a way to escape temptation horrified him and he sought less drastic remedies for his plight. Neriah, the most knowing of his fellows in matters of the heart, had declared it impossible for anyone to recapture the excitement of a first encounter, which was why King Solomon had had a thousand wives and concubines and King Nebuchadrezzar maintained his harem. So, after much deliberation, Jared chose to confront his passion head-on and, like a carpenter driving out one nail with another, use a new visit to the temple to dislodge the memory of the old, trusting that once disillusioned with Zakir, he would be able to restore his higher organs to their rightful primacy.

He was wrong. Despite the difficulty of slipping away unnoticed and the need to take gifts, which, lacking resources, he had to purloin from his family, he returned to the temple three times during the next two weeks. But, far from cloying his appetite, his visits sharpened it. The more relaxed he felt in Zakir's presence, the freer he felt to express his desires. The more accustomed he grew to Zakir's body, the less ashamed he grew of his own. He found himself honouring Ishtar in pleasure more devoutly than he had ever done Yahweh in prayer. Although dismayed both by Zakir's coldness after he had spent, and his claim that his only interest in him lay in his gifts, Jared sensed a powerful bond between them. He was determined to break it and, while wary of invoking Yahweh, he prayed that he might be more like his companions – not Sheshbazaar, which would have been presumptuous, or Jehozadak, who, he suspected, was already more like him than he cared to admit, but, Hushai, Omri and Neriah, three guileless men who slept easily at night with dreams that they could joke about in the morning.

The Lord did not answer his prayers but then, according to Micaiah, He would not answer any prayer, however deserving, until the Judeans had returned to Jerusalem, rebuilt the

Temple and performed the ordained sacrifices. It was therefore even more urgent that Jared set aside his own concerns to work on the scrolls, the one place where the exiles could still hear the voice of Yahweh. To complicate matters, even as he was battling his own desires, he was working on the part of Abraham's story that pertained to Sodom.

When teaching them the sacred stories in Tel-Abib, the elders had skimmed over Sodom. Even after Ezekiel forced the issue during a particularly savage harangue in which he likened both it and Jerusalem to whores, they preferred to dwell on the Lord's acceptance of Abraham's challenge to stay His hand if He found as many as ten righteous men living there, than on the wickedness of the city itself. Although they presented it as proof of the Lord's regard for His chosen people, Jared remained unconvinced and subjected his father to a battery of questions. First, how had Abraham, who obeyed the Lord in everything, plucked up the courage to confront Him, and not on behalf of his kinsmen but of strangers? Second, if the city were so corrupt, why had Lot stayed there, exposing his wife and daughters to its influence? Third, even if the men of Sodom were depraved, what about the women and, especially pertinent to him, the children? Why did the innocent have to suffer? Fourth and most important, in what exactly did the wickedness consist?

While his father dismissed his questions even more brusquely than those about the loquacity of Balaam's ass, Asaph had been happy to fill in the gaps. He explained, so graphically that Jared was grateful for Micaiah's reticence, that the men of Sodom had grown bored with their wives and lusted first after one another and then after the angels whom the Lord had sent to investigate them. Jared, who as a boy had recoiled from any intimacy that was neither familial nor playful, was appalled by such coupling; now that he had known it himself, he was appalled by its punishment. As he copied the story, he pictured the unsuspecting Sodomites consumed by fire and crushed by falling masonry, and he wondered about the status of a scroll streaked with tears.

Seeking distraction, he rummaged in the chest of discarded scrolls, where he chanced on one that put the story in a very different light. Here, the Sodomites' transgression lay not in their lusts but in the worship of their own god, Baal. It was not Yahweh who denounced them but Abraham and his steward Eliezer. The men were not trying to molest the angels but to discover whether they were Abraham's spies, and Lot did not offer up his daughters to satisfy their jaded appetites, but used the spectre of their violation to underline the horror of mistreating his guests. Not only did it exonerate Lot but it explained the Lord's goodwill towards him, since it was impossible to believe that He would rescue a man who made such a monstrous proposal while punishing those who rejected it.

The questions that exercised him now were not about the sin but about the scroll and, above all, why it had been placed in the chest, which, once filled, would have been buried in the Temple precinct, condemning the story to oblivion. He scrutinised every line for a sacrilegious smudge or error. Unable to find the slightest flaw, he deduced that this was not an aberrant or imperfect copy but the original account, which had been rejected at the time of King Josiah's reforms in favour of the one he had been taught in Tel-Abib. If he were right, by restoring it he would not only be honouring Yahweh but reversing the deception perpetrated by his ancestors. He had, however, reckoned without Jehozadak, who snatched the half-finished copy from his writing board while he was talking to Hushai.

'This is impious!' Jehozadak said, scanning it. 'You've pulled the teeth from the story, as if it were one of the king's pet lions.'

'I've written what I've found. See for yourself!' Jared replied, passing him the scroll.

'You've found what you wanted to write,' Jehozadak said, knocking away his hand. 'Is this how you plan to impress the king? By painting the Sodomites as Babylonians, worshipping false gods? Just as you do yourself. And what does Moses tell us in the Book of Law? That it's our duty – our sacred duty – to kill all those who proclaim false gods, no matter if they're our wives or our sons or our daughters or our closest friends. To kill you!'

Jared bristled at hearing words that might even have been devised by his grandfather imbued with a spurious authority and directed at him.

'So what are you waiting for?' Jehozadak turned to Hushai, rheum dripping from his nose and spittle from his lips. 'Go ahead! Kill him!'

'You're overwrought,' Hushai said. 'Why quarrel? It's only a story.'

'It's our story! It's what the Lord wants from us and therefore from the world. The sin of Sodom is spelt out – not in an abandoned scroll unearthed from an ancient chest where it was placed for a reason—'

'Yes, to stop us finding it,' Jared said.

'But in the words of Moses himself. The Sodomites were filled with such unnatural lusts that they even sought to ravish the angels of the Lord when they assumed the shape of men. What's more, the sin didn't die with them. It persists to this day, and not just among the Hittites and Babylonians but among the Lord's own people. Some of them known to us.'

Jared shuddered at the force of the invective. But even at the height of his fury, even in the depth of his disgust, Jehozadak could not bring himself to accuse him, as though the implications were too grave. He clung to the fact that Jehozadak had no proof, unless it were his unconvincing ribaldry about the women in the harem. And not everyone would support Jehozadak's argument, as Hushai, swallowing his discomfort, made clear.

'How can you be so sure that the Sodomites' transgression was unnatural lust? You said yourself, the Lord punished them for trying to ravish His angels.'

'Welcome, Hushai the peacemaker!' Jehozadak said scornfully. 'But you're wrong. Their transgression can't have been against the angels since the Lord had decided to destroy the city before He sent them.'

'So why send them?' Jared asked.

'Because He'd made a promise to Abraham.'

'Why should the Lord God, creator of the universe, defer to a mere man?'

'Not any man – Abraham! The man He chose to be the father of His people. Why did He save Lot, who'd aligned himself with the wicked city, if not because he was of the house of Abraham? In the same way He'll save all of the house of Abraham who obey His laws. But you not only break those laws, you encourage others to break them. Your offence is worse – far worse – than the Sodomites' because you perpetuate theirs. You seek to justify it. But not any more! I shall tear this scroll in two—'

'No!' Jared shouted.

'No!' Hushai echoed. 'It contains the holy name.'

Jared had never felt such reason to be grateful for the laws governing his craft.

'Very well,' said Jehozadak, breathing heavily. 'You have a choice, Jared. Either you can put both these false scrolls in the chest with all the other forgeries and rubbish, and return to the teachings of your father – and of mine. Or I shall go to Ashpenaz and tell him that you're fabricating stories in an attempt to delude the king.'

Jehozadak left the library, followed after a moment's hesitation by Hushai. Jared sat despondently, watching the ink cake on his pen. He considered his options. He could ignore Jehozadak's warning and put his own case to Ashpenaz, thereby revealing dissension in the Judean ranks and giving the steward a pretext for cancelling a project of which he had always been doubtful. Or he could comply with Jehozadak's demands and submit the standard story to the king who, if he approved it, would sanction the transcription of all the scrolls, which in turn would provide solace to the exiles. Yet to do so would be to deny not only his own deepest feelings, but the truth.

With his head cracking like a tablet left too long in the kiln, he was eager to escape. Ashpenaz had arranged for the Judeans to attend a display of hawking, but Jared had no wish to confront his friends, who would already have received a report of the dispute, coloured either by Hushai's embarrassment or Jehozadak's sanctimony. He was equally reluctant to visit his family, since his father was sure to question him about the scrolls and his aunt to be fretting over her missing jewellery. So instead, he took the well-trodden path through the blistering streets to the one place where he could be certain of a welcome: the place that he had most been seeking to avoid.

He entered the temple courtyard to find it busier than ever. Drawn by the furious drumbeat, he elbowed his way through the crowd to find a group of priests, including Zakir, dancing ecstatically, skin torn and robes splattered, slashing their arms and chests and scourging their backs. Jared watched with a mixture of fascination and abhorrence, while the ravening spectators urged them on. In the centre, largely hidden by the adults, was a boy of indeterminate age, stark naked, with his member bandaged to his belly. Blood sprayed from his wounds as he whirled and writhed, leaping and stumbling, frenziedly slicing himself. With the drums and timbrels growing louder, the priests stepped aside, leaving the boy alone. Finally, one of their number approached him from behind and, steadying him with one hand, placed the other on the hilt of his knife and guided it towards his loins. For a moment the boy resisted and then, with a single sweep, he slit open his own sack. His mouth gaped in agony, emitting a lupine howl, before his head slumped to his chest. With the boy insensible in his arms, the priest leant forward and, plunging his hands in the butchered flesh, plucked out his two stones, which he brandished to deafening cheers. Two of his fellow priests advanced and wrapped the boy in a white cloth that swiftly turned scarlet. Lifting him high above their heads, they made a circuit of the rapturous onlookers, many of whom reached up to touch the inert body. Then, as one, they parted to allow the priests to carry him into the temple. The third priest walked behind, arms sleeved with blood, shouting 'A gift to Ishtar!', although Jared was unsure whether he meant the boy or his stones.

He recoiled from the barbarism, which had left the temple courtyard as gory as the one in Jerusalem. There, at least the sacrifices had been goats or rams rather than children. For the first time, Jehozadak's charge of idol-worship rang true, but he put it from his mind as he rushed to intercept Zakir, who was climbing the temple steps.

'I'm so glad I've found you,' he said, averting his eyes from the blood-soaked robe.

'It shouldn't be hard. I cannot leave the precinct without permission from the Entu.'

'May we speak?'

'We are speaking.'

'You know what I mean.'

'Be quick then! I have to welcome a new devotee to Ishtar.'

'What about afterwards?'

'You're free to wait. Anyone who brings a gift to the goddess has the right to the services of one of her priests.'

'Yes, of course,' Jared replied, horrified by his lack of foresight. 'I brought a jewel – a ruby – but it was lost in the crush. I promise I'll bring another tomorrow.'

'Then I'll be waiting for you tomorrow.'

'You can trust me. I promise I won't cheat you.'

'Ishtar puts no value on promises.'

'But I need to see you today.'

'What do I care for your needs?' Zakir asked, his cheeks as red as his arms. 'My only concern is Ishtar.'

'But you said yourself that I'd given you pleasure as well as Ishtar.'

'Perhaps. For a moment that was as meaningless as it was brief.'

Zakir wrapped his shawl around his head and entered the temple. Jared watched, his gaze lingering on the great bronze door until the lions, owls and stars on its panels began to merge. Narrowing his eyes, he turned back to the courtyard, which, as the crowd dispersed, was filling with doves who, to his disgust, were gobbling up the blood-speckled crumbs. He strode along the arcade, telling himself that he should be glad that his connection with Zakir had been severed as permanently as the boy's sack, but the words rang hollow. He was so sunk in gloom that he failed to spot the four men waiting for him immediately outside the gates, as if weighing the risk of his escape against that of their own pollution. Accosted by Sheshbazaar, Jehozadak, Omri and Neriah, he could think only of Hushai and whether he were absent by chance or by choice.

'What did I tell you?' Jehozadak asked his companions, gripping Jared's wrist with unnecessary force.

'I thought you were watching the hawking,' Jared said, shaking him off. 'Did you come to the ceremony instead?'

'Don't act the innocent,' Jehozadak said. 'The temple of Ishtar. The most debauched, the most profane of all their idols.'

'No, you don't understand. There's a peace, a harmony—' He broke off at the thought of the doves' bloodstained beaks. 'How did you know I was here?'

'The eyes of the righteous are sharp,' Jehozadak said.

'We followed you,' Neriah interposed bluntly.

'This is the reason you tried to distort the sacred story,' Jehozadak said. 'You've been corrupted by the Babylonians just as Lot was by the Sodomites, lingering in the sinful city even after the Lord ordered him to leave. What will your uncle say when he learns the truth about the nephew he recommended to Ashpenaz? And your father?'

Jared felt as helpless as the boy before the baying crowd. 'No! You mustn't say anything to my father. It would destroy him. Sheshbazaar, please tell him. He'll listen to you.'

'My father, together with my entire family, is confined to four rooms. One king, two queens, four princes and three princesses. I'm the only one allowed to leave without a guard. And you expect me to concern myself with the feelings of a scribe?' he asked, in a voice dripping with contempt.

'Then I beg you myself,' Jared said to Jehozadak, 'in the name of your own father.'

'My father, really? My father, who was murdered at Riblah, while yours was released? My father, who didn't have a prophet to intercede for him? It's bad enough that I've had to sit with you, to study with you, to sleep in the same room as you, to listen to your lies … yes, we spoke to Ashpenaz. He took us into the kitchens and showed us where the meat was prepared. Not a single piece comes from Esagila. Now he too knows the sort of man you are.'

'That was a low trick, Jared,' Omri said sadly.

'I'm sorry. It was just that you were all being so superior.'

'We are superior,' Jehozadak said. 'Superior to a man who's betrayed his friends and his family and his king and his nation and …' He stumbled over the words in his desperation not to omit any of Jared's victims. 'And above all, the Lord. Let's go,' he said to the others. 'Before we're thoroughly contaminated.'

Jehozadak led Sheshbazaar, Omri and Neriah away, leaving Jared to wait at the gates until he felt safe to follow them back to the palace. Rejected, first by Zakir and then by his fellows, he had never felt so alone. At least now he understood Jehozadak's hostility towards him. Far from being the only way to express feelings stronger than friendship, it reflected his deep-rooted envy and resentment. Nothing in the Law was more unjust than to blame a son for his father's transgressions. But it was even more unjust of Jehozadak to blame him for his father's preservation. Every Judean saved was a reason to rejoice, yet he had turned it into a reproach. And this was the man who, should the exiles return to Jerusalem, would assume his place as high priest.

The next day Jehozadak made good his threat, obtaining permission from Asardin, the spindle-legged scribe who taught calculations, to miss the lesson in order to meet Jaazaniah. Jared, charged with predicting the annual level of the Euphrates based on its fluctuations during the king's reign, received a stinging rap on the knuckles when he worked out that in five years it would have dried up. He was trying to avoid a similar blunder with barley yields when Jehozadak returned, looking smug. Soon afterwards, an under-steward summoned Jared to Ashpenaz's room, where he was confronted not by the man himself but by a grim-faced Jaazaniah who, after repeating what Jehozadak had told him, asked if he had anything to add. Eager to unburden himself, he admitted having taken his aunt's earrings as a gift for Ishtar, but his relief at confessing vanished when Jaazaniah berated him for both stealing his own betrothal gift and allowing suspicion to fall on a servant, who had been flogged and dismissed.

After begging forgiveness, which his uncle grudgingly granted, because 'at your age, I did as bad – worse – although in a better cause,' Jared turned his mind to the servant. 'Can we try to find her, explain what happened (that is, some of it), and invite her back?'

'Would you have me root around the city's taverns? You need to learn, Jared, that being a man means admitting your mistakes and accepting the consequences, for others as well as yourself.'

'I'll do whatever you ask.'

'Will you? You've brought shame on us all. You've made us complicit in your crimes.'

'By dismissing the servant?' Jared asked, too queasy to mention the flogging.

'Would that were all! I was bitterly attacked for marrying Beletsarrausur by many in our community, who appeared to forget that King Solomon himself took foreign wives. But I was in love, whereas you are in lust – and lust of the most degenerate sort. You mock everything our people hold dear.'

Despite Jaazaniah's revulsion at Zakir and his fellow priests during the New Year procession, Jared had hoped that he would show more sympathy for his own nephew. Was he afraid that any impropriety would reflect on him? Or was he genuinely shocked by Jared's behaviour?

'Are you listening to me, boy?' Jaazaniah asked.

'Yes, of course,' Jared replied, blenching.

'You've broken faith with me and your friends, and you'll break your father's heart.'

'You won't tell him? Surely there's no need? If I promise never again to go near the temple: if I promise never even to think about it.'

'That's easy to say.'

'If I swear by my love for the Lord.'

'And what of your love for Ishtar? No, don't speak! I'm going to tell you something very painful and, in doing so, I shall break an oath myself: an oath that I made to your father. It wasn't the official reports of Asaph's disappearance that took me to Tel-Abib but the word I received from your mother.'

'I knew it!'

'What?' Jaazaniah asked in surprise.

'I mean I suspected it.'

'She told me what had happened to your father.'

'I was there; I saw.'

'You saw part of it.'

'I saw him beaten ... stripped ... humiliated,' Jared said, struggling with both the words and the memories.

'But you didn't see him violated,' Jaazaniah said quietly. 'That was the real humiliation. That was a torment far worse than any beating. They took his manhood away. Do you understand?'

'Yes,' replied Jared, at last understanding the sullenness and the silences, the sudden bursts of rage and, worse, of tears.

'And, if you persist in your defiance: if you flout the Law yourself and seek to rewrite it for others, then you'll be doing everything that the soldiers did to him – and worse.'

Jared felt as if he had been shackled at the neck and bound at the wrists and flung into the foulest dungeon beside King Zedekiah, his eye sockets crawling with insects. This was the true curse of seeing his father's nakedness: to know that an act that had given his own life meaning had destroyed Micaiah's. Desperate to atone, he agreed to all Jaazaniah's demands: to relinquish control of the copying to Jehozadak, helping him when asked and without argument; to devote himself to his studies, proving worthy of the trust placed in him and of a post in the administration; and, most importantly, never again to set foot in Ishtar's temple or to have dealings with her priests. Satisfied, Jaazaniah sent him back to his fellows who, in time, came to treat him much as they had done in the past: Jehozadak with antipathy; Sheshbazaar with disdain; Neriah and Omri with indifference; Hushai with warmth, except in the dormitory where even he kept aloof.

Jehozadak's transcription of the Abraham stories met with the king's approval. According to Ashpenaz, who ignored the irony, he was especially intrigued by the adoption of circumcision, which he credited with sapping the strength of many of his enemies. He expressed interest in hearing more stories of the Judeans and their god Yahweh, although Jared doubted that his enthusiasm would last should Jehozadak present him with a full account of King David's victories. Meanwhile, he consoled himself with the thought that, despite excluding his version of the Sodom story, Jehozadak could not expunge it completely. With the scrolls protected by the holy name, he had stored them in the Temple chest. And every time that Jared visited the library, either to assist with the copying or to study the ancient Assyrian tablets of whose script he had developed a mastery, he let his eyes stray to the rusty, rough-hewn chest and prayed that someday someone would recover its riches.

TWO

The Presentation of the Pageant

'The Ignorance of priests casteth the people into the ditch of error.'

Constitutions of Lambeth, 1281

That I am still with you attests to the power of the myth. The wings you gave me enable me to move not only through space but through time. I am, however, a shadow of my former selves. Where once I announced momentous events and shattered great cities, I am now 'guaranteed to deliver a personal message of Divine Inspiration' to everyone who purchases a set of Angel Gabriel cards. But in the late Middle Ages that inspiration was not so easily bought. Of all the eras of human history, it was then that we exerted the most profound influence over your everyday lives. Not only did you credit us with governing the seven planets and the four seasons, but you endowed every blade of grass with its own guardian angel. Ordinary people offered prayers and incantations to gain our favour. Theologians at the newly founded universities hotly debated the celestial hierarchy: whether Thrones ranked above Dominions or Dominions above Thrones. So abstruse were these debates that, in later years, they were said to have included one on how many of us could dance on a pinhead. But that is as apocryphal as the tale of the friars who revered my moulted feathers as relics. The one is a scholarly fabrication, the other a literary fantasy, both designed to demonstrate the superiority of the rationalist mind.

The most tortuous debates concerned our material nature. In the early Christian centuries we were classed as animals, albeit ones with no oesophagus, duodenum, stomach, small or large intestine or, of course, genitalia. Then, at the Lateran council of 1215, we were proclaimed to be pure spirit. The doctrine was refined by St Thomas Aquinas, who declared that, when necessary, we assumed a body that we could manipulate like a marionette. We had no actual physical functions. We did not speak but rather fashioned sounds in the air, which were perceived as words. We did not eat, so that when the Bible describes our dining with Abraham in his tent and Lot in Sodom, we were merely going through the motions, presumably to avoid offending our hosts. I should add that the issue, however vexed for Christians and Jews, was irrelevant to Muslims, since there is no mention of our eating in the Qur'an.

Without bodies, we had neither gender nor sex. Although Aquinas and his followers based their doctrine on Christ's teaching that, at the Resurrection, people would not marry but be like the angels, the association of sexlessness and purity stretches as far back as Genesis and the serpent's seduction of Eve. It baffles me that a belief in innate human evil maintains its hold on the imaginations of even those of you who have long since abandoned the Scriptures. Like the serpent condemned to crawl on its belly, for whom detumescence does not signal impotence, it continues to spit its venom. Equally baffling is that you have made sexuality, the most elemental form of God's creativity, into the root of that evil, transforming it from a blessing to a curse.

My own imagination may be restricted by the roles in which you have cast me, but I am at a loss to understand why you no sooner asserted your unique place in the divine order, declaring that you were made in God's image, than you pictured yourselves in thrall to your baser nature, defining yourselves not by the God who created you but by the earth into which He breathed. To explain this discrepancy, you introduced an external agent – whether Lucifer, Iblis, Satan or the Devil – and to explain his power, you introduced an earlier fall in heaven, a state of perfect bliss in which rebellion is inconceivable. Try as I might, I find no logic in making a character of your own invention the agent of your undoing. The truth is not that evil is stronger than good but that a belief in evil is stronger than a belief in good. Lucifer's power is over your perception not your fate. Although, as so often, perception determines fate.

I too played a part in the Eden story, albeit non-canonically, for according to tradition I was one of the angels whom God sent to oversee the Garden. On his deathbed, Adam told his son Seth how the Devil took advantage of our temporary absence in heaven to tempt Eve. Since I must therefore bear a measure of blame for what ensued, I trust that you will permit me to offer a corrective. Just as I have accrued characteristics from the many paintings, poems and plays in which I have featured over the years, so I have developed a degree of understanding from the various theological treatises in which I have been cited. In my version of the story, when Adam and Eve eat the forbidden fruit, their eyes would be opened not to their nakedness, with all the shame that that has bequeathed to subsequent generations, but to age and pain and frailty and decay. The knowledge that they gained would be not of sin but of time. It is time that gives human life meaning but that also manifests your distance from God. It is time that introduces imperfection into the universe. It is time that will, in time, be redeemed by eternity.

You have coupled my role at the beginning of time with one at the end of it. It is I who am to herald the Last Judgement, when all of you, past, present and to come, will be held to account for your deeds on earth. In recent years, judgement has fallen from fashion. You are more likely to hear me blowing my horn in a popular song than in a Sunday sermon. But in the late fourteenth century, when consciousness of sin and fear of retribution were universal, my apocalyptic role was much in evidence, from the Doom painting on the chancel arch of the parish church, which separated you from the priest at the altar, to the final pageant in the annual Corpus Christi Day cycle, when you watched your fellow townsmen enact God's reckoning and wondered whether you were destined for a place on the right of the wagon with the saved or on the left with the damned.

THE SALTERS

Lot's Wife or The Destruction of Sodom

Gabriel: Good people all to me take tent
I Gabriel am.
Raphael: I Raphael hight.
Gabriel: Bright angels twain from Heaven sent
By gracious God of main and might.
To Sodom borough have we hied
Where men do dwell in loathliest sin
As black as buboes on the skin.
Covetise, gluttony and pride,
Sloth and lechery here abide.
And God would it confound.
To Abraham his darling dear
Yet hath he pledged his troth
If ten straight-fingered men appear
He will foreswear his wrath
And all the rest scape safe and sound.
Raphael: Now quick, descend we to the ground.

Lot: The chapel bell hath chimed eight
To end my wonted sweat and swink
So sit I down by city gate
To rest my weary corse and think.
But lo, what fellows have we here
Of raiment bright and golden hair
And countenance so pink?
Gabriel: We greet thee, Lot, thou worthy wight!

Lot: How kennest thou my name?
Gabriel: With Abraham were we last night
And Sarah his reverenced dame.
For we are come from God on high
To this most naughty city
To see if all herein must die
Or else procure his pity.
Lot: Alas! I like not this to hear
But bow I to my dread Lord's will.
His word to me is ever dear,
I promise to obey it still.
But see, the night upon us falls,
I bid ye lodge within my house.
Tarry a wink beside these walls
Whiles I go hence to rouse my spouse.
Gabriel: Stir not, thou deft and doughty swain,
Of murk we are not craven.
Here in the street we will remain,
The heavens be our haven.
Lot: Prithee with me be not aloof
Ye men so fair and limber,
But pass the night beneath my roof
With drink and belly-timber.
Raphael: I thank thee, Lot, upon my life
And here we will not lag.
But shroud our purpose from thy wife
For women's tongues do ever wag.
Lot: Fear not my masters both,
My helpmeet I will handle,
Though she be crabbed and loath
And apt to scold and brandle.
So enter now my hall
Albeit mean and humble.
Wife, come thee hither when I call
And make nor moan nor mumble.

Wife: To rend my rest what right hast thou,
Old Lot, thou ancient looby?
I rue the day I didst thee trow,
Thou ever dost beshrew me.
Lot: These strangers met I on the road,
So show them parfait courtesy
And welcome them to our abode
Lest we by God accursed be.
Wife: Wouldst thou to every waif and straif
Dispose of all our chattel?
Lot: Now take them in and keep them safe
And cease thy foolish prattle.
To give what cheer my house may find
It is my bounden duty.
Wife: I say thee nay … I change my mind.
I ne'er have seen such beauty.
Lot: Bring pease pudding and stottie cake
And all my pantry doth afford.
And, woman, see thou undertake
To whisper not a word abroad.
Wife: Nay husband, wouldst thou have me be
A tainted leper in this land?
Raphael: Good mistress, hie thee silently
For we have mighty hefts in hand.
Wife: Pray masters, do not frown,
No word will I repeat.
Draw near the fire and sit ye down
While I fetch forth some meat.

Wife: Alack, I wish that I were blind!
I see we have no salt.
I fear that these good men must find
My provender at fault.
As all this company doth know
'Tis salt gives food its flavour.

Into the street I now will go
To beg some from a neighbour.
Good gossips all, to ye I plead
To lend that blessed condiment
That I my noble guests may feed
And suffer no impediment.

1 Gossip: What guests be these? For thou kenn'st well
The law of this our borough,
No traveller herein may dwell
Without inspection thorough.

Wife: Such men as ne'er mine eyes did spy,
Fine of figure, fair of face,
Beauteous as the butterfly,
Ornaments of Heaven's grace.
Diamonds, rubies, sapphires, pearls,
Of all mankind they bear the flower.
These peerless knights, these precious earls,
To my two girls shall bring the dower.

1 Gossip: Fret not, thou beldame sweet,
Accept this peck of salt
That thou might spice thy meat
And thy fairheads exalt.

Wife: Gramercy, honest friends,
To home repair I fast
To season their viands
And furnish their repast.

1 Gossip: Forsooth, I fain would shed a tear
That men so meet to marry
Of all the houses far and near
In hers do choose to tarry.

2 Gossip: My beds are just as soft as hers
My daughters just as comely.

1 Gossip: Then let us hasten to our sirs
Lest they should linger dumbly.
Goodman give ear, I prithee,

To tidings thou wist not,
Two foreigners in privity
This night do bide with Lot.

1 Man: Thou dightest me in deepest dole
For 'tis against our laws.
All foreigners must pay a toll
That lean within our doors.

2 Man: So haste we to this varlet bold
That is himself a guest,
That robbeth us of righteous gold
And scorneth our behest.

Gabriel: Mistress, we thank thee for our food
So plenteous and hale.

Wife: Sirs, take ye more if it be good.
Some wine or Adam's ale?

Raphael: No more, for we have had our fill
(In truth we did but semble),
But wherefore haps this bruit so shrill
That makes the walls to tremble?

1 Daughter: The burgesses from wide and side
Are come to seek these strangers.
Alas, alack and woe betide,
That we must face such dangers.

Lot: But how ken they our company?

Wife: I craved of them some salt.

Lot: Thou blab-tale!

Wife: Keep in memory:
Soft fire maketh sweet malt.

1 Man: Open thy gate at our requests
Sir Lot, thou sorry minion.
And to our charge release thy guests
O'er whom we claim dominion.

Lot: Forsooth, good friends, forbear
To make such scathe and scorn.

The men ye seek are now at prayer.
Return ye in the morn.

1 Man: Eschew thy wrenches and thy wiles,
The morn will come too late.
By then an hundred miles
Will be they from thy gate.

2 Man: Withdraw thou lurdan lout,
And let me through the door,
Else I will fetch thy scalp a clout
To fell thee to the floor.

Lot: Good sirs, the honour of my house
I pray do not defile.
'Tis dear to me as is my spouse.
Renounce this place awhile.

1 Man: And who art thou – and what – and whence
To lord it over us?
Bring out these men. Cease thy pretence.
Else will I beat thee thus!

Lot: Daughters twain have I within
As fair as they are pure,
I yield ye my most precious kin
If ye this sin abjure.

Wife: Fie husband, dost thou wish to be
Of all the world reviled,
To pledge thy daughters' chastity
To men so rough and wild?
These maids I girdled in my womb
And nourished at my breast.
My rueful eyes o'erspread with rheum
For I am sore distressed.

Lot: Peace wife, do not me blame
For 'tis my wilful policy
To put these noisome men to shame
That they may do us courtesy.

1 Daughter: Good father, do not force us

With these rude men to go.
1 Man: Now by Mahomet, in we truss!
Raphael: Mark how these caitiffs madden so.
Gabriel: Still and mild here have I stood
And hearkened to this wanton rout.
'Tis time to whelm them – by the rood!
And send them groping round about.
By God's good grace their eyes I brass
That they no solid shape shall see.
1 Man: Is this the grass?
2 Man: No, 'tis my arse.
1 Man: Say wellaway, alack is me!
For I am blind as stone.
He hath skelped us full sore.
2 Man: Now for the nonce we are undone
And driven sightless from the door.
Wife: I wit that ye be angels bright,
To ye I fealty give.
I laud your name this hallowed night
And aye while I do live.
Raphael: Let not my words be wrought in waste,
Lot, wife and daughters twain,
But quit this place in highest haste
For fear that ye be slain.
Gabriel: This city like is to the plum
That pleasing looketh to the eye,
But inwardly there lurks the worm
That causes all to putrefy.
The men of Sodom for their faults
Yet showeth no contrition,
So God doth send from Heaven's vaults
His mightiest malison.
Raphael: Then gird ye up and flee this town
That is of God accursed.
The towers all shall be torn down

And folk in fire immersed.
But turn ye not your hindward gaze
On this sin-blackened city
Lest sight of bodies all ablaze
Should move your hearts to pity.
Lot: My daughters dear and froward wife,
God biddeth us this bodeword,
We who would scape this bitter strife
Must flee and glent not backward.
Wife: Nay press me not this place to quit
Hereby I still will settle,
For I have meat that roasts on spit
And wort that boils in kettle.
I must ceruse put on my face
And kirtle o'er my smock.
To wend like this will me abase,
The neighbours all make mock.
Lot: They now are blind and soon will die
In sulphur and in reek.
Within an hour we hence must fly.
Wife: Ask me anew next week!
1 Daughter: Sweet mother mine, forsake thy sloth
Since we this wicked lieu must leave.
Wife: Thou dotest, daughter, by my troth,
Lief were I to sit here and weave.
Lot: Did not great God at Adam's fall
That followed from Eve's hand
Make him her lord for aye and all
To practise aught he did command?
So now, beldame, to end this broil
I thrust thee through the gate.
That we may set our feet on soil
Afore it be too late.

Wife: My game, my glee, from me is reft.
I tramp and trape o'er down and dale,
O'er frith and fell and cliff and cleft.
What man can boot me of my bale?
2 Daughter: Kind mother take my heed,
Thy dolour mortify,
All-wielding God is good indeed.
Wife: Hold! Dost thou hear that cry?
1 Man: In dungeon of dole are we cast,
We fear to step out of the door.
Lightning doth flame and thunder blast
And pitch from the welkin doth pour.
2 Man: The city steeples melt
Like snow in an April morn.
And we shall all be keit—
Wife: Whence comes this shout forlorn?
Alas, alack, I must look back,
The solemn walls do crumble.
Roofs rive and chimneys crack,
As to the earth they tumble.
And I do crumble with the rest
So grievous is my fault.
My foot, my leg, my arm, my breast
Are turned into salt.
Lot: Adieu thou stiff and headstrong dame
That ne'er attended me.
For aye and o shall be thy shame
Transformed thus to be.
1 Daughter: I weep to see thee, mother dear
That ne'er from hence may roam,
But aye will be interred here
In sad and salty tomb.
Lot: Wipe dry thy brine, my daughters twain.
In this drear bailiwick,
A mildful stone she will remain

For hungry kine to lick.
Now let us busk and press ahead
Whiles yet the sun be bright
For divers beasts of mickle dread
Do prowl this stead at night.

1 Daughter: Look father, I a cave espy!
The great Lord sans mistake
Doth grant to us a sanctuary
Where we our cares may slake.

Lot: Then shortly hie we in to kneel
All-puissant God to bless,
That wendeth all wights to his weal
And easeth their distress.

1

Ralf clasped the angel's crown and tapped the bronze wings on the door. He was greeted by the Underwoods' steward with the mixture of disdain and deference due to one with so little sway in this world and so much in the next. He walked through the great hall where, notwithstanding the warmth of the June morning and the absence of company, a fire blazed in the grate, doubtless to show off the chimney that was Marjorie's latest indulgence. He climbed the stairs, noting dispassionately the ache in his knees, and entered the gallery. His hosts stood in the centre: Walter in a samite tunic and purple robe trimmed with ermine; Marjorie in a silver caul and the green-and-yellow gown she had worn at Lammas. Their guests were likewise resplendent, as though vying with the players in the pageants. Only Edmund had eschewed such pomp and, despite his contempt for outward appearance, confined himself to the colour of his grief.

For the third successive year, Walter had procured the right to have the Corpus Christi pageants presented outside his house. His was the sixth station, midway along the route, immediately after the most perilous passage for the wagons where they turned sharp left from Ouse Bridge into Coney Street. Despite the station-holder's fee, the cost of scaffolding and the Chamberlain's levy of every third penny from the lease of the seats, he was satisfied that he would make a fair profit. Ralf would have preferred to watch from the street where the air was cooler and the view less obscured, since he was obliged to stand back from the window in deference to more honoured guests, but he could not refuse an invitation from his patrons. Besides, the well-furnished sideboard had its compensations. Gazing at the venison, mutton, goose, stuffed carp, wheels of cheese, pies, honeyed fruits and custards, he prayed that he would not succumb to the sin to which he was most prone.

To his dismay, his gaze was intercepted by Edmund: the same Edmund who once declared that, had he known Ralf's appetite, his grandfather would have waived the provision in the chantry ordinances for his chaplain to dine with the family every feast day. For now he contented himself with a sardonic smile before turning back to his companions, two thickset men whose unfamiliar caps and hoods marked them out as merchants from Norway or Zeeland. Although Ralf disapproved of his using the pageants to further trade, he acknowledged that without trade there would be no pageants. Walter had paid his silver for twenty years and it was widely rumoured that his affairs were foundering. Peace with France had favoured rivals such as Simon Muskham, who transported salt from Bourgneuf Bay. Walter and Edmund dealt exclusively with the Hanse, where the mining and shipping costs were high and the threat of piracy constant. So they had to take every opportunity to persuade their associates to grant them the most beneficial terms.

Ralf's relief that he did not belong to the merchantable world vanished when he was beckoned by Edmund. Conscious that he was not one of the distinguished townsmen who would inspire the foreigners with a sense of their hosts' renown, he suspected that he was to be the butt of mockery, affording them a brief distraction before the pageants began. And so it proved.

'Do not be misled by the gaunt cheeks and ragged gown,' Edmund said. 'Sir Ralf is the most fortunate man in the room. While the rest of us toil day and night, he prays. Prayers he has repeated so often that they are like the humming of drone bees.'

'Did not Alfred, the greatest of all English kings, say that a monarch had need of three kinds of subject?' Ralf replied. 'Those who pray, those who fight and those who work. Remember whom he placed first.'

'Well spoken, Sir Ralf,' said Walter, who, unlike his wife, liked to see his son chastened, provided that it was only with words.

'It is halfway Prime,' Marjorie said sharply to her cousin, Frances Skirlaw. 'The first wagon should be here soon.'

'Is it the same in your country? Priests; bishops; chaplains; clerks; monks; friars; to say nothing of their children,' Edmund said, the last clause tearing Ralf's heart, 'all robbing honest men. Taking a tenth of our revenue in tithes while we live and a third of our estates in mortuaries when we die.'

'Pray have some breakfast,' Marjorie interposed. 'Do not hold back.'

'And as if one priest in a church is not enough, they have two … sometimes three or four, each with his own chapel, squinting past the pillars to the high altar to be sure that one of them is not raising Christ's body at the same time as another is devouring it.'

'Peace now,' Walter said, gripping his son's shoulder and turning to the merchants. 'Gentleman, please eat something. Have you tried plover pie? It is a dainty in these parts.'

Walter led the men to the sideboard, leaving Edmund scowling, until Agnes Muskham's arrival transformed his mood as markedly as Lazarus's resurrection did Martha and Mary's in the cap-makers' pageant. Ralf wavered between gratitude that there was someone to ease Edmund's troubled spirit, and apprehension that it was Agnes, who had not only been his wife Constance's dearest friend but was married to his lifelong foe. Walter, blind to how his favour towards Simon had fanned Edmund's jealousy, had prayed that the women's affection would spread to their husbands. Since Constance's death, however, he had come to mistrust

Edmund's familiarity with Agnes and urged Ralf to counsel Simon on his duty to govern his wife. Stammering like Moses he had tried, only for Simon to scorn his concern, although whether from faith in Agnes's innocence or indifference to her guilt, Ralf could not say.

After waiting in vain for the steward to pour him a cup of ale, Ralf crept towards the window where crabbed voices filtered up from the street. With the first pageant setting off from Holy Trinity at daybreak, it should already have reached Coney Street and, even if the wagon had yet to trundle into view, the cries of Lucifer and his doomed companions should have wafted from the fifth station. Every year brought complaints from the final stations that *The Coronation of the Virgin* and *Doomsday* took place in the dark. Any further delay and they would extend to *The Resurrection* itself.

'For sure we are waiting on the king,' Edmund said disparagingly. 'It is still too early for one who retires at an hour when all honest men rise.'

'The king is the flower of courtesy!' Marjorie chided her son more severely than was her wont. 'Master Underwood and I were presented to him at Easter. He told me that the queen herself did not have a kirtle so fine as mine.'

'And me that he would be content to hold his court permanently in York,' Walter said.

'So that he might drain our coffers dry within the year?' Edmund asked, avoiding his mother's eye.

While presuming that a king so prone to flattery was apt to flatter in turn, Ralf did not doubt the affection in which he held the city. He had visited it twice this year, first to grant it the dignity of a county and then to attend the Passion Week masses in the Minster. He had given a hundred marks from his privy purse for the rebuilding of the choir and paid for the renovation of his great-grandfather, Edward II's chantry. But he had quarrelled with the Dean and Chapter, who refused to support his petition to have King Edward canonised, hence he was watching the pageants at Holy Trinity rather than at the Minster Gate.

The tanners' wagon approached, prompting a roar of approval as loud as the one that had greeted the king at Micklegate Bar three days earlier. The company in the gallery moved to the windows, which Marjorie declared safe to open since the streets had been newly cleansed and the seats at their station leased only to the most wholesome persons. Ralf held back, until he was summoned by Agnes to a place at her side. He tried to allay the suspicion that her kindness to him was a ploy to provoke Edmund. The pageant bearers, dripping sweat although the sun was still low in the sky, set down the wagon, narrowly missing the jetties on the tenements opposite. Musicians in craft livery played a measure on trumpet, shawm and regal. The leaves of the wooden cloud high on the mansion creaked open, and a burst of applause hailed Jack Sawyer, a master tanner from Barkergate, wearing the familiar golden mask and white robe of God. Silence fell as he spoke the lines with which the whole play – indeed, the whole of creation – began: *Ego sum alpha et O, Vita, Via, Veritas, Primus et Novissimus.* They were among the smattering of Latin words to be found in the pageants, which were written not in the language of the Church but that of the people. Yet it was fitting that the Almighty's first utterance should have a grandeur that all would recognise if few comprehend.

The tanners' God was attended by five angels, boys with flaxen tresses and peacock-feather wings, singing a canticle of praise. Ralf recalled when he himself had been part of just such a celestial choir, in the *Creed* play more than fifty years before. He had been dressed much as the boys were now, although his wings had been made of swansdown and his mask only covered the top of his face. He was paid four pence, a detail that he wished had not fixed so fast in his memory. He had watched the priests who represented God and Christ and Mary and imagined joining them on his ordination. Since then, however, clergy had been forbidden to take part lest they be defiled by unseemly emotion.

He turned back to the pageant, where Lucifer's baleful pride met with the regulation hisses. Undeterred, the soon-to-be devil was hoarsely bewailing his plight, when four or five men (Ralf's view was partially blocked by Agnes's shoulder) beset the wagon. The good and bad angels combined to repel them, while God retreated hastily into the cloud. Four wagon bearers and two stytelers entered the fray, buffeting the assailants, whom they dragged off as roughly as the devils did the damned in the *Doomsday* pageant. Peace was restored to loud cheers, as the good angels, their feathers ruffled, and Lucifer, limping, gathered around God, his majesty diminished by his flight. Although such attacks occurred every year, Ralf had never before known one so early in the day. Even the archbishop's pledge of a forty-day indulgence for every spectator failed to ensure good behaviour from the drunken apprentices and emulous craftsmen, more inclined to run riot and settle old scores than to shorten their term in purgatory.

Walter, ever jealous of his city's honour, looked relieved when his visitors not only commended the presentation but assumed that the disturbance was planned, a discord on earth to mirror that in the skies. There was less spectacle, licensed or otherwise, for them to laud in the second pageant. Although six richly painted curtains were drawn across the mansion, one for each day of Creation, God, as was only proper, stood alone. Ned Capstick, whose hoary beard required no added horse-hair, was no longer master of his speeches and had to be loudly prompted to bring forth the birds and fishes. Ralf trusted that Sir Robert Palfrayman, in whose church his chantry was housed, had expressed his disdain for the pageants by staying away. His objections to a common plasterer representing God would have been compounded by such infirmity.

The plasterers were succeeded by the cardmarkers with

The Creation of Man, the fullers with *Adam and Eve in Eden* and the coopers with *The Fall*. A palpable excitement filled the gallery as Satan, scaled and tailed, rose from the trap to reveal his dark design. Not only was *The Fall* a perpetual favourite, the vain excuses of Adam and Eve and crooked cunning of Satan alleviating the horror of Original Sin, but the coopers' arrival at the sixth station meant that the salters' own pageant of *Lot's Wife* would be starting at the first. After *The Fall* came the armourers' *Expulsion from Eden*. Marjorie, who had fought a long and bootless battle to oust a noisome forge from Davygate, refused to see any virtue in the offending craft. No sooner had Gabriel stepped forward to proclaim God's purposes for the pair than she abandoned the window and once again exhorted the company to eat. Disturbed by her rancour but loath to decline the request, Ralf took his platter to the sideboard, where she rewarded him with a slice of the sturgeon reserved for more eminent guests.

The armourers' Adam and Eve were followed by the glovers' Cain and Abel. Thankful for any distraction from the evil of the first murder, Ralf observed the return of the scullion whom Walter had sent to Holy Trinity to report on the reception of *Lot's Wife*. Bounding up the stairs with a want of breath worthy of one of Herod's messengers, he pronounced it a success. 'The king smiled.'

'You were close enough to see, were you?' Edmund asked.

'I saw his teeth,' the boy replied pertly.

'And how do you know he wasn't removing a piece of honey cake?'

'Hurry along, Crispin. Ask Sarah to give you some pie,' Walter said. 'And I will thank you to keep your thoughts to yourself,' he added sternly to his son.

Edmund bristled, no doubt adding paternal authority to his list of grievances. Mindful that, however blank his countenance, Edmund was sure to read it as a rebuke, Ralf turned back to the pageant where, having dispatched his brother,

Cain was drinking himself into oblivion with his servant Brewbarret. The respite proved to be brief, and the angel exiled him in his turn, after which the play moved forward hundreds of years to the two pageants about Noah: *The Building of the Ark* and *The Flood*, presented by the shipwrights, and the fishers and mariners respectively. They were among the most popular in the whole play, although last year *The Flood* had had to be abandoned at the third station, when two monkeys borrowed from the menagerie at Thornhill Hall tore down the painted canvas. This year the animals were limited to two lions, two unicorns and two donkeys, represented by six boys from St Sampson's song school. Yet, as though the pageant were as doomed as the world it portrayed, the top of the rainbow stuck at the crucial moment, reducing God's covenant with mankind to three colours: green, blue and violet.

'Our pageant comes next,' Walter informed the foreigners, as the fishers and mariners hauled off their wagon.

'I cannot watch,' Edmund muttered to Agnes. 'Simon Muskham wreathed in glory.'

'He takes the wife's part. It is all he is fit for,' she replied, in a whisper that Ralf wished he had not overheard.

The signs of affection between Edmund and Agnes made him uneasy. While not their priest, he was by virtue of his chantry Edmund's family chaplain and, having known Edmund and Simon since they were boys, he had a care for their temporal as well as their spiritual welfare. Moreover, he had heard both their confessions every Passiontide for almost twenty years and, unless either had confessed to Sir Robert privately, he alone before God had a true understanding of their feud.

They had grown up together when Simon served his apprenticehood in Walter's shop and Walter kept Edmund at home rather than binding him to a fellow salter. The two boys had shared a schooling, in part at Ralf's hand, and an instruction in the mysteries of their craft at Walter's. They had shared prayers and pastimes and friends and, at night, they had shared a bed – Ralf looked away from the street, where the pageant bearers were securing the salters' wagon, and up to the garret. It was there one night, as Simon had hesitantly divulged, that Edmund stretched out his hand and stroked his belly. Simon, the more timorous of the two although the elder by eighteen months, felt his body grow numb, except for the one part that quickened. Thereafter they committed the sin every night, with one or other of them reaching out as if at hazard. Simon was in dread of punishment, both for the sin itself and the pleasure he took in it. Assuring him that God forgave every contrite heart, Ralf sought to discover the nature of the offence: whether it had been limited to the hands or extended to the mouth, thighs and fundament. Simon swore that theirs was a solely manual transgression, horrified as much that such other practices existed as that Ralf knew of them. But Ralf's knowledge was drawn entirely from the penitentials. He had never felt another's hands on his privy flesh in all his sixty-four years.

He had imposed a penance of fasting and prayers on Simon who, either because he was afraid of laying up punishment in the life to come or because he sought privation as much as pleasure, appeared disappointed by the lenience. Despite giving him every opportunity he could short of betraying his office, he had failed to obtain a similar confession from Edmund. Fearful for the boy's eternal soul, he allowed himself to hope that his offence had been unwitting. Given Simon's assertion that no words had been spoken, might he even have been asleep?

Ralf wondered at his eagerness to pardon – if only in his own mind – a man who did not trouble to conceal his contempt for him. It was clear that, whatever else, the prospect of purgatory held fewer terrors for Edmund than for his fellow miscreant. Not two years after Simon's confession, Marjorie's young maidservant, Rose or Marigold (he remembered only that it was a flower), found herself with child, naming the seventeen-year-old Edmund as the father. The couple were arraigned in the archdeacon's court for fornication. Edmund was acquitted after purging himself before six neighbours. The maid was less fortunate. With no compurgators to vouch for her, she was further accused of perjury and slander and sentenced to be whipped around the churchyard and driven from the parish. Ralf was called upon to witness, although his vision was clouded by the memory of a whipping in another churchyard fifty years earlier and the woman who had died not of her stripes but of her shame.

He turned back to the pageant just as Gabriel and Raphael descended the mansion by means of a jouncing winch. Their fresh faces, golden locks and long white gowns drew lewd whistles from several of the more unruly spectators, who would no doubt shortly revile the Sodomites for similar wantonness. Ralf wished that the angels had been presented as more manly, not simply to accord with the biblical verse, but to challenge the common misconception that the Sodomites' sin was lust. As a confessor, however, he knew that people oppressed by their own sins took comfort from the thought of others who had committed worse, not least a sin so grave that, according to St Augustine, it had led Christ to defer his Incarnation; a sin more deadly than murder since it threatened the very survival of mankind. Yet, while echoing St Augustine's revulsion, he could not forget the two scholars with whom he had shared a hostel at Michaelhouse, gentle souls whom he would never have suspected of such vice. Caught in rank lust, they had been arraigned before the Chancellor, excommunicated, and handed to the city sergeants, who had cut off their ears, branded and gelded them.

Heart-sore, he forced his attention back to the pageant, where Lot's wife, ignorant of the angels' true nature, chided her husband for harbouring more waifs and strays. The crowd whooped as Simon rolled his eyes at Lot's credulity, hid a pie beneath his apron and swooned like a maid on beholding the strangers' beauty. Pouting, he prepared a meal of bacon and pottage as the Sodomites encircled the house, pressing Lot to yield up his guests like drunken journeymen calling for whores outside a brothel-house. Ralf was surprised that the clerk who penned the pageant in Walter's father's day had failed to draw on the legend that it was Lot's wife herself who betrayed the angels' presence by soliciting salt from her neighbours, which would have both presaged her transformation and given the craftsmen a chance to display their wares. Instead, he had dwelt on the men's fleshly appetites with all the horror of one who lived in the shadow of the Great Pestilence, when such lewdness was blamed for inciting God's wrath.

Lot denounced his neighbours as:
'*Saracens so hot and haught,*
Who, glutted with all licensed love,
For wanton lust do set at naught
The benison of God above.'

The men, in turn, scorned his reproofs, one beating the mansion curtain so hard that the door to Lot's house shook like Abraham's tent.

The Sodomites' assault was met by even louder hisses than Lucifer's fall.

'I do not understand this,' the Zeelander said. 'Are these also devils?'

'Worse than devils,' Marjorie said.

'The basest of men,' Walter added.

'It is hard for your players who must speak above the bruit.'

'Not at all,' Walter said, with the assurance of one safely indoors. 'We are doing God's work. When the people shout, they are denouncing sin.'

'A sin that is not of Master Underwood's choosing,' Marjorie said quickly.

'We receive our charge from the Corporation,' Walter explained to the Zeelander. 'Just as the shipwrights have *The*

Building of the Ark and the vintners *The Marriage at Cana*, so we have *Lot's Wife*.'

'A peevish woman turned to salt does not compare with a pot of water turned to wine,' Marjorie said sourly. 'I sometimes wish that God had transformed her into a sheaf of wheat and Christ made his sacrament of salt and wine. Then we might trade pageants with the bakers.' She laughed, as though to lessen the impiety.

'How you women prate!' Walter said, torn between silencing his wife and reassuring his guests. 'Would you sooner I were a girdler and my fellows slaughtered the Innocents or, worse, a butcher and they crucified the Lord?'

'At least those are daylight sins. Whereas this is a sin so foul that it is found only in the black Mahometans.'

'Not so, Mother,' Edmund interposed. 'It is rooted in our native soil, rife in every abbey dormitory. Am I not right, Sir Ralf?'

'That, as you well know, Edmund, is a Lollard slander.' With a last look at the wagon, where Raphael was commanding Lot to flee the city, Ralf moved to the centre of the room, determined not only to meet Edmund's challenge but to correct the error on which the pageant itself was based. 'You have not studied the sacred page like those of us who were at the university.'

'Even those who were excluded?'

'Edmund!' Walter said, blushing as much at his own indiscretion as his son's discourtesy.

'Stop taunting Sir Ralf, Edmund, and come here!' Marjorie called from the window, where the mirth had reconciled her to the pageant. 'Simon is on the ground, refusing to stir. You can see his great boots under his gown. The sleeves are just like yours, Agnes dear.'

'They are mine,' Agnes said quietly.

'I knew I had seen them before.'

'We can start by abandoning the fable that, at Our Lord's

nativity, all the sodomites in the world fell down dead,' Ralf said, pursuing his theme.

'They are about to die again,' Randall Clayton, the salters' warden, interjected. 'We shall see how they accomplish the fire and brimstone this year.'

'At Michaelhouse we were told never to breathe the word Sodom out of doors for fear the grass would wither. But is that what we find in the Bible?' Ralf left them no time to reply. 'Not at all. If you read Ezekiel, you see that the sins of Sodom were arrogance and gluttony and contempt for those in need. Would not the same be true of York today?'

'Quick!' Frances said, 'or you will miss Master Muskham's transformation.' Returning to the window, Ralf gazed out at the wagon where, with a thunderclap, a tower collapsed and four Sodomites rolled into a monstrous hell-mouth. As neatly as if he were dancing a carole, Simon whirled round to look, emitting a piteous scream as he fell through a trap in the rush-strewn floor. Moments later, a pillar of salt sprang up in his place.

'The very image of Master Muskham,' Randall's wife Janet said. 'Would you not say so, mistress?' she asked Frances.

'Indeed,' Frances replied, although both knew that it had been fashioned on old Giles Sweetmouth and the pageant master had resisted Simon's pleas to replace it.

On the wagon, Lot led his weeping daughters away from their transmuted mother with a haste that would have been unfitting in anyone not favoured by God. They took refuge in a cave, where the pageant drew to a close, the clerk having wisely recoiled from depicting what ensued. Marjorie praised Simon's representation to Agnes and enjoined her guests to replenish their platters before the sacrifice of Isaac. 'It is too doleful a tale to watch without victuals.'

Ralf, thankful to see both the Louths and the Skirlaws moving towards the sideboard, made to follow when Walter seized his arm.

'What you said about Ezekiel and the sin of Sodom: was it just to goad Edmund?'

'On the contrary. I could have said much more had I had the chance.'

'You have it now.'

'Really?' Ralf asked in surprise. 'Then look at the gospels. Both St Matthew and St Luke make it clear that Our Lord condemned Sodom for its unkindness to strangers.'

'What about St Mark and St John?'

'Neither speaks of it.'

'Then it might not be the sin against nature?'

'Not unless it be a sin against human nature, since hospitality was second nature to the ancient Israelites. Say nothing to Edmund' – Ralf immediately regretted naming him as he followed Walter's gaze to the tapestry where he was huddled with Agnes – 'but this is one occasion when I might wish to turn Lollard and make the Scriptures plain to all.' Walter stared at him in amazement. 'I only said "might".'

'So it would be possible to make a different pageant of *Lot's Wife*, one that removes the stain from the Sodomites and, as Mistress Underwood sees it, from those who represent them?'

'Certainly. If your fellow salters are willing to open their purses. But remembering how many of them carped at the raising of the pageant silver this year …'

'Leave me to treat with them. Thank you, Sir Ralf, you have given me much to think on. But you must be hungry,' he said with a laugh. 'Have some sweetmeats. The bookmen will shortly be here with *Abraham and Isaac*. And then it is but a twinkling till the birth of the Lord.'

2

The church was always cold on Candlemas, the celebration forty days after Christmas of the Purification of the Virgin and the Presentation of the Lord. As he rubbed his numb nose and shuffled his tingling feet, Ralf, who was assisting at Mass, watched Sir Robert, imperious in purple, bless the candles, both those that would be lit in the church and those that the congregation had brought from home. The latter were fewer than last year when Sir Robert had spurned Joan Dernwater's tallow candle, insisting that only beeswax was permitted by law. Had he been bolder, Ralf would have cited the parable of the widow's mite.

The Mass over, the people dispersed. Those with rustic memories returned home to gather up any Christmas greenery left after Twelfth Night, lest a single berry found indoors should portend a death in the parish. Others walked up to the Minster or the Abbey to pick a bunch of Candlemas Bells, the pure white flowers that the Angel Gabriel had grown to assuage Eve's despair at the wintry bleakness her sin had brought into the world. In the countryside, farmers moved cattle from the hay meadows and prepared the fields for first planting. In the forests, wolves tentatively sniffed the air, their swift retreat into their lairs signalling a further forty days of cold.

Ralf had no such recourse, being due at the Underwoods' to hear Walter's deathbed contrition and to administer the last rites. Keen to avoid Sir Robert, who made no secret of resenting his presence in the sacristy, he divested himself of his cope and stole and hurried out, only to be accosted in the porch by a beggar who had survived the rector's purge. The rasping request for alms filled him with the desire to emulate the church's patron and tear his cape in two, but a voice, barely recognisable as his own, countered that St Martin had been a young and hardy soldier, whereas he was an old and feeble clerk. It proceeded to list his ailments: aching joints; bladder stones; bleeding gums; cataracts; skin lesions; until, sickened by the subterfuge, he gave the man a farthing and fled into the churchyard, where the bitter wind battered his cheeks. Pulling open the lychgate, he stepped into the street, narrowly avoiding a frozen sump.

Arriving at the Underwoods', he clasped the door knocker with his usual unease, wondering why, when the Great Lateran Council had decreed that angels had neither shape nor substance, the citizens of York should be so eager to cast them in bronze. He was admitted by Thomas, Walter's young apprentice who, left in charge of the shop, looked overwhelmed, either by his own unexpected authority or his master's imminent decease. Pausing to reassure him, Ralf made his way up to the chamber, where he hesitated on the threshold. Years of attendance at deathbeds had failed to reconcile him to the smell. It was as pungent in the homes of the rich, where it was imperfectly masked by herbs, as in those of the poor, where it was heightened by vermin and refuse.

The room was murky as well as musty, lit solely by a candle at each corner of the bed. The hangings were drawn back and Walter lay propped on the pillows, his cheeks sunken and body shrivelled as though he had already shed his flesh in readiness for his final journey. Marjorie sat to his left, staring at his face, her distress manifest in her disarray. Edmund stood behind her, grasping the bedpost as though seeking to become one with the wood. To the right, an apothecary held a flask of Walter's urine, which, after swirling, sniffing and sipping, he declared to contain a surplus of bile, requiring the application of hot irons to the legs, although, according to Walter's horoscope, it would not be propitious to do so until sundown. The shallowness of his old friend's breathing assured Ralf that he would be spared that ordeal. Meanwhile, he was to transcribe Walter's last will and testament, hear his confession and give him extreme unction. Leaving the apothecary to complete his tasks, he moved away from the bed and nodded a sombre greeting to Simon Muskham who, present as an executor but bowing to Edmund's primacy, sat discreetly in the corner. Ralf prayed that Walter would not allow his fondness for his former apprentice to influence his bequests. Even in extremis, he must be aware that any show of amity between the two young men would not survive his funeral.

For all his grief, Ralf could not regret Walter's death, which would save him from the scandal that threatened both the Underwoods and the Muskhams and into which he feared that he himself must be drawn. He gazed at Agnes, sitting on the far side of the room from Simon, although the few wooden boards were no measure of the distance between them. Four months ago, shortly after the black bile had swollen Walter's belly, she had brought an action against Simon in the dean's court, claiming that he was frigid and that they had never lain together as husband and wife. Simon's proctor had replied to the libel and the registrar begun to take depositions. Ralf, convinced of Agnes's adultery with Edmund and afraid that Simon would enter a counterplea, begged her to recant. He reminded her that there had been no carnality in the Virgin Mary's marriage, but she remained unmoved. A judgement of frigidity was the only way for her to obtain her annulment while retaining her dower.

Loath to peer into their chamber, Ralf urged Simon to perform his marital duty.

'But surely that is to procreate?' Simon replied. 'At my betrothal, Sir Aidan told me that a man should desire his wife purely in order to engender children. I have tried; I have vanquished my disgust at her sour flesh and peppery smell and the

Saracen's moustaches under her arms. I have ploughed her like a frosty field in March. But not once has she released her seed. So how can she conceive? And if she is barren, then my duty must be to abstain, for it would be a mortal sin to lie with her.'

Seeing the warring couple together for the first time since Agnes's action, Ralf longed to act as peacemaker, but there was little hope when neither would listen to him, let alone to each other. He was pondering how to proceed when a cry of pain interrupted his musings and drew his attention back to the bed.

'My throat!' Walter screamed. 'Get it off my throat!'

'What? There's nothing. Edmund, water!' Marjorie grabbed the cup from her son and held it to Walter's lips. He slowly quietened.

'A bird – a great eagle – was carrying me off to the clouds.'

'It was a dream. You were dreaming,' Marjorie replied. 'What does it signify, Sir Ralf?'

'It was a dream, Mother,' Edmund interposed. 'It signifies no more than the figure of the ice on the window.'

Ralf, more conversant with omens than Edmund, suspected that it signified the fourth beast of the Apocalypse but, eager to console Walter, he named a kindlier spirit. 'Remember the cherubim whom Ezekiel saw surrounding the throne of God? Each had four aspects. It is the eagle aspect that watches over you.'

Edmund snorted, but even he was reluctant to pick a quarrel while his father was fighting for breath. Walter wheezed and hacked, letting slip his sheaf of indulgences. Retrieving it, Ralf smiled to see the one from Santiago de Compostela, the pilgrimage they had made together in their youth and which, in spite of flies the size of finches in Sabres, bouts of biliousness from the rancid pork in Languedoc, the ferrymen on the Sorde who robbed them of their horses, and the brigands in the Pyrenees who robbed them of their gold, had been the most glorious adventure of his life.

'Why worship St James in Spain when the Church teaches us he is in heaven?' Edmund had asked, after one of his father's feast-day reminiscences. Ralf trusted that the bill remitting a third of all his sins, which Walter clasped to his chest and with which he wished to be buried, was sufficient answer.

As Walter's breath grew shorter, Ralf asked him if he were minded to make his will. He nodded, whereupon Marjorie summoned the steward and, as calmly as if she were ordering a custard, instructed him to bring parchment, a writing board, inkhorn and quill. No sooner had Ralf drawn a chair up to the bedhead than Edmund, with rare solicitude, placed a candle behind him. The steward returned, handing the writing materials to Ralf who, anxious not to strain the dying man, cleared his throat in readiness.

Walter had attended enough deathbeds to need no guidance in framing his dispositions. He began by bequeathing his soul to Almighty God and the Blessed Virgin, and ordaining that daily prayers for himself and all those he had wronged be said in perpetuity in the family chantry, where his body was to be interred, wrapped in a cloth and laid beneath a flat stone. After bequests to the high altar of St Martin's, to his steward and scullion and towards the marriage portion of his maid, he left the house and its movables to Marjorie and twenty pounds to Simon, who wisely remained silent while an angry vein throbbed on Edmund's brow. His relief when his father left him the residue of his estate – lands and tenements, goods and chattels – was short-lived since, with his next breath, Walter confirmed Simon as his fellow executor. Having fiercely opposed the choice, Edmund was forced to watch as it was signed and sealed, with Ralf guiding a hand that was as light as the quill it clutched.

Preoccupied with the transcription, Ralf had little time to reflect on the two clauses of direct import to himself, until Walter, having relinquished his seal to his steward, lay back on the pillow, panting. To his surprise, Walter had invested the patronage of the chantry not in Edmund but in the warden and searchers of the salters. He imagined that he saw a smile play on Walter's lips, although it may have been the flicker of the candle, at the thought that he had saved him from a lifetime's subservience to his son. Still more unexpected was the legacy of twenty marks – untold riches for a cantarist with a stipend of seven marks a year – as payment for writing a new Corpus Christi Day pageant of *Lot's Wife*, one that would convey the true meaning of the bible story and bring credit to the craft.

'Must you, Father?' Edmund asked, no longer able to contain his fury. 'If you wish to leave money for the common weal, then repair bridges, build roads! Do not waste it on idle spectacles in which such as he may prance and prat.' His hand vanished into the shadows, but there was no doubt where it was pointing.

'Not now, Edmund, please!' Marjorie begged, as Walter gulped for air.

'Moreover, you hire this mouldy priest. Twenty marks! Why not bequeath it to the baker? That is where it will end up when he squanders it on pies and sweetmeats to swell his withered carcass.'

'Oh Edmund,' Walter said. 'What will become of you when I am gone?' He closed his eyes, and Ralf panicked that he had spoken his last. He grabbed his stole, kissed it and put it on, as the apothecary held a cup to Walter's lips, eliciting a welcome cough.

'A brewage of liquorice, lungwort, comfrey and garlic,' the apothecary said proudly, but the very names seemed to disgust Walter, who spewed up the mixture. He grimaced as Marjorie dabbed his chin.

'Sir Ralf,' he said, with due gravity. 'Will you confess me now?'

Ralf held up his crucifix, instructing Walter to gaze on it and take comfort from the knowledge that Christ died for him. He exhorted him not to fall into despair at the thought of his own depravity but to remember Mary Magdalene and Dismas, sinners who even at the foot of the cross had become saints. He asked him whether he rejected heresy and desired to die in the faith of the Holy Church; whether he recognised and truly repented of his wickedness; and whether, setting aside all merits of his own, he put his trust wholly in his Saviour; to all of which he answered with a clear, if hoarse, 'yes'. He asked him whether he were in charity with his neighbours, forgiving all those who had wronged him and intending to make reparations to all those whom he had wronged, to which he assented, less distinctly but still audibly. Assured of his penitence, Ralf absolved and anointed him. The sacred rite complete, Walter slipped into a stupor. The apothecary proposed to administer his most potent potion, a mixture of barberry, wormwood and arsenic, but Edmund, finally rebelling, dismissed him. He departed in a clatter of instruments, after which a resonant stillness filled the room broken only by Walter's fitful breathing. First, he panted like a running-hound after a kill, then fell so silent that Marjorie cried out that he was dead, and lastly rasped like a leper shaking his rattle. As Marjorie covered her ears against the sound and Edmund his nose against the boiled-beef odour that emanated from beneath the coverlet, Ralf promised them that it was an occasion for joy not sorrow. Walter was escaping from fleshly corruption and ascending to heavenly bliss.

As ever at such moments, time freed itself from the bells and took on a new measure. While Walter hovered between life and death, Ralf reflected on their fifty years of friendship. They had met as boys when Walter's father, another Ralf, whom he had often wondered if he had been named for, was one of his father's executors. Ralf never knew his father or rather he knew him before the age of cognisance. Gilbert Whitmore, rector of St Wilfrid's, Brayton, had lain with Dorothy Brigges, his parishioner. Ralf knew nothing of his parents' union, except for its end, when Gilbert was charged with incontinence and incest with his spiritual daughter, and Dorothy with fornication. They were arraigned before the Dean of Ainsty's court and ordered to purge themselves. Gilbert assembled the requisite six witnesses to affirm his innocence, but Dorothy stood alone. With women either less indulgent of their sex's transgressions or less willing to lie under oath, she found no one to testify for her. Convicted, she was sentenced to be whipped three times around the churchyard. The whole parish gathered to watch her chastisement. One of the wardens' wives took Ralf. It was his only memory of his mother.

She died and his father said *Placebo* and *Dirige* over her. Looking back at the obsequies, shrouded by time and his own recital of countless similar offices, Ralf brooded over whether Gilbert had invested the words with particular warmth, the slightest hint of a personal as well as a pastoral concern, but the effort was futile and he heaped all the scorn that he had spared his father on to himself. It was Gilbert who arranged for him to attend the Minster school in York, where he spent the next twelve years, first at the song school and then at the grammar school, singing in the choir, taking part in the processions and assisting the celebrant at Mass. He never saw his father again, although he long cherished the notion that he had come to the Minster in secret to watch him. It was Ralf Underwood who informed him of his death and explained that he had left a cottage and four cattle in Brayton to pay for his education, with the proviso that, having obtained his legitimisation, Ralf should take holy orders and pray for the souls of his father and his fellow compurgators.

He received his first tonsure at school, where he was ordained as a holy-water clerk. At fifteen, he was admitted to Michaelhouse, Cambridge, to further his studies. As Gilbert had foreseen, his birth barred him from a benefice and he applied to the archbishop for a dispensation, which to his chagrin was declined. Displaying a tenacity that he had hitherto not suspected and an eagerness to serve his father that perplexed him, he determined to circumvent the archbishop and appeal to the pope. Learning that the Prior of Ramsey Abbey had been summoned to a council in Avignon, he travelled to France in his retinue and obtained the necessary exemption.

He returned to Cambridge, where three months later he witnessed the public mutilation of his two friends in the market square. That night he was walking back to his hostel with four fellow scholars, when a group of townsmen, who had continued the revelry in the tavern, accused them of partaking in the men's vice. The outraged scholars drew their daggers and, in the ensuing brawl, two of them were wounded and one of the townsmen killed. Ralf escaped injury but not detection. He was expelled from the university and returned to York with no hope of preferment, until Ralf Underwood offered him the incumbency of his new chantry, presenting him for ordination to the archbishop. Even when, years later, Walter confessed in his cups that his father had sought to atone for abusing his executorship, Ralf remained grateful to him for the grant of his title.

He looked again at Walter, whose skin was as waxen as the candles, and intoned the psalms, but memories continued to distract him. Although the dispensation allowed him to attain any dignity short of a bishopric, he had spent forty years as priest of a perpetual chantry, which in the eyes of many – including his fellow clergy – amounted to little enough. He, however, could imagine no worthier task in this world than to ease a person's passage to the next. In addition, he had assisted two rectors of St Martin's in their parochial duties, said a daily morrow Mass, and kept a petty school, teaching generations of boys to read and write.

His reflections were interrupted by a sigh so long and deep that it seemed to drag the auditor down with it. In the silence that followed, he waited in vain for an echo. Finally, Marjorie leant over the pillow and, with a tenderness that stung Ralf like a scourge, planted a kiss on Walter's lips. 'He is gone,' she said, as simply as if he were visiting his ship in Hull. Agnes sobbed and Simon shuffled his feet. Edmund punched the bedpost twice as though trying to confine the pain. Agnes moved to him and, with a show of neighbourly condolence, touched his arm, but Edmund, fixing his eyes on his father, recoiled. He flung his hands to his face in a paroxysm of grief that was almost as shocking as Walter's death groan. With no pause for reflection, Ralf walked over and clasped his shoulder. Edmund leant his head on his chest and wept. Then, with startling abruptness, he shrugged him off. 'There,' he said, 'you have him where you want him. There is nothing left for him now but prayers.'

Needing no persuasion, Ralf drew up the prie-dieu and knelt. He was dimly aware of activity as two women came to wash Walter's body, which, within a few hours was blotched red, as though he had died of St Anthony's Fire. Shortly before dawn, Edmund and the steward carried him down to the hall, laying him on the high table, with a candle at either end. The bellman was sent to spread the news across the parish and as far afield as Petergate. Throughout the day, friends, neighbours, fellow salters and members of the Twelve arrived to pay their respects and, according to Edmund, consume their best wine, although it was clear to all who knew him that his deepest rancour was reserved for himself.

In keeping with Walter's wishes and to the fury of Sir Robert, Ralf was to officiate at the obsequies. Excommunicate, Edmund was forbidden to attend. Although the archdeacon offered to remit his public penance on payment of a fifteen-shilling fine, he remained obdurate. Ralf begged him to reconsider, if not for his father's sake, then for his own.

'Do you mean to meet your end with your sins unshriven?' he asked.

'Only God can grant absolution. Only He knows if we are foredestined to salvation or to doom.'

'That is heresy!' Ralf said, shuddering.

'Is it any greater heresy than that committed by your Church – a heresy against nature, against love, against God Himself – when it denies Christian burial to an abortive child?'

'The Church cannot commit heresy. It is the body of Christ; it is the truth,' Ralf replied, reluctant to rake up the past.

'Words. Empty words. And what pains me most is that he believed them,' Edmund said, pointing to his father's corpse before striding from the hall.

Removing the cushion the better to concentrate his mind, Ralf knelt, picked up his psalter and recited Psalm 113. But, like a conjuror whose voice issued from across his booth, his words were distanced from his thoughts, which lingered on the bitter aftermath of Constance's death. Edmund's grief at the loss of his wife had turned to fury at Sir Robert's refusal to bury his stillborn child in hallowed ground. Ralf had witnessed their confrontation in St Martin's sacristy.

'She is an innocent,' Edmund said.

'Who was conceived in lust and fed on clotted blood and slime in her mother's womb,' Sir Robert replied.

Edmund lunged at the priest, and Ralf, leaping forward, pinioned his arms to prevent his committing a greater sacrilege.

'Love! She was conceived in love,' Edmund shouted. 'Is that not what God commands?'

Ralf ushered Edmund out of the church and into the chantry house, seating him by the brazier with a gourd of ale, but his words of conciliation fell flat as Edmund inveighed against priests and cantarists, bishops and popes and, at times, even the Creator Himself. Although wounded, Ralf listened quietly in the hope that his anger would burn itself out. That hope proved to be misplaced. The night after Constance was entombed in St Martin's chancel, her daughter was buried in unconsecrated ground at the north of the churchyard. The following night, aided by two equally reckless friends, Edmund dug up the tiny coffin, broke into the church and descended into the crypt, reuniting mother and child. But they were apprehended by the sexton, reported to the wardens and brought before the archdeacon's court, where they were condemned to stand at the lychgate on three successive Sundays, bare-headed and bare-legged, scourging themselves. His accomplices performed the penance, but Edmund remained defiant. Since then he had neither confessed his sins nor received the Sacrament.

Edmund attended the first part of his father's obsequies, even joining in the antiphons, when Ralf said *Placebo* in the hall on the eve of the funeral. The next morning, he watched from the gallery window as the mourners set off, his face its own effigy when Simon gave Marjorie his arm.

The bellman led the procession to the church. As Ralf entered, his eye was ineluctably drawn to the chancel arch, where grinning devils with flame-red skins were busily thrusting the souls of the damned into hell. He stood to one side as the bier was laid before the high altar. Once the congregation was settled and his fellow priests prepared, he said *Dirige* and Lauds and celebrated Mass, striving not to wince at Sir Robert's limping Latin. The ceremony over, he escorted the chief mourners through the north transept to the chantry. The bearers lurched as they lifted the bier up the three steep steps and through the narrow arch in the tracery screen that enclosed the two-tiered tomb of its founder. On the lid, he and his wife lay in sumptuous robes, their hands clasped in prayer and clutching rosaries; inside, they cast off their finery in favour of shrouds, opened to reveal their putrefying corpses slithering with worms. Mistrusting such elaborate self-abasement, Ralf welcomed Walter's more modest memorial, a brass plaque beneath the window of the Seven Works of Mercy, inscribed *Vos estis sal terræ*.

The bearers detached the gold-and-red patterned pall and lifted the body off the bier and into the hole in the chantry floor. Ralf reeled as twenty people crammed into a chapel where he was accustomed to pray alone. Hoping that his voice would hold out, he committed Walter's body to the ground and commended his soul to God. He then blessed and dismissed the mourners, exhorting them to return in seven days to repeat the office. After ceding the chantry to the sexton, he crossed to the south transept, where, in a further vexation to Sir Robert, a door led directly to the chantry house, enabling Ralf to come and go without muddying his boots, whereas he had to wade through the mire at the bottom of Stonegate.

Ralf entered his chamber and lit the brazier. He relished the rare luxury of a fire at midday, but it was easier to warm his hands than his heart. He should never have questioned the truth of the salters' pageant. Had he kept silent, Walter might have made his bequest as a token of friendship rather than on conditions that both his executors for different reasons – Edmund's antipathy and Simon's ambition – would insist on his fulfilling, thus leaving him no choice but to refuse it. He swiftly doused the coals and, shunning solitude, quit the house and walked down Coney Street, where the shroud of snow had thawed to reveal a festering midden. He continued along Spurriergate to the Ouse Bridge, gagging at the stench of the newly built privies, before turning up Coppergate to Pavement, where a grey friar was preaching to a rowdy crowd at the market cross. Idling on the periphery, he was startled to hear the friar addressing the very subject that was preoccupying him. He clearly shared none of the Master of Michaelhouse's qualms, since he not only spoke of sodomy out of doors but rent the air with condemnation of a sin so odious that every trace of the city that had given it its name had been buried beneath the Dead Sea.

Egged on by the crowd, he diverted his invective from the sin to the sinners: men who bore themselves like women, scorning the flesh in which God had clothed them, the flesh that Christ himself had assumed; men who flouted the divine commandment to go forth and multiply. Even as the crowd roared its approval, Ralf longed for someone to point out that the friar himself had flouted the commandment. Listening to his castigation of sodomites, he was troubled by the naming of a new class of sinner. Forty years of hearing confessions from husbands eager to keep their wives from conceiving had taught him not to locate the sin solely among womanish men. He had first come across *sodomites* in the heretical writings of Wycliffe, who had identified them with clergy. Was the friar denouncing them so vehemently in order to deflect attention elsewhere? And what of his own two Michaelhouse friends? Were they no more than their transgression? They had shown him a pattern of love from which he had shrunk, as though their kisses were as noisome as Judas's. He had walled himself up in his priesthood like an anchorite in his cell. But what virtue was there in vows made in fear? His friends were not the only ones to have been gelded.

He realised that, whatever his qualms, he must write the pageant. He would base it on the authentic account of Sodom, as recorded by Moses and affirmed by Christ. He would write it not to honour Walter, or to secure his legacy, or even to vindicate his butchered friends, but because he knew with unshakeable conviction that it was the truth.

3

Lent was the season for lice. Ralf shared his infestation with his pupils. As he stood in the church porch, instructing them in the difference between bad, bade, bed, bide, bode and bud, he resisted the urge to scratch himself, since they already exhibited an unwholesome fascination with the creatures. He had even come across Nicholas Haxey and Dickon Barbour competing as to how many they could pluck from each other's scalp. Now, while the rest of the form chanted 'The bad lad bided in bed when his master bade him bring the bud without bode,' Dickon, an inveterate nose picker, was nibbling a louse he had extracted from Adam Inglish's matted hair.

'Leave that, Dickon!'

'Why, master?' Dickon asked, with the truculence that would lead him to either the pulpit or the stocks. 'Is it Lent? Are lice meat?'

Ralf feared that he must equivocate, reprimanding the boy rather than answering his question, when a distant memory came to his aid. 'They are insects. Moses taught us that the only insects we are allowed to eat are locusts and grasshoppers.'

'There are grasshoppers in Bedern,' Dickon said, as if planning a forage.

'I should stick to your mother's stottie cake.'

As the form burst out laughing, Ralf had an inspiration. The homely reference that had delighted them would be equally effective in the pageant. Telling the boys to recite 'The bad lad bided …' ten times, he picked up his writing board and tried to transcribe the phrase that had sprung into his head like a jest during Mass, but his ink had congealed in the cold, so he repeated the line to himself while the boys spoke theirs out loud.

Church bells across the city rang out for Vespers and Ralf dismissed the boys for the day. He longed to return home and replace 'fatted calf and barley cake' in Lot's list of provender with the local dishes of 'pease pudding and stottie cake', but first he must go to Goodramgate to collect the rents from the seven tenements with which his chantry was endowed. Setting off on this most dispiriting of tasks, he wished that, like the cantarists of St William's chapel, he might receive his stipend directly from the city chamberlain, or else that Ralf Underwood, so diligent in furnishing his revenues, had shown equal foresight in appointing an agent to gather them. He trudged through the streets, taking the longer route down Davygate, preferring the stinking flesh from the butchers in Haymongergate to the fleshly stink from the brothel-houses in Grapcunt Lane, but, as he passed the mounds of carcasses thick with flies, he feared lest he should vomit. No wonder the rector of St John's in the Marsh had sued the butchers, whose discarded offal exuded such a fetor that several of his parishioners had refused to attend Mass.

Twice a year, Ralf collected the noble that was due on each of the properties, although it was a rare tenant who paid without pleading for either a reduction or a period of grace. Last autumn, one claimed that the money had been stolen during the night by goblins and showed him the scorch marks on the rushes. Another swore that he had used it to bury his mother who, to Ralf's certain knowledge, had been two years in the grave. His resolve that this time he would brook no excuses wavered when the only signs of life in the first house he approached came from the mouse holes in the walls. A midwife forbade him to enter the second, where a fifty-year-old grandmother was miraculously at her birthing stool; and a neighbour stood guard at the third to prevent his entering a place of 'ague'. In the fourth, a woman tearfully recounted how her husband was rotting in St Peter's prison after assaulting the rector of St John del Pike for driving the demons into Holy Trinity during the Rogationtide procession. Far from paying her rent, she begged him to spare some coins to feed her three starving children, who stared at him in silent reproach. Threepence the poorer, he crossed the street to the fifth and sixth houses, both occupied by weavers, who besought him to accept a half-noble, citing the fall in the price of cloth for the deficit. Stifling a conviction that no lay landlord would accept such excuses, Ralf agreed, before making his final call, on a thatcher's widow, whose prompt payment humbled him.

Walking home by the more salubrious route down Colliergate, he turned into Peter Lane and stopped at Ned Hodges' shop for a carrot-and-root pie. He was as inured to a diet of vegetables as mankind before the Flood, but the carrots chafed his mouth and, while he knew it was God's will that he should suffer, especially during Lent, he longed for a bowl of fish or curds, which would be kinder to his gums. Ned greeted him warmly. The affection in which he held his former schoolmaster had deepened since his five-year-old son Toby started petty school. Besides which, Ralf was one of his most faithful customers. Lacking a hearth on which to cook, he came every evening for his pie, which Ned not only heated without charge but, whenever his wife was distracted, supplemented with quincebread or waffres.

'I have tidings, Sir Ralf,' Ned said, his cheeks more flushed than usual, as he called him to the front of the line.

'Is it Toby?' Ralf asked.

'I am to represent Christ in our pageant.'

'*The Last Supper*?'

'The same. It is I who am to institute the Blessed Sacrament in York this summer.'

'That is blessing indeed!'

'For the last four years I was St Andrew, with no more than

a dozen speeches. Before that I was St Simon the Zealot, with no speeches at all.'

'God hears what is in our hearts, not on our lips.'

'But, with more words, I will have more chance to say them right,' Ned replied, and Ralf could not bring himself to disabuse him. 'Davy Chetmill, who has been our Christ these eight years, was indicted for stealing an axe on Plough Monday. The warden and searchers did not think it fit for a felon to take part in the pageant.'

'Has he been convicted?'

'Not yet, but he is sure to be. He must needs be! Or does that make me unworthy too?'

'It is a venial fault.'

'Master Hodges!' Ned was summoned by his wife, whose tart tongue and sour manner made Ralf impatient to return to the termagant in his own pageant. 'You are wanted.'

'I will be with you straight.' He handed Ralf the pie. 'Stop there!' he said, as Ralf untied his purse. 'This is a gift. And this.' He added a ginger tart.

'Master Hodges!' his wife said. 'It is the Last Supper that you are presenting, not the Feeding of the Five Thousand.'

Ned's excitement infected Ralf, who hurried back to the chantry house where he devoured both pie and tart, which tasted of blood from his inflamed ulcers. He lit the brazier to warm the ink, fearing that he had added too much gum to the mixture of oak galls and iron salt, causing it to harden. He laid out his parchment on the writing board and fetched his pumice stone to scratch out any traces of the previous script. As ever before starting work, he read a few speeches at random. He relished a simile between the angels' beauty and a butterfly, before reminding himself that he was a mere conduit for words that came from God. He turned to where he had left off the day before, the passage in which Lot's wife begged salt from her neighbours, which was sure to please the audience, who welcomed any connection between character and craft. He prayed that inspiration would flow as freely when, with Lot's wife having returned home, the neighbours informed their husbands about her mysterious guests and the men, furious at such furtiveness, demanded that they pay the statutory toll.

He dipped his quill in the inkhorn and began to write. Speed was of the essence. Last week, the Common Clerk had dispatched the sergeants-at-mace across York with billets informing each craft of the pageant that it was to present on Corpus Christi Day. The salters, electing a new pageant master to replace Sidney Berwick, had chosen Simon Muskham. To nobody's surprise, Edmund had objected, arguing, more shrewdly than usual, that if Simon accepted, he would be unable to take part, leaving the craft without its most skilled player. Simon, equally politic, pledged to renounce his private renown for the sake of the craft, knowing – or so he later told Ralf – that Edmund's real objection was that, should he be elected, he might expect to follow his predecessors as warden, a member of the Twelve and even mayor.

Having failed to halt Simon's appointment, Edmund did his utmost to frustrate his schemes. The day after his election, Simon sent his wily apprentice Hamo to all his fellow salters with a proposal to raise the pageant silver from two shillings to two and sixpence for each master, threepence to sixpence for each journeyman, and, for the first time, to charge a master twopence for each apprentice. He cited the need both to repair the wagon and to refurbish the mansions so as to compete with the goldsmiths' gilded caskets, the saddlers' red damask flames and the tapissers' embroidered bed-hangings. Edmund had protested, swearing that he would dismiss his apprentice rather than pay a farthing to feed Simon's vanity. But Thomas's place was secure, since the salters' loyalty to their new pageant master stopped short of opening their purses. They insisted that he make do with the existing levy, declaring that his skill in the presentation would outshine their rivals' profligacy.

His scenic ambitions thwarted, Simon was all the more determined to make his mark with the new speeches. Showing enviable faith in the audience's discernment, he pressed Ralf for an account of his changes. Ralf tried to explain that he was replacing the erroneous *concupiscence* with the authentic *want of charity*, only to find himself floundering. Agnes's action had left him with a deep, if undefined, sense of unease and, although Simon's youthful transgression with Edmund was long in the past – repented and acquitted – he worried lest he should mistake his purpose and suppose that, by removing the carnal slur from the Sodomites, he was somehow excusing the sin to which they had lent their name. His fears proved to be groundless since Simon was more concerned with the pageant's novelty than its meaning. He decided that, rather than wait until 1399 as Ralf had assumed, they should present his script this summer, which, with the first practice set for Passiontide, left him with less than a month in which to complete it.

Even as Simon was urging haste, Sir Robert was expressing disapproval. It was hard to avoid the suspicion that, behind his measured opposition to the pageants, lay an innate hatred of the pleasure they afforded to players and spectators alike. He was the only priest of Ralf's acquaintance whose preferred season was Lent, when the chastity that he embraced from choice was enforced on his parishioners. Woe betide the parents of any baby born between eight and nine months after Ash Wednesday unless it were preternaturally small! He never published the banns without preaching that men who married for sensual gratification or had immoderate intercourse within marriage were as guilty of fornication as those who lay with harlots. He instructed the betrothed couple that had Adam and Eve not fallen, their children would have been born from mud like Adam or air like the angels and, furthermore, that when Satan tempted Eve, he infected the apple with his venom, which was why men spat out their seed from an organ that resembled a snake.

His aversion to the pageants may not have been as fierce as his aversion to the flesh, but it strengthened once he knew that Ralf was not only to write one but to profit by it. Instead of ignoring him as was his wont, he questioned him on his progress, pouring scorn on both his tardiness and the enterprise itself. On the morning after Ralf's doleful visit to Goodramgate, he arrived at church two hours early, accosting him in the sacristy at the end of the morrow Mass.

'I am glad to see you attend to your spiritual duties. Your mind is not wholly given over to your script.'

'The script is a spiritual duty. It is designed to bring people closer to God,' Ralf replied evenly.

'How, when the words you write are as soiled by the uncouth men who utter them as the paintings on our pillars by the candle smoke?'

'No, the paintings remain fixed, but the words are spoken afresh each year.'

'The words should be spoken only by priests, God's ministers, and in a tongue that is pleasing to Him.' Ralf smiled at the thought of Sir Robert's song-school Latin delighting the divine ears. 'But you and your accomplices have taken the word of God out of the church and into the world of the tug-of-war.'

'So that the people can play their parts in a story far greater than their own: the history of the world from Creation to Judgement.'

'Exactly! It is blasphemy from the first words of the first pageant when a common draper stands before a painted firmament, representing God.'

'The first words are Latin: *Ego sum alpha et O, Vita, Via, Veritas, Primus et Novissimus*. Surely you with your respect for the language must approve?'

'It is easy to mock me but unwise to mock God,' Sir Robert said, his eyes narrowing. 'As you who were blessed to study at the university should know as well as we who did so by our own base efforts, Lucifer, the brightest of the angels, fell because he sought to counterfeit the Creator. Yet you have rough, unlettered men counterfeiting Him throughout the play. They know no better; it is you who betray them. But what do you care when, like Judas, you have procured your fee?'

Ralf was aghast at the accusation but, before he could reply, Sir Robert withdrew to the high altar, where he sank heavily to his knees. Mistrusting the show of piety, Ralf returned to the chantry house to fetch his cape before setting off for the Dean of the Christianity's court in the undercroft of the Minster.

While not expecting Agnes to rejoice at Simon's success, Ralf had hoped that his election as pageant master and her own prospective dignities would finally persuade her to abandon her action. Instead, she appeared intent on damaging her estranged husband no matter the cost to herself. Although the frigidity suit had not deterred the salters from electing him, she was sure that a judgement in her favour would halt his advancement, since no town would appoint to its governing body, let alone to its highest office, a man whose member had been pronounced 'of little worth'. Moreover, having obtained her annulment, she would be free to marry again, and Ralf was in no doubt where her choice would lie.

He walked through the Minster precinct, past priests and pilgrims, chandlers hawking candles and beggars who spurned his prayers, to the great West door where, with the effigies of Adam and Eve to remind him of his sinfulness, he entered the church that had fired his imagination for sixty years. As a boy singing the eight daily offices, he had watched the solemn processions of canons and vicars choral, and dreamt that one day he would stand among them. But for that he would have needed a patron as powerful as Sir Thomas Ingram, whose tomb was newly installed in the nave. As it was, he had not even been permitted to take his father's name. Banishing melancholy, he crossed the aisle, past the shrine of St William Fitzherbert, its rows of wax limbs redolent of a butcher's shop, and paused to examine the building works in the choir.

'Sir Ralf!' A familiar voice cut short his contemplation. 'Sir Ralf!' He turned to find Marjorie, in mourning weeds and widow's wimple, struggling to make herself heard above masons winching a tomb-shaped stone up a scaffold, carpenters sawing planks beside a plinth, and the wind whistling through the canvas sheets at the top of the tower. She greeted him grimly, awaiting a court judgement which, whether it were the humiliation of a man whom Walter, wanting tact, had called his 'second son', or the annulment of his marriage with all that that boded for Edmund, would only cause her pain.

They made their way down the uneven steps to the undercroft and through the scriptorium to the consistory room, where Simon and Agnes, with their proctors and advocates, were sitting at a large oak table in the centre of a wooden enclosure, which bore a disconcerting resemblance to the cattle pen at the Thursday market. The Official, Master Thomas Munkgate, wearing a scarlet-and-black gown and a white coif topped with a violet skullcap, was enthroned in front of the altar to the Virgin, his scribe seated on the step beneath. A surprisingly large crowd pressed against the pales, among them several of the warring couple's neighbours. For the first time, Ralf was thankful that Edmund was excommunicate and forbidden to bear witness. He accompanied Marjorie to a space directly opposite Agnes, who did not return his smile. No sooner had they settled than Frances Skirlaw approached, as full of excitement as if she were watching the mummers playing at the staff on St John's Day, although the bruises that Simon and Agnes inflicted on each other would outlast any arising from that brutal game.

Frances's excitement was understandable since, after seven hearings, with the registrar having taken all the depositions and the Official having ordered both parties to undergo a corporal examination, the suit was drawing to a close. Declaring that he had proved his mistress's intentions, Agnes's proctor appealed to the Official to publish the depositions, which were solemnly delivered to the court, bound and sealed, by the registrar himself, who proceeded to read them out. The three main witnesses were Agnes's maid, Lucy, and her former maid, Matilda, attesting to her articles, and Simon's apprentice, Hamo, attesting to his allegation. Each had been subjected to interrogatories from the opposing proctor, with Simon's proctor eliciting damaging admissions from Lucy, first that she had served in the household for a mere four months and, second, that Agnes had beaten her twice in one week for idle conversation with the gong-farmer. He similarly discredited Matilda by summoning two neighbours, who swore that Agnes had given her a bale of stuff worth five shillings after she testified. When Matilda countered that it was to make herself a gown so that she was not shamed before the registrar, he summoned a third neighbour, who swore that Agnes had given her a linen gown on leaving her service, whereupon she recanted, claiming that 'I was tormented by the sickness of fever when I spake before but I am now better advised.' Agnes's proctor, meanwhile, failed to impugn Hamo, who declared that he had seen the couple exchange many tokens of affection and that, although his master slept beside him in the garret, he prayed every night, on his bare knees, that his mistress would take him back to her bed.

Flustered at hearing the deponents' halting English transcribed into fluent Latin, Ralf wondered how much the two principals could comprehend and whether Simon, whose face was hidden from view, was as dependent as Agnes on the proctor's frequent nods and occasional whispers. He himself translated for Marjorie, whose impatience, together with the legal vocabulary, complicated the task. His difficulties deepened when the registrar read the depositions of the two corporal examiners. Agnes had been inspected by Avice

Paynell, a widow from the parish of St Sampson, who alleged that she had marks on her breasts that were not accordant with virginity. Furthermore, she had refused to let her search her 'secret places' (Ralf preferred 'generative organs'), spitting out a warning 'like a curse' that, should she touch them, her hand would wither like the midwife's who doubted Our Lady's purity. Ralf stole a glance at Agnes, who sat, oblivious to the damning testimony, while her proctor stared despondently at the table.

The registrar could barely stifle his contempt at the name of the next deponent, Violet Scholes, a common harlot who, along with two others of her 'tainted trade' familiar to the court from their frequent citations for fornication, had inspected Simon in the upper chamber of the Seven Stars tavern in Gregory Lane. Violet recounted how they kindled the fire to increase the heat in his blood before inflaming him further by lewd talk and exposing the wanton parts of their bodies, which Ralf rendered to Marjorie as 'making pretty speeches and folding him in their arms'. No paraphrase could suffice, however, when Violet attested that, after removing Simon's shirt, she embraced him fondly about the neck and stroked his member, which, far from being frigid, grew to the length of two of her fingers before spending copiously in her hand. In brief, she deemed that Simon's was as good and manly a member as she had seen and sufficient to satisfy any honest woman.

It was evident to anyone who understood the depositions that Simon had convincingly replied to Agnes's libel, so it came as no surprise that it was his proctor who asked the Official to grant a conclusion. Master Munkgate duly retired, together with the four lawyers, to consider his judgement. Agnes and Simon, excluded from the deliberations that would decide their fate, remained at either side of the table like pebbles in a game of queek. The spectators whiled away the time: some discussing the suit; others wandering up and down; one old couple sharing a halfpenny loaf. Mistress Skirlaw, whose Latin ended with her paternoster, advanced on Ralf who, dreading her questions, escaped into the enclosure. After charging Hamo to fetch them on the Official's return, he persuaded Simon to quit the fusty undercroft for the fresher nave. Emerging just as the master mason conducted a party of canons around the works, they entered St Sepulchre's chapel, where a lone priest was saying Sext.

'It is plain that Master Munkgate must declare for you,' Ralf whispered.

'The strumpet will pay for her infamy.'

'Be bounteous, Simon. You must now live together as husband and wife.'

'We have not lived as husband and wife these past three years.'

'What about your testimony … the testimony of your witnesses?'

'Poor Sir Ralf,' Simon said, shaking his head as the priest censed the altar. 'The one unsullied soul in York!'

'So Agnes's libel was just?'

'Shall I tell you here or wait until I am come to confession? Then you will be bound by your oath; now you but keep silent like a player of hoodman's bluff.'

'If you wish to unburden yourself, I pledge to keep your counsel.'

'It is no burden,' Simon replied, 'it is a joy.'

'So you did not pray that she would take you back to her bed?' Ralf asked in confusion.

'I would as lief she should take me to my grave!' Ralf gestured to him to lower his voice. 'Do you think that I would ever again meddle with her miry flesh?'

'But we heard how you meddled with a whore.'

'That was her hand, not her cunt!' Ralf looked around, but their only auditors were the angels gracing the vault. 'And my yard can be roused by many hands, even yours … yes, even yours, Sir Ralf, were you thirty years younger with a little more meat on your Lenten frame.' He drew so close that Ralf felt his breath like a blade at his throat. 'And there is more,' he added. 'Did you take note of the harlot's name?'

'Violet? Was it not Violet?' Ralf asked, recoiling.

'Violet Scholes. I see that means nothing. Let me quicken your memory. Ten years ago … when I was apprenticed to Master Underwood … a maidservant who accused Edmund of fathering her child?'

'A flower, of course!'

'I refused to be one of his compurgators, or rather perjurers,' Simon said, with rank hypocrisy. 'That is why he has never forgiven me. That and … I think you remember.' Ralf gazed at the floor. 'I felt sorry for the wench. As a prentice, I had no money, so I took two crowns from Master Underwood's chest to help her and the child.'

'It died.'

'I never thought of her again until I saw her in the Seven Stars. For the last ten years she has lived in Grapcunt Lane, not half a mile from Coney Street, although it might as well have been the Antipodes. But she had not forgotten me. She said I was the only man in all her life who had ever done her a kindness. So she was kind to me in return. She and her friends lit the fire, but that was all they lit. She felt no remorse about forswearing herself for me. After all, what is one sin among so many?'

'Poor soul.'

'Surely you see it is providence that of the hundreds of harlots in York – I speak only of those who are paid – she should be appointed to examine me? God has delivered me from my enemies!'

'His ways are indeed wonderful,' Ralf said slowly. 'Which is all the more reason to show compassion to Agnes. You must take her again to your heart.'

'I would rather take a basilisk to my bosom! No, Sir Ralf,

she shall pay for what she has done to me. And so shall he. After all,' he said, grinning like a devil on a choir stall, 'if I wink at their adultery, I shall be arraigned as her bawd.'

Hamo's arrival ended the exchange before Ralf could assess Simon's sincerity. They returned to the undercroft, where Simon took his place in the enclosure between his proctor and his advocate, and Ralf rejoined Marjorie opposite Agnes. One look at her disconsolate face showed that her proctor had informed her of her defeat, which was confirmed when the Official read out his judgement that her libel was unproven and Simon was her true and honest husband.

Agnes's muffled sobs gave way to shrieks of rage when, after handing in his bill of costs, Simon's proctor announced that they would bring a counter-petition against her for perjury and adultery with Edmund Underwood.

'No!' Marjorie cried. Ralf grabbed her arm as she tottered. 'If Master Underwood were alive, he would never have done this. He will destroy our house as well as his.'

'I begged him to be merciful, but his heart is hardened. He would rather his roof fell about his head than that Agnes should take refuge beneath it.'

4

Ralf shivered, from both cold and excitement, as he walked down Coney Street to Simon Muskham's house, where the first practice of *Lot's Wife* was to take place. In a rare neglect of duty, he had paid Andrew Oakham, a cantarist from St William's chapel, fourpence to say the morrow Mass in his stead. He hurried the final few yards to Simon's door, where he was greeted by Hamo, who led him straight to the hall. Averting his gaze from the plenteous breakfast on the table, he turned to the players gathered around Simon: Rylan Yafford as Lot; Eustace Inglish as his wife; John Helperby and Reginald Frost as the two gossips; Bartram Savage and Baldwin Louth as their husbands; along with four apprentices, Hugh Fleming and Hamo as the angels and Henry Bald and a bleary-eyed Paul Ruckshawe as the daughters. He apologised for his lateness, adding the hope that, like the householder in the parable of the vineyard, the pageant master would reward even his tardiest labourer, at which Eustace had the grace to laugh. Simon replied with a jest about priests hugging their pillows, which Ralf failed to follow but from the general mirth assumed to be ribald.

Reminding the company that it was his first year as pageant master, Simon begged their forbearance of any mishaps, while in the next breath assuring them that there would be none. After warning that time was short, he embarked on a lengthy account of his responsibilities, from inspecting the mansions, collecting the costumes and finding the wagon bearers, to conferring with the Common Clerk and the Twelve. For which reason, he would be entrusting the rule of the pageant to Ralf, although, given his own history of taking part, man and boy ('that is to say "wife and daughter"'), he urged them to come to him if they had any problems, an offer that Ralf found both generous and sinister. He explained that, because of the unfamiliar script, they would hold five practices: the first to familiarise themselves with the speeches; the second to set the movements; the third and fourth to combine the two; and, finally, the general, in full apparel on the wagon. He insisted on the need to arrive promptly at dawn so that they might work together for three hours before repairing to their separate labours. 'I know how hard it can be for some of you to rise from your beds, speaking of no one particular,' he said, staring at Hamo, who grinned wretchedly.

'Will we be paid more for the added practice?' Bartram asked.

'No,' Simon replied. 'If you wanted more, you should have agreed to raise the pageant silver.'

'In plain words, robbing Peter to pay Paul,' John said.

'Amen to that!' Paul interjected to a general groan.

After concluding his remarks, Simon asked Ralf to distribute the parts, which he did with trepidation. Not only did he fear that the words that had flowed so freely in his head would falter on the tongue, but he suspected that even those players who could read would struggle to make out their parts, which had been copied by his older pupils in widely diverse hands. As the men examined their parchments, with even the unlettered able to gauge their portion of lines, Ralf wondered whether he would have to work harder with the veterans who bemoaned the loss of the old script or the novices who lacked confidence. An early indication came from Reginald, who protested that the second gossip had been reduced to a single speech. Simon bluntly informed him that he was free to leave since there were plenty of men eager to take his place. Ralf was less sanguine, not least given the rift between Simon's and Edmund's supporters in the craft, which had deepened since Agnes's suit. So he reminded Reginald of the Passion pageants in which, with a mere handful of words, Christ dominated the action – a specious argument, as he privately acknowledged, given the relative importance of the parts, but one that seemed to satisfy Reginald.

He was cheered to see Rylan perusing his lines, his brow furrowed and lips silently moving. Eustace, meanwhile, frowned at his script as though it were a court citation. His unease was understandable given Simon's long delay in filling a part of which he deemed none of his fellow salters worthy. Indeed, after the recent ordinance licensing players to appear in more than one pageant, he had sought to engage Humphrey Baynbing, the tapissers' Procula, and by common consent the most credible 'woman' in York. When, after much deliberation, Master Baynbing instead accepted Noah's Wife in *The Flood*, Ralf consoled Simon with the thought that, as Eustace was closer in height to Giles Sweetmouth, he would make a more authentic pillar of salt.

Although he had failed to engage Master Baynbing, Simon achieved his wish to have the angels represented by boys. Ralf sought to dissuade him, citing both the biblical verse in which Lot addressed them as lords and the pageant tradition that, while the canticles were sung by boys, the words were spoken by men. Moreover, given the new script, it was foolish to have such youthful angels, who would lend credence to the fallacy that the Sodomites were driven by lust. Simon not only dismissed his arguments but exercised his right as pageant master to choose Hamo as Raphael. While respecting his loyalty, Ralf was amazed that, having toiled over every detail of the presentation, he should take as an image of perfection someone whose rabbit face and buck teeth prompted taunts that, when his mother lay with his father, she must have been thinking of the pot. Even Hamo's speech was discordant, the 'S's drawn out in a serpentine hiss. Besides which, he had never learnt to read so that, as well as his other duties, Simon would have to teach him his lines by rote.

Usurping Ralf's rule, Simon began the reading, adding gleefully that he would take the parts of Raphael, the first gossip and the first daughter, until the three unlettered players had mastered their lines. Ralf sat beside Hamo, who was troubled with the itch. He thrilled to hear his words out loud, even spoken with Thomas's dullness and Eustace's hesitancy, and was gratified by both the laughter that greeted Lot's exchanges with his wife, and the silence that met the angels' proclamation of the city's fate. Between readings, he suggested several amendments that were seized on by the players, especially Reginald, who took the extra syllable that the second gossip was given, when her 'fair' daughters became 'comely', as testament to his skill. After they had read the script twice, John declared that he was ready to assay the first gossip, since 'although I may not discern the words, I do hearken hard and am quick of study.' Simon grudgingly relinquished the part.

As the church bells chimed for Tierce, Simon drew the practice to a close, reminding the players that they would return in a fortnight to set the movements, by which time he expected everyone to have learnt his speeches. Rylan looked doubtful, which Ralf trusted sprang from concerns about his memory rather than his part. He was so enthralled by the reading that he dreaded the addition of the action and costumes and mansions and music, however much they might enhance the effect. He made his way to the table where Lucy, summoned from the pantry, poured ale for the players, who served themselves from the dishes of bread, fish, cheese and pottage. As ever, the presence of a priest constrained conversation, the men more sparing of their own words than they had been of his. Sensing their discomfiture, he moved to Simon, who stood alone.

'Please convey my thanks to Mistress Muskham for furnishing us with such a magnificent feast.'

'Mistress Muskham has furnished nothing,' Simon said. 'Mistress Muskham wishes as little to do with the pageant as with its master. Mistress Muskham keeps to her chamber, spewing as she has done every morning since she gorged herself on Simnel Sunday. It is Master Muskham whom you must thank.'

Ralf returned to St Martin's to assist with the Lenten confessions. He entered the church to find Sir Robert seated on the shriving stool in the chancel, Isobel Louth kneeling in front of him, and a large congregation gathered in the nave. As he crept down the side aisle, he was conscious of heads turning towards him and he trusted for Mistress Louth's sake that one was not the rector's, lest he allow his resentment of his cantarist to influence her penance. Donning his surplice and stole, he pondered the task ahead. It was thirty years since Archbishop John had licensed him to hear confessions, instituting him to the cure of souls that had been his principal object on entering the priesthood. Sir Aidan had welcomed his aid, since not even the most assiduous priest was able to shrive the several hundred parishioners who came between Holy Tuesday and Maundy Thursday to make their belated confessions. Sir Robert, however, scorned to acknowledge his help. He even accused him of lightening his penances in order to attract more suppliants.

'What sort of a priest would place his own vanity above another's immortal soul?' Ralf asked, affronted.

The rector's flushed cheeks were his reply.

Far from apologising for his lenience, Ralf was ready to justify it before the archdeacon … the archbishop if necessary: a claim that he hoped would not be put to the test. Had Sir Robert, who was twenty years his junior, forgotten his own youthful confessions? Or had he had a kindlier confessor than the canon precentor who had shriven the boys of the Minster school? Of the seven deadly sins, he had singled out one. Every year he questioned Ralf about his privy member, how often he touched it and whether it hardened of its own accord, barely hiding his incredulity at Ralf's protestations of innocence, warning him that to defile himself was a graver sin than incest since he was closer to himself than to anyone of his blood. When at fourteen Ralf confessed to an involuntary pollution during his sleep, the precentor appeared almost pleased, insisting that there was nothing involuntary about the demons at work on his flesh. As a penance, he enjoined him to sleep with a crucifix bound to his member, which, to Ralf's dismay, led to his polluting his Saviour's body as well as his own, and to stand before the rood screen on four successive Ember Days, clad only in his shift and holding a candle whose dripping wax would concentrate his mind on his sin.

Ralf knelt in the Lady Chapel, where the crowd awaiting him risked provoking Sir Robert further. He prayed that, although a sinner, he might through his sacred office be the means whereby the sins of others were forgiven. Then he drew up the shriving stool and summoned the first penitent to profess his faith and confess his faults. As Stephen Dugdale, an apprentice cooper whom he had taught at petty school, knelt before him, the rest of the congregation edged forward, feeding his misgivings about what should have been a private conversation between the penitent, priest and God. Ordering them back, he was grateful that despite the frailty of his other organs – not least the one that would render the attachment of a crucifix superfluous – his ears were unimpaired, permitting Stephen to whisper. In his final years, Sir Aidan had been so deaf that confession had resembled a midsummer fair. It was no wonder that certain merchants asked Sir Robert to shrive them at home.

Stephen sounded a familiar note when, averting his gaze from the cross, he confessed to nocturnal pollutions. Having heard a black friar at Kingstoft preach that every spilt seed was a drop of blood drained from his body, he was terrified that his emissions were so copious he must shortly die. He had stuffed his pallet with thistles to keep from sleeping too soundly, but the only result was that his master beat him for sluggishness during the day. No sooner had he closed his eyes than the devil reached out his hand and tugged at him like a cat with a ball of twine. Ralf, whose knowledge of natural philosophy, albeit small, exceeded Stephen's, assured him that, while a man's seed was indeed refined from his blood, that blood rapidly restored itself, hence the healthful bloodlettings on the feasts of the physician saints.

He gave him a mild penance of forty days' abstinence from meat, five paternosters, five *Aves* and one *Credo*, as he did his next penitent, who was equally tormented by concupiscence, a heavily sweating farrier whose name Ralf did not recall and who, like a boy dipping his toes in a brook to test its warmth, confessed to neglect of his prayers and breach of the Lenten fast, before plunging headlong into intemperate knowledge of his wife. Confirming to a shocked Ralf that it was his own wife of whom he spoke, he described how, after bathing his privy member in onion juice to reduce its potency, he lay with her two or three times each night. It was a great joy to them both, but last Lady Day the rector had preached that it was as sinful for a man to lie with his own wife, except for the purpose of procreation, as it was to lie with his neighbour's. Whilst wary of opposing Sir Robert, Ralf assured the farrier that he was no more a lecher for lingering in bed with his wife than a glutton for relishing her pies. St Augustine himself had taught that the blessings of marriage turned the iniquity of copulation into virtue.

As though afraid that to delay would expose him to a harsher penance, the farrier kissed Ralf's stole and scuttled away. His place was taken by Martha Seward, a friend of Marjorie Underwood and reputed to be the most pious woman in the parish. Ralf struggled to suppress his amazement when, lowering her gaze, she confessed to three instances of fornication.

'On three several days?'

'With three several men.'

Ralf had heard of priests who withheld absolution from

wanton women unless they lay with them, and from wanton men unless they revealed the names of their accomplices, that they might seek them out. Although assured that it was a Lollard calumny, he could not keep from wondering whether that was how his father had ensnared his mother. It was hard to imagine even the most dissolute priest seeking out Martha, a sixty-year-old grandmother afflicted with pearl-eye and gout. Loath to impose too strict a penance for fear of alerting her husband, he directed her to eat only dry bread and say six paternosters, nine *Aves* and three *Credos* every day until Pentecost.

The litany of fleshly sins rolled on, with the occasional respite when a woolpacker confessed to dressing as a pilgrim in order to avoid the toll on the road to Doncaster, a pinner confessed to feigning sickness to miss Mass, a hosteler confessed to backbiting her neighbours, and a miller to mixing his flour with chalk. By the middle of the afternoon when Lucy, Agnes Muskham's maid, knelt before him, Ralf's attention was waning. After examining her on the articles of the creed and hearing her stuttering paternoster, he exhorted her to confess her faults. She began with the theft of a potion of juniper, giant fennel and pennyroyal from her mistress's chest. Glancing at the assembled company, she whispered that it was to avoid conception, describing how she had lain with three men, whom she named, unbidden, as Diggory, the gong-farmer; Roger, the fishmonger's apprentice; and Hamo. As saddened to learn of such lewdness in the girl as in the grandmother, Ralf charged her to atone or else suffer infamy in this world and agony in the next, giving her a penance of six months' abstinence from meat to quell her carnality.

Whatever the power of the potion, Lucy had thus far escaped any issue of her sin. Agnes was not so fortunate, as became clear the following day when, kneeling in front of him, she confessed that she was with child. Although her penitence should have forewarned him, Ralf cleaved to the hope that, after the dismissal of her suit, she had been reconciled to Simon.

'The child is Edmund's.'

'Speak lower.'

'I do not fear discovery. My son will be proud of his father.'

'I speak as your friend as well as your confessor,' Ralf said, shifting uneasily on the stool. 'You must avow your sin to God but not to the parish. Accept that the child will be Simon's.'

'Never! You were in the court when he accused me of adultery. The registrar has taken depositions.'

'Surely you will find six compurgators?'

'Are you counselling me to perjure myself, Sir Ralf?' she asked, with a ghost of a smile. 'And to press others to do so on my behalf?'

Ralf scanned the crowd waiting by the parclose and felt his sympathies at variance with his vows. 'They need not lie,' he said slowly. 'They may be true to what they know of you.'

'But I shall not.'

'And I shall chastise you. But any penance I give you for falsehood will be far gentler than the one that the archdeacon gives you for adultery. He will instruct the wardens to whip you round the churchyard. Trust me, I know whereof I speak.'

'No one will whip me! I shall resist.'

'Then you will be excommunicate and denied the service of a midwife when you are brought to bed. And when your child is born – let us suppose that it survives,' he said, purposely playing on her fears, 'what then? You will never marry Edmund.'

'Do you mean while my husband lives?' she asked, so coldly that Ralf dreaded what other potions might be stowed in her chest.

'No, by reason of consanguinity. You were to have stood godmother to Edmund's daughter.' Her loud wail startled several suppliants, who looked up eager to discover the sin that had incurred such painful expiation. Ralf wondered whether, at the high altar, Sir Robert was according him a rare nod of approval. Nevertheless, he prescribed a penance of prayer, unwilling to deny her the meat, which, when the Lenten fast ended, she would need to nourish the child.

The men of the Muskham household made their confessions on Thursday morning. The first was Hamo, who sputtered that he had committed a sin too wicked to put into words. Setting his remorse against Lucy's assurance, Ralf was moved to pity. Unable to speak his lines as Simon had done at the practice, he sought to prompt him.

'Have you been corrupted by lust?'

'I have,' Hamo said, although, to Ralf's consternation, he named as his accomplice not Lucy but Simon. 'It was last Michaelmas, when Mistress Muskham banished him from her bed and he moved to the garret to sleep with me. He pushed our two pallets together for warmth,' he said, shivering. 'But his hands were so hot when … he reached out his hand to my ballocks – my belly. He seized my yard. I could not withhold my seed.' He started to whimper.

'This was on the night that he left Mistress Muskham?' Ralf asked, as though some confusion in Simon's mind might mitigate the fault.

'And every night since then. He does me much mischief.' Hamo covered his face as though to obscure the memory.

'The sin is always with his hand?'

'It begins so.'

'Then how does it proceed?'

'I am too ashamed.'

'Remember, you are speaking not to me, Sir Ralf, but to God.'

'He spends his seed inside me,' Hamo said, snot dripping on to his upper lip.

'Inside your mouth or inside your fundament?' Ralf asked, his penitentials appointing a harsher penalty for sinning in the place where one received the sacrament.

'I choked.'

'I understand.'

'Then I thought that I would split.'

'Should he assault you again, you must withstand him.'

'He is my master.'

'Tell him that you confessed and I said that his punishment would be doubled – tripled – for defiling an innocent.'

'But what of mine? I shall burn in everlasting hell. Like the Sodomites – the real ones on the chancel arch, not the ones in your pageant.' After an extended hiss on *Sodomites*, he stared at the confessor with blazing eyes as if he had also played a part in his damnation and, for the first time, Ralf questioned the merit of his script. As pageant master, Simon had sole right to choose the players, but would he have chosen Hamo if he had had the old speeches to remind him of the penalty for lust?

'You will be forgiven,' he said. 'Put your faith in the measureless mercy of God. Do you affirm that you have made a true and entire confession of your faults?'

'I do.'

Ralf thought of Lucy and wondered whether Hamo were trying to shield her or if he had overlooked their incontinence in the face of the more grievous fault. Trusting that one avowal of venery would serve for both, he gave him his penance. Although he rejected the severity of the manuals that condemned even a boy involuntarily oppressed to ten years' privation of meat, he knew that too mild a penance would fail to fulfil Hamo's need for atonement. So he imposed a fast of dry bread and water for three Lenten seasons and a daily charge of five paternosters and three *Aves*, omitting less familiar prayers lest, unsure of the words, he was obliged to seek guidance from Simon.

As he summoned the next penitent, Ralf was assailed by doubt. Sodomy was a reserved sin and by law he should have referred Hamo to the archbishop. But while granting its gravity, he refused to regard it as the equal of apostasy, heresy or murder. As with Simon twelve years before, he chose to shrive him himself, invoking the power invested in the humblest priest as much as in the proudest bishop. The thought of Simon troubled him and he wondered whether, in twelve years' time, he – or rather, his successor – might hear an apprentice confess to committing a similar offence with Hamo. Had his efforts to save one sinner from an earthly punishment consigned another to eternal torment? Then, in the midst of his perplexity, he pictured his mutilated friends and he knew that he was right to entrust Hamo to the mercy of God rather than the justice of the Church.

When Simon stood before him at midday, Ralf made no attempt to conceal his coldness. He contemplated walking away and leaving him to the ministrations of Sir Robert, but that would have been unfair to the remaining penitents. Kneeling, Simon professed his faith and affirmed that he made his confession with a true and contrite heart, but the limits of that contrition became clear when the only sins he acknowledged were impatience, intemperance and perjury.

'Do you have a pure and utter desire to amend your offences against God?' Ralf asked.

'I do.'

'Do you have faith that God can forgive you your sins if you confess and convert to him with your whole heart?'

'I do.'

'Have you confessed all the sins that weigh heavily upon you?'

'I have.'

'Have you committed no wicked fornications or the luxury against nature?'

'I have not.'

'Are you sure?' Ralf asked, fixing him with a look designed to pierce his soul.

'I have said so,' Simon replied, imperturbably.

'Not with a woman or a man or any person in your household?'

'With no one.'

Ralf longed to protest but, bound by the seal of the confessional, he could do no more than warn him that sins not admitted to a priest would be exposed before all mankind on the Day of Doom. Faced with Simon's obduracy, he absolved him of those sins that he had confessed and, imposing a heavier penance than they might otherwise have warranted, enjoined him to fast on dry bread until Pentecost and to say *Misere mei, Deus* once, *Pater Noster* seven times, and *Ave Maria* and *Laudatum* ten times a day, for a year. Simon crossed himself and went out, leaving Ralf with a gnawing emptiness, which grew into a hunger so intense that gluttony, his besetting sin, felt like the deadliest of the seven. With the chapel finally empty, he was kneeling to pray when Edmund Underwood entered.

'You are forbidden this place, Edmund,' Ralf said, blocking the altar steps.

'I am come to make my confession.'

'You are?'

'Do you refuse to hear it?'

'You have left it very late.' Ralf wondered if he had been struggling with his conscience or simply seeking to avoid the crowd.

'"So shall the last be first and the first last." Is not my penitence worth as much as those who confessed on Ash Wednesday?' Edmund asked, palpably enjoying Ralf's confusion.

'Of course. Provided that it is heartful.'

'Do you doubt me? Cleansed of my sins, I shall do the penance ordained for my sacrilege. I shall lash my back until it streams with blood, but it will feel as if it is bathed in myrrh. Then I shall be allowed to attend the court and speak against Simon Muskham.'

'You intend to reply to his libel?' Ralf asked, hopeful that, if he denied the adultery, Agnes must do the same and the threat of her chastisement be averted.

'I shall reply so forcefully that he will dissolve like salt in the ocean.'

'To receive absolution, you must bear no man malice … you must be at peace with all your neighbours.'

'Let God Himself be the judge of my verity.'

'Then I shall inform the wardens of your readiness to do penance this Eastertide, that you may be welcomed back into Holy Church.' Ralf moved to the shriving stool. 'Come, let us pray.'

5

For the third practice of *Lot's Wife* they had abandoned Simon's hall in the face of Agnes's open hostility. In a series of wilful provocations, she had twice summoned the launderer, who had stumped through Sodom as though collecting its soiled linen; cleaned the pantry with such a clatter that the players' voices were drowned long before the fateful thunder-clap; and sent Lucy in a loose kirtle to chase an imaginary rat. Worn down, Simon urged Ralf to seek Sir Robert's permission to use St Martin's. Dreading the response, Ralf was greatly relieved when Rylan Yafford proposed his own parish church of St John del Pyke. The rector readily agreed, even deferring the morrow Mass. As the early morning light crept through the clerestory windows, the company gathered in the chill nave, with no sign of either Simon or Hamo.

'Five more minutes and, if our pageant master is still absent, we will begin without him. Master Braithwaite is keen to judge our progress.' Ralf forced a smile at the surly man whose task was to dress the wagon.

'What about Hamo?' Hugh asked. 'He stands beside me on the mansion.'

'Now quick, desssscend we to the ground,' Henry lisped, to the delight of his fellow apprentices.

'I expect that he is with Master Muskham,' Ralf said.

'No doubt,' Eustace said. 'By now they are yoked together.'

'My master says that they may soon be together forever, in the Ouse kidcote,' Henry said.

'Nonsense! Master Muskham's affairs thrive; he has no debts,' Ralf replied sharply.

He was gripped by a sense of unease, which deepened as he turned towards the left transept where, beneath a grimy painting of Susannah and the Elders, Paul Ruckshawe was in private conversation with John Helperby and Baldwin Louth. Having rebelled against Ralf's demand that the daughters practise in gowns, he now relished the licence, hitching up his skirt and wiggling his hips as though he were a denizen of Grapcunt Lane. For all the evident mirth, Ralf was troubled. Did the gown transform Paul in more than appearance? How shrewd was his smile? And how base were the men's glances? Were they apprising the apparel or the boy? Christ himself taught that children belonged to the kingdom of God. Yet Sir Robert had denied Constance's baby sacred burial on account of her birth-sin. Watching Paul, with his crooked gestures and wanton winks, Ralf wondered whether he might have been right.

The whispering, which died away on his approach, made him feel like a Fishergate wife whose husband's ship had failed to reach port. Scorning his fancy, he resolved to start.

'Let us waste no more time. We will make Master Muskham proud.' Reginald snorted loudly, which surprised Ralf, who had supposed himself to be the sole object of his disdain. 'Our task today is to suit the words to the movements. Until Hamo arrives, I shall read Gabriel. Although I fear I am no Master Muskham.'

'I should hope not,' Baldwin said coldly.

'And remember that I am the only one permitted to carry his lines. The rest of you should know them by now. Those that stumble will incur my wrath – the wrath of Raphael that is, not Sir Ralf,' he said, with a lonely laugh. 'Has everyone marked where our properties are placed, just as in Master Muskham's hall? The sanctuary steps serve well for our mansion … Do you require a parchment?' he asked Adam Braithwaite, who looked bewildered.

'Fret not, Sir Ralf,' Adam replied. 'My parchment is here.' He tapped his skull.

Ralf moved to the sanctuary steps, where Hugh took the opportunity to plead again for wings.

'Have you forgotten what I taught you at school?' Ralf asked. 'Only God is moved by repeated entreaties.'

'But I feel incomplete. How can I be an angel without wings?'

Ralf chose not to point out his other shortcomings. Having deferred to Simon over the casting of the boys, he had stood firm over their attire. Last year they had worn golden masks and peacock-feather wings, with swan down on their hose, thereby drawing attention to the very member that angels blissfully lacked. Such a singular appearance made nonsense, not only of the Sodomites' assault, but of Lot's presumption that they were weary travellers. So Hugh and Hamo were to be dressed in plain, loose-fitting albs.

'How will people recognise us?' Hugh asked, while Rylan searched for his staff. 'The coopers' angels, the armourers' angels, the glovers' angels before us will all be winged and masked.'

'Everyone knows that angels can change shape,' Ralf said. 'And you have taken the shape of men.'

'But we are boys!'

'You are angels in the shape of men in the shape of boys. That is your mystery.'

'And how will we pass through the crowd? Without wings, they will use us naughtily.'

'Why? Wings are not swords.'

'With wings we can beat them off.'

'I will tell the stytelers to keep close by you throughout the procession,' Ralf said, perturbed that the passions he had excised from the pageant were rife on the streets. 'Now, shall we begin? As you recall, Hugh and Hamo – that is Gabriel and Raphael – enter at the top of the mansion. So, if you are ready …'

'Now dread ye not—' Hugh declaimed.

'Stop! Where do you find that?' Ralf asked.

'My friend Jack Chambers, he that is prenticed to Master Harpham the spicer, is Gabriel in the pageant of *The Annunciation*. We were conning our lines together. He says "Now dread ye not" when he appears to Our Blessed Lady. And he wears a mask.'

'Then it is no wonder that she is disturbed. Whereas when they see your fair countenance, the audience will cheer.'

'Might they not wear masks?' Eustace asked. 'I say nothing of young Hugh, who is as goodly a lad as any in York, but when I declare Hamo "beauteous as the butterfly", I fear that the people will laugh.'

'Or else cut off his foot for a charm against goblins,' Henry said, to general merriment.

'There will be no masks!' Ralf said. 'An angel's beauty rests as much in his spirit as his face, and Hamo—' He broke off at the memory of the boy's confession.

Quieting the dissension in his head as well as among the players, he called on Hugh to resume, speaking the words as written, which he did without a fault. Indeed, as the practice progressed, Ralf discovered to his surprise that the only player yet to master his lines was Rylan Yafford. He was wary of Rylan, a dour, beetle-browed merchant, who dealt in salt from the brine springs of Cheshire. There was a darkness about him which, had he been a cook or a water-leader, would have fitted him well to represent Judas. So Ralf was relieved when Lot led the angels into the mansion, leaving his wife to seek provisions from her neighbours. Eustace had laboured over his speeches and devised a distinct gait, like a dog shuffling on his hind legs to beg a morsel, but he lacked Simon's vigour, which, by some strange alchemy, made the wife at once abject and piteous and her fate all the crueller. By far the greater part of Eustace's representation lay in his voice, which he pinched and squeezed until, like so many of the women in the Corpus Christi play, including several Blessed Virgins, he squealed like a trapped fox.

While Eustace's diligence was roundly approved, John Helperby's hoarseness sparked ribaldry.

'I have a cold rheum and little voice,' he said.

'Better a little voice than none at all,' Ralf replied. Filling the silence with an uneasy laugh, he chid himself that, after thirty years of schoolroom failure, he still chose to jest.

The Sodomites surrounded Lot's house, an action that would remain incomplete until the next practice when the four mute players joined them. Lot appeared at the mansion door to remonstrate with them, but the lines that Rylan spoke did not accord with those on Ralf's parchment:

'Good sirs, the honour of my house
I pray do not defile,
With lust as loathsome as the louse
And violation vile.'

Ralf wondered whether Rylan had made the error unwittingly, unable to drown the echoes of the old script, which, after so many years, he had fixed in his mind. But, on reflection, it was clear that, as discreetly as possible (he must commend him for that if nothing else), he had returned to the former pageant.

'You are mistaken, Master Yafford,' Ralf said. 'Those are not the lines in the script.'

'They are not the lines in your script, Sir Ralf, but they are the lines in God's.'

'We have disputed this before,' Ralf said.

'And I have listened. I have done my best to abide by your wishes, but they are wrong. I am no scholar, Sir Ralf, but I know the truth. I can no longer represent Lot. You have wrested the purpose from the pageant.'

'You have corrupted it,' Reginald said, froward as ever.

'I find now that Lot is at fault,' Rylan added. 'His anger is immoderate. Why should he scold his neighbours when they seek only the rightful toll on foreigners who pass the night in the city? Are we not all bound to pay our taxes and tithes?'

'But they seek more than their right,' Ralf replied. 'They breach the sacred law of hospitality.'

'You say that the sins of Sodom are pride and greed, and contempt for the poor and the stranger. But what about the sin against nature?'

'I have already made it plain: that sin is not the one in the story.'

'Then forgive me, but God's anger is also immoderate,' Rylan said. 'Would He destroy a city purely on account of its pride and contempt? With no care for the innocent women and children?'

'But He did that anywise,' Henry said, 'since they had not sinned against nature.'

'Peace, boy!' Baldwin said. 'You are not at school.'

'If God were to destroy all prideful cities,' Rylan said, 'there would be none left in England.'

'Certainly not York,' Henry said, smarting at Baldwin's reproof.

'Why was Lot's wife turned into a pillar of salt?' Reginald asked. 'Surely it was for more than disobedience, a sin to which, as we know, women have been prone ever since our first mother?'

'Mistress Helperby bickers even when I buffet her,' John said, laughing.

'No,' Reginald added. 'She was punished because it was a sin to which no woman should bear witness.'

'And because God willed that no record of that sin should survive,' Rylan said. 'He well knew how women prate.'

'Then why did Moses recount it?' Ralf asked.

'He did so by stealth,' Rylan said, 'which is why you have been able to embellish it, bringing shame on us all.'

'No, you are wrong. If the pageant proves false, the fault will be mine alone.'

'Once we were mocked for presenting the story of Sodom,' Rylan said. 'Now we will be rebuked for altering it at the behest of the pageant master – one who is himself accused of sodomy.'

'What?' Ralf said, feeling his entrails melt. 'That is slander. Who is it that accuses him?'

'Ask young Hugh.'

'Who is it, lad?' Ralf asked. 'Tell me what you know.'

'Master Underwood,' Hugh mumbled.

'Edmund?' Ralf said, more to himself than Hugh.

'Master Muskham charged him with adultery. My master was one of his compurgators.'

'As was I,' Baldwin interjected.

'Yes,' Ralf said. 'He has purged himself and answered the libel. That is good … that is very good. But how does that pertain to the charge against Master Muskham? Have the wardens denounced him?'

'No,' Baldwin said, 'it was Edmund Underwood himself. He supplicated the archdeacon to prosecute the offence that has been much rumoured.'

'Rumoured by whom?' Ralf asked.

'Lucy, Mistress Muskham's maid.'

'She saw him together with Hamo, naked as needles,' Henry said.

'She had to change the linen on their pallets,' Paul said.

'Be still!' Ralf shouted, sounding more like Sir Robert than himself. 'Is this true?' he asked Baldwin, who shrugged.

'I can answer that, sir,' Hugh said, savouring his new authority. 'Hamo confessed his sin to Lucy. He was afraid that he must burn in hell.'

'For all eternity,' Paul added, as though he were striking the flint.

'Lucy disclosed the tale to her mistress who disclosed it to mine who disclosed it to my master who disclosed it to Master Underwood,' Hugh said.

Ralf doubted that the news had reached Edmund so indirectly and wondered how, given all the talk, he himself had heard nothing. But Hugh had at least solved the mystery of Edmund's change of heart. By purging his sin and recovering his fame, he was licensed to bring the charge against Simon.

'And is Master Muskham so discomfited that he cannot appear before us now?' he asked.

'No, he is arrested,' Reginald said.

'And Hamo too,' Paul added.

'They were taken to St Peter's prison by the archbishop's officers last night,' Eustace said.

'And no one thought to tell me?' Ralf asked, staring at Baldwin, who shifted his feet, just as he had done twenty years earlier when caught with another boy's slate.

'It was not my place,' he said sourly.

'We thought that you must know,' Reginald added.

'How? I am not in the archbishop's trust. He does not come to me and ask "Now Sir Ralf, should I indict such a fellow for such an offence?" – such a rumoured offence.'

'Rumoured among persons of repute,' John said.

'Now you see, Sir Ralf, why we cannot present this new script,' Reginald said. 'We will seem to be winking at sin.'

'Nonsense. The truth of the story does not bear upon the truth – or untruth – of the libel. We must proceed with our work,' Ralf said, as though they could avert the danger by ignoring it. 'We have but one more practice before the general. You will be rebuked, not for what you say but for failing to say it with assurance. Master Yafford, the lines are:

Good sirs, the honour of my house
I pray do not defile.
'Tis precious to me as my spouse.
Renounce this place awhile.
Prithee speak them.'

The threat of rebellion passed as the players, either impressed or confounded by Ralf's resolve, resumed the practice. He heard them recite the lines and himself correct their faults, but it was as though all their voices, including his own, were muffled like bells at a funeral. They had repeated the script twice when, with his thoughts fixed on St Peter's prison, he called a halt. After reminding them of their next practice, he left them to breakfast in the porch and hurried back to the parish, through streets filled with people whose friends and neighbours had not been charged with the most heinous sin. Having no express plan, he found himself at Marjorie's door and, when the steward led him up to the chamber, she appeared to be expecting him. Without uttering a word, she clasped his hand and wept.

'I will not believe it, not of Simon,' she said, moving away and wiping her eyes. 'Yet it is Edmund who accuses him. What cause does he have to lie?'

'We must pray for God's guidance,' replied Ralf, who had never felt more burdened by the secrets of men's hearts nor thankful for the seal of the confessional.

'I am glad that Walter is dead – yes, I must say it – for this news would have sorely grieved him. He loved Simon like a son.'

'I know it – and so did Edmund.'

'If the semblance of the sin brought shame on the craft, how much more must the sin itself? You remember the words he had inscribed on his stone?'

'*Vos estis sal terræ.*'

'"Ye are the salt of the earth," yes. Edmund transposed it into English for me, along with the rest of the verse: "But if the salt lose its savour, wherewith shall it be salted? It is good for nothing but to be cast out and to be trodden on by men."'

Ralf's fears that this would be Simon's and Hamo's fate increased the following week when, with the case whispered throughout the city, he discovered that men accused of sodomy were bound to defend themselves without recourse to a proctor. He suspected that Simon, who had shown no compunction about lying in confession, would show even less in court. He would answer the depositions as guilefully as he had done those in the frigidity action. His accomplice, however, was a boy without position or friends or even understanding.

Ralf was pondering how best to help him when he received a message from Hamo, asking him to testify on his behalf. Written by the kidcote almoner, it authorised Ralf to reveal his confession, relating how he was pressed into sin by his master. Had Simon confessed, Ralf would have had to refuse since, by assisting one penitent, he would have betrayed the other. Simon's deceit, however, gave him scope and he notified the registrar who, two days later, summoned him to give testimony in the lady chapel of St Martin's. He arrived to find four fellow deponents: Lucy, Isobel Louth and Guy and Agatha Dobbes, waiting beside the parclose as solemnly as if it were the chancel rail on Easter Day. They stirred briefly when Agnes left the chapel and, eyes lowered, hurried from the church. Then, as the clerk came to fetch him, Ralf gazed across the transept where Sir Robert stood smiling.

The trial was set for the ninth of June, ten days before Corpus Christi, at the archbishop's summer palace in Cawood. Ralf, whose deposition gnawed at his soul, had resolved to attend, and Marjorie offered to accompany him. Discounting her lack of Latin, she declared that she had no wish to hear any of the filthy charges but would go for Walter's sake. To Ralf's relief, Edmund was in Hull, seeking a writ to distrain French goods in restitution for a ship seized off Yarmouth. He vowed, however, that not even a royal summons would keep him from Simon's execution, as though both the judgement and the sentence were assured.

Approaching Marjorie's door at dawn on the appointed day, Ralf found the carter waiting with the wagon that was to take them the ten miles to Cawood. He had not set foot beyond the city walls for a dozen years and, had the occasion been less doleful, he would have delighted to see the hedgerows and meadows in full flower. They arrived at the palace gatehouse, newly emblazoned with the arms of Archbishop Robert Waldby, and entered the outer courtyard, which was as busy as the Thursday market. A maid shouldering pails of milk waved to a launderer hauling a crammed basket. Two turnspits carried a side of pork past a drift of indifferent hogs. A wheelwright and his apprentice replaced the spokes on an upturned cart. A butler and a scullion dragged a barrel of beer up the cellar steps. Two grooms tethered and watered horses. A solitary peacock strutted about, its tail resplendent, as if representing the archbishop, absent at the King's Parliament in London. A page struggled to restrain a chained mastiff whose snarl so startled Marjorie that she tripped. Stammering an apology, he escorted them to the great hall, where the court was in session. They crept up the bank of benches and sat opposite the Official Principal, Master Rudyard Senhouse, who looked up briefly before returning his gaze to his knees, where it remained throughout the trial. Four advocates occupied the seats on either side of him, studying their scrolls, as though the men before them were a distraction from their higher purpose. The men – Simon and Hamo – looked far more defenceless than Simon had done in the dean's court. Ralf stared at their backs, the one broad and square as if refusing to bend beneath the weight of obloquy; the other slender and bowed as if longing to shrug off its own flesh.

The Official's notary read out their answers to the allegations. Neither sought to deny them. Simon maintained that, in his stupor, he had mistaken his apprentice for his wife, provoking laughter on the clerks' bench, until Master Senhouse instructed them to remember the dignity of their office and the gravity of the case. Hamo swore that he had resisted his master but had been vanquished by his superior strength. With no proctors present, the Official asked the notary to publish the depositions. He stood and, with his back to the defendants, read out the testimony that would determine their fates. The first was from Lucy who, after relating Hamo's account of his violation, described his subsequent attempt to enter her as 'filthily as Master Muskham did enter him'. The next was from the launderer, who stated that she had examined the linen on Hamo's pallet and found it smeared with blood and dung. The third was from Agnes who, after asserting that Simon was frigid and that the dean's court had been deceived by the testimony of harlots, declared that his member had only served when he sought to use her in the sodomitical manner but, by the grace of the Virgin Mary to whom she had prayed for strength, she had withstood the assault. Simon's head sank and his shoulders sagged as the notary read on. However impenetrable the language, he could not have failed to comprehend the term *peccatum sodomiticum* and with it the tenor of the charge.

The remaining deponents had no direct knowledge of Simon and Hamo's sin but gave credit to Lucy's and Agnes's accounts. Finally, Ralf heard his own name read out, his words lent weight by both the measured tones of the registrar and the Latin rendering. He alone spoke on behalf of the defendants – or rather, one of them, since his support for Hamo further indicted Simon. He was thankful that they were compelled to face the Official and that no sharp noise or interjection caused Simon to turn and catch sight of him, his eyes as accusatory as those that had fixed on him forty years earlier in the market square.

After a brief exchange with his notary, Master Senhouse called on one of the advocates to advise him on any points of law arising from the case. Crossing to the floor of the court, the man doffed his cap to the Official and declared that the case was as simple as it was noisome. The sodomite, having failed to induce his wife to sin, had meddled with his apprentice. The boy had then subjected a virtuous serving maid to the like outrage. The law on such iniquity was clear.

The Official thanked him and proceeded to pass judgement. He ruled that the allegations had been proved and the malefactors should be confined in the Ouse kidcote and thence brought before the sheriffs for punishment. All that was missing, in Ralf's view, was a bowl of water in which he might wash his hands since, by delivering the prisoners to the sheriffs' court, he had absolved both himself and the Church of any blame for the shedding of blood. Simon's drooping head showed that he had sufficient Latin to understand the sentence, but Hamo remained in ignorance until the officers approached to lead him away. He howled and fell to the floor, kicking Simon who bent to help him. Marjorie covered her face as he was dragged from the room, swiftly followed by Simon, whose eyes as they met Ralf's were blank.

The news of the judgement reached York faster than Ralf and Marjorie. After a jolting journey, Ralf made his way to see Agnes, uncertain of his reception but trusting that, whatever her quarrel with Simon, she would pity his fate. He was met at the door by Lucy.

'I have come straight from the court at Cawood.' He waited for her to ask after Hamo, but she stood in dumb insolence. 'Both Master Muskham and Hamo were condemned.'

'They brought shame on this house,' she said flatly.

'I am here to see Mistress Muskham.'

'She is not to be seen. She has taken to her bed.'

'Who is it, Lucy?' The familiar voice filled Ralf with dismay.

'Sir Ralf,' Lucy replied.

'Tell him I come.'

As Edmund descended the stairs, Ralf noticed at once that the belt on his tunic was unbuckled and suspected that it had been left so on purpose. 'Making yourself master here already, Edmund?' he asked.

'I heard the news on my return from Hull. I came straight to comfort Mistress Muskham. You may go,' he said to Lucy, who left with a sly look at Edmund and a pert one at Ralf.

'Then I can see that I am not needed,' Ralf said.

'Oh no, you are always needed, Sir Ralf. But you have many more pressing duties. Should you not be choosing another angel now that Hamo has sunk so low? Or do you propose to return my father's legacy?'

'It was never a question of money, Edmund,' Ralf said.

'So says every priest.'

'But we do have to find another angel. Since there is no time to elect another pageant master, I shall beseech the warden to take charge himself. He will wish to show the city that there is no offence in the craft or in the script.'

'I too have a duty to the craft, as well as to my father. So I shall provide your angel.'

'You wish to play Raphael?' Ralf asked, confounded.

'I am no piping youth! I have an apprentice, Thomas Langham, a fair lad and an apt scholar. I will spare him from his labours to con the part.'

Ralf was not present the following Monday when Simon and Hamo were led through the streets to the common hall, preferring to remain in the chantry, in intercession for the living as well as the dead. He knew that he would hear news of the sentence soon enough but was not expecting that the bearer would be Sir Robert who, with scant regard for sanctity, burst into the chapel and interrupted his prayers.

'The two filthy men—'

'One was but a boy!'

'With a man's filthy lusts – were brought from the gaol. The good people of York had gathered to show their abhorrence. They assailed them with all manner of refuse so that the blood from the butchers' carcasses mingled with that from the caitiffs' own hurts.' Ralf was unable to dispel the thought that, two weeks hence, those same people should have been cheering Hamo's part in and Simon's presentation of the pageant. 'They entered the assize in all their foulness. The sheriff, informed of the judgement of His Excellency's court, straightway passed sentence. The apprentice, Hamo, whom you permitted to represent the blessed archangel, was deemed to be the lesser sinner and given the milder punishment. He is to have his nose, ears and stones cut off. The salter, Muskham, who incited the evil, is to be taken to the gallows at Knavesmire and hanged by the neck.'

'And may God have mercy on his soul,' Ralf said.

'Amen,' Sir Robert muttered.

Ralf was determined to offer the prisoners what comfort he could. He was pondering how best to gain entry to the kidcote, when Sir Robert added that the archdeacon wished to see him before Compline.

'Was the archdeacon in the court?'

'It was his duty and his delight.'

Troubled by the summons from a man who on his visitations to the parish had barely blinked at him, Ralf made his way that evening to the Minster Close. He tapped the bronze lion's head on the heavy door, trusting that its bared teeth did not presage his welcome. The steward led him into the dank chamber, where the archdeacon sat, leather spectacles propped on his carbuncled nose. He did not rise from his chair but beckoned him sharply, as if he were a boy caught playing at ball in the churchyard.

'I knew your father,' the archdeacon said.

'I did not,' Ralf replied, unnerved by the singular greeting.

'I was a boy in Brayton. He was my priest. A proper man, but frail. We should pray for strength to surmount our frailties, do you not agree, Sir Ralf?'

'Or rather to be relieved of them.'

'Do you have any frailties, Sir Ralf?'

'Many, I fear.'

'I speak of the flesh.'

'Gluttony. I strive to vanquish it. I pray that the Lord will surfeit me with his spirit.'

'You mistake me,' the archdeacon said, knitting his brows as though he suspected that the confusion were deliberate. 'I was present this morning at the sentencing of the two sodomites of St Martin's parish.' Ralf strove not to stir. 'I am told that you heard one of the condemned men's confessions.'

'He gave me leave to make my deposition. I broke no vow.'

'That is not what troubles me. You absolved him of a sin

that should have been reserved for the archbishop or his penitentiaries.'

'I crave your pardon,' Ralf said, shivering as he realised the reason for his summons, 'but Hamo is an innocent. He was lured into the sin for which he must now be so savagely punished. It was that I was seeking to avoid.'

'No man is innocent. We are all guilty of the sin that sunders us from Our Heavenly Father, most of all when we persist in wilful disobedience as, by your own admission, you yourself have done. Nevertheless, His Excellency is prepared to excuse your fault provided that you prove your penitence.'

'I am ready to do whatever is needful.'

'Good. But be warned, His Excellency wants more of you than a prayerful penance. I understand that you have written a pageant for the forthcoming *Play of Corpus Christi*.'

'That is true,' Ralf said, astounded that the report had ascended so high.

'It is a grave mishap that it should pertain to the sin of Sodom.'

'On the contrary, it is a boon, since it shows that the sin was not the one to which we have grown accustomed. God wreaked vengeance on the city for its cruelty to strangers.'

'In your judgement.'

'Not just in mine, but that of Our Lord himself when he foretold the fate of the towns that disdained his disciples. And for the Jews, hospitality was a sacred trust.'

'Those wicked Jews who betrayed every trust we bestowed upon them, until the first King Edward banished them these shores, for which his name be forever blessed.'

'I speak of the ancient Jews, the Jews of the Bible, from whom Our Lord was descended.'

'Enough! It is for you to remember your duty of obedience.'

'Forgive me but I do so, every hour of the day. Yet my first duty must be to God. When I wrote, I felt that my quill was wielded by somebody else.'

'An angel?'

'It may be,' Ralf replied, ignoring the mockery. 'I see lines that I have no memory of writing.'

'Come, Sir Ralf, that is the defence of every young sluggard distracted from his exercises. I have no doubt your purposes are pure, but that is not how they will be perceived in the city. We must make certain that the authority of the Church is not dimmed.'

'By one pageant?'

'A single spark can set a fortress ablaze. The archbishop has granted charge of the pageants to the crafts – that is, charge of the procedure, not the matter. The Common Clerk provides a copy of the scripts for his assent, which he has withheld from yours. With the recent action noised abroad, there is talk that sodomy is as rife among the salters as it was among the Templars of yore. You are concerned for your own enterprise, but His Excellency has care of the entire province.'

'Then he should not be guided by idle babble.'

'There must be nothing needless in the play. It already lasts long into the night. We cannot present every story in Holy Scripture. Some might question why we include *Lot's Wife*.'

'It is at the very heart of the matter. By showing God destroying the wicked and rescuing the righteous, it prefigures both the Day of Doom and the Harrowing of Hell.'

'Which we have just seen in the pageant of *The Flood*. No, the only argument for *Lot's Wife* is that it portrays the effects of a singular sin: a sin which of all sins is most loathsome to God. So you must return to the old script that has served for so many years, or else we will have to withdraw the pageant.'

'But it is not for me to decide,' Ralf said. 'It is for the warden and the pageant master.'

'The pageant master, precisely! Without him, the salters will look to you. And surely they will not wish to be doubly shamed by having the pageant annulled? Some of the players must have their old parts to hand. And we have a scroll in the Minster library that our scholars will copy for you.'

Ralf took his leave of the archdeacon and quit the house, crossing behind the Minster which, with the roof open to the sky, resounded with the strains of Compline. He made his way out of the precinct and down Loup Lane but, although the streets of the city were as familiar to him as the petitions of his paternoster, the blackness of the night and the turmoil in his mind disoriented him. He walked warily between the murky steps and the ditch, his measured tread heightening the nameless rustles and snaps underfoot. Wrestling with imagined dangers, he ignored the immediate one as a shrill shout of 'Look below!' heralded the voiding of a piss-pot. Narrowly escaping the ordure, he hurried on with a fierce yearning for home, which vanished when he arrived to find Edmund Underwood waiting unannounced in his chamber, as though for his bondman rather than his chaplain. Even seated, Edmund seemed too large for the room but, when he paced up and down, his presence was stifling.

'Why does God delight in persecuting me?' he asked bitterly. Ralf was about to rebuke his impiety when he remembered that Simon and Hamo were not the only couple to have been put on trial. While they were being sentenced in the sheriffs' court, Edmund and Agnes were answering charges of adultery in the dean's. Edmund had assembled his six compurgators without offering them so much as a peck of salt. Agnes, however, had not produced a single one. Even those who might have been moved by her plight or, at the very least, open to corruption, were confounded by the evidence of Simon's guilt. When a husband pursued such filthy practices, it was unsurprising that his wife should seek solace elsewhere. But that made her no less culpable. So while her alleged accomplice was acquitted, Agnes was condemned, as Ralf had foreseen, to public chastisement in the churchyard.

'And our child – our innocent child – will be whipped alongside her. Oh, I forgot! You do not believe in innocence. For you, he is already slimy with sin.'

'No, that is not my belief. It would be easier if it were.'

'A bastard!' Edmund said, as if Ralf were no more than an echo. 'He will not have my name or rank. He will not even have the right to enter the craft. A bastard! A nothing! It would be a mercy to drown him at birth.'

'He will have all that his mother can give him,' Ralf said, trusting that Edmund was too consumed by grief to have intended the insult. 'Simon Muskham is a man of substance. Whatever has passed between them, I am sure that he will not leave Agnes in want when he ...' Although eager to show Edmund that there were others more wretched than he was, he found that he could not utter the words.

'Are you in your wits, Sir Ralf? Do you not know that, as the wife of a convicted sodomite, she has no rights in the law? Any villain can abuse her – can assail her – and she has no redress. Her house and all her property are seized. And by whom? The Church.' He leant in so close that Ralf smelt the anise on his breath. 'He will be hanged, but hers is a creeping death. And the worst of it is that she blames me. She maintains that she would never have allowed me to bring the libel against him if she had known.'

'There may be a remedy. She must appeal to the archdeacon,' Ralf said, refusing to abandon hope.

'It is too late. She is to live with her aunt in Selby, where she is yet unknown. I will see neither her nor the child again.'

Edmund cursed his lot, resisting all Ralf's attempts to console him until, wearied by rancour, he fell asleep in his chair, leaving Ralf to watch over him through the night. For his pains, he was greeted at daybreak by lewd jests about ill-sorted bedfellows, which would have been odious even in happier circumstances. On Edmund's departure, he hastened to the chantry where, in addition to his prescribed prayers, he entreated God's pardon on Hamo and Simon. Seeking to serve their bodies as well as their souls, he then made his way to St Mary's Abbey, where he was received by the infirmarer, whose handshake left a yellow residue on his palm. Unperturbed, Ralf explained that he sought a powerful physic to relieve a patron in torment from St Fiacre's figs. Any scruples that the monk may have harboured were silenced by the payment of five marks, for which he gave Ralf a potion of belladonna, cowbane and mandrake, administered by the barber-surgeons when they severed corrupt limbs. Clasping the phial as reverently as a chalice, Ralf crossed the city to the Ouse Bridge, where the kidcote abutted uneasily on St William's chapel.

Without the authority of the archdeacon, who was awaiting news of his compliance, he had to trust to the venality of the gaoler. Any remorse that he felt at suborning the man vanished with the impudence of his demands. As he handed him four marks, two for each prisoner, he gave thanks to Walter who, even if the script were now suppressed, had furnished him with the means to assist Hamo and Simon, and he felt sure that, notwithstanding their transgression, he would have approved. As the gaoler led the way down the unwrought steps, he warned him that they had had to shackle Hamo's hands to inhibit his voluntary pollution. 'Although I had as lief let him be,' he said, grinning through blackened teeth. 'The villain will have little joy after Thursday.' He unlocked the door to the cell and Ralf was hit by a fouler stench than any since he had visited the anchorite at St Olave's. The gaoler, inured to the fetor, bent to enter and, kicking the boy like a sleeping cur, announced 'A priest,' before leaving Ralf alone with him. After stooping, which caused a crick in his neck, and crouching, which caused a cramp in his calves, he sat on the cold, rough, and, as he swiftly discovered, verminous slabs.

As the gaoler bolted the door, Ralf felt more confined than at any time since four of his fellow choristers had shut him in the unfinished tomb of Archbishop William Melton by the Minster font. Overcoming his terror, he raised Hamo's crusted head from the floor.

'It is Sir Ralf, Hamo.'

'I know.'

'I am very sorry to see you like this.'

'Come back on Friday. I shall have no nose. I shall have no ears. I shall have no stones!'

'You must make the penalty into a blessing.'

'What? How?' Hamo sat up and stared at him.

'No nose to smell the stink of mankind. No ears to hear their noisome jangle. No stones to draw you into Satan's snare.'

'But the hurt. The knife. The irons. The hurt!'

'Here,' Ralf said, removing the phial from his purse. 'I have brought a potion from the monks of St Mary's. You must drink this half an hour before they lead you away.'

'"Led in infamy to the horror of all who abjure sin and corruption": those were the sheriff's words.'

'It will assuage the pain. You will feel no more than if you cut your thumb.'

'Truly?'

'Truly.'

'But how will I drink it?' Hamo asked, raising his shackled wrists. 'I am chained.'

'I will seek permission – no, I will purchase permission, which is the surer way – to confess you on the day.'

'God bless you, Sir Ralf. But wait … tell me that you do not do the same for Master Muskham!'

'Do not trouble yourself. Like all of us, Simon Muskham will have to answer for his sins to God.'

'No, God will not hear him. He is the very Devil. God will stop His ears!' He shook his shackles.

'Peace, Hamo! Turn your thoughts beyond Thursday. You are young, with much life still to bear. You must leave for another town where you are not known.'

'They will know me by my scars. I will be marked as surely as Cain that killed his brother.'

'God marked Cain so that no one might harm him. It will

be the same with you. Now I must go, but be assured that I will return on Thursday. Meanwhile, spend your every waking breath – your every sleeping thought – in supplication for God's mercy.'

Ralf called the gaoler who led him out of Hamo's cell and up to Simon's, which, as accorded with his higher degree, if not his greater fault, was larger, lighter and more fragrant. As the gaoler locked the door and left them together, Ralf saw that Simon's hands were fettered as fast as Hamo's and trusted that it was not for the same offence.

'I am sorry that I cannot offer you a chair, Sir Ralf.'

'It is no matter.'

'Maybe not for one who passes his days on his knees. Some of us are customed to greater cheer.'

'I am glad to see that you have kept your spirits.'

'Have I? No doubt they are wise to deny me a chair. On Thursday, it would have to be burnt, for fear that it corrupt any felon or murderer who may be held in this place. Everything I have touched is to be burnt. The pallets on which Hamo and I slept are to be burnt. The records of my trial are to be burnt – did you know that? The very words on the scroll, lest they impair the register in which they are kept. I am not to be hanged on Thursday; I am to be annihilate.'

'I have been to visit Hamo.'

'How is he?' Simon's voice softened.

'He endures his punishment.'

'In truth? Is he reconciled?'

'He is fearful and bitter. Most bitter towards you.'

'He is unjust.'

'You led him into sin.'

'As you lead a child by the hand over a stile. We took our pleasure together. Hamo as much as me.'

'You must banish all thought of pleasure.'

'What else do I have? Everything has been stripped from me: my fame; my friends; my property. And soon my life.'

'Set your mind upon God. You must confess your sin: a sin so grievous that only death can remit it.'

'I can confess many sins; I can confess my great sin of not loving Agnes (you see, I am ready to admit that now). But I cannot confess to sinning against nature for that would be to sin against God.'

'You are too subtle!'

'The bliss – the blessedness – I felt when Hamo and I were as one – as one, Sir Ralf, not just together! – that can only have come from God. I lay with him as naked and pure as when I shall appear before the Throne of Judgement. You tell me not to think of pleasure because you see it as disobedience, but I see it as the Garden before disobedience, when neither the serpent nor his words were venomous.'

'For pity's sake, let me confess you now. Or you doom yourself to an eternity of torment.'

'Very well. I will admit my sins, if you will admit that it was you who disposed me to them.'

'Do not jest, Simon; you venture your immortal soul!'

'But I am in earnest. Remember when I confessed to offending with Edmund and you questioned me: was it in the hand? In the mouth? Between the thighs? In his privy flesh?'

'I was following the rule of the penitentials.'

'I had never thought that such things were possible.'

'You were sickened. I feared you would swoon.'

'I was a boy. I had years to dream of all the ways that a man could meddle with a man. Until I savoured them for myself. And it is you I must thank. Without you I might never have known.'

'You are rending my heart.'

'So shall I confess to you?'

'No, not while you remain obdurate. I will return on Thursday, in the hour before your soul meets its maker, when I trust that I shall find you humbled. Gaoler!'

He banged on the door as fiercely as a fugitive seeking

sanctuary. The gaoler led him out on to the bridge, where for once the stench from the privies seemed almost fresh. He returned to the chantry house and pondered Simon's charge as if he were back at the grammar school studying the works of the Church Fathers. Whether or not his questions had truly led Simon astray, he could not deny his account of the confession. Although his purpose in writing *Lot's Wife* had been to challenge the misconstruction of the bible story, he had never imagined that his own words might be similarly misconstrued. The one coin in which he thought himself rich had been counterfeit. So that afternoon, he sent Dickon Barbour to the archdeacon with a letter of submission. Dickon returned with his thanks and half a crow pie. Meanwhile, he himself met Sidney Berwick and informed him of the archdeacon's demands. Berwick, eager to defend the craft's renown, agreed to resume the office of pageant master and restore the discarded script. With five well-practised players, he was sure that the rest would learn the new – old – lines in readiness for the general in three weeks.

Early on Thursday morning Ralf arrived at the kidcote, where, for a further four marks, he was conducted to Hamo's cell. As he entered, Hamo hurled himself forward, so pitifully thin that it seemed as though his wrists might slip through their fetters.

'Do you have it?' he asked.

'As I promised. But, while it will relieve your pain, you must put your greater trust in God.'

'Show me!'

'Wait!' Ralf replied, aware of the gaoler gazing through the grate, suspicious that anyone, even a priest, should disburse so much on such a miscreant. Leaning against the door, he prayed with Hamo that he would have the strength to withstand his ordeal and vouched that, if he visited the chantry house after dark, he would give him his last four marks to furnish his exile. For a moment Hamo forgot where he was, as the thought of the money made him smile: the final time, Ralf realised with dismay, that he would do so with an unscathed face. Catching sight of the gaoler still staring, he covertly removed the phial from his purse, knelt and laid his hand on Hamo's head. Hamo opened his mouth as if to receive the Host and Ralf poured in half the potion. According to the infirmarer, it would take effect within the hour and Ralf trusted that, if Hamo swooned beforehand, the officers would presume that it was in dread.

'Make haste,' the gaoler called. 'The marshals are on their way.' Ralf stood and signed Hamo with the cross before, to his own surprise, bending and kissing the crown of his lousy head. The gaoler hurried him to Simon's cell, no doubt fearful that he would demand the return of half the fee if the officers arrived there first.

'Forgive my not standing, Sir Ralf,' Simon said, 'but I find myself somewhat encumbered.' He rattled his chains.

'We have little time, Simon. I come to ask if you are ready to confess.'

'What was it you told me at Easter: that sins not confessed to a priest will be revealed to the world on the Day of Doom? I prefer to take that chance. I will tell not of the pleasure but of the joy … the wholeness … the truth I felt in my passion, that for the first time in all my years I was my own man. The angels themselves will weep that they cannot know such passion.'

'This is damnable,' Ralf said. 'I beg you, repent!'

'There is nothing more to be said. I have no testament for you to take down, since all my property is forfeit to the Church. Christ profits by my sin.'

'Christ weeps for you.'

'We shall see.'

'If you will not save your soul, at least drink this potion. I have it from the monks at St Mary's. It will make you less sensible to the pain.'

'But surely you wish me to feel it, if not as my just penalty, then as a taste of what is to come?'

'Will you ever mock me, Simon?'

'It is my last hour on earth. May I not pass it as I choose? But if you truly wish to ease my pain, Sir Ralf, I am much afflicted with an itch that I cannot reach. If you would show me that charity …'

'Of course.' Ralf moved forward. 'Where?'

Simon gazed at his groin. 'There. Just where I am forked.'

'I shall pray for you,' Ralf said, turning to the door.

'But not, I trust, in the same breath as for the Underwoods.'

Ralf made the sign of the cross over him, but it felt of no more substance than a child tracing letters in the air. He left the kidcote and crossed the bridge to Micklegate Bar, where a large crowd had gathered. Soon afterwards, a roar of derision greeted the arrival of the prisoners, startling the horse that was drawing their hurdle. Bound hand and foot, Simon and Hamo lay together one last time, bruised by every rock and rut in the path and the rotten fruit and offal flung at them from all sides, along with a large stone that struck Hamo's doomed ear. The marshals whipped the horse along the two-mile road to Knavesmire, as though any delay might forestall the punishment. Ralf, feeling the weight of his years, lagged behind, finally arriving sore-footed and breathless at the marsh, where a large platform had been erected, furnished with a gallows and a post.

The lesser punishment took place first. Hamo was tied to the post, where, to Ralf's relief and the crowd's indignation, he underwent all three concisions with scarcely a scream. Ralf rejoiced in the monkish skill that made some amends for the episcopal cruelty. Hamo was dragged off the platform and across the marsh, while Simon, hitherto accustomed to the crowd's acclamation, was led to the gallows in ignominy. Displaying more dignity than his detractors, he mounted the platform, followed by the sheriff's chaplain intoning psalms.

He spoke a few words to the hangman before stepping on to a block and placing his neck in the noose as casually as if he were tying the strings of a coif. The hangman deftly removed the block, and the crowd's indignation turned to glee as Simon's eyes popped out of their sockets, his tongue lolled, his mouth slavered, and his arms and legs jerked as though in a fit. Ralf fell to his knees and, had it not been for his tonsure, he felt sure that he would have been assaulted by his neighbour, who contented himself with spitting into the dirt. The crowd bayed as the hangman pulled down Simon's hose to display the member that had caused his downfall disporting itself at his death.

Soul-seared, Ralf returned to the city, where he devoted himself to his chantry, assured that, whatever his son might say, Walter would not object to his adding a name to his daily prayers. He attended the two final practices of *Lot's Wife* although, with Sidney Berwick returned as pageant master, his own task was restricted to assisting the players when they forgot their words. He had planned to spend Corpus Christi Day indoors, but Marjorie Underwood, who had hired two seats at the Spurriergate station, begged him to accompany her, insisting that she would not go without him. Loath to disappoint her, he agreed, taking his place on an unusually chill June morning. As ever, he delighted in the conjunction of divine majesty and human frailty that marked the pageants from *The Creation of Man* to *The Flood*. No sooner had God sent forth his rainbow, restored to its full glory after last year's misadventure, than it was time for *Lot's Wife*. Ralf felt Marjorie stiffen as the salters' wagon rolled into view and took care not to catch her eye. He listened to Hugh Fleming speak Gabriel's opening lines, written thirty years earlier by a man whom he could no longer call his predecessor. He admired Thomas Langham's Raphael, worthy of all the epithets bestowed on him, even as he grieved for Hamo, who had exchanged a face that was mocked for one that was shunned. He joined in the laughter when Eustace as Lot's wife, fully justifying Simon's trust in him, defied her husband's demand to entertain the strangers, while regretting the loss of his own script in which her change of heart had come within one line rather than four. He marvelled at Master Braithwaite's skill as Sodom's towers tumbled with a resounding thunder-crack and Eustace was transformed in a flash of powder. But, when Rylan stepped forward to address the audience, he knew that everything for which he had striven was lost.

'My wife is turned to salt
My city into dust,
But I the Lord Above exalt
That punisheth foul lust.
Take tent, all ye who do aspire
In Abraham's bosom to dwell,
Men who burn with lewd desire
Shall roast in fires of hell.'

THREE

Bonfire of the Vanities

'Good government is punishing the evil one and getting sodomites and the wicked out of your city.'

Girolamo Savonarola, *Ruth* 1496

Renaissance Italy gave us our bodies back. Scholars may argue over the precise nature, sequence and, indeed, significance of what took place, but they all agree that the rediscovery of a classical culture that celebrated physical beauty produced a profound shift in human consciousness. And along with the change in the way that you perceived yourselves came a change in the way that you perceived us. For two hundred years under the sway of St Thomas Aquinas, you had viewed us as beings of pure spirit, without emotion, imagination or senses. Now that you no longer regarded the material world as, at best, a shadow and, at worst, a snare, you no longer confined us to incorporeity, preferring to picture us as the embodiment of God's beauty: the emblems of His grace.

Although the Church, seeking to retain its power over your minds, bodies and, above all, hopes of salvation, accused you of prizing the glories of this world over those of the next, the charge was false. Even the greatest humanists among you remained devoted to God. Moreover, you continued to honour us. Our influence may have waned in a world that set more store by natural law than celestial agency, but our presence was as strong as ever. Michael, Raphael, Uriel and myself, along with a host of our fellows, were to be seen everywhere around you, lamenting the dead Christ and lauding the living, heralding the Incarnation and attending the Dormition, chastening Balaam and vanquishing Satan, blowing trumpets, strumming harps and sometimes, it has to be said, merely supplying the background to the thousands of paintings that adorned the churches, palaces, courts and private homes.

Artists of all faiths have laboured down the ages to capture our image, but it is among Christians that we have been most prominent. Few early pictures of us survive and it is perhaps inevitable that those that do, deriving from a time of persecution, are to be found in burial sites. Indeed, the first likeness of any of us – I should say of me, since it depicts the Annunciation – is in the second-century Priscilla catacomb in Rome. Even if it were better preserved, however, you might be hard pressed to recognise me in my nondescript robe, without my now familiar insignia: the lily, sceptre, scroll and, of course, the wings.

Those wings first appeared two or three hundred years later when painters, inspired by the Mercuries and Cupids they saw in fragments of antique sculpture and mosaic, assigned them to the fleet, aerial creatures of their own tradition. But, for the Church Fathers, the burning question was not how we should be represented, but whether we should be represented at all. The issue was debated at the Second Council of Nicea in 787. The First Council had drawn up the Creed, which the church-goers among you recite to this day, with its ringing affirmation: 'I believe in one God, the Father Almighty, maker of heaven and earth and of all things visible and invisible.' I am one of those 'things invisible', although whether most of you who say the words believe in me as anything other than a literary device is a moot point. Nevertheless, just as the First Council gave us a doctrinal authority, so the Second Council gave us an aesthetic one, making us a legitimate subject for art.

Surprisingly, given its determination to impose rigid uniformity elsewhere, the Council left responsibility for representing us to the individual artists, although in effect there was considerable conformity. For the next five hundred years, our faces were illuminated, not from any natural source but from within, as though by our own sanctity. We were crowned with haloes and set against backgrounds of pure gold, which, ironically, gave the paintings as much of a material as a spiritual worth. It was not until the early glimmers of the Renaissance that we were portrayed in recognisable landscapes and in genuine interaction with people. For the first time in art, we bridged the divide between the human and the divine.

This new, richer – I forbear to say 'more realistic' – depiction revived the question of our gender. Paradoxically, given the emphasis on our immateriality, medieval theologians had agonised over whether we were male or female in accordance with the rest of creation, or unique asexual beings, the exemplars of Christ's teaching that there would be no marriages in heaven. The Bible was unusually explicit on the issue. Apart from a single contentious passage in Zechariah, we are always envisaged as male. Moreover in some stories, such as the destruction of Sodom, our masculinity is critical. Despite the ancient Israelites' reverence for the women warriors Deborah and Jael, their scribes would never have conceived of a female angel of the Lord who slew a hundred and eighty-five thousand Assyrians in a single night.

So we have been traditionally portrayed as masculine. Indeed, in another catacomb, dating only a century after Priscilla's, the angel blocking Balaam's path is bearded; admittedly, this is Michael, whom you have always regarded as the most martial of us. Over the years, our features grew softer, more androgynous but, even at the height of the Renaissance, artists pictured us as sensuous rather than sexual. The exception as so often was Leonardo who, in a drawing intended for private view, endowed me with an erection that would not have disgraced a Roman satyr. It was especially shocking since, of all the angels, I had been the most frequently feminised. In spite of a name that translates loosely into English as Warrior or Strength of God and my many retributive interventions in human affairs, I remain most closely identified with the Annunciation. As the cult of the Virgin Mary flourished, even minimal masculine traits were deemed inappropriate to the messenger of divine motherhood.

All of you who have seen the great artworks of the Renaissance will have your favourites. Given the hundreds of masterpieces in which I myself appear, it may seem invidious – ungrateful even – to express a preference. Nevertheless, I shall mention three. The first is a Fra Angelico Annunciation, *made for the convent of San Marco, which exquisitely conveys the awe that I felt on addressing the pregnant mother of God. The second is an earlier* Annunciation, *carved by Donatello for the church of Santa Croce, which, with equal subtlety, catches Mary's confusion when, for a moment, she recoiled from both me and her destiny. The third, in a different vein, is Titian's* Resurrection, *more familiar to you as the* Averoldi Altarpiece, *where I burst out of the frame, the panel too small to contain my exultation at greeting the risen Lord.*

But, if there is one Renaissance artist for whom I feel a singular affinity, it is Botticelli. In his studies both of me personally – and he was among the first painters to endow me with a personality – and of my fellows, he finds an ethereal beauty that is the perfect conjunction of his ideals and our nature. Indeed, it is when seeing myself on Botticelli's panels that I almost regret my lack of flesh.

TO THE MOST ILLUSTRIOUS MAESTRO GIORGIO VASARI

Most honoured Sir,
With humble reverence and due commendation I take up my pen to address you. I have of late passed many joyous hours in perusal of your incomparable *Lives of the Most Excellent Painters, Sculptors and Architects*, men whose glorious invention has dignified both our own city and the whole of Italy.

As an unfledged youth, I had occasion to converse with several such masters, for my father was Giusto Coverelli, of whom you may have heard speak. It was to his shop in the Via della' Acqua that many of the foremost painters, carvers and stone-cutters of Florence came to purchase the beaten gold that enriched their work. Among those I recollect most clearly were: Pietro Perugino, his narrow brow and arched eyebrows atop his fleshy cheeks and broad jaw, as though his face were formed of two parts like the hinged panels of an altarpiece; Domenico Ghirlandaio, ever disposed to consult my father on the mysteries of a craft of which his own father had been a notable practitioner; Filippo Lippi the younger, who kept about his person a packet of comfits that he would bountifully dispense to the serving boy, which is to say myself. But the patron who intrigued me the most was the one who marked me the least: Sandro Botticelli, always courteous but so distant, and possessed of the saddest smile I had ever seen, like a man entrusted with a grievous secret that he has sworn to the death not to reveal.

Once and again I conveyed the precious metal to the patrons myself. As I hied through the narrow streets, filled

– or so it seemed to my boyish fancy – with pickpurses, cut-throats and tricksters, I was keenly aware of the dangers. Nevertheless, I was ready to brave them for the chance to visit the shops and glimpse the prentices, some no older than myself, at work or play – that is at work and play, for to my untutored mind there was no distinction; to taste the sweet sourness of the air; to cover the unfinished panels with imagined brushstrokes. Whenever my father could spare me, I took up my blacklead and paper and, having proved my facility in making likenesses of our friends and neighbours, I besought him to let me study painting. My worthy father was hesitant, for although the magnificent Lorenzo, who showed such munificence to men of accomplishment, was then alive, Fra Girolamo of the Preaching Friars was already crying out against the fashioning of vain images and establishing a hold on the city, at the memory of which all men of honour and discretion must rebel. My father, however, seeing my resolve and knowing that my two older brothers would assist him in his labours, acceded to my request. You may picture my elation, followed by surprise, apprehension and every other emotion natural to one of such tender years, when he placed me with Botticelli, who had served not only the Medici and many of the most exalted families in Florence, but the pope himself in Rome. But his fame was not measured in riches and he owed my father payment for half a *libbra* of gold, in respect of which he had waived the prenticeship fee.

Most honoured Sir, I pray you will pardon the seemingly impertinent history of one, now in the crepuscule of life, unknown to you or indeed to any outside of his family and his *gonfalone*, for, despite such august training, no work of note has ever flowed from my brush. Nonetheless, I have deemed it needful to set forth how I entered Botticelli's shop in the year of our Lord 1492 and remained there for six years, during which time I observed his practice at first hand and assisted at the creation of what I am convinced would have been his most resplendent master-work had it survived. I shall attempt to redress that loss by describing it in every particular, although I am mindful that no pen save your own could do it justice.

It is with much trepidation that I alert you to an error in your account: one, however, which is not of your making but rather of those who furnished you with information of events that took place over half a century ago. You write that Botticelli became a fervid partisan of Fra Girolamo's sect, which led to his abandoning his brush and spending the remainder of his days in poverty. The error is, indeed, so grave that I would suspect it of having been perpetrated by his enemies were I not assured that he had none, for who could bear malice toward one of such a gentle disposition? It is true that he took a keen interest in Fra Girolamo's teachings, as did all those who dwelt in Florence at that time. But while there were some in his own family who numbered among the Friar's most ardent adherents, he himself remained aloof. It was unclear, even to those of us who lived alongside him, quite where his sympathies lay.

Despite the weight of advancing years – he was nigh on fifty when I joined him – and the turmoil in the city, which led to a slackening of his endeavours, he never ceased painting. He did, however, abandon four of his most remarkable panels and, it was whispered, consign them to the great pyre erected in the piazza della Signoria, although for that I lack the evidence of my own eyes. The panels, which presented the story of Lot and Sodom, had been ordered by the Office of the Night to adorn its new courtroom in the Palazzo del Podesta. The Office, which has long since been dissolved, had been established by the *Signoria* to punish that most pernicious vice to which Sodom has lent its name and which, in the last century, ran rife in our own city. There is not a shred of truth in the rumours bruited abroad by emulous rivals that he agreed to make the panels in return for having a charge that had been brought against him dismissed. There were those in the shop to whom such venery was not unknown and whom I blush to call my fellows, but our master was not among them.

At three and a half *braccia* in length and two in width, the panels would be the largest that Botticelli had made, not just during my prenticeship but in many a year. They were to be painted in distemper, to which our master remained ever faithful, even though his younger competitors were trumpeting the supremacy of oil. Work began directly, although Botticelli, who never displayed as much trust in his judgement as he did in his invention, was apt to be deflected by those among his friends who berated him for the choice of subject. Panels of the finest poplar were purchased, which I, as the least of the prentices, set about preparing. My joy was complete when my master complimented me on the smoothness of the gesso, adding that he had learnt in his youth that to take such pains was the mark of a true painter. I suspect now that he was consoling me for the meagreness of my contribution.

Contrary to his custom, he made a cartoon of the entire first panel, not just of the principal heads and draperies. It was inspected by three of the Officers who, after thumbing through the pile of drawings and enquiring after the distribution of the blue and the gold, declared themselves satisfied. For all his professed indifference, Botticelli was relieved and straightway directed my two fellow prentices, Gianpiero and Annibale, to pounce the cartoon on the panel. He himself commenced the underdrawing of the three remaining panels, while Bartolomeo di Giovanni, his most practised assistant, copied the head of Lot from the studies of Moses made years before for the pontiff's chapel.

Rest assured that I do not seek to vie with you by narrating the making of the panels, a task as far beyond my pen as to paint them would have been beyond my brush. I shall, nonetheless, attempt to describe them and render some account, however wanting, of their incalculable loss. You may wonder how it is that my memory of them remains strong when so much else has been devoured by time. I ask you to bear in mind that I was a mere stripling who watched in awe as day by day more peerless contrivances issued from my master's hand, just as the angels in the firmament watched the hand of God as He brought forth marvels from the void.

Two panels were achieved in their entirety. The first portrayed the meeting between Lot and the angels at the city gate, a most precise representation of the Porta a San Piero Gattolino, through which we had passed every day the previous July when Botticelli painted the portrait of St Francis in the new dormitory at Santa Maria di Monticelli. Lot was in the foreground in a cloak of bright green (mixed by my own hand from yellow lake, gypsum and azurite). His countenance, down to his long grey locks and sweeping beard, was bathed in joy at God's grace in sending the angels, who stood to his right, such delicacy in their line and hue that they appeared truly celestial. Gabriel, holding a sceptre, wore a pink doublet and green hose, with a golden cord around his waist. Raphael, holding a staff, wore an orange doublet with richly patterned sleeves, violet hose and a gauze mantle folded about his arms. Although he was wont to use only the yolk of egg in his paint, Botticelli taught us to add a touch of the white to effect such translucence.

On the left of the panel were seen the men of Sodom or of Florence (for it was impossible to distinguish the two) in sundry attitudes. Some gazed at each other in deep affection; others strolled arm in arm, as is still the custom with our young men today. Clasping hands were two greybeards who might have passed for brothers in another town, just as the thickset man pouring a cup for a comely youth might have been his father. A hook-nosed man held out an apple to his companion in token of the primal sin. Frisking at their feet was a pair of rabbits, further symbols of wantonness. In the window of a house adjoining the gate, a woman with braided hair looked up from her needlework to smile on the scene.

Although some in the shop maintained that the men's mild demeanour betrayed Botticelli's secret sympathy with their vice, he was merely keeping faith with the bible story, for their outward rectitude had long deluded Lot.

The second panel depicted Lot's house, which was expressly located in the Mercato Vecchio. When Bartolomeo, who alone dared to question our master's devices, asked him why he was so intent on portraying the biblical city as our own, he replied that he was both following Fra Girolamo, who coupled them week after week in the Duomo, and assisting the Officers of the Night, who were seeking to strengthen their position with the Friar. Whatever the cause, the effect was remarkable. The panel was divided by a row of marble pilasters, expertly wrought in chiaroscuro. To the left was the forum with the great column of Plenty, and through a window at the back could be glimpsed the portal of San Tommaso. To the right was a hall worthy of one of our most eminent merchants, with a high ceramic fireplace, oak dining table mounted on four crouching lions, inlaid ebony coffer and velvet-cushioned curule chairs. The walls were dotted with pictures, including a Madonna and Child and a St Anthony, which played havoc with my sense of history, and, most strikingly, one of the many copies of Botticelli's own Venus. While at the time I considered this to be an unworthy and even an immodest jest, I apprehend now that it was an artful riposte to Fra Girolamo, who had denounced such works as pagan. For what harm could there be in them if one hung in the house of the virtuous Lot?

At the table, Lot's wife was entertaining the angels to a feast, which, judging from the array of dishes, was more sumptuous than the city's laws allowed. She wore a pink pearl-encrusted cap and a robe of the richest red, obtained by laying the vermillion over a sheet of gold, for our master was not one of those who displayed all his gold on the surface. Lot's wife ate her fill but, despite the napkins on their laps, the angels sat with empty plates, the staff and sceptre gripped in their hands. Standing chastely to the side were Lot's two daughters, maidens of exceeding loveliness, with azure eyes, cherry-red lips and a roseate flush to their cheeks. Their tawny tresses fell freely to their breasts as befitted virgins. So strong was their resemblance that they might have been twins, Botticelli having used the same model from an ancient drawing book for both. I suspected she must be a lost love from his youth, a thought I kept from my fellows lest they mocked my ingenuousness, a practice to which they were much disposed.

The angels and their hostess were rapt in conversation, seemingly deaf to the disturbance at the door, where Lot was remonstrating with the Sodomites. Although exposed to the evening air, he had removed his cloak to reveal the full glory of his Venetian blue robe. His eyes blazed and his lips quivered with fury at having been summoned from his meal. In his right hand he clutched the wing of a chicken, rendered with such fidelity that one could almost savour its succulence. Fronting him and stretching far into the forum was a crowd of twenty or thirty men of diverse aspects: some full-face; some three-quarters; some in profile. In spite of their costly apparel, the hues he had chosen were simple: contrasting pairs of orange and blue, pink and green, violet and grey. His object as ever was not to dazzle the eye but to create an impression of harmony.

The third panel depicted the destruction of Sodom or, as it was here, the piazza della Signoria. All was chaos and carnage. The walls of the Podesta and the columns of the Loggia had collapsed like the tiers of a giant bonfire. The great tower of the *Vacca* was brought down like the dragon felled by St George. Donatello's statue of Judith and Holofernes, newly installed in the square, was so shattered that it was impossible to discern who had vanquished whom. A soldier emerged from the ruined Signoria bearing Donatello's statue of David as lovingly as if he were Jonathan delivering the youth himself from the wrath of Saul. Nearby, a lion, escaped from its cage, mauled its hapless keeper (red lake laid upon lamp black to represent its sanguinary claws). Across the square, the Sodomites lay dead and dying, some seeking solace in a last embrace, others tasting the desolation that would be theirs throughout eternity. In the foreground, a large crack had opened in the brown-washed pavement. A soot-smeared man was frantically trying to heave out his buried friend, the jutting vein on his brow an effect that I have never seen surpassed. So piteous were their visages that, in spite of their vice, it was hard not to weep for their fate.

At the centre of the square stood Gabriel, apparelled as before, although, to emphasise his divine agency, with the addition of a pair of wings, which, rather than unfurling, he thrust over his eyes as if to shroud the sight of such suffering. His fellow angel was behind him in the top right-hand corner, leading Lot and his wife and daughters away, past the flattened Tettoia dei Pisani. Even in such a doleful scene Botticelli saw fit to inject a note of humour. All four were shown from behind, Lot on foot and the three women on donkeys, with the donkey bearing Lot's wife buckling beneath the cumbrous burden, its legs bowed, tail swaying and rump buried in her voluminous robes – although I may have misconstrued the effect since the shading was unfinished.

My greatest regret is the loss of the fourth panel for, while it was the least complete, with much of the landscape and the ravaged city merely sketched in charcoal, it was the one to which I had contributed the most. On the far right was a cave in a cliff, and to my hand had been entrusted the grey underpainting, upon which one of my more seasoned fellows was to trace the rocks. But that is to put the cart before the oxen. The panel itself depicted two successive episodes of the story. On the left and centre, the family journeyed into the desert, with Lot's wife, like Eve before her, flouting the divine command; on the right, Lot and his daughters took shelter by the cave.

The figure of Lot's wife dominated the picture, even more so than if it had been finished, for the gold of her robe was yet to be overlaid with red. Dismounted from her donkey, she gazed back towards Sodom, gesturing to it with her right arm, which, from fingertips to shoulder, was painted lead white. So rare was Botticelli's skill that he did not, as a lesser master might, portray her metamorphosis from the head down or feet up but rather, contrived that the side closest to the sinful city was the one first transmuted to salt. Meanwhile Lot and his daughters, either oblivious or indifferent to her plight, continued on their way. The riderless donkey trotted beside them, grateful to be relieved of its load.

Their course took them to the cave on the right of the panel. Lot, rendered with faultless foreshortening, lay naked save for a loin-rag next to one of his daughters. At first, it appeared that, travel-soiled and weary, the daughters too had loosened their robes to rest, but closer examination revealed them to be in more explicit undress. The one beside her father had her bodice open and her breasts exposed; the other sat dishevelled, her torn veil on her knees, and her hand shielding her female parts. On the ground were plates of half-eaten figs, peaches and melons, which they could not have packed in their mean saddlebags or picked in the arid desert. Like the rabbits frolicking in the city streets, the fruit was there to betoken a deeper truth: the more intimate appetite that had been sated.

Callow youth that I was, I had known nothing of Sodom beyond its name before we commenced the panels. I was shocked therefore to discover that Lot had fled from the iniquitous city only to commit a further transgression by lying with his daughters. My fellow prentices had scorned my scruples, but our master, with wonted kindness, explained the purport of the story. It was not Lot but his daughters who had initiated the act, plying their father with drink both to quell his qualms and conceal their shame. They believed that the Lord God had annihilated not only Sodom but the whole world and, just as their father had been willing to sacrifice them to protect his angelic guests, so they were willing to sacrifice themselves to preserve mankind. Nevertheless, as I watched the scene take shape, my misgivings increased. Why were there no angels present, not even Raphael who had led Lot out of Sodom? Had they performed all that God required of them and been recalled to heaven? Or were they so horrified by the fate, first of Lot's wife and then of his daughters, that they could not bear to watch? I put my questions to Bartolomeo, who replied, even more tersely than was his wont, that our master would no doubt add an angel or two later. He must have known better than anyone that that was not his practice but, before I could investigate further, Botticelli had destroyed the entire work.

At some point on the twenty-sixth or twenty-seventh of February 1498, when the rest of us were celebrating Carnival, he removed the panels from the shop. On our return, he gave no explanation save that they had been displeasing to his patrons but, even after ascertaining that three of the Officers had visited him, I could not believe that they had found fault with the least particular. We later learnt from his brother's maid that the previous day he had received another visitor, but she could report nothing about him except that he had been accompanied by a very ill-mannered servant. Gianpiero and Annibale conjectured that he was an emissary from the pope who, wonderstruck by the panels and aware that they were bespoken, had offered our master a large reward if he might convey them forthwith to Rome. That accounted for neither the presence of the insolent servant nor the absence of so much as a *soldo* in the shop. So I clove to the view that, in a fit of the melancholia to which he was prone, he had judged the contrivances of his hands unworthy of the conceptions of his brain and had disposed of them.

While the loss of the panels affected me deeply, the arrest

and trial of the Friar and the end of that infamous chapter in our city's chronicle provided a distraction. The shop was not exempt from the tumult that engulfed Florence and, following the calumnies of one of my fellow prentices, Botticelli was himself arraigned before the Office of the Night. Notwithstanding his acquittal, my father saw fit to remove me from his tutelage and place me under that of Rafaellino Capponi, or del Garbo as he is named in another of your excellent *Lives*. I remained there but a short while before returning to my father's shop and thence to that of Antonio di Matteo, the frame maker. I perceived at once that I had found my calling, and I trust I may say without immodesty that it was one in which I did not lack renown. I set up my own shop in the piazza Santa Trinita and practised my craft for thirty years before surrendering it to my sons. My vision is failing but, God be praised, it was strong enough to read your estimable *Lives*. I thank you most profoundly for affording me such a rich recollection of my youth. I hope that you will find some merit in this protracted account of a matter of which I fear that I am the last remaining witness, although, given its unhappy outcome, that may be for the best. Whether you include it in any future edition of your work, I leave to your own discretion.

And so, praying for your continued health and deserved success in all your endeavours, I commend myself to you,

Your assured servant,
Lioncino di Giusto Coverelli

1

Politics were of no concern to painters. They dealt in eternal matters, from the *Annunciations*, *Transfigurations*, *Crucifixions* and *Entombments* that graced churches and monasteries to the allegories of *Love* and *Spring* that adorned palaces and courts. It was of little consequence to them whether the Medici or Strossi or Pazzi wielded power, so long as the demand for their services persisted. But with the advent of the Friar, everything had changed. Not only did the rich no longer sit for portraits, which he decried as vain, or plaster their walls with gods and nymphs, which he decried as sinful, but they no longer ordered altarpieces, after he repudiated the notion that it was as good to give money for devotional works as to give alms to the poor. He excoriated the usurers who sought to save their souls by furnishing chapels, thereby creating monuments to themselves as much as to God, but he reserved his strongest strictures for the painters who served them, portraying the Virgin in a harlot's trumpery and the Magdalene and St Sebastian as lewdly naked as Venus and Ganymede.

Alessandro di Mariano di Vanni, better known as Botticelli, a name he hated, feared for his future. At fifty-two, he was growing old and, while his strength was undimmed, his star was waning. Moreover, although Lorenzo himself had employed him rarely – a *Festival of Pan* for his villa at Careggi, a memorial portrait of his brother Giuliano and the mural of the Pazzi conspirators – he was closely associated with the old regime. The honour of being a Medici painter had faded in a world where the Great Council had proclaimed the eighth of November, the day on which Lorenzo's son Piero fled the city, a public holiday. Even Lorenzo di Pierfrancesco, his most generous patron, had distanced himself from his discredited cousins, changing his name from Medici to Popolano, a move that Sandro judged to be devious as well as disloyal.

Who would have thought that the Medici name would ever be a liability in Florence? As he prepared to join his brother and his family to walk to the Duomo, Sandro reflected on the circumstances that had led to Savonarola's ascendancy. The irony was that it was Lorenzo himself who had pressed for his return to the city. Encouraged by his friends, Poliziano and Pico della Mirandola, the one attracted by the Friar's rhetoric, the other by his reasoning, Lorenzo had entreated the Vicar General of the Dominicans to reinstate him at San Marco. His motives remained obscure. Some said that he hoped Savonarola would be a moderating influence on his fourteen-year-old son Giovanni, the recent recipient of a cardinal's hat; others that he thought his clarion call for a reformed church would help to curb papal ambitions. Either way, it was not to be. No sooner had Savonarola been elected prior than he preached a series of sermons containing thinly veiled attacks on Lorenzo's despotism, which Il Magnifico was obliged to suffer in order to disprove the charge.

There was a poignancy, at least to one of Sandro's stamp, in the sight of a man accustomed to a crowd of petitioners gathered at his gate, humbly attending Mass at San Marco in the hope that Savonarola would favour him with a word. It was not until he was on his deathbed that the Friar deigned to visit him, although what passed between them remained uncertain. According to Poliziano who was present, Savonarola enjoined Lorenzo to trust in God and gave him his blessing. But Poliziano was a poet and a scholar, two callings that filled Sandro with awe and, although he would never have dreamt of challenging him, which, in any case, was not possible since he had survived Il Magnifico by a mere two years, he acknowledged that, to such a man, poetic truth counted for more than plain fact.

Lorenzo's death in April 1492 marked a profound shift in the city's government. His son, Piero, assumed his father's mantle, only to be forced into exile after his abject submission to King Charles of France, who invaded the country in pursuit of his claim to the throne of Naples. In desperation, the *Signoria* chose Savonarola to lead a new embassy to Charles and, to everyone's astonishment but his own, this small, sallow-skinned man, with the hooked nose, beetle brows and sheep-shaped skull, won over the most glorious king in Christendom. Having stayed the threat of a French invasion, he consolidated his hold on the city, exercising power through the Great Council as ruthlessly as Lorenzo had done through the *Signoria*. Or so it appeared to Sandro. His brother Simone saw it differently. In his black-and-white view of the world – as alien to Sandro's temperament as to his craft – the Friar was a saviour, sent to deliver the people from both their shackles and their sins. Yet, for all his tirades against Lorenzo's tyranny, Simone had been absent for the greater part of his rule, having left Florence in 1470, less than a year after he had taken control, and returned in December 1493, just a few months before his death.

Although the closest of his three brothers to Sandro in age, Simone was the furthest from his heart. At twenty years his senior, his eldest brother Giovanni had been more like a father to him, and certainly more of one than his actual father, Mariano. His only fault was the tubbiness that had inspired the Botticelli sobriquet, which had been bestowed on his slenderer brothers. To his second brother Antonio, Sandro was, if anything, even more indebted, having been placed in his goldsmith's shop at fourteen. It was there that he learnt the basic techniques of engraving, chasing and enamelling, and first met the painters who brought their designs to be copied. Talking to them had convinced him that theirs was the craft he wished to practise and, with Giovanni's and Antonio's help, he had set about convincing Mariano.

Simone, his elder by barely a year, had been his boyhood rival, religiously cataloguing all his misdemeanours, leaving Sandro in no doubt that, had Giovanni not intervened, he would have denounced him to the Office of the Night. Sickened by Florence's depravity, he had gone to work for a cloth-merchant in Rome, where Sandro visited him ten years later when he was painting the pope's chapel. By then, Simone had come to loathe his adopted city, quitting it soon afterwards to take a position with a wine merchant in Naples. There he married Ippolita, the daughter of a pawnbroker, who was plump and plain with eyebrows that met in the middle. Although blessed with a fair complexion (more lime white than cinnabar), she accentuated her plainness, as though to remove any suspicion of carnality from the match. She shared Simone's mistrust of Florence, which she knew only by repute, until, fired by a book of Savonarola's sermons, he resolved to return to his native city and take part in the Friar's mission of reform. With his wife and three children, twelve-year-old Santi, eleven-year-old Crucifissa and ten-year-old Ildebrando, he moved into the family home, directly above Sandro's workshop, to the dismay of Ippolita, who maintained that the rowdy apprentices and profligate patrons were a danger to her daughter and a provocation to her sons.

However much he made light of it, Sandro perceived a change in his family's manner towards him after Piero's exile. Having been gilded by Medicean glory, he was now tarnished by their fall. In the wider world, his various *Madonna and Childs*, *Annunciations*, *Adorations* and *Nativities* notwithstanding, he was best known for pictures of pagan myth: the *Mars and Venus* for the marriage of Lucrezia de' Medici to Jacopo Salviati; the *Realm of Venus* and *Pallas and the Centaur*, which had drawn so many visitors to Lorenzo di Pierfrancesco's palace that his wife, Semiramide, quipped that she could no longer call her bedchamber her own. Even the *Venus on the Seashore*, locked away in their villa at Castello, was familiar from his workshop's numerous copies of the goddess. It would be a brave patron indeed who ordered a painting from one so out of favour at San Marco.

With the cloths up at the windows and shutters closed, the shop was stifling. His three apprentices had already left for the day: Lioncino returning to his parents; Annibale and Gianpiero meeting friends. Sandro made his way into the street, where the only effect of his fanning the air was to fluster the flies. Moments later he was joined by Simone, who squeezed his arm with his customary mixture of wariness and warmth, followed by his wife and children. Ippolita, modestly clad in a wine-coloured gown with charcoal sleeves, her bodice tightly laced and hair hidden beneath a white linen kerchief, was perspiring profusely. Crucifissa, in dress and manner a miniature version of her mother, trotted dutifully by her side, while the boys forged ahead, their enthusiasm for the two- or three-hour sermon putting their listless uncle to shame. 'Ready?' Simone asked him and, not for the first time, Sandro questioned his determination that the whole family should attend. Was it to prove to his fellow *Piagnoni* that he had redeemed his wayward brother? Or did he simply want him to share his devotion to the Friar?

Shortly after returning, Simone had taken him to two of the lectures that Savonarola gave after Sunday vespers to selected followers in the convent garden. For all his excitement at the irreverent – even irreligious – ideas he had encountered at Lorenzo's table (an excitement derived as much from his admittance to the charmed circle as from sympathy with its views), he held churchmen in high regard and was keen to hear what the Friar had to say. His asperity disappointed him. With so much beauty, joy and mystery in the world, it felt perverse to dwell on the negative. While he would not lay claim to a fraction of Savonarola's piety and perception, he refused to believe that women wearing open-work stockings or dancing on feast days were to blame for the succession of bad harvests, or that other more intimate vices were the cause of the city's decline. On their second visit, Simone had led him up to receive a blessing. The Friar had stared at him through great green eyes that seemed to penetrate his very soul (what he might have painted had he had those eyes!). There was such stillness about him that, although he spoke rapidly, his words did not sound rushed.

'What work do you do?' he asked, after Simone's introduction.

'A painter … I'm a painter … I paint.'

'What do you paint?'

'Sandro made the *Coronation of the Virgin* for the altar of St Eligius in your own church,' Simone interposed.

'The subject is finely and devoutly drawn,' Savonarola replied, studying him with more interest. 'But there's too much gold. Far too much gold.' Sandro wanted to explain that he had made the picture for the guild of goldsmiths, who had instructed him to use the maximum amount of gold leaf to honour their craft, but he feared that it would not satisfy him. 'We have many holy pictures at San Marco, some of the finest by a friar of our order, Fra Giovanni Angelico.'

'I've always admired his altarpiece in the church and, entering the cloister last month, I was struck by his fresco of St Dominic at the foot of the Cross. The remarkable way he's foreshortened Christ's body so that we seem to be gazing at it from below, and then elongated his torso to convey the full agony of the Crucifixion. And his use of azurite for the sky, just as effective as ultramarine and far less costly, to bring out the iridescence of Christ's skin.'

'It's an aid to devotion: an exhortation to the brothers to kneel in imitation of our founder and to contemplate the sacrifice of our Lord, not a subject for idle conjecture! You must pray that God will purge your heart of the pride to which painters are prone.'

'I shall, I swear it,' Sandro replied, kneeling for the Friar's blessing, which he felt as palpably as the rays of light in an *Annunciation*. But walking home in silence with Simone, he was racked by doubts as to how much of what he felt had been real and how much willed.

They joined the crowd heading towards the Duomo. Despite the August heat, there was a Lenten chill in the air. Few of them exchanged more than a nod or a word, as if obeying the Friar's instruction to turn the city itself into a shrine. On reaching the Mercato Vecchio, they found none of the jugglers, stilt-walkers and storytellers who were wont to fill the streets with colour. A solitary balladeer attracted a small audience as he sang of a knight's ill-fated love for a peasant girl. Sandro lingered for a moment before responding to the summons Simone issued to Ildebrando but aimed at him. As they walked down the via dei Calzaiuoli, Simone himself stopped at a tabernacle with a large painting of the Madonna flanked by Gabriel and Raphael. Sandro had often wondered about the unknown master who had painted faces that, though weatherworn, were worthy of Masaccio, but today he moved swiftly on to escape the stench where the wall had served for less sanctified purposes.

'Men are animals!' Ippolita said, curling her lip in disgust.

Sandro blinked as he emerged from the warren of dingy streets into the brightness of the piazza del Duomo. Shading his eyes, he gazed up at Brunelleschi's great dome, now so much a part of the landscape that it was easy to take for granted, but his father, a witness to its construction, had told him of the widespread conviction at the time that it would collapse. Yet even when, in a dire portent, lightning struck the building three days before Lorenzo's death, splitting the lantern in two and sending slabs of marble crashing to the ground, the dome was unscathed. It was the façade that looked unsafe since only the lower half had been clad in marble, the upper half remaining a shell. As he climbed the steps, Sandro found the effect both disconcerting and comical, as though a child had carefully picked the icing from the top of a cake, leaving the bottom intact so as to mitigate the crime.

No matter how frequent his visits, the starkness of the Duomo took him by surprise. Unlike the city's lesser churches, it had no need of him or even Giotto or Fra Filippo to imbue it with reverence. He followed Simone and his nephews to the right of the rail that Savonarola had erected along the nave, while Ippolita led Crucifissa off to the left. He squeezed against a pillar beside a malodorous old man but, with the space behind him swiftly occupied, there was no escape.

Sandro turned towards the high altar, which he could never see without recalling the moment eighteen years earlier when, midway through Mass, Lorenzo leapt across the sanctuary steps, blood streaming from his neck, his cloak wrapped around his arm like a shield and his sword drawn on two priests who had tried to murder him. He escaped with a flesh wound, beating back his would-be assassins to reach the sacristy, where Poliziano and others secured the door. Giuliano, also a target, was less fortunate. As he bowed his head in prayer, the butcher, Baroncelli, drove a dagger into his chest, while Francesco de' Pazzi repeatedly stabbed his gaping corpse. No death – not even those of his mother and Giovanni – would ever affect Sandro so deeply. Hailed throughout Florence as the flower of chivalry, Giuliano had chosen him to design his standard for the tournament in the piazza Santa Croce only three years before. He had worn the colours of Mario Vespucci's wife, Simonetta, whom Sandro portrayed on the standard as the chaste Pallas: the first of several Pallases and, indeed, Simonettas that he was to paint. Like Giuliano, Simonetta died lamentably young, but Sandro had honoured them both throughout his life and sought to emulate Giuliano's ideal of love, even if, in paying court to an unattainable lady, Giuliano had merely to transcend his desires, whereas he had to feign them.

Lorenzo rapidly recovered to wreak vengeance on the conspirators, while his followers executed summary justice on anyone even nominally connected to the Pazzi. Sandro, who had joined the general drift from the Duomo to the piazza della Signoria, watched aghast as young Medici supporters marched up and down with heads skewered on spears, like pilgrims bearing lanterns on the Feast of the Virgin's Nativity. Several leading conspirators were hanged from the windows of the Palazzo. In a particularly gruesome twist, the Archbishop of Pisa, who had sanctioned the plot, dug his teeth into Francesco de' Pazzi's thigh as they dangled from adjacent ropes. Whether this were an inadvertent entanglement or a deliberate assault on the man he blamed for his fate was unclear.

Painful as it was to admit it, even to himself, the Pazzi conspiracy had profited Sandro. He had been paid forty florins a piece by the *Signoria* to paint life-size effigies of the seven leading conspirators on the Porta della Dogana, six of them with nooses round their necks to indicate their punishment and the seventh, Napoleone Francesi, suspended by an ankle to indicate his escape. While mindful of the honour, he had had little relish for the task and was not sorry that none of the figures had survived. The first to be scraped off was the archbishop, victim of Lorenzo's peace negotiations with the pope. Then, after Piero's flight and the redefinition of *traitor*, the other six were effaced. Nothing had cemented his association with the Medici more than the renegades' effigies, so the return to Florence of the Pazzi, together with the Peruzzi, Barbadori, Strossi and others hostile to the family, was another reason to be grateful for their erasure. He wondered whether, granted free rein, one of them might take revenge on him or whether they would regard him as of no more consequence than the smith who shod Lorenzo's horses. Maybe he should imitate Lorenzo di Pierfrancesco and change his name? It would be one way of ridding himself of the injurious *Botticelli*. Simone glared at him as he laughed out loud.

Five minutes later and the glare would have been fiercer. He might even have been attacked by a rabid *Piagnone*, for the service had reached its climax with the arrival of the Friar. The anticipation in the nave reminded him of the moments before a hanging, not the frenzied dispatch of the Pazzi conspirators, but a solemn execution. As Savonarola mounted the pulpit, the entire congregation fell to its knees, crushing each other still further. Sandro, trusting that he had followed suit out of piety and not slavishness, found himself pressed against the ankles of his pungent neighbour, who gave him a toothless grin. A crucifix grazed his ear as the man behind him thrust it towards the Friar, who stood, eyes raised to heaven, nodding purposefully, while the air around him was rent by a babble of moans and shrieks and prayers. Silencing them with a sweep of his hands, he bade people stand and addressed them in a voice which, whether from practice or overuse, was gentler – the Ferrarese sibilants less pronounced – than when Sandro had first heard him in Lorenzo's day.

Although he had attended few of the Friar's sermons, Sandro recognised his familiar concerns. Foremost among them was the need for the city to repent if it were to escape the wrath of the Avenging Angel, who even now hovered overhead, brandishing a sword of fire. While half the congregation glanced upwards and one of Sandro's neighbours mopped his dripping brow, Savonarola listed their offences: 'Dicing, dancing, swearing and lechery abound in every tavern. Harlots – lumps of meat with eyes – parade their wares. So-called honest women come to church in low-cut gowns, their heads uncovered. Youths with curls reaching to their shoulders blur the divinely ordained divide between male and female. Fathers profane their daughters' weddings by giving them marriage chests painted with pagan gods. Rich felons purchase their freedom, while poor innocents languish in jail. Men gamble away their fortunes, leaving their wives and children to starve. Puffed-up scholars laud the new learning from Greece and

Rome, which is nothing but ancient superstition. They value Plato's dialogues above St Paul's letters; they extol the obscene Ovid over the virtuous Thomas; they quote Seneca, Martial, Catullus and Lucan rather than St Jerome, St Augustine and St Gregory. And worst of all – worse even than the worst of these – are the sodomites: dissolute men who make filthy assignations in shops and storerooms, who procure sons from unprincipled fathers, as if indenturing them to their crafts. I adjure you, wherever you see a sodomite, be it in the street, in the market or even in church, to spit on him. Spit once, twice, three times, so as to douse the flames of his lust.'

Savonarola had been speaking for more than an hour and, unlike his hearers, showed no sign of fatigue when he introduced a theme that, to judge by their murmuring, was as new to the rest of the congregation as it was to Sandro. 'Some of you may wish to go on pilgrimage to the holy cities of Rome or Jerusalem. Last night, I made an even more momentous journey. It was my joy – a joy beyond reckoning – to be transported to heaven to meet the Virgin Mary. My guide was the Archangel Gabriel and my four companions were Faith, Purity, Penitence and Prayer.'

'Aren't you forgetting Ignorance, Hypocrisy and Credulity?' a dissenting voice called from the back of the nave. Sandro turned to look, but Savonarola made no acknowledgement of either the question or the subsequent scuffle in which the man and his two confederates were ejected.

'Leaving my body on earth, I entered the empyrean in my spirit and saw countless wonders that I am not permitted to describe. But what I can tell you – what I must tell you – is that I was conducted before the Virgin, who was seated on a throne made of metal more precious than gold and decked with stones more dazzling than jewels. She spoke to me in a voice closer to light than to sound, and promised that Florence would be restored to her former glory, a hundred times richer and more powerful than ever.' The Duomo erupted in shouts of praise to the Virgin, God and the Friar himself, which seemed to enfold him like clouds of incense. '"The territories she has lost will be recovered. The Turk and the infidel will be converted and dedicate their lives to Christ."' The *Piagnoni*, Savonarola's most fervent followers, lived up to their name by weeping loudly. '"But first you must purge the city of vice" … I speak the Virgin's words, not my own. "Even the godly among you will not be spared unless you root out the gluttons, the gamblers, the blasphemers, the whores and, above all, the sodomites." It was then that I heard a gentle rustling and saw that she had stopped the ears of the babe she was cradling. Such was the radiant mystery of the place that, while we spoke, He had manifested Himself in His mother's arms. It was clear that she wished to shield Him as she cited the city's most loathsome sin, the sin that makes it reviled throughout Christendom. "If you, Florence, wish to regain God's favour," she said, "you must build a pyre in the piazza and pitch every sodomite into the flames, making their flesh a burnt offering to the Lord."'

As he listened to Savonarola's invective, Sandro felt like an exile suffering an insult to a homeland he had not seen for years. He refused to believe that Mary, the loving mother to whom the whole city had prayed when it was visited by plague during his childhood, was the same Mary who told the Friar 'to build a pyre so high that it will blaze across Italy'. But his doubts were not shared by his neighbours, who looked avid to chop the wood.

'How I longed to dwell forever in her blessed company, but I knew that I must return to do her bidding. And the angel carried me back on his silken wings. Open your ears, Florence, that you may heed the warning I bring you! Open your hearts, Florence, that you may give praise to the Lord! Open your minds, Florence, that you may see that, in this church today, there is a greater multitude of angels than of men! I beseech you all to entreat them to intercede with the Divine Majesty that He might show His mercy towards you.'

Sandro had painted many angels, which were among the proudest products of his brush. He had striven to capture the beauty, the innocence and truth of their celestial form, but they had been modelled, whether in memory or in person, on the very men whom Savonarola denounced. Had he depicted his angels in the colour of sin?

2

With three hungry apprentices to feed, Sandro would have welcomed even a request for Carnival masks or jousting armour but, under the new government, such vanities had been proscribed. Apart from a hanging for the processional cross at Orsanmichele and a *Flight into Egypt* for Messer Orlando de' Nobili, he was starved of orders. He had been working on a *Transfiguration* for the Niccolini chapel in Santa Croce but, after the mob attacked his palace and the *Signoria* began investigating his support for Piero, Agnolo Niccolini fled to Lombardy and his family abandoned all his projects, hence the huge, unfinished panel propped against the shop wall. Sandro gazed at the figures of Venus and Pallas that he would once have placed outside the windows to attract customers. Now even a Madonna was not safe from the Friar's followers should they deem her immodestly dressed.

Santi and Ildebrando would be in the vanguard of those throwing stones. Three months ago, Simone had sent them to catechism classes run by Fra Domenico da Pescia, Savonarola's closest associate. From what Sandro had gleaned, these differed markedly from the simple introduction to the sacraments that he had been given forty years earlier by the all-too-trusting Padre Matteo d'Antonio. Under Fra Domenico, boys aged between six and sixteen were divided into four companies, one for each of the city's quarters, in which they were drilled in virtue. They were encouraged to discipline themselves, the older boys forming tribunals that administered fraternal correction, punished minor offenders and expelled backsliders. Sandro listened, nonplussed, as Simone boasted that Santi, taking fraternal correction at its most literal, had given Ildebrando six strokes for eating during prayers and, moreover, that his brother had thanked him for it.

'Next time, maybe Santi will take on someone his own size,' he said coldly.

'He did. On his own initiative, he pelted a harlot with dung in the piazza San Giovanni.'

'You say that with approval.'

'Of course. He was doing God's work.'

'Really? I thought Christ stopped the crowd from stoning the adulteress.'

'He wasn't living in Florence!'

'Aren't they a little young to play magistrates? Ildebrando's twelve.'

'The Friar sets the innocence of children against the corruption of their elders.'

'It's not innocence, it's ignorance. Until it's tested, it's worthless. Remember St Augustine? Even if you condemn the rest of my work, you must exempt the portrait in the Ognissanti? He said that trials and temptations were an essential part of our spiritual journey.'

'I feel sorry for you, Sandro. Is this what mixing with all those philosophers has taught you? How to twist words, making good bad and black white?'

Returning to the shop, Sandro pondered whether his brother were right. Pico and Poliziano – doubtless the philosophers in question – had joked that, in any argument, Sandro always ended up siding with his adversary. It was true that, knowing he could never compete with them, he was reluctant to press his case, but he also tried to respect other points of view. Would that Simone kept such an open mind! Sodomy had always repulsed him, but was he correct to say that the sin (in his words), vice (in the words of the *Signoria*), or act (in the words of Sandro himself) was so much more prevalent in

Florence than elsewhere? Certainly in Rome, the only other city he had visited, it had been rife. One of his few consolations, as he laboured through the autumn and winter of 1481 on the frescoes of Christ and Moses for an ungenerous pope, had been the strains of the choir that Sixtus had founded to sing the liturgy and which his colleague Ghirlandaio, a Vatican veteran, explained, doubled as a brothel-house where the bishops and cardinals selected their favourites.

Sandro had never discovered how Pico and Poliziano reconciled their reverence for the Friar with the irregularities of their lives. He, who made no claim to intellectual rigour, approved Savonarola's vision of Florence as the city of God, while rueing the actuality. The lack of compassion towards offenders horrified him, especially when he contemplated his three apprentices: Lioncino, aged thirteen, Annibale fourteen and Gianpiero, the oldest if not wisest at fifteen. Shunning the catechism classes, they had fallen foul of his nephews, who accused them of profligacy for frying their ravioli with garlic and ostentation for wearing pockets with French pleats. He had urged them as best he could to guard against more serious charges, confiding that he too had known the snares of youth. But they found it as hard to see the fourteen-year-old Sandro beneath the wrinkles as an underdrawing beneath the paint.

For Sandro himself, the outline remained clear. He had been a feeble scholar, given to abandoning his books and roaming the city, drawn to the Chiassa de' Buoi and the via tra' Pellicciai like a bee to a blossom or, more strictly, a mouse to a piece of baited cheese. With his every thought fixed on forbidden pleasure, his studies suffered so badly that Mariano removed him from school and placed him in Antonio's shop where, although his mind was more engaged, even polishing a chain could give him an unseemly thrill.

One morning when he was filing the shank of a ring for Cosimo de' Medici, his father marched into the shop and, without a word, grabbed him and dragged him by the sleeve, shoulder and even earlobe back home, much to the merriment of their neighbours, to whom his fine airs had been a permanent affront. A youth who had been caught servicing a grocer on the Ponte Vecchio, had sought to save himself by incriminating his friends. Mariano, informed by the youth's father, was determined to beat the iniquity out of Sandro and, as soon as they stepped through the door, he flung him over a chair, tore down his hose, and proceeded to thrash him. Antonio, bewildered, ran to the broking-house to alert Giovanni, who accompanied him home, where Mariano, having paused for breath, was renewing the attack. Giovanni seized his arm and pulled him off, leaving Sandro, his eyes and nose dripping, smarting in parts that the belt had not touched, mortified to be so exposed before his brothers. Antonio helped him to dress, while Giovanni remonstrated with their father.

'You might have murdered him!'

'So? Better that than he should bring shame on my grey hairs.'

Sandro's snivels turned to snorts at the sight of their father's bald pate.

'Why? What's he done?'

'Your brother … your precious little brother has been playing the backside game with a pack of wastrels from Sant'Apollinaire.'

'I knew it!' said Simone, who had been drawn by Sandro's screams.

'He takes his pleasure where he pleases, like a bitch on heat. A glutton, with boys as wanton as himself!'

The thought of his profligacy made Mariano reach once more for his belt, so Antonio bustled Sandro away while Giovanni restrained their father. Although grateful for their intervention, Sandro knew that Mariano was right. Far from avoiding him, as Giovanni advised, he resolved to turn his fury to his own advantage. When Mariano railed that he did not know what to do with him, he offered a solution: apprentice him to a painter and he would swear to mend his ways. Then, showing him his latest drawing of the Madonna and Child, he insisted that he would be able to achieve far more in paint than he ever would in gold.

Whether Mariano were genuinely impressed, concerned for his son or relieved to have him off his hands, Sandro never knew. He consulted Ser Nastagio Vespucci, their most eminent neighbour, without whom no weighty decision in the di Vanni household was ever taken. Ser Nastagio not only approved of Sandro's ambition (and kept his drawing) but offered to recommend him to his friend, Fra Filippo Lippi. Although at fifteen, Sandro was somewhat old to begin his apprenticeship, Ser Nastagio was confident that at his behest Fra Filippo would waive his objections. Besides which, as Sandro soon discovered, the chronically improvident friar was in need of the fee. In recent years, he had been based in Prato where he was frescoing the choir of the *pieve* but, far from distance being an obstacle, Mariano was glad to remove Sandro from the lure of Florence. He struggled to convince his wife who, ignorant of her son's offence, was both dismayed at the prospect of losing him and appalled that he should be indentured to the infamous Filippo Lippi, a friar who had not only broken his own vows but persuaded a credulous novice to break hers. Yet the reputation that horrified her reassured Mariano. There was no man in Tuscany less inclined towards youths than Fra Filippo.

The five years that Sandro spent with his master were the happiest of his life. Fra Filippo and his wife Lucrezia took him to their hearts, while their son Filippino became his bosom companion. Although he quickly tired of the drudgery that was now the bane of his own apprentices (grinding pigments, priming panels and gathering eggs for the tempera), he impressed Fra Filippo with both his enthusiasm and his skill in copying from a drawing book. His master, in turn, took pains to teach him the rudiments of the craft: the illusion of space; the representation of due proportion; the principles of foreshortening. After a mere three years in the shop, Fra Filippo set him to work on the *Funeral of St Stephen* at the bottom left of the choir, giving him charge not just of the pillars and pavement but of two of the mourners (prominent among whom the painter had placed himself). Despite the ill-concealed hostility of the senior assistant, Fra Diamante, Sandro was utterly content, reproducing Fra Filippo's manner so perfectly that, years later when he returned to Prato, he was unable to detect his own work.

As well as teaching him to transcend the limitations of the plane, Fra Filippo taught him to transcend those of nature. At once uncouth and ungainly, he had painted some of the most sublime *Madonnas* in Florence. Moreover, the model for the finest of them was that same Lucrezia whom he had seduced from the convent. He showed how a painter could redeem himself in ways not open to other men: transforming flesh into form and form into spirit, just as he had transformed his mistress into a saint.

The last of his master's many gifts to him was an introduction to the Medici. Fra Filippo, who was a favourite of the whole family, took him to the palace to see his altarpiece of the *Adoration of the Christ-child*. With a show of confidence, Sandro followed him into the courtyard, its elegant colonnade framing an array of antique busts, statues and sarcophagi, attesting to the imperial cast of the family's ambitions. But for all the glory of the perimeter, his eyes were drawn to the centre, a naked bronze of David with his foot on Goliath's head. Despite his having lately quit the battlefield, there was nothing martial in his stance. On the contrary, he was all sensuousness and swagger, from the tilt of his neck to the twist of his elbow, and the curve of his hips to the bud of his breasts. Even the dead Philistine seemed to acknowledge his beauty, the feather on his helmet caressing the youth's thigh. Sandro felt a stirring in his blood and a tumult in his brain. He had never seen anything like it. Were it not for the subject, he would have sworn that, along with the rest of the sculpture, it had been unearthed in a pagan temple.

'Who could have made this miracle?' he whispered, as though afraid to break the spell.

'Donatello,' Fra Filippo said bluntly.

'Not the old man you greeted outside San Niccolo?'

'He was young once,' Fra Filippo replied, with a smile.

'But I've seen his David. The white marble statue in the Signoria.'

'I've painted many Madonnas.'

'But that's like an effigy on a tomb. This is so full of … life.' Sandro wished that he might use a more honest word.

'He was in love when he made it. With Verrocchio.'

'Your Verrocchio?'

'Yes. And, before you say anything, he was young too and Donatello's apprentice. I'm told – although not by Donatello himself; he's far too circumspect – that he modelled it on the lad.'

The knowledge that it was based on his master's friend, Andrea del Verrocchio, made Sandro even more uneasy about the feelings that the statue evoked in him. But he was grateful that, unlike so many men, Fra Filippo did not scorn those whose desires differed from his own; although, if he suspected Sandro to be one of them, he was too shrewd to say so. Like Fra Filippo, Donatello had used his work both to express and transcend his desires: to create a symbol of freedom and valour that Cosimo was moved to place at the very heart of his palace.

Reminding him of their mission, Fra Filippo led him up the steep flight of stairs. They entered the chapel, where Sandro was instantly entranced by the brilliant procession of the Magi that wound across three walls. The effect was heightened by the cramped confines of the room. Never before – not even in the side-chapels of San Lorenzo and Santa Maria Novella

– had he felt such a sense of standing inside a painting. With so many men and angels and horses and harts and dogs, he was torn as to where to look but, out of respect for his master, he turned first to the altar. Scarcely had he expressed his admiration for the painting – the harmony of the design, the subtlety of the shading, the power and restraint of the gilding – before two of the leading figures from the procession appeared in person, and he longed to vanish into the crowd.

He lowered his eyes as Fra Filippo introduced him to Cosimo's son Piero and grandson Lorenzo. He felt doubly uneasy at having disturbed them at prayer, until Piero explained that they had come to receive the Neapolitan ambassador (the splendour of the room clearly compensating for its size). As Fra Filippo exchanged pleasantries with their hosts, Sandro studied them: Piero, with his gout and goitre, barely able to stand upright in spite of his stick; Lorenzo, only three or four years younger than Sandro himself, his jutting jaw, snub nose and sallow skin accentuated by the candlelight. He spoke little and in a voice that was surprisingly shrill, but he accompanied his words with the most eloquent gestures that Sandro had ever seen.

He only painted him once, ten years later, in his own *Adoration of the Magi*, at the request of the banker, Gaspare di Zanobi del Lama, who wanted to proclaim his connection to the Medici. Marvelling at his own daring, he had placed himself on the periphery, something he would never have done without the example of Fra Filippo and St Stephen. Moreover, he doubted whether Fra Filippo, for all his assurance, would have had the courage for such a self-portrait had he not enjoyed the favour of the Medici.

Rousing himself from his reverie, he turned to his apprentices. Annibale and Lioncino were preparing to prime the panel for the *Flight into Egypt*: the one threading hog's hair for a gesso brush; the other boiling fish heads for glue. Gianpiero sat apart, making charcoal sketches of waxed drapery. A conspicuously well-favoured youth, he had been an excellent model for various angels and saints until Sandro, fearing to feed the self-regard that would once have marked him out as the perfect Narcissus, insisted that he spend more time drawing, much to the fury of Annibale, who accused him of shirking his share of chores.

'Master, there's someone here to see you. Master!'

Sandro looked up to find a tall man in a brown velvet robe trimmed with green taffeta, whose silver-grey hair sat so strangely on his youthful face that it seemed like a further embellishment. Sandro stood quickly, smoothed his hose and trusted that the stains on his shirt would pass for paint.

'Good day, Signor. What may I do for you?'

'I am Orlando di Orlando de' Nobili.'

'Of course, Signor. We weren't expecting you. I trust that all is well with your distinguished father. And all your distinguished family.' Gianpiero snickered. 'We are about to start work on his painting.'

'Is there somewhere we might talk in private?' Orlando asked.

'Of course. Had I known, I'd have welcomed you upstairs. But my brother's wife … If you'd care to come into my sanctum.' Sandro led him into the small room at the back of the house, whose brightness, usually a blessing, now dismayed him, since it exposed rumpled sheets, dirty plates and a brimming chamber pot that he nudged into a corner. His guest, however, appeared oblivious, sitting heavily on the stool without removing his hat, which Sandro, although sensitive to the least slight, felt to be justified given the mess.

'May I offer you a cup of wine?'

'No, nothing,' Orlando replied, transmitting his unease to Sandro, who perched on the edge of the bed.

'I've given a great deal of thought to the painting and made several preliminary sketches. Had I known you were coming, I'd have had them to hand. But as you can imagine with so many orders …' He doubted that Orlando was deceived by the claim, but once again he made no response. Despite – or perhaps because of – his inactivity, he had done nothing to prepare for the painting, except to study Gentile da Fabriano's version in Santa Trinita. 'So if you'd care to come back on Thursday or Friday.'

'I'm relieved – so very relieved – to hear that you haven't begun work.'

'Not on the panel, no,' Sandro said quickly. 'But it's all here.' He tapped his brow. 'Every brushstroke.'

'My father … we will not be wanting the painting.'

'I don't understand. Has something happened?'

'There's no point in pretending. You'll hear soon enough. The whole of Florence will hear. My father has been denounced for sodomy with my son's tutor.'

'Your father … your son … I see.'

'A man I trusted with my life.'

Sandro wondered if he were referring to his father or the tutor. 'But I thought … I must be wrong,' he said, unable to keep track of dignitaries whose tenure was so brief, 'but wasn't your father once an Officer of the Night?'

'Yes. We can add hypocrisy to his offences.'

'Your poor mother,' Sandro said, grateful once again that he had resisted the pressure to marry.

'She's almost as bad. Taken to her bed with the shock and the shame, yet she's known about his conduct for years. She didn't care as long as it was hidden. You know what they say: blind in one eye and winking with the other.'

'Has he appeared before the tribunal?'

'No, I have.'

'Were you also accused?'

'No! Forgive me, it's a reasonable mistake. My father sent my brother and me to appeal for clemency. His age … his standing … his honourable contribution to suppressing sodomy in the past. He even asked us to suggest that it was hearing so many cases that had corrupted him.'

'But you didn't?'

'And be laughed out of court? There were those among the Officers – the Friar's men – who wanted to impose the ultimate penalty. But at least five of the six have to agree if the culprit is to be burnt. They ruled that he was to be publicly disgraced, fined a thousand florins and confined among the madmen in San Bonifazio for the rest of his life.'

'Thank God they were so merciful!' Sandro said sourly.

'Yes,' Orlando replied. 'My brother and I must find the money. We have to cut out all waste … not that your painting is—'

'I understand.'

'I was afraid you'd be immersed in it. But we wouldn't wish you to suffer any losses. I see that, in the contract, there are separate sums for the blue and the gold.'

'Please don't give it another thought. We're always busy here. What we can't use on one panel we can use on another.'

'Thank you, Signor Botticelli. I'm surprised – and humbled – to find such delicacy in one of your profession.'

Sandro led Orlando back through the workshop, which the boiling fish scraps filled with a redundant fetor. Meeting the three eager stares, he felt a stab of regret at having refused payment for the pigments, but pity for Orlando's plight outweighed all other concerns. Having known a father's shame for his son, he understood the still greater shame that a son felt for his father, a shame soon to be blazoned abroad. The older Orlando would be subject to the public degradation at which the Florentines excelled. Sandro had seen men whipped and pilloried, paraded naked through the city, sometimes drawn by a cord tied to their member, sometimes mitred and riding on an ass. With the balladeers and tumblers dispersed on the Friar's orders, it was the only street entertainment left, and the crowd responded with gusto, insulting and tormenting the hapless victims. Years before, Poliziano had castigated people who hung pictures of Jupiter and Ganymede on their walls while recoiling from their flesh-and-blood counterparts. Now the pictures had vanished – some hidden away; others repainted as Abraham and Isaac – but the duplicity remained.

Of the many such degradations he had witnessed, there was one that stuck in his mind, less on account of the victim, whom he could barely recall, than of his companion. He had been leaning against a column in the Loggia dell' Orcagna when he felt a hand on his shoulder. The jasper ring, brocaded sleeves, lilac tunic and scent of rose-water could only belong to one man, and he spun round to meet the gently mocking smile of Leonardo.

'You're supposed to be in the Stinche!' he said, amazed.

'Do I look like a phantasm?'

'You look remarkable … that is you look yourself. When were you let out?'

'This morning.'

'This morning?'

'I'm not your grammar master. You don't have to repeat every word.'

The casual acerbity dispelled any doubts about his friend's identity. But it was hard to credit that this elegant, fragrant man with the cascade of perfectly primped curls had just emerged from two months in jail, not lodged in a well-appointed cell but chained to the wall of an unlit dungeon. Verrocchio, distraught at the fate of his beloved assistant (and some said at the threat of sharing it), had bribed the guards to let him visit, returning with tales of brutal conditions, leaving Sandro to wonder whether the shackles or the darkness were the crueller punishment for a man who rarely sat still to eat and had built his life on the clarity of his vision.

'But you haven't explained how you got out! Maestro Verrocchio went to see Ser Piero, who was dandling his new baby. He begged him to help but he refused.'

'What are you saying? That because I was born out of wedlock and my father has a new family he would abandon me?' Leonardo asked, nostrils flaring. 'He worked night and day for my freedom: visiting officials; calling in favours. He wasn't going to risk all that by confiding in a tattletale like Verrocchio.'

'No, of course not.'

'He should learn to keep his tongue to himself. Someone might rip it out,' Leonardo said darkly.

'He's devoted to you. And you owe him a lot. Just as I do Fra Filippo.'

'Too true,' Leonardo replied, with a smile. 'Be bold, Sandro! It's time to break with your master and make your own rules.'

Returning his friend's smile through gritted teeth, Sandro felt the joy at his release begin to fade. Of all the painters he had known, Leonardo was the most singular. They first met in Verrocchio's shop, where he had spent a few months between leaving Prato and setting up on his own. Although his fellow apprentices included Ghirlandaio and Perugino, with whom Sandro was later to collaborate in Rome, Leonardo had established himself as Verrocchio's chief assistant, with a private workspace at the side of the shop to which no one, not even the master himself, might enter unbidden. By the time of Sandro's arrival, Verrocchio's infatuation was an increasing irritant to Leonardo, who regularly threatened to leave. Desperate to prevent him, Verrocchio gave him ever more responsibility. When asked to make a *Baptism* for the monks of San Salvi, he entrusted him not only with the rocky landscape but with one of the angels who held Christ's robe. On its completion, he declared himself so in awe of his skill that he would never again take up his brush. However flippant, the remark was widely trumpeted by Leonardo, leaving Verrocchio little choice but to comply. Years later when, stricken with an ague, Sandro consigned much of his first *Magi* to Filippino, he warmly commended his assistant's work, but not so much as to injure his own reputation or swell the youth's head.

Leonardo's head was swollen enough, without help from

Verrocchio or anyone else. Were Apelles himself to return from Hades, he would remain unimpressed. Nevertheless they became friends, that is Leonardo sought him out more than anyone else in the shop. 'You're the only one here for whose work I would give a *soldo*,' he said to Sandro one day.

'Why's that?' he replied, feigning nonchalance.

'The gesso,' Leonardo said, broadening his smile. 'I always admire the smoothness of your gesso.'

They kept up with each other's work after Sandro moved away, or rather Leonardo kept up with his, since he himself produced almost nothing. It was as though for all his outward assurance he was afraid of being judged: of failing to fulfil expectations, not least his own. Did he seriously believe that there was a painter alive whose achievement matched his invention?

They differed as much in practice as in temperament. Leonardo held that observation was all: a painter (although he preferred *artist*) found both his subject and his purpose in nature. Sandro believed that, once a painter had grasped the rudiments of anatomy, the effect of light and shade on a body and its positioning in space, he should trust to the power of his imagination.

'You spend too long among Lorenzo's statues, my friend,' Leonardo said. 'Forget all those gods and goddesses with their perfectly sculpted muscles. Take a look at the people around you.'

'You mean search out their flaws?'

'No, their truths.'

'We should rise above nature, not be its slave.'

'Careful who you call a slave!' Leonardo said, clenching his fists. 'I aim to master nature, but out of respect: to capture the divine flow of creation. But you … you want to prettify it—'

'To improve on it!'

'Like a merchant's wife painting her face.'

'Take your Virgin: the one with the Christ-child clutching the flower – and when do you plan to finish it by the way?' Sandro asked boldly. 'She's toothless and practically bald. That may be the truth of a peasant girl but not of the mother of God.'

'The mother of God was a peasant girl!'

'But who can gain comfort from that? Who can look to a higher nature and make such a figure the focus of their devotion?'

'Why should they? It's nonsense to talk to a picture – a pattern of brushstrokes on a panel – and expect a response.'

'So says the man who bragged to the entire shop that he intended to paint a portrait so perfect that a dog would recognise its master and bark!'

For once Leonardo was lost for words, a reticence that, to Sandro's regret, did not extend to his meeting with Poliziano. They were sitting outside a tavern at the Porta San Gallo watching a group of youths playing *calcio*, when he caught sight of the poet, the last person he would have expected to find in this hinterland. Poliziano looked equally taken aback but, swiftly recovering, he greeted Sandro who, with a mixture of pride and apprehension, introduced him to Leonardo, listing Poliziano's accomplishments like an ambassador reciting his sovereign's titles. He knew that it was foolish but he could not help himself. This was the man whose friendship he numbered among the greatest privileges of his life, the man universally acknowledged as the finest poet, scholar and translator of the age.

'It is I who am honoured to claim kinship with you, Sandro,' said Poliziano, who, either because of the unforeseen meeting or Leonardo's pugnacity, had affected diffidence. 'You are a poet among painters.'

'Is that meant to be a compliment?' Leonardo asked contrarily.

'Why wouldn't it be?'

'A painter appeals to the eye, a poet to the ear, which is the lesser organ. Ergo poetry is the lesser art.'

'I see ... or should I say I hear?' said Poliziano, who, to Sandro's relief, sounded amused rather than offended. 'But where would painters be without poets to praise them? Even Apelles, the greatest of them all, would be forgotten if it weren't for Pliny.'

Sandro could not tell whether the tension between the two men sprang from attraction or hostility or both. Feeling like a schoolmaster at once admiring and resentful of his quick-witted pupils, he sat in silence as they sparred with each other until, in an unspoken truce, they turned their attention to the youths playing *calcio*, assessing them in the coarsest manner, comparing their teeth and flanks as though they were colts in a stall. To make matters worse, when he refused to join in, they condemned his prudery, questioned his sincerity and mocked his blushes. He would have expected it from Leonardo but was horrified by Poliziano, who had known Giuliano de' Medici.

Although Poliziano had been implicated in cases of sodomy, Lorenzo's protection ensured that he was never prosecuted. The lowlier Leonardo was less fortunate. Two months before, while modelling a terracotta head of the young Christ on Jacopo Saltarelli, a goldsmith's apprentice, he was one of four men denounced for violating the youth. Unusually, Leonardo was imprisoned prior to the case being heard, leading Sandro to conclude that he had offended some high-ranking official who was taking revenge. Verrocchio had worked tirelessly – and seemingly in vain – to secure his release, imploring every great man for whom he had so much as designed a button to intercede on his assistant's behalf. Happily for Leonardo, one of his fellow accused was Lorenzo's cousin, Leonardo Tornabuoni. So, despite his insistence that he had been freed as a result of his father's efforts, Sandro suspected that the charges were dropped at Il Magnifico's behest.

'Have you seen Maestro Verrocchio?' Sandro asked, fearing that it would be quite like Leonardo to neglect his champion.

'Of course,' Leonardo replied shortly. 'I went even before going to the baths. He held me close and stroked me like a stray cat. He didn't seem to notice the smell.'

'But why are you here?'

'The same reason as you.'

'I doubt it,' said Sandro, who was reminding himself of the penalty for lust.

'So you happened to be passing on the way to the market?'

'No, but I haven't just been released from prison for—'

'The charges were dropped. I may well seek reparation.'

'I wouldn't if I were you.'

'Perhaps not,' Leonardo said. Then, with a composure that Sandro did not know whether to applaud or decry, he took out his drawing book and a stick of red chalk and sketched faces in the crowd, as the mitred prisoner, sitting naked and backwards on an ass, was led past.

'How can you be so calm?'

'See that woman with the cabbage! And that old man shouting abuse. Look at his snarl. Perfect if I'm ever asked to paint a road to Calvary.'

'I find it hard enough to watch, let alone draw.'

'Don't be so feeble! Come on, they're pillorying him in the Mercato Vecchio.'

They followed the crowd into the teeming marketplace where, in a macabre spectacle, cobblers and clothiers, goldsmiths and printers, cooks and vintners hawked their wares; scriveners and moneychangers offered their services; one barber shaved a priest and another examined a hunchback covered in weeping sores; while, beneath the central column crowned by the goddess of plenty, the prisoner, the red B for *Buggerone* on his mitre now visible, was locked in the pillory.

'This is hopeless. Too cramped! Come on!' Leonardo said. Dragging his feet, Sandro accompanied him through the throng, past butchers and fishmongers doing a brisk trade in produce that would otherwise be discarded. 'This is perfect. Out of the way!' Dismissing the protests of an elderly woman, her face as wizened as the apple in her hands, Leonardo pushed forward and opened his drawing book. 'Have you ever seen an expression like it?'

Gazing at the man's rictus of pain and incredulity, Sandro thought that he had once: in Prato, on a sheep at the moment its throat was cut. 'Have you no compassion?' he asked.

'Is that another word for cowardice?'

'It might have been you.'

'No!' Leonardo turned on him so furiously that the old woman gasped. 'That man is a pathic. He let himself be entered. He serviced other men – younger men. He broke the natural law.'

A moment later, the woman threw her apple, striking the prisoner on the chest with a force that the youths playing *calcio* would have envied. As he shrieked and the onlookers jeered, Sandro brooded on Leonardo's words and knew that he must never reveal, let alone indulge, his desires.

'I'm surprised to see you two in this rabble.' A young woman sidled up to them. The trappings, which in normal circumstances would have classed her as an outcast, were here almost a badge of respectability.

'Do I know you?' Leonardo asked.

'Maybe not with my gown on,' she replied, in a voice striving for outrage.

'You have the wrong man,' he said coldly.

'No, I never forget a face. Thankfully, I can't say the same for other parts. Delfina from the apothecary's shop in via Ghibellina. I modelled for Maestro Verrocchio.'

'Then for me you were just planes and contours.'

'And for you?' Delfina asked Sandro.

'What happened to the apothecary?' he asked.

'He was bitten by a snake.' She tossed back her head and

the bells on her hood jangled. 'I mustn't laugh.' She stared at the prisoner. 'Poor soul. I know I shouldn't feel sorry for him. Many more like him and women like me will starve. It makes no sense. They license us so they can curb unnatural vice, but we attract the most customers by dressing as boys. Then they fine us for wearing improper clothes.'

'It's a hard life for a philosophical whore,' Leonardo said.

'That's cruel,' Sandro said.

'What? You're still after compassion?' He turned to Delfina. 'Scram! If I ever need a Magdalene, I'll know where to look.'

'How about you, Signor?' she asked Sandro. 'Would you like company?'

'It'll take more than a doublet and hose to attract him,' Leonardo said. 'You'll need wings and a halo.'

'Since I like you, I'll give you a special price. Two *soldi*.'

'That's very kind, but no.'

'I said "Scram!" We'll put our dough in a cleaner oven.'

Delfina flicked her hand beneath her chin and spat, before pushing through the parting crowd.

'Ding-a-ling-a-ling, and she clears a path like a leper!'

'Or a priest taking the sacrament to a dying man.'

'Only you, Sandro!' Leonardo said, smiling, before turning back to the blood-streaked prisoner.

3

'Your louts are murdering my sons!' Ippolita screeched from the doorway. The antipathy between his apprentices and his nephews was such that, even allowing for his sister-in-law's embellishment, Sandro feared the worst. He ran into the shop where Annibale was crouching on Ildebrando's chest, pinning down his elbows and banging his head on the floor, and Gianpiero and Santi, more evenly matched, each had one hand on his adversary's throat as they lashed out with the other. Meanwhile, Lioncino chased after three ruffled chickens, whose squawking increased at Ippolita's approach. The spasms in his spine forgotten, Sandro pulled Annibale up and flung him roughly across the room. He was less successful at separating the others, not least because of Ippolita's frenzied swipes at Gianpiero, her particular aversion ever since he had placed two wax modelling hands under the lid of her marriage chest. Sandro ducked so often to evade the blows that he began to wonder whether she were aiming at him on purpose.

'Ow!' Gianpiero jumped away as Ippolita sank her teeth into his arm. 'She bit me!'

'Don't!' Sandro said, stopping Santi taking advantage of his mother's attack. 'Everyone calm down. What on earth's going on? Don't!' he repeated, as they shouted at once. 'Quiet, all of you!'

'I'm wounded,' Gianpiero said.

'Let me see,' Sandro asked. 'A scratch,' he said, grabbing a rag to staunch the blood. 'You'll live. Lioncino, you're the most sensible person here.' A glance at Ippolita made it clear that he included her in the reckoning. 'Tell me what's going on.'

'Santi and Ildebrando came downstairs and tried to steal one of the chickens.'

'Is that true?' Sandro asked his elder nephew, trusting that the catechism classes would ensure his honesty.

'Yes,' he replied sullenly. 'But not for ourselves, for the farmers.'

'I told you to stay away from them,' Ippolita interjected. 'They're filthy, flea-ridden peasants who bring pestilence into the city.'

'They have nothing. No food. No beds. They sleep in gutters,' Santi replied.

'In the rain,' Ildebrando added.

'I understand,' Sandro said. Eleven months of the worst storms on record had devastated the harvest and driven hordes of starving villagers into the city. Their presence, together with the rumours of plague and the rise in the price of grain, had sown discontent even among Savonarola's supporters. 'Your intentions were honourable.' Far more so than your mother's, he might have added. 'But you of all people should remember the Commandment "Thou shalt not steal."'

'Yes,' Santi said, 'but Jesus said "Feed my lambs."'

Sandro, whose knowledge of the Bible derived largely from his painting, was at a loss.

'But what about the Friar?' Gianpiero asked scornfully. 'Didn't he tell us that, as long as we obeyed his orders, all would be well? Why did he lie to us?'

'Gianpiero …' Sandro warned.

'No!' Santi said tearfully. 'Fra Girolamo hasn't betrayed us; it's us who've betrayed him. This city is a midden. Look at you with your lewd pictures!'

'My pictures are not lewd!' Sandro said, fuming at the familiar calumny.

'Not yours, Uncle. His!' He pointed at Gianpiero.

'Gianpiero hasn't made any pictures yet. Whatever he may think, he still has a lot to learn.'

'Drawings ... sketches then. What difference does it make? Filth showing Fra Girolamo and Fra Domenico ... No, I can't say it.'

'Force yourself!' Ippolita said.

'Fra Girolamo mounting Fra Domenico.' Santi burst into tears.

'He's crying!' Annibale said, with a smirk.

'Where is this drawing?' Ippolita asked.

'Not anywhere you'll find it,' Gianpiero replied.

'He hid it down the front of his hose,' Ildebrando said.

Ippolita lunged; Gianpiero leapt away. But his agility was no match for her determination and she cut him off behind a table, thrusting her hand down his hose and triumphantly pulling out a paper. Equally brazen, Sandro grabbed it from her, leaving her with a virginal corner. A glance confirmed his nephew's charge. Not even the most innocent observer could misconstrue such a ribald pose.

'Let me see!' Ippolita demanded.

'No,' Sandro replied, ripping the drawing into such small pieces that one of the chickens pecked at them. All five boys protested, albeit for different reasons.

'Quick thinking!' Ippolita said bitterly. 'You wouldn't want it to fall into the wrong hands.'

'Quite. The hands of the Confraternity of San Giorgio. They've ordered a St John's Day banner showing the Friar and two of his fellows venerating the Cross. I asked Gianpiero for a preparatory sketch. It's my fault for putting my trust in him. Far, far too much trust.' He cuffed the apprentice's ear. Ignoring his yelp, he turned to his nephews. 'And you two should know better. You're so eager to sniff out mischief, you find it when it isn't there. Learn to leave well alone.'

'That's not what Fra Domenico tells us,' Santi replied. 'He says it's the duty of the righteous to unmask the guilty.'

'As I've explained, the only guilt here is in your imaginings. And if I were your mother,' he said purposefully, 'I'd be disturbed.'

Ippolita glared at him, as though trying to find a suitable riposte. Failing, she addressed her sons. 'Santi, Ildebrando, upstairs!'

'Won't you all shake hands first?' Sandro asked.

'No,' Gianpiero said, rubbing his ear.

'That wasn't a question.'

'You said "Won't you?"' Annibale replied.

'Then it wasn't a question with any answer but yes. Come on, we all have to share a house.'

Ippolita harrumphed. 'Lioncino, Ildebrando!'

They warily shook hands, after which Santi reached out to Gianpiero, only to spring forward and tug the hair that covered his uninjured ear.

'Fra Domenico says that any boy with long hair is a girl,' he said, dodging Gianpiero's fist.

'What about Samson?' Gianpiero taunted, as Sandro restrained him. 'Can't answer that, can you?'

Whether or not he could, he was denied the chance, since Ippolita propelled both him and his brother out of the room and up the stairs. A series of shrieks indicated that she had found a target for her rage.

'Right, fun's over,' Sandro said. 'Let's clear up and get back to work.'

'You hit me!' Gianpiero said.

'You're lucky it was only me. You're lucky I didn't take off my belt and beat it out of you.'

'What? The lewdness?' Gianpiero asked, sardonically.

'No, the stupidity. Do you have any idea what might have happened to you if some fervent *Piagnone* found that paper? Whipping, pillorying, branding, worse! The city's gone mad. Besides, paper's too expensive to waste,' he added, at the sight of the three chastened faces.

'The *Piagnoni* won't be persecuting us much longer,' Gianpiero said. 'I've heard stories.'

'Then don't repeat them. Whatever you know' – and Sandro

suspected that it was little more than prattle – 'don't say anything to anyone you can't trust. Don't say anything to anyone you can trust!'

'If only they'd left the spikes on the Friar's May Day pulpit,' Annibale said. 'Bang!' He slammed down his fist with a mock grimace.

'Lioncino, will you go to the Velluti and see if they have any bones for the ground?' Sandro asked, ignoring the foolery. 'If they don't, try Mona Francesca.'

'Do I have to?'

'Better still, try everyone on the street,' Sandro said, eager to send his youngest and most impressionable apprentice out of earshot.

'But the maids all make fun of me. They muss my hair and put their hands …'

'Look how red he's gone!' Annibale said. 'Shame we can't use his cheeks as a pigment.'

'Don't be mean! And you, boy, hurry up. Take that bucket and don't come back till it's full.' Grumbling, Lioncino left the shop. 'You two had better watch your step. It's not just that tawdry drawing—'

'You must admit it was well done,' Gianpiero said smugly. 'You knew at once who they were.'

'Their faces were passable. Some of their other parts left a lot to be desired.'

'That's what Fra Domenico said when Fra Girolamo was frigging him,' Annibale interjected, to Gianpiero's delight.

'Have you been listening to a word I've said?'

'Think though,' Annibale added, 'if they hadn't discovered the nails before the service and Savonarola had hammered on the pulpit. Aargh!' He shuddered.

'He might never have noticed,' Sandro said, with a hint of admiration. 'When he preaches, he seems to be transported to another world.'

'Pity he doesn't stay there!' Gianpiero said.

'But with blood pouring from his hands …' Annibale said.

'The *Piagnoni* would have seen it as a stigmata. It'll take more than a few infantile pranks to loosen his grip on power, let alone break his spirit.'

'Why infantile?' Annibale asked.

'It's all very well fixing nails on the pulpit – well it's not, but for the sake of argument … But if you do, why smear it with dung? Why cover it with a rotting donkey skin? Isn't that bound to rouse any sacristan's suspicions?'

Taking their silence for assent, he left them to their tasks and went upstairs to speak to Simone, anxious to ensure that his nephews laid no formal charge against Gianpiero. Dreading a further clash with Ippolita, he was relieved to see her heading to the well, where she was sure to stay and gossip. He found his brother in his study, reading the Bible that had been his constant companion since its first printing in their native tongue twenty-five years earlier.

'I gather there's been more trouble,' Simone said, looking up.

'You'll only have heard half the story.'

'I'm not a fool!'

'No, of course not – not at all. It's just … Where are the boys?' he asked, mistrustful of the quiet, as well as keen to clear the air.

'Out.'

'But Ippolita was furious with them. Surely she didn't allow them to go and play?'

'They don't play, Sandro. You should know that. They have serious matters in hand.'

'What is it now?'

'Two boys from their company collected them. They've gone to lime-wash the tabernacle on the corner of the piazza Santa Maria Novella.'

'Not the one on the crossing with the via della Scala?'

'I didn't ask.'

'With the Madonna in glory surrounded by saints?'

'I said, I didn't ask.'

'And you don't care?'

'I care that every day men untie their hose and piss on that wall in full view of the Holy Mother.'

'I doubt she's watching them. And at least they have something beautiful to look at when they piss.'

'Is that supposed to be funny?'

'Not at all. Besides she'll understand. I presume she had to change Our Lord's clouts.'

'For pity's sake, Sandro! Is that what you teach your apprentices? No wonder they're out of control.'

'Says who? It's your sons who provoke them. Just as they provoke me. Always asking why I'm not married.'

'I assure you that doesn't come from me.'

'I told them they might as well ask the same of their precious friars.'

'They've taken vows!'

'So have I, Simone,' Sandro said sadly, 'if you only knew.'

'Nonsense! You're a painter, or at least you were. The closest you've come to vows is joining the Confraternity of St Luke. I know that you have no respect for the Friar.'

'I respect him sometimes.'

'This isn't a time for *sometimes.* You had your *sometimes* under the Medici and look where it left us. I'm proud of my sons. Don't you remember what we were like at their age? Those games of *calcio* when boys broke their arms, legs and teeth. The stone fight against San Paolo when Attaviano was killed. Those two brothers – I forget their names – in the Borgo Ognissanti, who dug up a corpse and laid it on the sanctuary steps.'

'Scarfo – Piero and Matteo Scarfo.'

'Right. We ran wild.'

'Just as they do now, but with impunity. No, I'm wrong,' Sandro said firmly. 'Not wild but vicious. Where in the Bible does it say we should break into an old woman's house and berate her for eating pastries? Where does it say we should ambush a fat man in the street, beat him with staves and tell him that his body is an affront to God?'

'My boys? You're telling me they were my boys?'

'No … I don't know. Maybe. They're part of the gangs.'

'Not gangs, companies. Well-disciplined companies.'

'Well, one of those well-disciplined companies attacked two Soderini servants last week because they misheard their guardian and thought they were sodomites.'

'They should have listened more carefully.'

'No, they should have considered more deeply.'

After securing Simone's promise to speak to his sons, Sandro returned to the workshop to find Lioncino still absent and Annibale and Gianpiero busy on the banner for the Confraternity of San Giorgio. This, needless to say, depicted not a trio of reverent friars but rather St George defeating the dragon, a beast that Sandro, whose fancy did not rise to the fantastical, had based on the magnificent green-winged, twisted-tailed creature that Paolo Uccello had painted for Cosimo. He praised their efforts before reminding Gianpiero that, until such time as he had his own shop, it was his duty to reproduce his master's manner and not to depart from the underdrawing in the smallest detail, let alone pick out the dragon's green scales in red.

'I told you he wouldn't like it,' Annibale said.

'And you were right. So first thing tomorrow, Gianpiero, you can paint over it.'

'It's no wonder the shop's floundering when you refuse to recognise true brilliance.'

'I'll bear that in mind. Meanwhile, it's time I started work on the tondo. Mix me some orpiment and red lake, will you?'

'That's Lioncino's job!'

'In case it's escaped your notice, he isn't here. Annibale, as soon as you've finished that *G*, help me lift the panel on to the easel.'

The ornate frame made the balance precarious, but Sandro knew better than to complain. He had made the tondo of the *Madonna and Child with St Francis, St John the Baptist and Eight Angels*, for Francesco Albizzi, in whose hall it had hung for the past ten years, attracting many plaudits and generating several orders. Recently, however, there had been murmurings about the direction – and even the intent – of two of the angels' gazes, away from the Mother and Son and towards one another. Sandro was appalled that anyone should confuse pure angelic affection with base human lust, but Niccolo Albizzi, Francesco's son, bowing to pressure from his *Piagnone* wife, had asked him to alter the two offending figures, secretly paying him twenty florins.

'Are you ready for the egg?' Gianpiero asked, tipping the powdered pigment into a shell.

'Yes. And a drop of yolk. The same amount you used for St Zenobius's flowers. You know what that means, Annibale!'

'Oh no,' he replied, feigning a groan.

'Poke away!'

When Fra Filippo first asked him to add a pinch of earwax to the paint, Sandro had assumed that he was jesting. But having seen how it smoothed the froth in the egg white, he had adopted the practice himself. With a shop full of youthful apprentices, there was never any shortage of supply.

He painted through the night, the boys' heavy breathing providing both a stimulus and a reassurance. By morning, he had realigned the angels to his and, he trusted, his patron's satisfaction, with two of them holding a golden crown over the Madonna's head and a third who, for reasons he no longer recalled, had been staring out of the frame, now playing a *lira da braccio*. The apprentices were impressed, although Lioncino who, against all the evidence, still saw painting as a sacred mystery, half-believed Gianpiero's claim that Sandro had summoned a familiar spirit to assist him.

'No, nothing but this aching back and sore fingers,' Sandro

assured him. 'So if one of you idlers would fetch me a cup of wine ...'

'Me,' Lioncino insisted.

They laid the tondo against the wall, leaving a gap that was swiftly filled, not by another picture but by a man who might well have posed for one. Although it was a painter's shop, he infused it with colour that, in present-day Florence, was not just a delight but a defiance. He wore a lemon doublet and a blue cape trimmed with velvet, white silk sleeves and hose both closely worked in silver, an emerald green cap set off with a spray of peacock feathers, gold buckled shoes, a sword, a dagger, a heavy gold chain with a medallion of Julius Caesar and so many rings that his hand glistered. While upbraiding himself for a delusion born of too little sleep, Sandro immediately saw something in him of the long-lamented Giuliano.

'Doffo d'Agnolo Spini,' the visitor said, bowing with an elegance that the shop had not witnessed in years.

'I'm the one who should introduce you,' Gianpiero said. 'It was me you picked out in the Corso Adimari.'

'Who would have failed to pick out such a delicious creature?' Doffo said, twining a lock of Gianpiero's hair around his fingers until Sandro longed for a pair of Savonarola's scissors. 'But it was when you told me that you worked for Maestro Botticelli that your charms were fully manifest.' Gianpiero's expression soured as Annibale's brightened. 'I've been asking him to bring me here for months without success.'

'I didn't think he'd support your aims,' Gianpiero said.

'Which are?' Sandro asked.

'To destroy tyranny and return Florence to her ancient liberty.'

'No one could find fault with those,' Sandro said guardedly, although as Doffo stroked Gianpiero's breast, he seemed to be confusing liberty with licence.

'Doffo is the leader of the *Compagnacci*,' Gianpiero said with pride.

Sandro started. He knew of the group, who were increasingly open in their opposition to the Friar, but he had not expected its leader to be so high-born. 'So it was one of your supporters who stole my nephews' caps in the piazza San Paolo?'

'Not just your nephews, unless you have twenty or thirty.'

'He has two,' Annibale said, 'which is bad enough.'

'They came home distraught,' Sandro said. 'It was very cruel.'

'As cruel as tearing the veil off a terrified young girl or the wig off a humiliated old woman?'

'You don't have to fight like with like.'

'Maybe not, but you won't win if you fight it with anything else. So your nephews are two of the Friar's boys?'

'I told you,' Gianpiero said, 'his brother is a rabid *Piagnone*.'

'And you?' Doffo asked Sandro.

'I'm nothing. But I recognise the Friar's sincerity.'

'Wasn't Brutus sincere when he murdered Caesar? Wasn't Cassius?' Doffo asked, clasping his medallion. 'Besides you're wrong. His so-called sincerity is just self-interest. No wonder he sets such store by abstinence when he's too ugly to enjoy anything else.'

'You're being unjust,' said Sandro who, faced with the arrogance of youth and beauty, found himself leaping to Savonarola's defence more readily than he might have wished. 'Even his enemies acknowledge that he's a holy man, spending night after night on his knees in prayer and fasting.'

'If he wants to mortify his flesh, that's fine. Frankly, it's fit for nothing else,' Doffo said, to an accompaniment of sniggers. 'But he has no right to persecute the rest of us.'

'The people of Florence have put their trust in him.'

'The people of Florence are fools,' Doffo replied. 'But I expected more from its painters. And one in particular.'

'Why me?' Sandro asked.

'You're everything we're fighting for. With Lorenzo dead,

with Pico dead, with Poliziano dead, you alone are left to remind us of the world we've lost – no, that's been wrested from us. I can't begin to tell you how much your paintings mean to me. The first time I saw them, it was like – I suppose if he's as sincere as you say – what Savonarola feels when he gazes on the Cross.'

'No painter could ask for more,' Sandro replied warily. 'It's what we all hope for when you contemplate an *Annunciation* or a *Lamentation* or a *Madonna and Child*.'

'No, I was speaking of your *Realm of Venus*. The ancient Gods filled with the joys of springtime. The grace. The beauty. The fecundity. And painted with a freshness that makes them seem not ancient at all but part of the world we live in. After that I sought out all your pictures in the city.'

'In the churches?'

'And the palaces. Although our fathers haven't spoken for twenty years, I called on Jacopo Salviati and humbly requested to see the *Mars and Venus* you made for his wedding. Once again I was overawed by the figures: the beautiful Venus watching tenderly over her paramour, so sated by the joys of love and congress that he'd fallen asleep.'

'Don't you mean grumpily?' Gianpiero asked. 'We had to make a copy three years ago. I thought she was sulking because Mars was so bored with her he couldn't keep awake.'

'You're too young to understand such things,' Doffo said, giving him a playful punch.

'Or too wanton,' Sandro added, fearing that he should have made his purposes more explicit. 'It's an emblem of spiritual love vanquishing sensuality.'

'But nothing can compare with the day when, knowing of my interest, Lorenzo di Pierfrancesco invited me to see his – that is your – *Venus on the Seashore* at Castello. Of course I'd seen copies of the goddess around the city – very inferior ones, probably painted by this lot.' He gestured good-humouredly to the apprentices.

'Impudence!' Gianpiero said.

'They couldn't prepare me for the picture itself. Please don't take this amiss but, for all the beauty of the goddess and the exquisite depiction of Zephyr and Aura and Horae, my first thought was of a baptism – actually, the one that Verrocchio and his pupil painted for Santa Salvi – with the two winds in place of the attendant angels and Horae bringing Venus her cloak in place of the Baptist pouring his pan of water. What's more, Venus herself put me in mind of Christ: the way she stands so still at the heart of the painting, although not with her head bent and her knee bowed, not with her loins draped in a cloth, but naked and unashamed, her modesty preserved only by her sumptuous tresses. Of course I said nothing to Lorenzo – I was afraid he'd think me mad – but then I realised that whatever he thought, indeed whatever you intended, it is a baptism, for it's the birth of a new way of thinking. You've freed us from the old superstitions. Through you, Republican Florence has taken on the mantle of Republican Rome.'

'But Republican Rome with the blessing of fifteen hundred years of Christ,' Sandro said quickly. 'My Venus is no lewd enchantress but the quintessence of virtue. She has no shame in her nakedness because her body and soul are pure. She is Eve before the Fall. She is the eternal Madonna. The Friar condemns painters for depicting the saints as if they were pagan gods and goddesses, yet when I painted Venus, I was condemned for depicting a pagan goddess as if she were a saint. But she is the goddess of love, and it is love that leads us to God.'

Sandro wished that his tongue were as eloquent as his brush. He had been taught by Pico and Poliziano, who had in turn been taught by Marsilio Ficino, the one member of Lorenzo's circle to intimidate him more than Il Magnifico himself, that beauty was the manifestation of love and love was the sustaining principle of the universe. The contemplation of beauty was therefore the pathway to the divine. So in painting – if not in life – he made no distinction between a Venus and a Virgin.

He had never heard Ficino in the lecture hall, but he had listened spellbound to him at the dinner table, although even then it was on sufferance. He had spent the autumn of 1486 at Lorenzo's villa at Careggi, painting a *Festival of Pan* in the central loggia, which had taken longer than anticipated. The November dampness was not conducive to fresco, but the delay meant that he was present for the annual banquet in honour of Plato's birthday. There were nine guests, one for each of the Muses, with Lorenzo himself presiding. Pico and Poliziano, who were of the party, greeted him warmly on their arrival before commiserating with him on his exclusion from the feast. Poliziano declared that his attendance would be inappropriate since there was no muse of painting, any more than of basket-weaving or candle-making, but Pico wondered whether they might make an exception provided that he promised not to talk. Sandro, for whom such a proviso was no hardship, readily agreed, and with their host's approval a place was laid for him at the bottom of the table.

Poliziano warned him that they would be discussing philosophy as though they would be speaking Hungarian but, to Sandro's relief, the primary subject was love. Ficino, to whom even Lorenzo deferred, explained that love had two natures, the spiritual and the sensual, and it was the duty of everyone to nurture the first and suppress the second. Having fought his desires for years, Sandro was astounded to hear that, far from being more depraved than those of other men, they were purer. Since men lived more in their minds than women and were less bound than them to their flesh, their affections were innately more spiritual and the highest form of love was that between men. Yet for all Ficino's eminence as a philosopher and authority as a priest, Sandro found his argument self-serving, not least when he suggested boldly – even recklessly – that such love had reached its pinnacle in that of Christ and his disciples.

He reminded himself that the love that Ficino extolled was an intellectual ideal and not a physical passion, and that, should any passion creep in, it involved an older man's love for a youth, such as Leonardo had once described as the natural order, and not its perversion, such as he himself felt in the longing for another man's embrace: a longing that he kept locked in his breast, not even releasing it in conversation with his most trusted friends. Pico and Poliziano mocked his meekness. Even Lorenzo questioned the nature of his sentiments. Was he a neuter or a saint? He replied that he responded to form rather than flesh. Whereas others looked at a picture and saw the man it portrayed, he looked at a man and saw the picture he would make. But that was not the whole truth. After the shame of his youthful carnality, he had vowed to subdue his appetites as completely as Pallas had the Centaur and Venus had Mars.

Doffo continued to heap praise on Sandro, without any indication that he would order a painting. Why was it that men who gorged themselves at their own tables presumed that painters were able to live on air? Sandro felt a rush of resentment first towards him and then towards Gianpiero for not acquainting him with the parlousness of their position, which was doubly unjust given the pains that he himself had taken to conceal it.

'Should you wish for a Venus of your own, I could make one,' he ventured to Doffo.

'I have no plans to marry.'

'It doesn't have to be a wedding gift. She's the goddess of love not of marriage.'

'No, the next time you paint Zephyr, he should be blowing on Hyacinth, the beautiful youth he adored.'

'And I must be the model!' Gianpiero said.

'But didn't Zephyr end by killing him?' Sandro asked, struggling to recollect the story.

'All youth dies but not all has the fortune to be loved by a god,' Doffo said. Then, kissing Gianpiero with a ferocity that left him breathless, Lioncino wide-eyed and Annibale scowling, he quit the shop.

'So that's the famous Doffo,' Annibale said. 'I pictured him taller.'

'He's big where it counts.'

'He'll soon lose interest when you have a beard,' Annibale replied, stroking his chin.

'You sell yourself too cheaply,' Sandro said, aiming his words as much at the susceptible Lioncino as at Gianpiero himself.

'Does a silver chain come cheap? Does a leather belt come cheap? Do a velvet doublet and rose-coloured hose come cheap?' Gianpiero asked, reassigning gifts for which he had previously credited his 'uncle'.

'You know the saying: a golden key opens every door but the one to heaven.'

'You sound like the Friar,' Gianpiero replied, with disgust.

'You have far greater gifts in yourself than anything anyone else can offer. You have it in you to become a fine painter.'

'You've never said that before.'

'I'm saying it now.'

'Then give me a chance to show it! What do you want me to do?'

'Clean out the chicken coop,' Sandro replied stonily.

'But that's the brat's job!' Gianpiero said, outraged.

'I need Lioncino for something else. And the chickens must be tended. No eggs, no paint. No paint, no food.'

'Then we'll eat the chickens.'

'And don't startle them or they won't lay.'

Gianpiero moved towards Sandro until their mouths were almost touching, before snapping his fingers and backing away. 'Not in your wildest dreams!'

Doffo's visit was followed the next day by that of Messer Donato Davanzati. He was the son of Dietaiuto di Donato Davanzati, who had bought a *Madonna with a Pomegranate* and a marriage chest for his daughter shortly after Sandro's return from Rome. Sandro's first thought was of a new order and the opportunity to use some of the gold and ultramarine from last year's abortive *Flight into Egypt*, but his visitor was scarcely through the door when he announced that he was an Officer of the Night come on court business. Despite his gracious – even affable – tone, Sandro quailed like a boy of fourteen threatened with public exposure. Forty years of guilt and fear rose up in him like bones buried in a flooded field. Refusing to indulge his apprentices' curiosity, he sent them away before inviting Messer Donato to sit on a stool, from which he hastily snatched one of Gianpiero's sketches that might have incriminated them all.

'Believe me, it's not the best time to have taken up the post,' Donato said, his confidential tone bemusing Sandro further. 'The Great Council, guided by the Friar, can't make up its mind how to punish offenders. First they abolish fines in favour of prison sentences, with the result that denunciations decrease. Which, let's face it, you and I could have foretold.' Sandro nodded uncertainly. 'Without their share of the fines, there's less incentive for people to inform. So they reintroduce fines but set them far higher. I ask you, what's the point of imposing a fine of five hundred florins on a shoemaker or a weaver who makes at most fifty or sixty a year? How will he pay? How will his children eat?'

'They won't.'

'So with convictions falling, who do the councillors blame? Us. The Officers of the Night. They accuse us of being too lenient, which is absurd. No other city in Italy takes unnatural vice as seriously as we do. No other city has its own designated magistracy. But it seems that that's no longer enough. We're to divide our responsibilities with the Eight of Watch and the Guardians of the Law.'

'I understand your frustration,' Sandro said, 'but I'm still not sure what it has to do with me.'

'Didn't I say? I'm sorry. We're moving from makeshift courts in the guildhalls to a permanent one in the Podesta. So it's the perfect time to reassert our authority.'

'And?'

'And we've decided to decorate the chamber with scenes from the story of Lot. To show the Eight and the Guardians and the Council that Sodom is our private preserve.'

'And you want me to make them?' Sandro asked, the visit suddenly making thrilling sense.

'We'd like to discuss it with you. To be honest, there was no obvious candidate. Someone suggested di Credi, someone else Baccio. He's much in favour at San Marco.'

'Too much.'

'Quite. There was talk of Filippino, but he has more work than his shop can handle.'

'So I've heard.'

'Then I remembered you and the paintings you'd made for my father and sister. No one was sure if you still had your shop.'

'What?' Sandro regretted having sent the apprentices away. 'I've never been busier. Look!' Straining every muscle in his back, he lifted the tondo, thanking God and his own indolence that he had not yet summoned the porters to collect it. 'I've just painted this for Francesco Albizzi.'

'Let me see. Why, it's exactly like ours!'

'Really?' Sandro struggled to remember which of his many *Madonnas* he had made for Donato's father.

'Different saints. One of ours is a woman: St Catherine of Sienna.' Sandro was none the wiser. 'And this may have an extra angel.'

'I'm sorry. It's what the patrons expect. There's not much scope for variety.'

'Don't apologise. Consistency is a virtue. And it's for your *Virtues* that we want you.' He emphasised the word with a chuckle.

'I'm confused,' Sandro said, laying down the tondo.

'*Charity*, *Fortitude*, *Prudence* and the rest that you painted for the Tribunale della Mercanzia. We trust you'll do as well for our court as you did for theirs.'

Sandro wondered whether to admit that he could only claim *Fortitude* and that the other six virtues had been painted by Piero Pollaiuolo. But Piero was dead and, given the *Charity* he had manifested on the panel if not in person, he should not object to Sandro's reaping the reward. After arranging to meet the next day at the Podesta, Messer Donato departed, leaving Sandro to contemplate a project that filled him with a mixture of excitement and dread. The benefits were clear. It would replenish his purse and restore his reputation, banishing the cloud that had hung over him since the advent of the Friar. The subject, although an unusual one, had rich possibilities. He could already envisage the doomed city: no pagan temples, just churches and palaces, the flames that lapped the tumbling towers enhanced by a spot of oil in the yolk. Lot's wife's transformation would be as thrilling to effect as that of Chloris into Flora in his *Realm of Venus*. Nevertheless, he remained wary of an association with a tribunal before which, without the saving grace of his work, he might have appeared himself.

The story of Sodom was, understandably, not one that the priests had instilled in him as a boy. Eager to flesh out what was to him little more than a word or rather, an anathema, he made his way upstairs to borrow his brother's Bible. Simone's mistrust of his sudden interest in Holy Writ was only partially allayed by his report of Messer Donato's visit. Loath to let his treasured Bible out of his hands, let alone into the paint-splattered workshop, he offered to read aloud the passage in question. Although his dull delivery rendered the destruction of the city as humdrum as the preparations for the angels' supper, Sandro was taken aback by the ending, which he had either never known or else long forgotten, when Lot's two daughters seduced their father in the belief that he was the last man left on earth. Their action was doubly perverse after they had spent the previous night among the people – the men – of Zoar. But Simone, true to form, dismissed his objections, describing it as an act of heroic self-sacrifice designed to perpetuate the nation.

Returning downstairs, Sandro reflected on the girls' behaviour. He thought about Delfina, whose image had haunted him ever since he saw her last in the Mercato Vecchio, working to suppress the vice that was blamed for sapping the city's manhood and depleting its population. Whether she were driven by heroic self-sacrifice or, more likely, by desperation and poverty, he knew that he had found the pattern for Lot's daughters and leafed through his ancient drawing books to find the studies he had made of her in Verrocchio's shop.

The following morning he crossed the sombre courtyard of the Podesta, past the packed cells and up to the tribunal, where he stood like a prisoner behind the barriers while Messer Donato and two of his fellow Officers questioned him from the bench. Messer Donato, clearly regarding himself as the project's progenitor, displayed growing enthusiasm as Sandro outlined his scheme for each of the panels. His colleagues were more circumspect: one, who wheezed so heavily that Sandro trusted he was never called upon to pronounce sentence, stipulated that he undertake to paint all the figures 'men, women and angels' himself and not assign them to assistants; the other, smiling deceptively, that he make a cartoon of the first panel, 'to exhibit his manner and his discretion' before they paid any of his fee. They summoned the notary, who drew up the contract as though disappointed to be condemning Sandro to nothing more severe than a twelve-florin penalty should he fail to deliver the panels within the specified ten months.

Despite the pressure, Sandro was keen to complete the work (and receive the final payment) during the current magistracy, rather than trust to their replacements who might favour a different design or even painter. The contract signed, he took his leave of the Officers and returned home, where he made a series of preliminary drawings in chalk, which after initial reservations he found more serviceable than silverpoint. By the end of three weeks he had produced a full-size cartoon of Lot's meeting with the angels, which Messer Donato and his two fellows came to inspect. As they questioned him about colour and composition, he felt like a condottiere explaining his battle plan to the sedentary *Signoria*. Honour satisfied, they confirmed his appointment. For the first time in months, everyone in the shop was fully occupied: preparing the panels, pouncing the cartoon and shading the background, while he himself embarked on the underdrawing.

The work invigorated him but, however hard he tried, he could not escape the babble of the city and, like everyone else, he was gripped by the saga of Savonarola's excommunication. Given his challenge to the pope, it had been long expected, but the edict still came as a shock. On 18 June 1497, it was solemnly proclaimed in five of the city's main churches. Sandro accompanied his family to Santa Maria Novella to attend the doleful ritual when, first, a death knell was tolled; then, the great Bible was slammed shut; finally, two large candles were turned upside down and snuffed out. Many of the congregation, including Santi and Ildebrando pressed uncomfortably against Sandro's ribs, were openly weeping. Others gazed at the ground as though wary of betraying any emotion that might be held against them later.

During the following weeks, debate raged across Florence, officially in the Great Council and unofficially in every house, street and square, over Savonarola's right to preach. Eventually, the *Signoria* ruled that he was forbidden to speak in the cathedral but permitted to do so at San Marco. To Sandro's surprise, a man who had built his life on moral certitudes agreed to the compromise, and his Sunday sermons continued to draw vast crowds. Simone, whose faith in the Friar's rectitude had never wavered, invited Sandro to a service and, although he longed to work on the one day that the shop was not filled with the bleating and banter of his apprentices, he accepted. Despite having set off half an hour early, they arrived to find the church crammed and, as they passed through the women in the porch, Sandro was astounded to see Delfina, instantly recognisable, even in unfamiliar dress and after a gap of twenty years. Her presence was uncanny and he could not shake off the fancy, at once exhilarating and alarming, that he had conjured her up.

'I'll be with you in a moment,' he told Simone, 'there's someone I must speak to.'

'Who?'

'That woman over there. You don't know her.'

'I should hope not. She's indecent.'

'She's a nun!' Sandro said, trying to moderate his voice.

'A convertite. She might as well be wearing yellow gloves.'

'So much for Mary Magdalene! Excuse me, but I painted her once' – he felt it wiser not to mention that he was planning to do so again – 'and I'd like to pay my respects.'

He edged through a group of censorious women, one of whom poked him in the side, and reached Delfina, her skin as mottled and scarred as Fra Filippo's fingers, a few wisps of grey escaping from her wimple, and yet undeniably herself.

'Sandro,' he said. 'Do you remember me?'

'Should I?'

'I was an assistant in Maestro Verrocchio's shop,' he said, reluctant to remind her of their later, less cordial meeting. 'Does that help?'

'I used to model there. First I lost my modesty, then my maidenhead, then my position and my livelihood, until I had nothing.'

'But you've found God.'

'Have I?'

'Why else have you come to church?'

'You mean rather than spend another morning making lace, which the abbess has us toiling at from dawn to dusk to pay for our sins – and our keep – and to praise God for His infinite mercy?'

Sandro blushed.

'I was curious to see how the Friar deals with his own degradation.'

'Damnation.'

'That too. After all, he was the one who banned us from the streets and taverns and herded us into brothel-houses, which he then shut down. He calls us lumps of meat, but there was so little flesh on my bones that any man who visited me would have done as well to go to the graveyard. So I joined the Convertites.'

Looking closely, Sandro saw that she was still emaciated. 'Does your order require regular fasting?'

'Of necessity,' she said, with a laugh, 'not choice. We're not a rich order. Indeed, in the eyes of many we're not an order at all.'

'But you're recognised by the Church.'

'Tell that to these women.' She lowered her voice. 'Women who've wasted their lives being proper and resent us slipping into heaven through the back gate. Huh!' Her snarl startled her apple-cheeked neighbour. 'We make a little by our lace-work and embroidery, but most of our income has always come from court fines.'

'Surely, since the Friar took power those have increased?'

'I should have said "fines imposed by the Office of the Night". Having sanctioned our trade in order to stem the tide of sodomy, some ancient *gonfaloniere*, who must have had a sense of humour, decreed that those of us who abandoned it should be sustained by the fines on sodomites.'

'In other words, having renounced sin yourselves, you rely on others to sin on your behalf,' Sandro said, pondering the irony. 'It must make prayer very difficult.'

'Prayer is difficult,' she replied. A loud hush alerted them to the entrance of the friars. 'But it may be easier tonight.'

As the thurifer censed the congregation, Sandro moved away from the women, several of whom regarded him with suspicion, and joined the men. Unable to detect Simone in the array of hoods, he squeezed beside a young man who spluttered in the clouds of incense. The Mass proceeded without incident, until a storm of hallelujahs heralded Savonarola's arrival. He stumbled on the pulpit steps provoking a collective gasp, but recovered swiftly and addressed the people with a mixture of bitterness and defiance.

'I am the messenger of God. Believe me, it is not I who speak to you today but Christ.' Allowing his gaze to drift towards the altar, Sandro tried to work out how the Friar's assurance differed – as he knew that it did – from that of Fra Giovanni Angelico, who had maintained that God was in his brush. 'The Lord brought me here to proclaim His Word. Other cities in Italy know me only by report, but you, Florence, have heard the truth from my own lips. Woe betide you if you fail to heed it! Woe betide you if you yield me up to Rome! Just as the Lord delivered Lot from Sodom before He reduced it to rubble so, once I am gone, He will pour down tribulations on this wicked place.

'You may ask why I say this. How can I stay silent when I see blasphemy and abomination all around? And nowhere is it more manifest than in the Church. The Church that should be the light of the world plunges the world into darkness. The Church that should be the solace of widows and the defender of orphans ravishes the widows and sodomises the orphans. The high priests of Rome live in lust and luxury, passing their nights with their concubines and catamites and celebrating Mass the next morning. Rome, I tell you, will be wiped out like the cities of the plain. The sun will be shrouded and the sky will rain fire and brimstone until not a single house remains standing. The angels in heaven will rejoice at the destruction of such iniquity. And any one of you who looks back – any one of you who feels the least drop of pity for those miserable sinners – will be turned into a pillar of salt … no, not even a pillar, a heap of grains upon the ground.'

As the faithful invoked blessings on the Friar, Sandro mused on his own time in Rome, which lent credence to the litany of charges. He recalled the contrast between the purity of the light, which seemed to emanate from the gilded cupolas and bone-white columns, and the squalor of the streets. Crossing the Ponte Sant'Angelo, he had passed the corpses of executed criminals, their faces every colour but the one God had given them. The stench was foul, but it was nothing to the reek of corruption that issued from the Vatican and had clung to him down the years. Evidence of papal perversity swelled like the effluence in the Tiber. Laxity not piety was the path to preferment, as Sixtus raised compliant young men to the cardinalate, several of whom were his nephews. Those cardinals who were spared Sixtus's vice in their veins were equally venal: rank embodiments of the sins with which they shared a name. Worst of all, their depravity had licensed Sandro's. By day, he had worked diligently on the *Temptation of Christ* and the *Trials of Moses* for the pope's new chapel; by night, he had sought pleasure in the taverns and bathhouses of the Ortaccio. The Holy City became his Babylon until, by the time he left for Florence, desire had turned to disgust and he pledged himself to chastity – but a painter's chastity, not a friar's. He would honour the flesh, not deny it. Unlike Savonarola, whose hectoring cadences hammered at his brain, he acknowledged no dichotomy between passion and piety, poems and psalms, or Hadrian's and Peter's Rome. He would find unity – and sanctity – through his brush.

4

Although the air was so cold that the water in the buckets had frozen and the apprentices fought to fire the charcoal, Sandro was elated. His stiff joints made it increasingly hard for him to stand, giving him a valid reason to miss church, even when the preacher was less prolix than the Friar, but, once he was at the easel, every ache and pain vanished. After his busiest autumn and winter for a dozen years, he had completed two of the Sodom panels, with the third awaiting minor adjustments and only the fourth still in outline. Provided that the Carnival did not cause undue disruption, it would be ready by the middle of March. That was two weeks later than set out in the contract, but he was confident that, when they saw the paintings, the Officers would forgive the delay.

His first task was to redraw Lot's daughters, whose robes were far too neat for girls who had lately lain with their father. He crumpled the fabric on the clay model that displayed the drapery but, as he sketched the new folds, he realised that the true problem lay in the figures not the clothes. Dawdling, he scanned the room where the two finished panels were propped against the walls and the two others mounted on easels. His eyes rested on the third panel, where Bartolomeo di Giovanni was mottling the donkeys' flanks and Gianpiero shading the shattered columns of the Loggia. A man of few words, Bartolomeo had been his most trusted assistant since Rome, where he had painted the figure of Moses slaying the Egyptian in the pope's chapel. Three years ago he had set up on his own and last summer he had matriculated in the guild but, to his wife's fury, he had interrupted his own work to help Sandro.

Whereas Bartolomeo laboured diligently, Gianpiero was already in Carnival mode, his mind and brush constantly straying from the panel. In token of the imminent festivities, he sported a new pair of silk hose, a present from Doffo, the left leg plum-coloured and the right chequered, arousing Lioncino's admiration and Annibale's envy. They, meanwhile, worked together on the fourth panel: Lioncino, ever eager, underpainting the rocks; Annibale laying the gold for Lot's wife's robe.

'Will it be covered in red like the others?' he asked Sandro, who moved across to check on the precious metal.

'Why? Do you think she'd have changed her apparel in the desert?'

'It seems such a waste.'

'On the contrary. Look over there, where she's leaving the Signoria – if you can see past the dazzle of Gianpiero's legs.'

'No chance!' Gianpiero interjected.

'The robe has a warmth – a glow – that you'd never achieve with red alone, either lake or vermillion. I learnt that from Fra Filippo who learnt it from Maestro Uccello.'

'Who?'

'Piero Uccello. He died some twenty years ago … a great favourite of Lorenzo de' Medici or haven't you heard of him either?'

'I'm not stupid!'

'His work lacked harmony and was full of strange foreshortenings, but he was always generous to younger painters and ready to share his secrets.'

'I still say it's a waste.'

Sandro despaired of his apprentices' lack of curiosity, even about a painter whose work they could see in the Duomo and churches throughout the city. He suspected that if, by some miracle, Gianpiero, the most gifted of the three, should show a commitment equal to his talent and, forty years hence, mention something he had learnt from his master Botticelli, he would meet with similar bemusement or, worse, sniggers at the comical name. Dismissing the thought, he crossed the room to the third panel.

'That's far too dark!' he said, studying the columns. 'What happened to the colour I mixed?'

'I added more umber,' Gianpiero replied. 'I thought it looked better.'

'Your job is to paint, not think,' said Bartolomeo, who understood the meaning of *assistant*.

'How often have you walked through the square?' Sandro asked. 'Haven't you ever looked at the stone?'

'So? You always say that it's the effect of a picture, not its accuracy, that matters and that buildings are just a backdrop.'

'This time it's different.' Indeed, it was so different that, although his practice was to work by the eye alone, he had instructed Annibale to map out the grid lines on the ground.

'Why are you so keen to turn Florence into Sodom? Doffo says it's a betrayal.'

'You have no right to discuss your work with him or anyone else outside the shop.'

'Don't worry. It's not his conversation Doffo's interested in,' Annibale said.

'He called you the Friar's lackey.'

'That's absurd. When my brother asked me to sign the petition urging the pope to rescind Savonarola's excommunication, I refused.'

'Doffo said—'

'Did your father indenture you to Doffo or to me?' Sandro asked. 'Forgive me if I haven't seen fit to explain my intentions to you but, to clear up any confusion, I am not "turning Florence into Sodom". It happens to be where we live. If we lived in Siena, I'd have painted the piazza del Campo. Don't forget we're making these panels for a courtroom. The people who see them every day will be the magistrates and they won't be trying Sodomites but Florentines … that is the sodomites they try will be Florentine. Look at the victims strewn across the square! They're not the damned in an ancient Day of Doom, but men like you and me – and the magistrates themselves. Even Gabriel can't bring himself to witness their suffering. Don't you suppose that it might move the Officers to clemency?'

'Whatever you say,' Gianpiero muttered.

'And unless you mend your ways,' Sandro said, seizing the moment, 'you – and Doffo – might one day soon be grateful for it.'

Gianpiero fetched another shell and mixed a brown with more sienna. The altercation had concentrated all their minds and they worked without pause or complaint until dusk.

The following day they broke off at noon when Sandro gave them leave to prepare for Carnival: Bartolomeo returning to his wife and children; the three apprentices to their parents. Sandro himself intended to work. Having finally solved the problem of the daughters, he was amending the underdrawing – undoing the older girl's bodice and shading the blush of her breast – when the maid came to tell him that he had a visitor.

'What visitor?' asked Sandro, who had closed the shutters to prevent any such intrusion.

'He said you'd know if I told you his name was Dede … Dede … something.'

'Daedalus?'

'So you do know him?'

'No!' Sandro said, feeling his throat constrict. 'What sort of a man?'

'A gentleman. Very handsome, very charming. He made me a little bow. Which is more than you can say for his servant! Should I bring them down?'

'No!' The prospect of Leonardo – the allusion left no doubt as to his identity – appraising his work was unbearable. 'Are your master and mistress at home?'

'They've gone to San Marco with Signorina Crucifissa. The young masters are collecting vanities for the great fire.'

'Then I'll come upstairs.'

He followed the maid up to the hall where he found Leonardo, trimly bearded, elegantly coiffed and more extravagantly dressed than ever, as though he had stepped out of his own portrait.

'Good Lord!' Sandro said. 'How long has it been? Ten years? Twelve?'

'The only time that counts for an artist is eternity,' Leonardo said solemnly, before roaring with laughter and striding up to him. 'It's fifteen … fifteen and a half to be precise. I could tell you in months and days but I'd be lying. Come here, you dolt!' He clasped Sandro in a bone-crushing embrace. 'Still sticking to Saturday baths, I see.' He shoved him away with a shudder. 'And I hear you're permanently drunk.'

'Oh yes, and I'm married with seven children,' Sandro replied, affecting levity. He thought it politic not to offer him wine. 'Would you like some almond milk? Are you hungry? We have an excellent prosciutto.'

'I no longer eat meat. It's a sin to deprive animals of their nature.'

Sandro winced at the choice of word, which had to be deliberate since he might just as easily have said *life*. But then Leonardo had always cited nature to disconcert him. He claimed that, as the embodiment of God's perfect plan, it was the only subject worthy of a painter's craft. At the same time he sought to transform it with machines that moved mountains and drained rivers, and even to transcend it through his burning desire to fly. Was he trying to honour God or to supplant Him? As Sandro grappled with the question, the servant crouching malignly at his master's feet gave a loud yelp and leapt on to one of Ippolita's best chairs. Leonardo rebuked him with a warmth which suggested that the one nature he had yet to transcend was his own.

'Let me introduce my pupil, Gian Giacomo Caprotti, although his friends call him Salai.'

'Satan?' Sandro asked, wondering if the malice were in the youth or the friends.

'In person! A liar, a thief, a reprobate and a glutton,' Leonardo said, as though enumerating his virtues. 'Where are your manners, Salai? Salute a great artist.'

Unsure whether the past fifteen years had mellowed Leonardo or whether master and pupil were enjoying a joke at his expense, Sandro hesitantly held out his hand. Salai approached, only to ignore the greeting and run his fingers over Sandro's face.

'Is he blind?' Sandro asked, seeing the apprenticeship as the latest sign of Leonardo's caprice.

'We've been discussing whether the Ancient Greeks were right to say that a man's nature can be found in his face.'

'And have you decided?'

'What do you find, Salai?'

'Hot skin. Thick hair. Wrinkles round the lips and eyes. Too much blood. Much too much blood.'

Leonardo laughed as Sandro recoiled, both from the youth's peaty smell, which must have been a permanent affront to his fastidious master, and his insolent appraisal. He longed for a little of Leonardo's learning so that he might respond with a remark about Salai's own distinctive physiognomy: the tightly packed curls, heavy-lidded eyes and lack of any discernible bridge to his nose.

'I had no idea you were back,' he said, recovering himself. 'When you left for Milan, you insisted that it was a one-way journey; Florence was too small for you. Or was it too small-minded?'

'Both. And I can see it's got worse. The city is in thrall to a mountebank in a cowl.'

'So why have you returned?'

'It was less that I wanted to return here than that I had to leave Milan. I was working on the new apartments Ludovico – the Duke – has built over the castle moat when there was a misunderstanding with one of the apprentices.' Jiggling his thumb between his lips, Salai graphically illustrated its cause. 'Just a temporary setback,' Leonardo declared with his customary aplomb. 'But the Archbishop of Milan has been asked to use his influence to persuade Perugino to take my place. Part of my reason for coming is to urge him to decline. Remind him of our days together in Verrocchio's shop.'

'I doubt that'll help. You were forever disparaging him.'

'Was I? Was I really?' Leonardo's surprise sounded genuine. 'Then I'll just have to threaten that Salai here will break his arms.' Salai grinned and cracked his knuckles.

'Aside from this present setback' – Sandro was careful to use Leonardo's word – 'have you found work in Milan?'

'I'm Ludovico's chief military engineer. I've designed machines and weapons that will make him the most powerful man in Italy.'

'I meant pictures,' Sandro said, recognising Leonardo's habitual tactic. No doubt if he were talking to a military engineer he would emphasise his painting.

'Some. An altarpiece of the *Virgin and Child in a Cave* for the Church of San Francesco Grande. A fresco of *The Last Supper* for the refectory of Santa Maria delle Grazie.'

'Is it finished?' Sandro asked disingenuously.

'Almost. I'm having trouble with Christ's head. Come away from there!' He turned to Salai, who was warming his hands at the grate, admonishing him as though he were a boy of seven rather than a youth some ten years older. 'Like all his kind, he's drawn to fire.'

'And you don't find fresco too fast for you? Eternity's not much use if the plaster's set.'

'Mock all you like. But I'm working in oil.'

'Straight on to the wall?'

'Your problem, Sandro – one of your problems – is that

you stick to the rules. It's not enough to reproduce; you have to experiment. Now no more questions! As Salai can vouch, I hate talking about myself.' The youth looked at him incredulously. 'What about you? What have you been up to? No, you don't need to tell me. I went to see Lorenzo di Pierfrancesco.'

'I didn't know you knew him.'

'I don't. I carried a letter to him from the Duke. You don't think I came all this way just to twist Perugino's arm? He showed me your *Pallas and the Centaur* and *Realm of Venus*. You have been busy.'

'It's fifteen years! I wish you'd seen some of my sacred paintings,' Sandro said, drawing a distinction for Leonardo that he refused to draw for himself. 'There's a *Coronation of the Virgin* in San Marco, an *Assumption* in San Pier Maggiore, a *Pieta* in—'

'But I have seen them,' Leonardo said, thrilling Sandro with the thought of his most stringent critic roaming the city in search of his work. 'I saw them all in the face of your Venus. At any moment, she might have been lifted up from her realm to heaven – to sit beside the Father, Son and Holy Spirit, not Jupiter and Mars.'

'Is that a fault?'

'You tell me.'

'Then no. In different – very different – ways, Venus and the Virgin both bring forth the love that governs the universe. Just as there's a sadness in the Virgin who knows that she's dooming her son to suffering and death, so there's a sadness in Venus who knows that she's dooming mankind to heartache and rancour.'

'And have you received that gift of love, Sandro? Have you tasted the heartache and rancour?'

'You've seen the picture.'

'Other men sin and go to confession. You sin and do penance in paint.'

'You've lost me.'

'I recognised her in both Flora and the Graces.'

'Who?'

'Simonetta Vespucci, who else? You must admit it's odd that twenty years on you're still haunted by the lover of the man you loved.'

'An intrigue!' Salai interpolated with glee.

'Nonsense! Like everyone else in Florence, I admired Giuliano. He was an ideal – that's to say, an idealist. He pledged his heart to Simonetta, even though her loyalty to her husband dashed any hope of consummation. He worshipped her with a purity that someone like you will never understand. I can see him now in the tournament in Santa Croce, his silver armour glistening in the sun, bowing to Simonetta, exquisite in a green-and-red silk gown studded with pearls. And the standard he presented her with was painted by me.'

'Exactly. You're an artist who painted his colours, not a servant who wore them! What's more, it's Giuliano de' Medici we're talking about, not Savonarola. He may have pledged his heart to Simonetta, but nothing else. Or how do you explain the son born a month after his death and given a loophole legitimacy?'

'More intrigue!' Salai said.

'Silence! His Simonetta was a fantasy and yours, Sandro … yours is the fantasy of a fantasy.'

Even after fifteen years, Leonardo knew how to goad him. Relenting, Sandro invited him downstairs to see the Sodom cycle, proof of the audacity of his scheme and the reality of his sentiments.

'How can you of all people work for the Office of the Night? Or do you think it's a way to escape their notice?'

'There's nothing for them to notice.'

'No, I suppose not,' Leonardo replied coldly. 'You're the most daylight person I know.'

'I'm trying to do two things – come down and see! To boost their authority in the eyes of the Friar and to encourage – even inspire – them to clemency.'

'By depicting the annihilation of an entire city?'

'I thought of you while I was painting,' Sandro added, in an attempt to disarm him. 'Your two months in the Stinche.'

'What's the Stinche?' Salai asked.

'A prison,' Leonardo replied, to Salai's visible horror. 'Though it should be the Styx. Crossing its portals, you're plunged into Hades. The stench. The vermin. The squalor. The man chained to the wall beside you, two days dead of typhus. And the darkness – worst of all, the darkness. Being deprived of the most precious of the senses.' Salai squeezed his head through the crook of Leonardo's arm and nestled against his shoulder. 'That's why you must take care never to come before the courts.'

'Was it really as bad as that? I saw you the day you were released – or was it the day after? You came to the Mercato Vecchio to draw.'

'To draw, yes. Maybe now you understand?'

Sandro nodded hesitantly and led them down to the shop. He opened the shutters to so little effect that he lit three candles, handing one to Leonardo, keeping one for himself and placing one on the table, which was immediately seized by Salai, who took it over to the fourth panel. 'Ignore that,' Sandro said, 'it's not finished.' But even the barely sketched breast of the half-naked daughter excited the youth's lust – or his derision – and, licking his lips, he pressed his mouth to the panel, as though trying to taste the newly applied wash. As Leonardo laughed and gently chided him, Sandro understood the reason for his indulgence. He was not just his apprentice, servant and apparent bedfellow; he was the natural man that Leonardo acknowledged in himself but was forced to conceal.

Interrupting Salai's display, Sandro asked him to help lift the first panel. Leonardo stood back to assess the whole before stepping forward to inspect the detail, holding the candle to the surface like a merchant appraising a rug. As Salai's arms sagged, Leonardo, showing more regard for the painting than the painter, exhorted him to keep it still. He was rewarded with a savage scowl that Sandro was thankful had not been aimed at him. Brooking no complaint from Salai, Leonardo asked Sandro to show him the second panel. He reluctantly agreed, bracing himself for both the shooting pains in his side and the inevitable censure.

'I'm impressed,' Leonardo said, after several minutes of close study, almost causing Sandro to drop the panel. 'You've presented the Mercato Vecchio with great fidelity. You've caught the dignity and supplication of the ancient Lot. Which is no surprise since you've taken his attitude straight from my St Jerome.' Basking in a rare – almost unique – instance of Leonardo's praise, Sandro bit back the demurral that he had not looked at that painting since Leonardo left it unfinished in Verrocchio's shop on his departure for Milan. 'Your angels are paragons of grace and beauty. Your wife … Lot's wife' – he said sternly to a snickering Salai – 'is resplendent in her lustrous robe. But as ever, you reserve your finest effects for your maidens, standing modestly by the table, oblivious to the fateful offer that their father is making at the door. If I were a Sodomite – that's enough!' he said to Salai, whose snickers had become guffaws, 'I'd be tempted to accept it, if only to lift their perfectly rendered veils from their perfectly rendered breasts. You've put your heart and soul in these panels. You affirm and condemn yourself at the same time. They're good, Sandro … truly. I can't speak for the Officers of the Night – especially if they're as perverse as their predecessors – but I for one salute you.'

Relieving Salai of his burden, Leonardo helped Sandro to prop the panels against the walls and left with the promise to return after Carnival. Sandro contemplated the paintings in the light of his friend's comments, suddenly worried they might be misinterpreted. He stared at the dying Sodomites in the square until his eyes watered, but he found no answer. He stared into the shadows in the hope that they would concentrate his mind, but they merely unsettled it. He was roused by a deep curse and a loud cry as Doffo and Gianpiero stumbled into the shop.

'Don't be alarmed,' Sandro said. 'I'm not a ghost.'

'That's not what your friends say,' Doffo replied brusquely.

'Are you praying, Master?' Gianpiero asked.

'No, thinking.'

'You should have warned us.'

'How? By putting up a sign, like a fortune-teller in the market? Thinking from twelve till six.'

'He's mad,' Gianpiero said.

'Just drunk,' Doffo said.

'You're the second person to say that today.'

'You mean to your face! Come on, Gianni. Fetch what you came for.'

'Shouldn't you be with your parents?'

'I'm staying with Doffo,' Gianpiero replied, as he rummaged in the alcove.

'The rest of my family have gone to the country to escape Carnival. So we have the house to ourselves.'

'What about the servants?' Gianpiero asked. 'You said there'd be servants.'

'Don't worry, my sweet. There'll be servants to satisfy your every whim.'

'Tomorrow we've been invited to dinner in Parione. Each of the *Compagnacci* can take a guest. Guess who Doffo's taking!'

'Hurry up, Gianni, we don't have all night.'

'It's to celebrate liberty and sodomy.'

'Two very different things,' Sandro said.

'Not in Savonarola's Florence,' Doffo replied.

'When you reach my age, you'll see that yielding to passion – any passion – imprisons a man, body and spirit.'

'Your age! You said it. Your body's withered and rotten and stinks like the corpse it'll soon become,' Doffo said, with the full force of the scorn to which he had treated him ever since his contract with the Officers of the Night. 'Your pizzle dribbles and droops—'

'Let's go, Doffo. I've found what I need.' Gianpiero, carrying a handful of clothes, grabbed his arm.

Flicking him aside, Doffo held his dagger to Sandro's throat. For all his fear, Sandro felt a tingle in his blood.

'No!' Gianpiero shouted.

'You're too old for passion so you seek to deny it to everyone else. You're as bad as the Friar … worse. At least he's no hypocrite.'

'Nor am I!'

'No? Where was Venus when you agreed to destroy Sodom?'

'You misunderstand her; you misunderstand me.'

'I understand you all too well. Come here, Gianpiero!' The youth stood still. 'Now.'

Trembling, Gianpiero approached them. Doffo pressed him against Sandro's chest. 'Tell me you don't want him!'

'It will never happen,' Gianpiero said, breaking away.

'The hot mouth. The smooth skin. The welcoming hollows.'

'Not if he were the last man on earth,' Gianpiero said, putting Sandro in mind of Lot.

'I swear to you on my life … on the Bible … on everything I hold dear, that I have no desire for this boy.'

Gianpiero looked insulted.

'You're worse than a eunuch,' Doffo said. Then, releasing his hand and sheathing his dagger, he led Gianpiero out.

Sandro, for whom the thrill of the hold had blunted the threat of the blade, felt strangely empty. He was relieved at least to have kept his secret. Not even Leonardo, for all his cunning, had been able to wrest it from him. He might have confided in him once, but his contempt for the pilloried pathic had hurt him more deeply than the harshest punishment. For he too transgressed the natural order, as sacred to Leonardo as to Savonarola, which held not just that the woman served the man, but that the younger served the older, the smaller the larger, and the weaker the stronger. So he had looked upon his passions as a poison to be purged by his own hand. But what if those passions were no contagion but the core of his being? What if Marsilio Ficino had been right when he said at Careggi that men who desired other men were not rebels against heaven but governed by the heavens, being born under the conjunction of Venus and Saturn? What if his passions were neither unnatural nor blasphemous but subject to a rare planetary influence?

The thought was so exhilarating that he began to devise an allegory, its meaning open to a select few but its beauty plain to all. Venus, at her most serene, would lie with Saturn, the big-bellied god of the Golden Age. Unlike her tryst with Mars, she would not be watching over him but snuggling in his arms, and surrounded not by mischievous Cupids but by handsome men, the products of their union. The picture was so vivid that he downed a flagon of wine to keep from sketching all night. Passing out almost at once, he slept through the church bells and street cries, waking to the sound of hammering, which he took several minutes to locate. Sweeping the offending flagon to the ground, he staggered to the door and struggled with the latch, which was as stiff as he was. To his dismay, he found himself facing Messer Donato Davanzati; the Officer with the deceptive smile; and a third man whom he had never met, graced with the snowy hair and beard of St Bernard in Fra Filippo's *Adoration*.

'This is an honour, Messeri,' he said, turning sideways to spare them the blast of his vinegary breath. 'Was I expecting you?'

'We sent a messenger last week,' the white-haired Officer replied. 'Your brother's wife said she'd tell you.'

'It must have slipped her mind,' Sandro said, swallowing his anger. 'Is there something you want?'

'Naturally,' the Officer said. 'Do you mean to keep us standing here all day?'

'No, no, please come in.' Sandro stepped aside, running his hand through his hair as though that were enough to fit him for company. He threw open the shutters, to his instant regret. 'Forgive the mess. We've been working so hard we've not had a moment to clear up. But if any of you would care to take a stool.'

'No, thank you,' Donato said, his eyes resting on the flagon. 'Tomorrow is February the twenty-seventh.'

'Carnival,' Sandro said uneasily.

'Hence our visit. You're due to deliver the panels on the twenty-eighth. Last month, when you asked for the final instalment of the fee, you assured us there'd be no delay. So I presume they're ready?'

'As near as makes no difference,' Sandro said, forcing a smile. 'Two of them completely. Work like this can't be rushed.'

'Work can't be rushed,' the smiling Officer echoed flatly.

'Then please show us what you've done,' Donato said. 'Flatter our curiosity.'

'The cloths are up at the windows. The light's bad. The shop's not swept. Wouldn't you rather wait until you can see them in place?'

'You try our patience,' the white-haired Officer said.

'What's this?' Donato asked, gazing at the fourth panel.

'You're coming to them in the wrong order,' Sandro said, as all three Officers studied the figures. 'It begins with the panel behind you. If someone would help me lift it off the floor ...'

'The girl is naked,' Donato said, ignoring him.

'She has just seduced her father.'

'That wasn't in the drawing. I distinctly recall that she was asleep.'

'Asleep,' the smiling Officer echoed.

'Asleep after seducing her father,' Sandro replied. 'It was just a sketch. When I came to effect it, I couldn't believe she'd be able to sleep after such wantonness.'

'And who asked you to portray this wantonness?'

'You did.'

'One of us?' The white-haired Officer turned to his two companions, who shook their head aghast.

'You asked me to illustrate the story. And it's the conclusion … the climax. When Lot and his daughters shelter in the cave, they ply him with wine and—'

'We're educated men,' Donato said. 'We know what occurs.'

'Too well,' the white-haired Officer said.

'We didn't ask you to ornament the room according to your fancy,' Donato said, 'but to express the function of the court. Which is to hear cases of sodomy, not incest.'

'But this shows the final consequence of sodomy,' Sandro said, terror loosening his tongue. 'With the men doomed, the girls must sacrifice themselves to their own father to repopulate the world. Just as in Florence we've sanctioned brothel-houses to safeguard the city. So I modelled the daughters on one of the women—'

'You have put a harlot on our walls?' Donato asked.

'She's a Convertite.'

'He has placed a harlot on our walls,' the smiling Officer said faintly.

Entreating the Officers to examine the story in sequence, Sandro pressed each of them in turn to help him hold the panels. As he strained to keep up his end, the pain in Sandro's right shoulder grew so acute that he failed to catch several of their questions, irritating them further. While admitting his skill, they took issue with his choices, even though, according to the contract: 'The distribution of the figures, their manner and attitudes are to be left to the painter's discretion.'

'You've made the Sodomites as harmless as rustics at a fair,' Donato said. 'You've made David, the symbol of the city's liberty into the symbol of its lust. You've made Gabriel avert his eyes from his own righteous retribution. You've made Lot's wife a second Rachel weeping for her children. And you have made us a laughing stock in the eyes of the entire magistracy.'

Listening to the tirade, Sandro felt his arms grow numb and the panel fall on his foot. 'Take care!' cried the white-haired Officer, whose warning sliced through the pain to give him hope, since such concern implied that they did not intend to reject the panels, let alone demand the return of the fee. And so it proved. They gave him two weeks to make the requisite changes, which they promised to put in writing that afternoon. As he meekly assented to all their demands, he concluded that his discretion was as worthless as his honour. Henceforth, Doffo's contempt would be justified.

With a mere fortnight's grace, there was no time to lose and he fetched charcoal and paper to begin the revised drawings. First, he poured a cup of wine to dull the pain in his bones and the shame of his compliance, but the drink was slow to take effect and, after seven or eight cups, he found that he had wasted the entire day, the squiggles and swirls on his page like Chaos before Creation. He was sitting stock-still at the table when Santi burst into the shop.

'You must help me, Uncle,' he said, in rare acknowledgement of their relationship. 'It's Ildebrando. He's been taken.'

'Who by? What do you mean?' Sandro asked, struggling to clear his head.

'It's my fault. I promised to look after him. He's only fifteen.'

'What happened? Where? Would you like . . .?' Sandro glanced at the flagon. 'No, of course not.'

'We were walking through Baldracca, searching out any last vanities for tomorrow's bonfire—'

'You should know better than to go there.'

'What's the good of only visiting reputable districts? Christ dwelt among sinners.'

'You're not Christ.'

'But Fra Girolamo—'

'Nor is Fra Girolamo. Tell me what happened.'

'We were attacked by a gang of men. I don't know if they were *Bigi* or *Arrabbiati*; all I know is that they hate the Friar.

They tore the crosses off our necks. They said they were sorcerer's charms and we were casting spells on the city.' He started to cry.

'Was it just you and Ildebrando?'

'No, there were two others,' Santi said snuffling, 'but they managed to escape. You must help me find him. What if they kill him? How can I tell Father and Mother? I promised to take care of him.'

'They know you were doing … doing your best. Come on, I'll take you upstairs.' Sandro tried to stand, only to discover that he was unable to move. His head hit the table and looking up, he saw a trio of Santis, as though he had made a series of portraits but all with the same expression: disgust.

'You're drunk!'

'How can you tell? Or are you a secret sot?' Sandro laughed, spilling his cup in his lap. But as a sticky warmth seeped through his hose, he realised with horror that it was not just wine.

'Stop it!' Santi shouted, as Sandro's laughter grew wilder. 'You're damned!' Stupefied, Sandro watched from the corner of his eye as his nephew fled the room.

The table was hard and rough but surprisingly comfortable, as he lay devoid of all sense but touch. Suddenly, he was aware of more liquid, cold and sharp, which scratched his face like slivers of glass. He opened his eyes to find Simone leaning over him with a pail of water. Sobriety returned in an instant, as his brother explained that Ildebrando had come home, his face bruised and battered, his clothes tattered and torn, and his backside bleeding. He had been violated by four or five men – he had lost count – in the Campanile.

'The Campanile?' Sandro asked, striving to make sense of it.

'What does the place matter?' Simone asked. But sitting up and rubbing the sleep from his eyes and the water from his face, Sandro knew that it mattered a great deal. Disdaining the dark alleys, empty stables and secluded gardens, they were as intent on making perversity a part of their pleasure as the pope when he debauched his own nephews, or the nephews themselves when they abandoned their whores and mistresses to ravish respectable Roman wives.

Hit by a wave of nausea, he grabbed the pail and retched, emitting nothing but a trickle of bile. 'Where is he now?' he asked.

'In bed. His mother's attending to him.'

'Is he very hurt?'

'In ways he'll never comprehend.'

'And Santi?'

'Crucifissa's with him. He's taken it very badly.'

'Fetch me my hammer!'

'Don't be ridiculous! You've no idea who they are. Look at you! You can barely stand.'

'No. Not for the attackers. I'll leave them to the court. Ha! For my pictures.' The Officers' cavils paled beside the true objections to his reclamation of the Sodomites. 'I know what I must do.'

'You're raving! I was talking about Ildebrando. Have you understood a word I've said?'

'Oh yes, I've understood now what I should have done a long time ago. Those men weren't born under Venus and Saturn but Venus and Satan.'

'What?'

'You never approved of my making the panels for the Office of the Night, did you?'

'Since when did you care a jot about my approval?'

'Since now. I should have refused them. If the Officers want to resist the Eight of Watch, let them pass stricter penalties … let them bring down the full force of the law – God's law, as he revealed it in Sodom. I want no part in moving them to mercy. I shall be no apologist for sin.'

'I'm lost. Are you planning to assault the Officers?'

'No, the panels!' Sandro said, ascribing his brother's obtuseness to shock. 'They're good for nothing but firewood – bonfire wood. Is the pyre in the Signoria built?'

'Haven't you seen it? It's seven tiers high. They say that it's bigger than last year.'

'Now it's going to be bigger still.'

'But you can't get near it. It's surrounded by guards.'

'Don't you know them?'

'Some of them, I expect.'

'Then surely you can ask them to let us through? There must be room for more vanities.'

'There's always room for more vanities.'

'From the vainest painter in Florence. They're too heavy to carry. I'll break them up.'

'No, we'll borrow Nencio's cart,' Simone said, with an enthusiasm that Sandro distrusted despite its expedience. 'They need to be seen in order to have the most effect. Ildebrando will bless his violation if it leads you to the light.'

'No, to the fire. I've stared into the inferno. Better that my pictures should burn than my soul!'

5

The Friar had redefined Carnival as a season in Lent. For most of Sandro's life, the weeks from Epiphany to Ash Wednesday had been given over to riot and revelry in preparation for the forty days of abstinence ahead. Men and women would gather around bonfires in the squares to dance, sing and carouse, as in the *Festival of Pan* Sandro painted at Careggi. Boys would build barriers across the entrances to their neighbourhoods and exact a toll from everyone who passed. Rival gangs would attempt to demolish them, provoking violent clashes that sent sober citizens scurrying indoors. But on Carnival Tuesday, even the mildest of them would don masks and line the streets to watch the elaborate parade of wagons on which guildsmen displayed their wares, youths portrayed legendary warriors, tumblers performed tricks, and buffoons sang bawdy songs.

Savonarola had long attacked such antics as ungodly and, from the first Carnival of his ascendancy three years earlier, he had sought to suppress them. He took the most unruly element, the boys, and put them at the heart of his reform, instructing them to build altars in place of barriers where, rather than menacing passers-by, they entreated them to pray with them and, rather than extorting money, they solicited alms for the poor. He combined the local bonfires into a central one in the piazza della Signoria, which rose thirty *braccia* high. Moreover, instead of decorating it with a few tokens of the pleasures to be given up for Lent, he enjoined the boys to range the city, demanding that people hand over the various 'vanities' that he condemned as Satan's snares. These were not just the usual perfumes, jewels and mirrors, masks, dice and playing cards, but musical instruments and scores, manuscripts and books, ancient sculptures and, as his nephews took great delight in telling him, two copies of Sandro's *Venus*. They even coerced an old woman into relinquishing her false teeth, insisting that she had no right to put back what God had taken from her. Then on the day itself, the gnarled, grotesque figure of Carnival came forward to concede defeat and beg the crowd's forgiveness. After the pyre was set alight, women and girls crowned with olive wreaths danced around it in a state of ecstasy, which, to Sandro's eyes, looked little different from the intoxication of the past.

With the panels loaded on the cart, he and Simone entered the square at dawn to find a monstrous figure, either Carnival or the Devil, perched on top of the seven-tiered pyre. They were intercepted by two guards, who had received warning of an *Arrabbiati* attack. But the name of Botticelli – the *Piagnone* rather than the painter – wielded influence and they were permitted to pass. On reaching the pyre, Simone explained that each of the tiers represented one of the deadly sins, and Sandro considered whether his vanities were better suited to Pride or Lust. In the event, he had no choice but to wedge them in the tightly packed bottom layer, between a chess table and a carpet and on copies of the *Decameron* and the *Poetics*. Catching sight of the latter, Sandro wondered whether he might have been overhasty and ought to retrieve the panels, however scratched and split. But grabbing one of the struts, he found it as rigid as a wall. As if privy to his doubts, Simone reminded him that St Paul himself had presided over the burning of books at Ephesus, and St Gregory had ordered pagan statues to be smashed in Rome.

In the early afternoon Sandro returned to the square, which was now crammed with people, although the fervour of past years had been replaced by disquiet. He gazed at the Palazzo, the rough-hewn, russet-stoned bulwark of his liberty, with its sinister, serrated parapet behind which stood the eight

Signoria, resplendent in their crimson coats, grouped around the *gonfaloniere*, who was further distinguished by his gold embroidered stars. The procession was delayed and the spectators grew restive. Sandro, never at ease in crowds, searched for a quick escape-route in case of trouble, fixing on the same alley beside the Tettoia dei Pisani down which he had sent Lot. Rumours of a pitched battle between the *Piagnoni* and *Arrabbiati* on Ponte Santa Trinita, which had left dozens drowned, were supplanted by reports of brief skirmishes at makeshift barricades. Finally the procession reached the square, headed by four young boys dressed as angels, bearing a statue of the Christ-child, one hand raised in blessing and the other clasping the Cross. Four companies, each several hundred strong, followed behind the standards of their respective quarters. First came the boys, next the men, then the girls, and finally the women. All were barefoot, clad in white, and garlanded with olive leaves, their stained robes and ragged wreaths the only sign of the earlier scuffles. Some held candles, few of which remained lit, and all sang psalms.

Even the most fervent opponent of the Friar could not fail to be moved by the purity of their voices and the strength of their devotion. Sandro, aware that by adding his panels to the pyre he was making a commitment he had hitherto resisted, felt a tingling in his eyes, which he chose to attribute to fatigue. When the Santa Maria Novella company drew close, he failed to spot Santi in the serried ranks of the boys, but he did see Simone striding resolutely among the men and Crucifissa trudging glumly among the girls, as though her thoughts were with Ildebrando, hurt at home. The procession was due to circle the square and proceed to the Duomo but, to forestall further disruption, the *Signoria* had ruled that the bonfire should be lit at once. So the marchers assembled around the pyre, which, in Savonarola's absence, was blessed by Fra Domenico. Twelve youths, three from each company, stepped forward with burning torches and ignited the kindling. Trumpets sounded and the *Vacca* tolled lugubriously, but even that could not muffle the jeers and ribaldry, previously unthinkable, which rose from sections of the crowd. For several minutes nothing could be seen but a faint glow and the odd wisp of smoke. One of the boys approached Fra Domenico and, although they were too far away for Sandro to hear, his gestures suggested that he was seeking permission to light it again. Fra Domenico shook his head, and his confidence was rewarded by a burst of flames at the base. The faithful sang the Te Deum, not faltering when three masked men broke through the guards and poured a sack of black powder on to the blaze, which filled the vicinity with a noxious, garlicky stench.

Sandro fixed his eyes on his panels, resolved to watch until they were reduced to ashes. But with so many vanities to burn, the crowd around him began to lose interest. The occasional excitement, as when a melting clavichord hurtled to the ground and a glass ball exploded, failed to check the growing exodus. Only the faithful seemed set to remain, clasping hands and singing hymns, until the diabolic figure above the pyre was consumed in his own corruption. Sandro returned home, where his sense of emptiness was compounded by the desolation of the shop. He sought the only comfort he knew but restricted himself to four cups, so as to be fully alert when he faced Bartolomeo and the apprentices in the morning.

Having promised Simone to conceal Ildebrando's shame and reluctant to reveal his own contribution to the bonfire, he came up with the story that, distraught at the Officers' rejection of the panels, he had destroyed them. Responding to the expressions of outrage (Gianpiero), incredulity (Annibale), horror (Lioncino), and resignation (Bartolomeo), he lavished praise on each of their efforts and assured them that he had never before failed to fulfil an order (he could not afford to, he added, in a vain attempt to raise a smile). He was not like his friend Leonardo, who dithered over a *Last Supper* because he felt unequal to depicting Christ's sacred countenance, which had been the stock-in-trade of every Florentine painter since Cimabue. He had done his best – they all had – but he was forced to agree with the Officers that his sympathies were at odds with the subject.

At any other time he would have shut the shop, but his apprentices had just had two days' leave for Carnival. So he set them to work, sweeping the floors, scrubbing the walls and clearing the chicken coop, scouring the models and mussel shells, and salvaging the sketches for future use: Lot for St Joseph or St Augustine; the donkey for a *Flight into Egypt* or an *Entry to Jerusalem*; the angels for any number of celestial scenes. Meanwhile, having called Bartolomeo for an interview that he dreaded almost as much as the one he must seek with the Officers of the Night, he was greatly relieved when the assistant announced that he wished to quit of his own accord, explaining that Lausanna di Noldo Sassetti, for whom he had painted a bedstead of nymphs to Sandro's design, had ordered a *Madonna and Child* for her pregnant sister. He had said nothing earlier for fear that Sandro would insist on releasing him before the panels were finished, but there was no longer any reason to delay.

Sandro was deeply touched by his solicitude and even more so when Bartolomeo asked if, rather than the four florins due to him, he might take the cartoon of Lot's daughters.

'Gladly. Make use of it in any way you choose! But what will Palmina say?'

'She'll call me a fool and then tell me she loves me,' Bartolomeo replied, and Sandro had rarely felt so alone.

The apprentices too paid him a tribute of sorts by refusing to believe that the Officers of the Night had rejected the work, speculating instead that he had sold it to one of the papal envoys, in Florence to demand the surrender of the Friar. By their account, the man had chanced upon the shop on his way to the Ognissanti and been so captivated by the panels that he had offered Sandro twice his original fee. He had of course accepted but dared not admit it for fear of offending the Officers. Finding their fantasies less fatiguing than their questions, Sandro made no attempt to disabuse them. The empty coffers would do that soon enough. Meanwhile, they had one outstanding order to fulfil: the design for a tapestry of *Pallas* for Guy de Baudreuil, abbot of Saint-Martin-aux-Bois in Burgundy. He had seen the *Pallas and the Centaur* when he visited the city in King Charles's retinue and now requested a figure of the goddess alone, since even chastened sensuality had no place on an abbey wall.

Moreover, two days after Carnival, he received a summons from Lorenzo di Pierfrancesco himself, from whom he had heard nothing since Piero's flight. It was as if he had abandoned his former life along with his name, spending much of the past three years sequestered in his villas at Castello and Caffagiolo, not even sending Sandro the customary gift of wild game. Yet there was no denying the warmth of his welcome as he ushered him into his study and informed him that the Friar's support was dwindling daily both among the populace and in the *Signoria*, where the *Arrabbiati* had a majority for the first time. While flattered by the confidence, Sandro failed to see how it concerned him until Lorenzo explained that he wanted to mark the occasion with a new work. With the Friar in the ascendant he had been unable to turn his mind to beauty, but his mood had changed in line with that of the city. Sandro, excited but apprehensive at the thought of another large piece, was first relieved, then disappointed and then excited again when he requested an illustrated edition of Dante.

The characteristically generous fee of thirty florins each for the *Inferno* and *Purgatorio* and forty for the *Paradiso* (an earthly as well as a heavenly reward) would not only sustain the shop but help to reimburse the Officers of the Night. Sandro returned to give the good news to the apprentices, who were less enthusiastic than expected, no doubt because the small scale meant that he would work on it alone.

'No wonder you're happy,' Gianpiero said, 'condemning more sodomites to hell.'

'Not just sodomites,' Sandro replied. 'All sinners.'

He immersed himself in the poem in an effort both to formulate his drawings and silence the growing clamour of the city. But the challenge of an ordeal by fire, issued to Savonarola by his arch-rival, the Franciscan monk, Francesco da Puglia, drowned out even Dante. Savonarola ignored it, but hundreds of his supporters professed their eagerness to accept it on his behalf, chief among them his most devoted disciple, Fra Domenico da Pescia. So, despite the misgivings of both the Great Council and the *Signoria*, the ordeal was sanctioned. Sandro was appalled that two such learned men should seek to resolve their differences in a manner that had been discredited by the time of Giotto. It was as if Petrarch and Boccaccio, Masaccio and Brunelleschi, Cosimo and Lorenzo, Donatello, Verrocchio and Fra Filippo had never lived. Surely, fifteen hundred years after the birth of Christ, God's will could be established in less barbaric ways? In the event, moments before the fires were lit, God made His displeasure felt by raising a thunderstorm, which drenched not only the participants, officials and spectators but also the specially constructed platform, piled with logs and brushwood.

The rain fell on both factions alike, but it was the Friar who fared the worst, since his enemies, scenting blood, pressed home their advantage. The next morning, a gang of youths stoned his representative, Fra Mariano, as he left San Marco to preach the Psalm Sunday sermon in the Duomo. His reception there was equally hostile. According to Gianpiero, who attended the service in order to catch a glimpse of Doffo, the *Compagnacci* repeatedly heckled him before engaging in fist fights with some of the bolder *Piagnoni*. The uproar continued throughout the day, with the houses of leading *Piagnoni* ransacked and several of the owners killed. A terrified Ippolita put on the embroidered sleeves she had not worn since arriving in Florence and begged Sandro, who had regained some of his Medicean status, to intercede on the family's behalf.

In the early evening, a fellow *Piagnone* brought Simone the news that the *Compagnacci* were marching on San Marco. Simone, more agitated than Sandro had ever known him, resolved to rush to its defence, until the friend repeated the *Signoria*'s proclamation that any layman found within the convent's walls would be charged with sedition and hanged. In an attempt to reassure him, he added that the friars had amassed a large cache of weapons. Dumbfounded, Sandro declined to join the family prayers, retreating to the shop, where his dismay at finding that Annibale and Gianpiero had defied the curfew increased with Lioncino's disclosure that they had gone to watch the attack. Reflecting on the irony that the Florentines had more to fear from one another than they had ever had from the French, Sandro sought solace in his flagon. He was roused by the roar of explosions and the crackle of gunfire. With Lioncino shivering at his side, he stood in the shop doorway as smoke billowed over the rooftops and a crimson glow suffused the sky. He dismissed Lioncino's fears that they would be murdered in their beds with a gruff 'In that case we may as well get a good night's sleep first.' After dispatching the boy to his pallet, he slumped at the table, exhaustion vying with concern for the two apprentices. Sometime before dawn, Annibale returned, flushed from both the defeat of the friars and the wine he had pillaged from their cellar.

'We won,' he said, swaying on the doorpost. 'Savonarola's been captured. Soldiers dragged him off to jail. You should have seen it. He was punched and kicked. His arm was twisted. I was close enough to spit on him. Me! Myself! I spat in his face.'

'That was brave of you.'

Annibale sank into a stupor. Gianpiero arrived an hour later, his elation tempered only by his failure to reach Doffo whom, in one of his wilder fantasies, he had installed as the new ruler of Florence with himself as his consort. Savonarola, meanwhile, was imprisoned in the bell-tower. The pope, sensing victory, demanded his rendition to Rome, which the *Signoria*, eager to assert their autonomy, resisted. Instead, they appointed seventeen commissioners to preside over his interrogation, one of whom, in the closest he came to fulfilling Gianpiero's hopes, was Doffo.

Elsewhere in the city, old scores were settled. Sandro, wrestling with the intricacies of Dante's imagery, was disturbed one evening by the sounds of a scuffle overhead. Hurrying upstairs, he found Lotto Lotti, a notorious felon, his dagger at Simone's throat, threatening to murder him for having endorsed his uncle's execution. With unexpected eloquence and a pledge that Simone would pay him twenty florins reparation, Sandro succeeded in placating him. Simone, fearing a second visit, fled with Ippolita and their children to Bologna, assuring Sandro that they would soon be back, since 'God will not let Florence fall once again into the hands of idolaters.'

After escorting them to the Porta San Gallo, Sandro returned to the shop, where he was intercepted by Gianpiero. 'They're lucky to have got away,' he said. 'One word from me and they'd have been rounded up and thrown in the Podesta.'

'I thank you on their behalf,' Sandro said, feeling almost as sorry for Gianpiero as for Simone. Misery had made him vindictive. Not only had his hopes for a part in Doffo's victory come to naught, but the recently appointed commissioner had apprised him that with his new responsibilities, he was renouncing his old ways.

The law took its course and Savonarola was sentenced to death, along with Fra Domenico and another close associate, Fra Silvestro Maruffi. While a few loyal *Piagnoni* decried the injustice, the majority of Florentines rejoiced. On the eve of the executions, the city was in festive mood. Balladeers composed songs recounting the Friar's crimes. Tumblers and dancers performed in the squares. People took to the streets in whatever finery they had saved from the fire. Finding the merriment unseemly, Sandro returned home, planning to spend the morrow indoors, but at eight o'clock a mixture of compassion, curiosity and the desire to bear witness drew him to the piazza della Signoria. Passing through the Mercato Vecchio, he saw a crippled Convertite nun begging for alms. He was about to cross the street when he remembered Delfina, whom he had encountered in the selfsame spot, in the garb of a very different calling, when he and Leonardo attended the pillorying of the sodomite. As he approached, he grew increasingly convinced that it was Delfina herself and addressed her by name, only to be rebuked in a voice as dry and cracked as her face.

'I am Suor Celestina, Signor. Spare me a few *soldi*.'

Unsure if the error were his or if she had been given a new name in the convent, he declined to press her. 'You are ill.'

'They call it the French boils. I don't know why. I have racking pains in every bone and pustules all over my skin, but mostly in my place of sin. Just a few *soldi* ...'

'You should be in bed.'

'The abbess sent me out to beg. The convent has nothing. We're living on dried figs and bread made of oak bark. Many of the sisters have died. Now that they're hanging the Friar, maybe men will feel free to sodomise again. They'll be fined and we shall have food.'

Disturbed by the connection, Sandro emptied his purse into her bowl. He recalled the youthful beauty he had confined to the flames and felt as if he had done her as great a wrong as the men who had defiled her and the Friar who had starved her.

He made his way into the piazza della Signoria where the ceremony of degradation had begun. The steps of St Cecilia afforded him an excellent vantage point from which to watch the three friars being stripped of their vestments, their heads, faces and hands symbolically shaved, while a bishop intoned the charges of heresy and schism. They were then led before the papal envoy, who proclaimed that the pope in his mercy had granted them a plenary indulgence and, to Sandro's surprise, all three signalled their readiness to accept it. Finally, they were delivered to the *Signoria* for sentencing, a mere formality given the gallows that dominated the square. Having been publicly condemned, they were ushered up to the scaffold, barefoot and in thin white shifts, so that from a distance they resembled three of their boys. First Fra Silvestro, then Fra Domenico, and finally Fra Girolamo were hanged. 'Why are there no last words?' a man beside Sandro exclaimed, as Savonarola stepped up to the noose. 'I've been waiting here three hours. Don't I deserve a speech?' But the Friar's hopes of a dignified death were dashed by the hangman, who yanked the rope around his neck, jerking his body as in some travesty of the dancing he had proscribed. The hangman then climbed down the long ladder to light the bonfire that was to consume the three choking, flailing bodies. But before he reached the ground, a man with a blazing torch broke through the cordon and set fire to the kindling, shouting 'At last I can burn the man who would have burnt me.'

In the following weeks the city ran amok, as though to make up for the three lost years of Carnival licence. Nothing was sacred. One gang filled holy-water stoups with filth and burnt a rancid resin in thuribles. Another stole the crown from the statue of the Virgin Mary in San Marco and placed it on a harlot whom they led in triumph through the streets. Woodcuts of Savonarola sodomising novices in both the mouth and the anus were plastered on church walls. Sandro pondered whether his sensibilities or his craft were the more offended, and he hankered for the days when they were the same.

One evening he was working late on the *Inferno*, soothed

by the gentle snores of Annibale and Lioncino as he sketched the panders in the eighth circle, when Gianpiero staggered through the door.

'Where have you been?' Sandro asked as the youth righted himself, cheeks red, eyes glazed and hose smeared with dirt.

'With Doffo,' Gianpiero replied, as if daring Sandro to challenge him.

'Your father entrusted you to my care. I give you fair warning. If you don't mend your ways, I'm sending you home. For your own sake as well as Annibale's and Lioncino's.'

'What's it to do with them?'

'It's not good for them to see the way you behave.'

'I can't help it if I'm appreciated.' He pranced round the room swaying his hips.

'Is that all you think you're worth? I've told you before, you have a fine talent and it's not in your arse.'

'Oh yes! I should spend my time imitating you and end up what? A destitute drunkard whom no one respects and no one wants.' He thrust his buttocks in Sandro's face, exuding an odour of the tavern and something more earthy. 'I sometimes think I should give it you just once, so you know what you're missing.'

'There was a time when I was very like you.'

'Don't insult me!'

'If only you knew how soon your charms will fade.'

'Then paint me – you know you want to. Paint me before we're both too old. David … the young St John the Baptist … an Antinous to outshine your Venus.'

'Or St Sebastian,' Sandro said, as a plan took shape in his mind.

'You just want to see me naked.'

'I've seen you naked.'

'Only at the baths. Not at night when we're alone.'

'You mean now?'

'Why not? You're still working. Or are you too tired, old man?'

'No, I'm wide awake,' Sandro said, conscious that if he were to effect the plan, he should give himself no time to reconsider. 'I need to tie you up.'

'What?'

'For the line of the arms. I had such trouble with my first St Sebastian. Wait there!' He brought out the rope that they had used to secure the panels on Nencio's cart. 'Take off your doublet and shirt.'

'Not my hose?' Gianpiero asked, teasingly.

'Just the top will do.'

As Gianpiero fumbled with his shirt, it was clear he was so intoxicated that only a scoundrel would take advantage of him – and Sandro feared that several had. When he finally slipped it off, Sandro bound his wrists tight, feeling him wince even while insisting that it was painless. He led him to the door, where he tied him to the lintel. 'There,' he said, stretching his clammy arms above his head. 'Now relax. First, you'll need this.' He rolled up a paint-stained rag and held it to Gianpiero's mouth.

'Why? You're not going to use real arrows?'

Sandro laughed with a mixture of joy and despair at his vestigial innocence. 'Don't worry. But the pose may hurt and we don't want to wake the others.' He thrust the rag into Gianpiero's mouth and knotted it around his head, before leaving the room to fetch his razor. The youth's eyes widened in terror on his return. 'There's been a change of plan. Something you said long ago has convinced me you'd make the perfect Samson.' Without further ado, he began to cut through the opulent curls. After the initial shock, Gianpiero squirmed and kicked as Sandro hacked at the hair, which was coarser than in his paintings. He avoided all but one kick, which caught him hard on his shin. After responding with a sharp slap, he put his hand on the youth's neck, holding him fast as he lopped off the locks. Tears welled in Gianpiero's eyes, snot dripped from his nose and his tongue clucked as he continued to resist, causing Sandro to nick his ear. 'Take care,' he said, as a bead of blood formed. 'No, it's only a flesh wound. And I've saved you from so much worse.' He paused for a draught of wine. 'It's thirsty work,' he said to the youth, whose eyes blazed with hatred. He continued to cut, reaching Gianpiero's scalp, where he wielded the razor more delicately. 'Don't worry. I shan't give you a tonsure.' He stood back to admire his handiwork. 'It's a little uneven, but you can always ask Annibale or Lioncino to trim it, since I doubt you'll trust me. And I know it'll grow, but by then I hope that you will have done too. You'll realise that I haven't destroyed your beauty but helped you to find a truer one.' He moved to pull off Gianpiero's gag, only to be rewarded with a knee in his groin so violent that he could barely suppress a yelp. He limped to the table and drained a cup of wine. 'It's your own fault; I'm going to leave you there until you calm down.' He poured another cup to numb the pain.

The next thing he knew, it was morning. He was shaken awake by Lioncino, his face filled with reproach. Taking a moment to adjust, he turned abruptly to the door, but there was no sign of Gianpiero nor a single lock of hair on the floor. Lioncino told him sombrely that Gianpiero and Annibale had left, stealing two candlesticks, two drawing books and a shell of Venetian blue. Affecting indifference, Sandro assured him that they would soon be back. In the meantime, he urged him to make the most of their absence since, while he drew the illustrations to the *Divina Commedia*, Lioncino would work on *Balaam's Ass* for the Compagnia del Vangelista.

Lioncino's enthusiasm exceeded his skill, so Sandro himself had to pounce the cartoon, which would have been a simple task for Gianpiero, Annibale or any number of past apprentices. Nevertheless, he was confident that in time he would be able to train him. His tranquil presence was, moreover, a boon after the tumult of recent months. Then, three days after Gianpiero and Annibale's flight, when Sandro was increasingly perturbed at having heard nothing from either of their fathers, he received a visit from the Sergeant of the Office of the Night.

As he led him in, he insisted that there must have been a mistake, since the Officers had agreed to defer his first repayment of thirty florins for six months. Silencing him with a gesture, the Sergeant handed him a writ.

'Alessandro di Mariano di Vanni,' he said, addressing him by a name that in other circumstances would have been welcome. 'You are hereby summoned to appear before the tribunal of the Office of the Night on Tuesday next to answer the accusation of Gianpiero di Carlo that, on the evening of the eighteenth of June 1498, you did bind and gag him against his will and seek to commit an act of vile sodomy upon his person.'

FOUR

The Salt Mountain

'Take care, do not gaze at beardless youths, for
they have eyes more tempting than houris.'

Muhammad, *The Arabian Nights*

So far I have addressed myself primarily – but not, I trust, exclusively – to those of you who know me as Gabriel. Now I wish to compensate by favouring those who know me as Jibril, the angel whom Allah chose to reveal His holy book to His Prophet. I did so first on Laylat Al-Qadr, the Night of Power, visiting him as he kept vigil in the Cave of Hira. I asked him to read and when he replied that he could not, I clasped him to my breast and taught him to recite. Over the next twenty-three years, I recited the entire Qur'an to him, verse by verse and sura by sura, and, although he sometimes heard my words like a muffled bell, by his death he had them by heart.

There are those who doubt Muhammad's illiteracy, insisting that he overstated his ignorance in order to protect the divine provenance of his revelation. I, however, refuse to believe that he misled me in the least particular and I remind the sceptics that he learnt about Christianity from the monks he met on the caravan routes in Syria and about Judaism from the merchants and scholars in Medina. So, in framing the message that he took from me, he drew freely on their scriptures, reworking many of their best-loved myths. I myself repeated my role in the lives of Abraham, Lot and Zechariah and even enjoyed an expanded one in that of Jesus (now Isa), breathing into his mother's vagina rather than simply announcing his birth. Often the variations were more striking than the parallels. Some were intriguing, such as Allah's adding congealed blood and semen to the clay from which Adam was formed, with all that that implied for the human constitution, and others perplexing, such as the identification of Moses's sister, Miriam, with Isa's mother, Maryam, when even according to a literalist chronology, they lived fifteen hundred years apart.

Of all the changes, none were more marked than those

concerning Abraham and his sons, Ishmael and Isaac. Despite some ambiguity in the text (an ambiguity I attribute to the Prophet's awareness of the project's audacity), it is Ishmael, rather than Isaac, whom Abraham was preparing to sacrifice on Mount Moriah and who, with preternatural docility, sought to strengthen his father's resolve. Likewise when, at Sarah's behest, Abraham banished Ishmael and his mother, Hagar, into the desert, the water I found to slake their thirst came from no ordinary spring but Zamzam, the sacred well near Mecca. And it was there that years later, when father and son were reunited, I led them to build the kabba. Given that his own tribe was one of several to claim descent from Ishmael, the outcast of the Jewish scriptures, it was no surprise that the Prophet sought to rehabilitate him but, in the process, he brought about an enmity between the children of Ishmael and the children of Isaac that endures to this day.

How often since I was sent to avert the sacrifice on Mount Moriah have I longed to exploit the ambiguity over the victim in order to reconcile the two traditions! But it is one of the paradoxes of Islam that, while you make belief in angels one of its binding tenets, you deny us the individual agency we possess in Judaism and Christianity. In contrast to the rabbis and monks who disputed for centuries over whether and in what part we assisted God in His creation, you deem us to be created beings like yourselves and equally subject to mortality. There was never any question of our rebelling against Allah since, unlike humans and djinns, we lack free will and are mere instruments of His design. You are of course familiar with the story that we counselled Allah against the creation of Adam – advice that, given the course of human history, you might consider to have been prudent – but He punished us for our presumption by endowing Adam with knowledge greater than our own, whereupon we bowed down before him, all that is except for Iblis who, by his defiance, revealed that he was no angel but a djinn.

I am privileged to have been the divine messenger to several prophets, but it was with Muhammad that I formed the closest bond. Having overwhelmed him with a vision of my eternal nature, when my six hundred wings spanned the horizon outside the Cave of Hira, I subsequently chose to appear to him in human form, sometimes in the white robes of a Bedouin and sometimes as Dihyah al-Kalbi, an exceptionally handsome youth from Mecca – indeed, I like to think that it was my beauty which inspired his assertion that one of the three things most pleasing to the eye is an attractive face. I was his guide in matters of the heart as well as of the spirit, allaying his qualms about marrying his daughter-in-law, Zaynab, and revealing his child-bride, Aisha, to him in a dream. I accompanied him to war, exhorting him to attack his enemies and leading the angelic forces at the Battle of Badr, my yellow turban conspicuous in a sea of white.

From the start there were those who cast doubt on our relationship, even maintaining that he put peas in his ear and trained a pigeon to peck at them in the hope that, from a distance, its wings would be mistaken for mine. But for all the pains that he took to assert the divine origin of his revelation, he was curiously casual about its transcription. The suras were written on scraps of papyrus, palm leaves and camel bones and even scratched on stones. Whole suras were lost when the huffaz – the disciples who learnt them by heart – fell at the battle of Yamama. Aisha herself confessed that, in her grief at the Prophet's death, she failed to spot a sheep chewing a parchment hidden beneath her pillow. I am well aware of the verse that states that the Qur'an will be safeguarded from corruption (it was, after all, first attributed to me), but I am also aware that celestial power has to contend with human frailty. Just as your scholars accuse Jewish scribes of confusing the son whom Abraham intended to sacrifice and Greek translators of concealing Jesus's claim that Muhammad would be the one to come after him, so you must acknowledge the flaws in your own sacred text.

To my deep regret, my favour towards Muhammad led to my loss of credit among the Jews. Ever since my guardianship of Eden, I had occupied a special place in their affections, but when Omar, one of the Prophet's boon companions, mentioned my name to a group of rabbinical scholars in Medina, they reviled me for betraying their secrets to Muhammad, calling me the agent of wrath and retribution, forgetting all the wrath and retribution that I had wreaked on their behalf. But nothing that I did at Jehovah's bidding – not the wholesale slaughter of the Assyrian army nor even the destruction of Sodom – had such fateful consequences as my escorting Muhammad on his night journey to the empyrean. I had assumed that it would resemble Enoch's four thousand years earlier, arousing wonder at the time and subsequently dismissed as apocryphal. Little did I know as I transported him on the winged steed Buraq from his home in Mecca to the ruins of the Temple in Jerusalem, and thence to heaven, that the point of departure would prove to be more contentious than anything we encountered along the way.

I have no quarrel with those who allege that our ascent was ecstatic, since to me the distinction between matter and spirit is notional. I know, however, that for many of you, such a view has far-reaching implications. The night journey has defined not just your religious but your cultural identity. Critics ask why, after spending his entire life in Southern Arabia, Muhammad should have chosen to begin the account of his most profound revelation in a city with which he had no previous connection. I can only suppose that he wanted to associate his new creed with the holiest site of its two precursors. In so doing, he gravely underestimated the human capacity for sectarianism and strife. By setting foot in Jerusalem – by literally leaving his footprint to inspire and confound in equal measure – he condemned its already bloodstained stones to fresh assault. Archangel, saint and messenger, I hover helplessly as the three faiths to which I owe my diverse existence take turns to tear each other apart.

THE DISCOVERY OF SODOM

An address delivered by the Reverend Gilbert Lightfoot at St Peter's church, Whatcombe, Berkshire, Sunday, 17 July 1859

It is with much pleasure that I welcome you here this afternoon, both my friends from Whatcombe and those who have journeyed from as far afield as Compton and Blewbury. I am beholden to my patron, Sir William Dalrymple, who, together with Lady Dalrymple and their daughters, Clementine and Henrietta, has graced us with his presence. I am mindful of Sir William's sentiments on prolixity in the pulpit and can assure him that he need feel no disquiet. Those of you who attended divine worship this morning will recall the opening words of the gospel: 'Be ye therefore merciful, as your father also is merciful.' If brevity is a mercy, I intend to exhibit it.

Sir William, if I may make so bold, has only himself to blame for his return to St Peter's this afternoon. It was his munificence that enabled me to undertake the recent voyage to the Holy Land on which I now report. There can be few in this assembly who are ignorant of the grave loss suffered by my family last year. I refuse to use the facile word *tragedy*, since how can it be a tragedy for a soul to be gathered to its maker? Yet, although I spoke to myself the exalting sentence that I have spoken to many of you during similar afflictions: 'Blessed are they that mourn, for they shall be comforted,' I struggled to hear it in my heart. Even as I sought to fulfil my duties in the church, in the parish and in the rectory, I sank ever deeper into torpor, whereupon my dear wife, with the sympathy and solicitude that she has displayed towards me during twenty-four years of cloudless marriage, voiced her concerns to Sir William. I am forever indebted to her, as I am to Mr Clarkson who, fresh from Cambridge, has ministered to you so ably during my absence, and of course to Sir William who, on determining that what I needed was 'a change of air', insisted that it should not be the somnolent air of a German spa but the bracing air breathed by Abraham, Isaac and Jacob, David and Solomon, and Our Saviour Himself.

I shall not tax your patience with trivial traveller's tales. What had been proposed as a solace for a bereaved father turned into a sojourn of far greater consequence when, compassing the dismal shore of the aptly named Dead Sea, I lighted upon the ruins of Sodom. Well may you gasp, and it was precisely to protect their innocence that I gave instructions that no children should be admitted to this talk. It has fallen to me to be the first man since the ancients to visit the site with true cognisance of its import. I planned to wait until I had edited my copious journal to present my findings to the world but, with well-disposed if ill-considered zeal, my friends in Jerusalem hastened to trumpet them abroad. Thus the sceptics and the scoffers, ever eager to refute the immutable word of the Bible, seized the opportunity to malign me before I had marshalled my argument. Fear not! When the full account is published, I shall rout them as roundly as Joshua did the Amorites. Meanwhile, I am happy to offer you, my faithful flock, a foretaste of the evidence.

I had expected my achievement to be greeted with delight, not derision. When Dr Livingstone announced four years ago that, while rowing down the Zambezi River, he was the first civilised man to gaze upon a waterfall so magnificent that it must have stopped the angels in mid-flight, the world applauded. When Captain Speke disclosed last August that he had located the long elusive source of the Nile, he was widely praised. But when the site of Sodom was revealed, even my fellow clergy expressed misgivings. How, they asked, had a humble Berkshire rector chanced to make such a momentous discovery? With respect, the answer is simple. Although the Ottoman sultan has of late opened up the Holy Land to Western travellers, very few have braved the inhospitality of the Dead Sea terrain and its tribes; and, of those who have, none has taken Moses as his guide. To a man, they have subscribed to the fable that the ruins of the iniquitous Cities of the Plain lie on the seabed: a fable no worthier of credence than that of Atlantis, yet one that has done far greater damage for, without tangible remains, unbelievers feel free to deny that the cities ever existed, leaving the Bible likewise submerged in a sea of doubt.

So potent is the fable that, when the French nobleman, Francis Chateaubriand, visited the region during Bonaparte's tyranny, he believed that in the breaking of the waves on the sands, he heard the drowned Sodomites groaning for all eternity: a belief we must impute to the incontinence of the Gallic imagination. More recently, the wretched death of the Irishman, Costigan, who rowed the length and breadth of the sea in his quest for the ruins has further convinced the credulous that no man can survive on its waters, when the plain truth is that, with the excess of enthusiasm and lack of foresight characteristic of his race, he failed to take adequate supplies. Otherwise reliable witnesses claim that the rubble from the pestilential city has so poisoned the sea that no bird can fly above it nor fish swim in it and its noxious vapours sap the strength of any Christian gentleman or Bedouin savage in its purlieus. How then do they account for the water fowl diving into it and the pigeons winging over it that I saw with my own eyes? And while it is true that no fish can survive in the brine, I myself have bathed in it and live to tell the tale.

You are most kind! I fear, however, that your approbation is unmerited since I was never in the slightest peril. I cannot reiterate too often that neither Moses nor any inspired writer, nor any ancient Father, nor even any pagan historian supports the notion that the Cities of the Plain lie buried beneath the Dead Sea. The truth is to be found in the pages of the Bible, which should be our sole authority on this as on all things. There, it is clearly stated that the Cities of the Plain were consumed by flames. Abraham looked towards Sodom and Gomorrah: 'and, lo, the smoke of the country went up as the smoke of a furnace.' Are we to suppose that the father of his race was as purblind as our modern theologians? And if, in deference to those gentlemen – not all of whom, we grant, are rogues – we allow that, despite the immaculate source, an error may have been introduced by the scribes who copied it, are we to lay a similar charge against St Peter, who, in his Second Epistle, attested to the incineration? And what of Our Saviour Himself? Was He at fault when He reported how 'the same day that Lot went out of Sodom, it rained fire and brimstone from heaven, and destroyed them all'? Perish the thought!

Consider carefully! Having taken such pains to destroy the cities, would the Most High then destroy the proof? By no means! Having raised His hand in retribution, He was determined to reveal His handiwork to the world. Both Ezekiel in the Old Testament and Our Saviour in the New suggest as much when they direct us to think on the fate of Sodom. St Peter is still more explicit when he calls the downfall of the cities 'an example unto those that after should live ungodly'. As your rector of twenty-two years, I know that no matter how I may chastise you from the pulpit, it is the sentences I pass from the bench that best serve to curb the wickedness of the parish. It is no whim of Sir William's that, while they may have fallen into desuetude, he has left the stocks standing on the village green. When the word alone does not suffice, we need the evidence of punishment to save us from sin.

In the case of Sodom, the evidence has long been there for those with the wit to look. We read in Genesis that the city was located in the vicinity of the Dead Sea. Since the mountain ranges on both the east and west extend almost to the shore, the choice is narrowed to the north or south. The reference in the fourteenth chapter to slimepits – that is bitumen pits – in the nearby Vale of Siddim tips the balance towards the south, where large deposits of bitumen are still to be found.

I shall not detain you by detailing the support for my discovery in the works of Strabo and Josephus – the one placing the city 'in the region near Moasada', that is Masada, the site of the final defeat of the Jews, and the other in the environs of 'Zoara in Arabia' – since I mean to review it at length in my book, which I trust that those of you who are able will soon have occasion to read. I must, however, make mention of Jebel Usdum, a long low mountain composed principally of salt, situated on the south-western seashore. I see from your faces that several of you have already made the connection. And yes, there is a pillar in the shape of a woman although, at sixty feet high, it is far too large to be that of Lot's wayward wife. My native guide who, supposing her to have been elongated as well as calcified, drew it to my attention. And, while I take his interpretation with, if you will forgive the pleasantry, a pinch of salt, it nevertheless attests to a Bedouin tradition that carries all the more weight since her metamorphosis does not feature in their own scriptures. Is it not shameful that, when reputable Christian ministers seek to 'rationalise' the workings of divine providence by postulating that the woman stumbled into the sea and the thick salt stiffened her clothing, or that her body turned rigid with shock at the sight of the devastated city, or even that the pillar was a statue erected to her memory by her husband and daughters, it should fall to the Muhammadans to remind us of the truth? Their designated pillar may be a counterfeit, but it is manifest to any judicious observer that, given the profusion of the mineral in the region, the Almighty chose to transform her into salt so that she might blend the better with the landscape.

A short step along the shore from the Salt Mountain we

come to a set of stones of much the same shape as those that comprise the sanctuary enclosures of Jerusalem and Hebron, but smashed and scattered as if by a ferocious onslaught. Unprompted, my guide informed me that this was Kharbet Usdum, the ruins of Sodom. You may surmise how my heart leapt but, I pray you, contain your excitement as we travel a further mile and a half to another extensive ruin, which my guide named as Zouera-el-Tahtah. Yes indeed, Dorothy Critchley, I see that you have come to the only logical conclusion … although, as I discovered on my return, there are those who charge that, in my enthusiasm, I myself came to it too readily. But if, in the very place where both scripture and history lead us to locate Sodom, we find a huge salt mountain and, fast by, the ruins first of Kharbet Usdum and then of Zouera (knowing, as we do, that Lot and his daughters sought refuge in nearby Zoar), what fair-minded man will deny it? Besides, if they are not the ruins of Sodom, then what are they? Not only is no alternative city named in the Bible or in any ancient chronicle, but it is clear at a glance that no city could have existed in the midst of such desolation unless, like Sodom, it were itself the cause of that desolation.

You may ask what of Gomorrah, the city forever yoked with it in infamy? Here I must crave your indulgence since a local difficulty prevented my proceeding with my mission and making what I am assured would have been a definitive identification. It is my heartfelt wish that the publication of my findings spur Her Majesty's Government into providing funds for further expeditions that will establish the locations beyond doubt – along with a gunboat to ensure that the natural malevolence of the Arabs is held in check.

I firmly believe that it was the Most High Himself who led me to Sodom in order that I might bear witness since, in an age when the truths of the Bible are assailed on all sides, it is imperative that men of good faith have the weapons with which to fight back. As I stood in Kharbet Usdum, surrounded by battered stones and charred boulders, my feet sinking into the thick black ash that was all that remained of the once proud city, I gave thanks to God who had sent His angels to punish the men who had sinned so foully four thousand years ago and prayed that He would wreak similar vengeance on those who flout His commandments today.

1

The ancient tower of Abu Seer slid into view, followed by groves of palm trees, each bare trunk crowned with a canopy of leaves as if an exploding firework had been caught in mid-air and transformed into foliage. Gilbert stood on the sun-soaked deck as the *Pera* entered the delta, vying with his fellow passengers for the first glimpse of Alexandria. A shout went up as a keen-eyed cornet discerned the marble monolith glimmering in the haze.

'It's Pompey's Pillar,' Gilbert announced to young Lizzie Frobisher, who was on route to meet her brother in Calcutta.

'Actually it's Diocletian's,' Captain Perry interposed as he stole behind them, prompting Lizzie to twirl her parasol so violently that Gilbert was torn between deploring her susceptibility and welcoming the breeze. 'It was mistakenly attributed to Pompey by the Crusaders who, like many ignorant intruders, knew nothing of the history and named it after one of the few ancient generals of whom they had heard.' His heavy stress on *intruders* made it clear that he intended his remark to have a broader application. He had made no secret of his rancour after Gilbert twice intervened to warn Lizzie and her cabin-mate that an unchaperoned stroll around the deck with a young officer would not be proper. Gilbert was indifferent to his hostility. They had been thrown together more closely at sea than they would ever have been on shore, but in a few hours the ship would dock at Alexandria and he would never have to suffer that supercilious drawl again.

He had held a Sunday service in the saloon as they crossed the Strait of Gibraltar, adapting his popular sermon on Jonah.

He suspected that some of the younger passengers had only come because the deck was too slippery to play shovel-board or quoits, but it became clear that one at least had paid close attention. Scarcely had he pronounced the concluding blessing than Perry launched a scathing attack on the chances of anyone surviving in an airless, blubbery cavern swilling in noxious acids, let alone negotiating the thirty-foot jaws lined with eight-inch teeth if it were a sperm whale (a creature he named solely in order to shock). Dr Triplow, with misplaced solicitude, interjected that the story was to be read not as a literal account but as an allegory prefiguring Christ's descent into hell and resurrection. Gilbert had little more patience with such spineless apologists for the faith than he did with its detractors. With the Bible under attack from an unholy alliance of scientists, scholars and political agitators, the solution was not to make niggling distinctions between spiritual and historical truth but to proclaim vehemently that the truth was absolute and indivisible.

Before leaving Southampton, he had impressed on his companion, Hugh Fletcher, that, should anyone ask about their reasons for the voyage, he was not to mention Theo's death. Now he found himself an object of sympathy on account not of his bereavement but of his beleaguered faith. He had been amazed to discover that only three of his fellow passengers were travelling to the Holy Land: the two Misses Smythe from Bethlehem, Pennsylvania, who were visiting their brother on an American settlement near the Sea of Galilee; and Joshua Kaufman, agent to Sir Moses Montefiore, who was to report on the almshouses that the great philanthropist was building for his co-religionists outside Jerusalem. Of the remainder, those who were not heading straight to India were staying in Egypt, more intrigued by the land of Antony and Cleopatra than that of David and Bathsheba. People who were happy to despatch Jacob's ladder and Balaam's ass to the world of Anderson's *Wonderful Stories* listened enthralled as Perry described Indian deities who had elephant heads or multiple arms or, even more obscenely, bodies that were both male and female. It was no surprise that the sepoys had mutinied when their masters permitted them to persist in such dangerous delusions.

Catching sight of Hugh leaning over the starboard rail, he joined him to watch the pilot gingerly steer the ship into harbour amid the fleet of Ottoman, Austrian, French and British merchantmen and men-of-war, the latter now blessedly at anchor. The air was filled with noise – the blasts of the ship's horn and shouts of the stevedores, messengers and donkey-boys – above which a strange rhythmic chant, at once guttural and plaintive, insinuated itself. All at once the fishermen, porters, traders and natives of every description stopped whatever they were doing and walked to the sea, some kneeling at the edge and others wading in, cupping water in their hands and washing their faces, ears, arms and feet, even poking their briny fingers into their nostrils. They then retreated up the shore, where some spread out mats the size of napkins and others dusted a patch of stone or smoothed the sand, before engaging in what to the unpractised eye resembled a cross between devotion and calisthenics. They then resumed their activities, as if released from a momentary trance that had left no impression. In spite of himself, Gilbert was moved.

One of the perquisites of a first-class berth was early disembarkation. With his blood still swirling to the swell, Gilbert took his first steps on dry land since leaving Malta. 'Watch out for your pocketbook,' he warned Hugh, as the quay swarmed with clamorous Arabs eager to take their money and, from the look of them, none too particular as to how they went about it. Fortunately, the major-domo of the Hotel de l'Europe, recognised them at once.

'Are we that obvious?' Hugh asked.

'Yes,' Gilbert replied, 'as English gentlemen.'

After admirably laconic greetings in near intelligible

English, the major-domo summoned two Nubians to carry their chests, claiming that they would be quicker and more reliable than camels, and then, with a sharp thwack of his fly whisk, roused a bedraggled boy to carry Gilbert's valise. He escorted them to the customs house for an inspection that he dismissed as routine. The officers did, indeed, pay little attention to the two eight-barrelled pistols, which Sir William had given Gilbert with the jocular instruction to test them on some insolent Arabs. They showed far more interest in his stock of cigars, sniffing them, weighing them in their hands and rolling them behind their ears like parvenus in the smoking room of the Athenaeum. Following the major-domo's advice, Gilbert offered a consideration (a word he preferred to Hugh's brusquer *bribe*) of three cigars to each of the officers, thereby ensuring safe passage for the rest.

Promising that the hotel was just a few steps away, the major-domo urged them to make the journey on foot since the streets in the Turkish quarter were so cramped and overhung that taking a camel or even a donkey was hazardous. Gilbert trudged behind the Nubians, eager to avert his gaze from their sweating, straining backs, each of which bore a load that two English porters had struggled to lift between them. But every stray glance encouraged the hordes of traders along the way to importune him with silks and satins, gold and silver, beads and glassware, and trays of pungent spices, seemingly oblivious to his dishevelment, fatigue and longing for a more substantial bath than the two-minute hose-down from the boatswain's mate who had sluiced the decks at dawn. Hearing his protest, the major-domo rushed to his aid and wielded his whisk in all directions, provoking a flurry of curses and a jet of spittle. Picturing the full-scale riot that would have erupted at home, Gilbert supposed that this was what was meant by Arab fatalism.

Escaping from the dingy warren, they arrived at an elegant square lined with sturdy, westernised buildings, among them their hotel. Pleading exhaustion, Gilbert insisted on being taken straight to his room. Although the air was stale with a trace of almonds, the bed a nightmare of flounces and frills, and the walls a dizzying pattern of interweaving flowers, it had one supreme advantage: privacy. He had never appreciated Celia's forbearance more than after spending two weeks in a cabin with Hugh. It was not just the snores and scratches, the belches and the smells, but the fatuous conversation that repelled him. The man was amiable enough but irrevocably coarsened by twenty years as a scene-painter at Drury Lane. He had abandoned the scene-room for the easel after the manager, recognising his facility, asked him to paint a series of theatrical tableaux to adorn the green room, which caught the attention of several wealthy connoisseurs. His forte was landscapes, domestic and foreign. Now the vogue for biblical subjects had brought him to Palestine. Gilbert had been wary of his companionship, but Sir William personally vouched for his propriety. Moreover, with the dual authority of brother-in-law and patron, he asserted that the Holy Land was far too dangerous and uncharted a region for Gilbert to explore alone.

Truth to tell, Gilbert welcomed the danger. Although Celia and Sir William, along with others less qualified to judge, had ascribed his dejection to a crisis of faith following Theo's death, they were mistaken. Hs faith was as steadfast as ever. It would survive the death of not just one child but all his children. It would survive disgrace, disaster, mental decline, bodily affliction and whatever else might befall him. Far from losing his faith, he suffered because his faith had not been shaken. While Theo's mother and brothers and sisters and friends mourned his death, his father could not but be grateful that he had gone to a better place. He had died while he was doing God's work – he had died because he was doing God's work – and in a primitive land free from temptation. Yet, while his heart and soul rejoiced for his son's salvation, his flesh rebelled. The hands with which he had lifted him, the arms in which he had cradled him, the knees on which he had dandled him, all held ineradicable memories. They accused him of being unnatural, inhuman, monstrous. In the Holy Land, they would be silenced. Amid the perils and privations of the desert, his faith would be vindicated.

After a dinner during which Hugh described at length his backdrop of the Temple of Isis for a production of *Azael, the Prodigal Son* that, by his own account, was prodigal both on and off the stage, Gilbert returned to his room to write to Celia. They had already been apart for longer than at any time since the terrifying weeks after Emilia's birth, but he felt their separation in far more than miles. Never before had he had to keep such a secret from her. He had longed to share it, not least when, in a swiftly repented remonstrance after hearing the news from Poverty Bay, she blamed him for exposing Theo to the Maoris, but to have done so would have been unconscionable. The burden was his to bear alone … He rubbed his eyes and an image flashed before them of a coffin strapped to his back like the chests to the Nubians. He turned to the miniature portrait of Celia by his bedside, but even that brought no relief, for her features refashioned themselves as Theo's. Of all their children, he had most resembled his mother – and not only in looks. As a boy, he had always been happy to help in the parish. Then he went up to Cambridge and everything changed. If only Hugh had mentioned any play but the *Prodigal Son*!

A good night's sleep restored his spirits and, after a hearty breakfast with no rough sea to inhibit his appetite, he took Hugh to call on the British consul. He was eager to proceed on the journey as swiftly as possible but first, he had to obtain the services of a reputable dragoman and to make contact with his nephew, Benet, who was due to join him from Cairo. Despite his much-vaunted valour during the late Indian Mutiny, Benet was a permanent worry to his family, and, without wishing to impugn Sir William's generosity, Gilbert suspected that one of his motives for funding this trip was to receive up-to-date news of his son. To Gilbert's dismay, the consul was, according to his secretary, 'very sick with pain', his words accompanied by extensive eye-rolling and stomach-rubbing, which Hugh declared would have earned him a round at Drury Lane but which, to Gilbert, looked embarrassingly insincere. The secretary suggested that they use the opportunity to visit the 'pleasings of the city', the absence of three front teeth giving the suggestion a sinister edge. While Gilbert was wondering how they might do so safe from exigent Arabs, Hugh, with rare resourcefulness, engaged the secretary as a guide, inducing him to forsake his desk for a modest fee.

The secretary, sibilantly naming himself as Salm, maintained that the best way to see Alexandria was by camel. 'It might be the best but it's certainly not the quickest,' Gilbert muttered to Hugh as they waited for the drivers to respond to Salm's summons.

'Relax!' Hugh replied. 'Everything's relative.'

'But not time.'

At last the drivers arrived, and Gilbert and Hugh went outside to find them crouching beside their recumbent camels. While the men were all salutations and obsequiousness, the beasts eyed them with a mixture of malevolence and disdain, one greeting Gilbert's forced smile with a loud sneeze and the other with a bubble of slaver. At Salm's behest, he walked up to the first and prepared to mount. A former rider with the Old Berks Hunt, he had not anticipated the awkwardness and, after several failed attempts, he was forced to call on the drivers for help. With one holding his left foot in the stirrup and the other heaving his buttocks, he managed to swing his right leg over the hump. Perched on the acutely uncomfortable saddle, he gripped the reins to adjust his position, prompting the camel to jerk its neck, almost flinging him off. He worried for Hugh who had never even ridden a horse. Shuffling round to encourage him, he saw that, with the confidence of the neophyte, he had approached the camel from behind and straddled it in a kind of leapfrog. 'Giddy up,' he said, with further tomfoolery, at which the two drivers cheered, before goading the beasts to their feet. Gilbert trusted that their seeming indifference to his safety was warranted as his camel rose first on its hind legs, throwing him forward, and then on its front ones, pushing him back. It trundled away, swinging each flank in turn with deceptive languor, disconcerting him both by his distance from the ground and his unimpeded view over its head. Despite the Turkey-work rug, the saddle chafed his thighs and the constant lurching made him ache from shoulder to calf. Hugh, true to form, declared that it was the only way to travel.

Even with the perilous descent, he was grateful for the respite when they reached Cleopatra's Needles, two huge red granite obelisks a few yards from the shore, which, needless to say, had no closer link with the infamous queen than Pompey's Column had with the great general. After studying the hieroglyphs, they mounted the camels, an operation that was no easier than before, and proceeded north, where Salm promised to show them some 'exceedingly ancient cataclysms'.

'Do you think he means *catacombs*?' Gilbert asked Hugh.

'Could be,' Hugh replied. 'How good's your Arabic?'

'That is beside the point. I am not employed by the sultan's representative in London,' Gilbert said sharply.

In fact *cataclysms* did not seem so wide of the mark for the vault had been subject to a violent convulsion, either natural or man-made, and like so much else in the city, was covered in debris. After a brief confabulation with Salm, who proposed to take them to further *cataclysms*, and Hugh, who preferred to remain to sketch the site, Gilbert decided to return to the hotel. He longed to walk, but his legs were so stiff that he could hardly bend his knees and, bowing to the inevitable, he made his way to the camel. On his approach, the prostrate beast, its back rising like the sand dunes at Southwold, turned to him with such a vindictive sneer that, regardless of the divine plan, he found himself wishing that its forebears had been excluded from the Ark. He failed to suppress a yelp as the drivers hauled him on to the hump and, while mindful of his woeful state, he was not prepared for Salm's emphatic 'You want hammam?'

'I beg your pardon.'

'You need washings, yes?'

'No doubt, when I'm back in my room. Not that it's any concern of yours.'

'No, he's suggesting you visit a hammam,' Hugh said, explaining that it was one of the famed oriental washhouses, where he could repose in the vapour and have his aching muscles relieved. Gilbert's fears that it might not be reputable were not wholly allayed by Salm's claim that 'all the big men in this city go there before prayer', but the pain in his back and thighs overrode any routine considerations of propriety.

Salm escorted him back to the Turkish Quarter and a ramshackle building that, apart from the wisps of steam escaping from a high pipe, had nothing to distinguish it from its neighbours. Descending from the camel for what he swore would be the final time, he followed Salm to the door, which was opened by a burly man with a single eye and a forbidding aspect. Salm engaged him in a spirited conversation to which Gilbert would have felt more indulgent had he not been standing beside a noisome beggar who, he trusted, understood his elaborate mime of empty pockets. His deceit was exposed when, with a smile as broad as if he had secured him an invitation to the sultan's palace, Salm said 'You must penetrate now. Three piastres.' He would have preferred to pay inside, but the attendant held out his hand, obliging him to count out the coins in the street. The camel's opportune bray reminded him of one of Christ's most unsettling precepts and, without looking down, he dropped a fourth coin in the beggar's lap.

After a hurried farewell to Salm, he entered the dank vestibule where his mimetic skills were put to further use since, with no common tongue, he was reduced to rubbing his arms and thighs, wiping his face and combing his fingers through his hair to indicate what he required. With what might have been either a smile or a leer in a face less defined by deformity, the attendant picked a napkin and a sack from a pile and ushered him through a dingy corridor into a surprisingly airy chamber with a red-and-white tiled ceiling, geometrically patterned walls and a cracked marble floor. Dappled light seeped in from the lantern, illuminating a central fountain as delicately carved as a cathedral font, flanked by four divans, on one of which an old man lay asleep beneath a patchwork of napkins and on another a brawny man, his briary beard melding with his hirsute body, was removing his robe. The attendant led him to a third divan and handed him the napkin and sack. 'No, no,' he insisted, 'I must have a room to myself.' The attendant looked blank so, with an ingenuity that made him regret his refusal to join in the shipboard charades, Gilbert mimed stepping through a door and shutting it behind him.

His face as inscrutable as ever, the attendant led him into an alcove, which exuded an odour of sweat mingled with spices. He held up two fingers and Gilbert, recognising the one universal language to have survived Babel, handed him a further two piastres, whereupon the attendant pointed to a pair of pattens on the floor and left him alone. After taking stock of his surroundings, Gilbert undressed as smoothly as his aching joints allowed and placed his belongings in the sack. He slipped into the pattens, which, though hard to secure, were preferable to stepping barefoot on to the torn, grimy matting. He struggled to knot the napkin around his hips. Then, with the uneasy realisation that no one – not even Celia – had seen him in anything less ample than a nightshirt for thirty years, he tottered into the corridor, his left hand clasping the two top corners of the napkin and his right arm hanging with studied insouciance over his nipples.

The attendant, waiting outside the room, collected the sack, filling Gilbert with foreboding for his watch and pocketbook but, short of miming shooting him through the temple (which might have been misinterpreted), there was no way to indicate the fate that would befall him if either went astray. Reminding himself that the object was to relax, he followed the attendant into the steam room. He soon acclimatised himself and, as he lay on the wooden ledge, a gentle lassitude crept over him. He must have fallen asleep for he was jolted back to consciousness by a boy who seized his arm and pointed to the door. Scrambling up, he dropped his napkin, but the boy seemed scarcely to notice, let alone take offence. Gripping it tighter than ever, Gilbert allowed the boy to guide him along the corridor as though they were treading a path through quicksand. Entering another alcove, the boy beckoned him to the marble slab in the middle and, despite the oddity of deferring to one no older than his senior Sunday School pupils, Gilbert obeyed. Holding fast to the napkin, he sat on the slab, whereupon the boy abruptly grabbed his legs, forcing him on to his back. The stone was hard, cold and ominously moist. The boy took a napkin from the pile and hung it across the doorway, giving Gilbert a moment to adjust the one on his loins. He lay flat, a cross between an effigy and a sacrifice, waiting for the boy to ease his tender muscles, only to recoil when, without warning, the boy flung a bucket of icy water over him. Ignoring his protests, he pushed him down on the slab and, picking up a bar of soap and a bunch of palm leaves, lathered his chest and shoulders, arms and legs. After dousing him with a second bucket, he gestured to him to turn over and repeated the process on his back. He followed this by stretching his arms and legs as if trying to wrench them from his torso, kneading his shoulders and spine, twisting his neck and even wriggling his ears. Gilbert, who had expected something far gentler, felt like the rag doll on whom Laetitia, the more hoydenish of his two daughters, had deflected any punishment that he had inflicted on her.

Despite the sparse hairs on his scrawny chest resembling the brushes that Laetitia, now in the bloom of maidenhood, used for her miniatures, the boy could have been no more than fourteen or fifteen, yet such was his expertise that Gilbert was happy to place himself in his hands. Even as he worked, he conversed in high-pitched Arabic with an unseen interlocutor, displaying a detachment from the flesh in front of him that, after a moment's indignation, Gilbert found reassuring. For all the pokes and prods, he was sinking into a stupor when the boy slapped him over-familiarly on the rump and indicated that he should turn over. Gilbert grew uneasy as he drenched and lathered him once again, and the promised solace for his aching limbs came to feel more like a feminine indulgence. Wiping his hands on his napkin, the boy fetched a blade and Gilbert's terror that he meant to cut his throat was little assuaged by the realisation that he wished to shave his armpits. 'No!' he shouted, hugging his arms to his chest, at which the boy shrugged, put down the blade and resumed rubbing his legs. Barely had Gilbert's heartbeat stilled when the boy extended his strokes first to his thighs and then to those parts that were reserved for Celia. He sat bolt upright but, as if it were some sort of game, the boy pushed him down and rubbed with renewed vigour. Gilbert sprang up, flung the boy aside and, grabbing one of the pattens, slapped him across the head. The shrieking boy cowered in the corner but, even while showing his true colours, he held out his hand with a cry of 'Baksheesh, baksheesh!' Gilbert towered over him, as heedless of his own nakedness as the warriors on the Parthenon marbles.

'Degenerate boy! You ought to be flogged within an inch of your life!'

The memory of having spoken the words before compounded his fury and, with no whip to hand, he picked up the razor, brandishing it in front of the boy who screamed 'Ya

Allah!' The appeal to God – even an infidel God – placated Gilbert, who laid down the razor. At that moment a well-built European with a full beard and an ugly scar on his shoulder pulled the napkin from the doorway and entered the room.

'My sainted aunt!' he exclaimed with a laugh.

'Your sainted uncle, Benet,' Gilbert replied, struggling to take command of the situation. Scarcely had he recognised his nephew than he recollected that he was naked and, grabbing the spumy napkin from the slab, pressed it to his loins. The boy, meanwhile, escaped from the corner and cringed behind Benet, who muttered something in Arabic that sent him scurrying from the room.

'My mother wrote and asked me to look out for you. I doubt that this is where she had in mind.'

'Your mother asked me to look out for you too,' Gilbert replied. He might have added that, given his suspicions of Benet's character, it was precisely where he would have expected to find him, but he had no wish to sour his first meeting with his nephew in three years. 'I came here in good faith to recover from the travails of the day, when I was subjected to the most vicious assault. Why? I did nothing to encourage it.'

'You mustn't blame yourself. It's one of the services the hammam provides.'

'You sound as if you're excusing it!'

'It's not for me to condemn the local customs.'

'On the contrary, that is precisely what your race, your rank and your religion entitle – no, require – you to do.'

Benet studied him for longer than would have been comfortable even were he not half-naked. 'You're shivering. Temperatures in the East can be treacherous. You need to get dressed and back to your hotel.'

Clapping his hands, Benet summoned the attendant who, eye lowered, returned Gilbert his sack of clothes and sidled away.

'Take your time. I'll meet you in the lobby.' Benet moved to the entrance. 'It's good to see you, Uncle. Truly.'

He walked out, leaving Gilbert staring vacantly at the sack. Rousing himself, he rubbed his chest with the sopping napkin, before giving up and pulling his undershirt and drawers over his clammy flesh. Banishing the memory of the assault, he reflected on Benet's propitious arrival. Even as a boy, he had had a flair for the unexpected. Gilbert had first encountered him springing from the trunk of a long-case clock when old Lady Dalrymple, with whom he had struck up a friendship during Missionary Society meetings at Exeter Hall, invited him to spend Easter at the Dower House. There he met, wooed and wed Celia, and the following year, her elder brother, William, presented him to the Whatcombe living. From the start, Benet had been his favourite of the five Dalrymple children and not just because, as a third son like himself, he was destined for the Church. His intelligence and spirit would have guaranteed his precedence whether he had been Bertram, heir to the title, or Thomas, bound for the Law. They had spent many happy hours in the rectory study mulling over Bible texts and commentaries until it was clear to both of them that the pupil had outstripped the master. Gilbert, who lacked ambition, had predicted that Benet would end his days as a bishop. Then, in his second year at Oxford, everything changed. The doubts that were blighting many of the brightest minds of his generation infected him. To the despair of all who loved him, he was sent down – and not for driving a coach-and-four into hall or some such puerility, but for answering the New Testament questions in his Moderations in Hebrew.

To the astonishment of his friends, he applied for a writership with the East India Company. Sir William's regret at the lowly posting was outweighed by relief that he was gainfully employed. For his part Gilbert, while mourning the loss to the Church, was grateful for the removal of a dangerous influence on his own children, especially Theo, who revered his older cousin. Contrary to expectations, he proved to be a devoted Company servant and, within five years, he rose from Assistant Collector to Magistrate of Muttra in the North-Western Provinces.

Even his sternest critic – a role that Gilbert had assigned to himself – could not deny his courage during the Mutiny. He had escorted the women and children from both Muttra and neighbouring Goorgoan to the safety of Agra before returning through rebel territory to rescue the treasury. The sepoys guarding it professed loyalty to their masters, only to attack them during lunch. But their muskets were as rusty as their marksmanship and they were rapidly disarmed, although not before Benet was shot in the shoulder. By God's grace, the wound had not festered, but it left him with limited movement in his right arm.

His sympathy for his nephew vanished when he found him in the vestibule, attired in Arab robes, which looked more like concealment than clothing.

'Is anything wrong?' Benet asked disingenuously.

'Is it your intention to renounce your heritage?'

'When in Rome …'

'But we're not in Rome. Even the iniquities of the Papists are nothing to those of the infidels.'

'You've had a shock, Uncle. I'll take you back to the hotel.'

It came as no surprise to Gilbert that, with two hotels in the city, Benet should have chosen to stay at the Hotel d'Orient rather than the Hotel de l'Europe. Nevertheless, he ventured into the l'Europe at eight for dinner with Gilbert and Hugh who, despite his theatrical training, was visibly taken aback by Benet's dress and demeanour. Rallying, he questioned him about his exploits during the Mutiny, eager for a first-hand account of events that continued to excite outrage at home.

'Will you be returning to England?' he asked, as Benet described his subsequent resignation.

'Oh, I think England's happy to keep me at arm's length.

I have my house in Cairo. I study ancient texts, both Arabic and Hebrew. I translate poetry – you should approve of that, Uncle. I converse with my neighbours.'

'It sounds a good life,' Hugh said.

'You mean an easy one,' Gilbert said.

'Shouldn't we try to make them the same?' Benet asked, a question that Gilbert refused to dignify with a reply. His initial relief as Benet and Hugh warmed to one another faded when he found that, without his realising, Benet had convinced Hugh that it was unthinkable that anyone – let alone a painter – should come to Egypt without visiting the pyramids. 'If you're fascinated by the sphinxes here, just wait till you see the Great Sphinx of Giza.'

'What about me?' Gilbert asked. 'I can't take an extra two weeks to sail down the Nile or twiddle my thumbs until Hugh finishes sketching. And your father was adamant that I was not to travel to Palestine on my own.'

'Quite right. I shall accompany you.'

'You!'

'Is the prospect so dire?'

'No, of course not,' Gilbert replied, gulping. 'It's just … are you sure that you can afford the time?'

'For you, always,' Benet replied. 'After all, you were the one who fired my imagination with stories of the Holy Land as a boy. It was your rhymes that breathed life into Cain and Abel, and Joseph and his brothers, and David and Goliath.'

'That's most gratifying. But it's not a pleasure jaunt. This trip means a great deal to me.'

'That's why I want to come. I owe it to you … and to Theo.'

Gilbert looked into Benet's face, the limpid green eyes still those of a carefree boy, despite all that life – or simply life in the East – had etched under them. It was the first time that he had mentioned Theo, his first acknowledgement of his death other than the formal condolences that had arrived from Cairo six weeks after the funeral. He was deeply moved and struggled to choke back the treacherous sob in his throat. Notwithstanding the danger that the devil in Benet (an all too apposite metaphor) would emerge as they stepped on to Palestinian soil, he welcomed the chance to share the journey with someone to whom he had once been close. Who could say what visiting the sacred sites would do to bolster – or, in the worst case, restore – his nephew's faith? Moreover, Benet had skills that Hugh lacked. Not only was he proficient in Arabic and Muhammadanism but he was practised in subduing subversive natives.

'Thank you,' Gilbert said. 'I should welcome your company.'

Hugh returned to his room to plan his trip to Cairo, which, after Benet offered to loan him his house, was largely a matter of finding a berth on a Nile barge. Gilbert and Benet remained at table to discuss their more arduous journey.

'The first thing is to find an expert dragoman,' Benet said. 'Someone who'll take care of the arrangements and act as a guide.'

'I'm well aware of that,' Gilbert replied testily, anxious that Benet should realise that, in accepting his offer, he was not relinquishing control. 'The consul was indisposed when we called on him this morning. I shall go back tomorrow to see if he knows of any suitable candidates. If not, we're sure to find one in Jaffa.'

'No need. I have just the man. Fuad.'

'Does he have only one name?' Gilbert asked, mistrusting the familiarity.

'Fuad Dhimel. He runs a coffee house.'

'A shopkeeper?'

'For heaven's sake, it's not Mrs Pagett's tearooms in Didcot! If anything, it's more like your precious Athenaeum. Patronised by clerics and poets. He's a poet himself, so you'll have a lot in common.'

'As you've pointed out more than once, Benet, mine is just a nodding acquaintance with the Muse. Besides, we need someone of a practical bent.'

'Who says poets can't be practical? Look at all your projects in the village.'

'Are you sure that he'll want to come? Who'll manage his shop in his absence?'

'His wife?'

'So he's married?'

'Why ever not? Would you have me restrict my acquaintance to bachelors?'

'No, of course not,' Gilbert said, chiding himself for his suspicions. 'So must we summon him from Cairo?'

'Not at all. There's the joy of it. He's already here. He had to leave Cairo post-haste.'

'Why? What had he done?'

'Nothing, except to be born a Druze and antagonise his Muhammadan competitors. I'll bring him here to meet you first thing.'

The next morning Gilbert breakfasted with Hugh, more forbearing of his company now that it was finite. He lingered over his coffee after Hugh went off to sketch, but took little pleasure in the gritty texture, bitter taste and sediment that filled half the cup. Leaving the dining room, he found Benet and Fuad waiting in the lobby. Taking a moment to study them unobserved, he wondered whether Fuad had dressed up for the occasion. In contrast to Benet's plain white headscarf and robe, he wore a red-and-white chequered scarf, faded blue silk jacket and, most arrestingly, baggy blue trousers tied at the ankles, with a scimitar in a silver scabbard hanging from his waist. There was more of the pugilist than the poet in his features: the bushy moustaches and stubbled chin beneath flushed, spider-veined cheeks that in a Christian would have signified crapulence. On Gilbert's approach, he stood and bowed deeply, reaching for his right hand, which he touched with his forehead.

'*Marhaba*,' he said.

'I have no Arabic.'

'Don't worry,' Benet interjected. 'It's a simple greeting. Besides, Fuad speaks excellent English.'

'Speak English, yes. Only excellent perhaps,' Fuad said, standing dutifully until Gilbert sat. Benet called for coffee, which he drank with an alacrity that said little for either his palate or the brew that he had been served in Fuad's shop. Fuad, meanwhile, chattered away with an assurance that Gilbert blamed on Benet, who doubtless told him that the interview was a mere formality. Nevertheless, his passion was persuasive and, for all his nephew's faults, Gilbert doubted that he would entrust their safety to either a blackguard or a fool.

'You'd be content to leave your shop in the charge of your wife for the next month?'

'Is good wife. Is very clever with all customers. Is good woman. All Druze wife is good woman. If not …' He raised the hilt of his scimitar a few inches before ramming it back in the scabbard.

'I know very little of your practices,' Gilbert said, willing to believe the worst of any infidel, despite Benet's laughter.

'Is good. This is what we wish. Is no good for all peoples to have our secrets.'

'Why? Do you have something to hide?'

'No, no things to hide. Druze is like open doorway. But is best you do not look inside because you do not understand. And when you do not understand, you make up stories.'

'Is it such a story that you worship the Golden Calf?'

'Always this Calf. Moo!' He laughed. 'Yes, is true if you wish. For Druze, Allah is in all things, so why must we worship Him in only one? We are most close to Islams because we live in his lands and we are happy to say his prayers. But I am happy to wear your cross and say your prayers if you wish for it.'

'That's not worship, it is promiscuity.'

'I do not know this word. Explain please, fellow!'

'What?'

As Gilbert spluttered, Benet answered Fuad's request, with a translation that, to judge by Fuad's grin, was extremely loose.

'There's one thing you should know, if we're to employ you,' said Gilbert, irritated by their complicity. 'In England, *fellow* is not a respectful form of address.'

'Is not?' Fuad looked to Benet, who shook his head. 'A thousand pardons. Ten thousand pardons. Ten hundred thousand pardons.'

'Granted,' Gilbert said, eager to curb such extravagance before they discussed terms.

'Then you will have me, yes? You will not be deceived. Most dragoman, he will take you only simple way. He is too afraid of you learning his ignorance, so he will tell you other way is dangerous because of thieves or throat-cutters. But I will take you all ways. Is good, yes? I know when I am waking up that this is good day for me because of dream I have this night that sultan, he enter me.'

'Enter?'

'Inspire,' Benet interposed. 'An Arabic metaphor. He dreamt that the sultan appeared and inspired him.'

Alerted by dark tales of Arab malpractice, Gilbert insisted on drawing up a binding contract. Dismissing Fuad's proposal that 'we spit on hands and shake them in way of the Franks', he led them to the British consulate, where they were greeted by the newly recovered consul, Herbert Reedy. Having witnessed many similar agreements, Reedy, whose name was so indicative of his manner that it might have been conferred on him at school, proved invaluable in handling Fuad. After declaring at the hotel that he would be 'pleasing to work for nothing for such fine English bishop', Fuad now fought for every last piastre. Gilbert was unmoved, refusing to pay anything above the hundred a day that Reedy maintained was more than generous and which, after realising that further haggling was futile, Fuad was 'pleasing' to accept. With the trip due to last a month, he would receive one thousand piastres in advance and the remaining two thousand on their return. Satisfied, he signed his name with a flourish, demonstrating that his hand, at least, was that of a poet.

The business concluded, Reedy drew Gilbert aside. 'You do realise that the cove is more inclined to the turban than the veil.'

Struggling to unravel the idiom, Gilbert was offended that Reedy should think of him as one of those milk-and-water clergymen who paled at the sight of blood. 'He gave himself away this morning when he talked about punishing his wife,' he said sternly. 'Some might object, but if the reports of marauding Bedouin are correct, he'll be more useful than a ladies' man.'

'Really? Then I wish you joy,' Reedy replied, his abrupt withdrawal suggesting otherwise.

With his joints still aching from the camel ride, Gilbert agreed to Benet's suggestion of a gentle stroll through the town, while Fuad, in the first of his dragoman's duties, set about booking their passage to Jaffa. They reached the souk, where a man stood at the entrance, a green-and-grey snake coiled so neatly on his head that Gilbert took it for a turban, until all at once the snake shot out its tongue and the man his hand with a demand for baksheesh. Hurrying on, Gilbert was stopped by a boy of six or seven.

'M'sieur, m'sieur,' he said, in such a thick accent that it took a moment for Gilbert to realise he was speaking French.

'Que voulez-vous?' he asked.

'Visiter ma mère?'

'Does he wish me to see his mother?' he asked Benet. 'Is she ill?'

'I suspect that he's offering her to you.'

'What for?'

'Baiser! Baiser!'

'I don't understand.'

'I daren't spell it out in case you take the whip to me as you did to Theo when he uttered the word: a word you told him that no self-respecting Englishman would ever use, let alone within earshot of his mother and sisters.'

'And he was grateful,' Gilbert replied, his eyes misting at the memory, 'grateful to be taught what was right, to have the Old Adam beaten out of him. Spare the rod—'

'No need to elaborate. Whatever economy you may have practised at the rectory, it didn't extend to the means of correction.'

Gilbert was so taken aback by Benet's rancour that he failed to notice the boy tugging ever more urgently at his trouser leg. 'Allez-vous en!' he shouted with such force that the boy fled with a scream and he found himself the focus of malignant stares and murmurs.

'In here,' Benet said, pushing him into a nearby bookstall, whose owner welcomed them with several salaams and the offer of coffee, which Gilbert, fearful of being compromised, insisted that they refuse. His nephew looked on in amusement as the owner, mistaking the older for the richer man and unfamiliar with the British custom of browsing, plied him with book after book and manuscript after manuscript. He presented each volume as though he could not bear to part with it and yet his life depended on its sale. Midway through his patter, the noonday call for prayer sounded and he shooed them out of the stall. They watched from the street as he laid out a small carpet and, after sprinkling water on his face, hands and feet, began to recite. With his words and movements echoed throughout the market, Gilbert stood still, respecting the act of worship if not its object, but Benet exhorted him to walk on, explaining that Muhammadans were as offended by people who stopped to observe them at prayer as Christians were by those who ignored them and continued with their own pursuits.

They watched a caravan of camels lumber past, as if the landscape itself were shifting. Their ears were assailed by a swelling cacophony, which Gilbert feared might signal a revolt, but it gradually took on a distinct, if dissonant, pattern, and a quartet of musicians appeared, the first playing a drum, the second a tambourine, the third a kind of twisted zither and the fourth a violin with an elongated neck and a body the size of a coconut shell. They were followed by a slight, opulently dressed figure astride a majestic grey horse. Gilbert's initial thought was that it must be the pasha but, as he approached, it grew clear that his minuscule size was no illusion. It was a child, bewilderingly dressed in both a turban and a veil. Four women accompanied him, their braided hair brushing their waists, eyes ringed with black, and arms heavily tattooed. As they moved, they wove their hands back and forth and clicked castanets, shook their hips and undulated their bellies, small strips of which were visible between their incongruously flat bodices and layered skirts.

Keeping a discreet distance, Gilbert and Benet followed the procession into a large, residential square, where it stopped in front of an imposing house with a red-and-black tiled façade and intricate latticework shutters. A heavy door swung open to admit the rider and his retinue before slamming shut, whereupon the musicians took up position outside, playing their ear-piercing discords as the dancers swirled and swayed to disturbingly hypnotic effect.

'Is it some kind of barbarous initiation rite?' Gilbert asked Benet, the child's ambiguous dress putting him in mind of Herodotus's account of the eunuchs of Babylon.

'Some might say so. It's a circumcision.'

'But the boy was veiled.'

'All the better to mark his passage into manhood when the veil's removed – and not just the veil.'

Gilbert shuddered. Such ostentation was a far cry from the sober Temple ceremony depicted in Sir William's gallery. He felt newly grateful for the din that would drown out any screams when the boy, more cognisant than the eight-day-old Christ-child, underwent his ordeal.

'What about the dancing girls?' he asked. 'I understood that the pasha had banned them as no better than prostitutes.'

'So he did.'

'Then what … ?'

'The people protested against the ban, so the authorities with an ingenuity that even you must admire decreed that the impropriety lay in the dances being performed by women. They'd have the same effect but cause less offence if they were performed by boys.'

'These women are boys?'

'Take a look at their chins; you'll see where they've plucked their beards. Look lower down and you'll find conclusive evidence of their anatomy.'

'It's perverted!'

'What a shame that you can't open a branch of your Vice Society here!'

'I forbid you to use that detestable diminutive! It sounds as if we're promulgating wickedness rather than suppressing it.'

'My mistake. But think of all the souls you'd be able to save. You wouldn't have to set your parishioners to denouncing one another. There'd be so much blatant depravity for you to sink your teeth into.'

'How can you bear to live here?'

'I think you know the answer to that.'

'You're thirty-one. You should come home … marry.'

'That's as may be, but it's not the *should* that's the issue, it's the *can* and the *will*.'

'Your father misses you.'

'So much so that he pays me a very handsome allowance to stay here. Besides, what would I do with myself? Bertram has the estate; Thomas has Parliament.'

'You were intended for the Church.'

'Remind me of the road that's paved with good intentions!'

'I'm in earnest.'

'So am I.'

'You never told me why you abandoned your studies. Did you have doubts?'

'Many.'

'About your own fitness or the Bible?'

'It amounted to the same.'

'And did you ever discuss them with Theo?' Gilbert asked hesitantly. 'Was it similar for him?'

'How could it have been? Wasn't he killed while preaching the gospel in New Zealand?'

'Then you dishonour him as well as yourself by living here, condoning such filthy practices. "The woman shall not wear that which pertaineth unto a man, neither shall a man put on a woman's garment. For all that do so are abomination unto the Lord thy God."'

'Yes, but with respect, Uncle, it isn't the Lord their God. Their scriptures are the Qur'an.'

'Falsehoods and delusions! The laws of Deuteronomy come straight from the pen of Moses.'

'And, to the Muhammadans, the Qur'an comes straight from the lips of Gabriel.'

'And does their Qur'an permit degeneracy such as this?' Gilbert pointed to the dancers, who continued to wriggle and writhe their sweat-stained arms and bellies before an enthusiastic crowd, including several women and children.

'The Qur'an is equivocal on that as on much else.'

'I thought you said it was the Word of God.'

'No, they say it is the Word of God. I merely mine its riches.'

'Which are fool's gold.'

'Whereas the Bible is a flawless gem?'

'Precisely.'

'Setting aside the kangaroos who apparently hopped eight thousand miles from Australia to ensure their place on the Ark, what of Christ Himself who told us to turn the other cheek and yet that He brought not peace but a sword; who charged us to emulate the ravens who neither sowed nor reaped and then condemned idlers in the parable of the Talents?'

'Have you turned apostate?' Gilbert asked, his heart like a stone in his chest.

'Let's leave it at doubts. And on your question of degeneracy, the Qur'an includes the story of Sodom, although it calls Lot Lut.'

'Names are the least of my concerns.'

'Its fate is treated differently in different passages. The most extensive might best be described as mildly condemnatory, emphasising Allah's mercy to all those who repent. Another sura – that's a chapter – contains a call for the flagellation or stoning of all fornicators, including sodomites. Even so, sodomy is not in the list of abominations offensive to Allah; although Muhammad himself spoke of it more harshly in the Hadith.'

'What's that?'

'The compendium of his sayings.'

'You mean, rather than Gabriel's?' Gilbert asked sourly.

'All in all, their religion is more sensuous than ours. You need only look to heaven where Christ tells us that we'll be like the angels and apprehend God in spirit. Muhammadans, on the other hand, believe in a paradise of fleshly delights, crossed by rivers of milk and wine and honey, filled with perfumes and jewels and peopled by beautiful virgins.'

'I presume that they don't remain virgins for long.'

'On the contrary. After each bout of pleasure, Allah repairs their hymens.'

'Are you serious?'

'What's more, there are comely youths, known as *ghilman*, whose role is enigmatic but, among the scholars in Cairo, the consensus is that they're there to fulfil our desires. If not, why would the Qur'an underline their beauty, "as fair as virgin pearls"?'

'To fulfil whose desires?' Gilbert looked at his nephew, the jarring, jangling music now pushed to the back of his mind. 'I'm very glad that you're coming with me, Benet. How arrogant of me to assume that the Lord brought me here for my own sake! It's you, not me, that he wants to walk in the land where He himself once walked with Abraham. And, in restoring you to the faith, I shall recover my purpose.'

2

Battling violent squalls, the small paddle steamer pitched its way up the coast from Alexandria to Jaffa, the ancient city from which Jonah set sail on his fateful voyage and through which Solomon brought the cedars to build his temple. Despite its exalted history, the port had no natural harbour and the steamer dropped anchor half a mile from the shore, where the passengers disembarked into a flotilla of waiting fishing boats. Gilbert said a hasty prayer as two of the crew hauled him over the rail and levered him into the outstretched arms of the half-naked fishermen below. 'Think of yourself as a sack of potatoes,' Benet shouted unhelpfully. As if the descent were not hazardous enough, his ankles were grabbed by rival fishermen vying for such a valuable prize. Kicking out at an especially insistent ruffian, who seemed intent on overturning both his own boat and that of his competitor, he feared that their reward would not be for rowing him to shore but for recovering his body from the seabed.

Slumped on a slimy seat as the boat plunged through the choppy waters, he strove to regain his composure. Ignoring Benet's superior and Fuad's supportive smiles, he gazed towards the shore, inhaling a heavy scent of orange blossom, which masked the reek of the recent catch. No sooner had they passed a narrow breakwater than the fishermen downed oars and remonstrated with Fuad.

'Fishmen, he say he throw us over the board if we do not give him more baksheesh,' Fuad explained, with remarkable equanimity.

'Then pay them and have done!' Gilbert said, too queasy to quibble.

'Is no problem. I tell him I put curse on himselves, his wife, his children. Is very silly people; he believe in everything.' As if in proof, the men picked up their oars.

'Didn't I say he was invaluable?' Benet asked.

For once Gilbert gave thanks for native superstition as the men rowed them swiftly to the shore, where he scrambled over the side and staggered though the shallow water. Although not the august arrival he had envisaged, it was a model of restraint compared to the antics of the French pilgrims, who leapt from their boats and threw themselves on to the sand, kissing it and rubbing it in their hair. Hurrying on, they walked the short distance to the Hotel of the Twelve Tribes, passing a row of tents, which, by luck (Benet), kismet (Fuad) and providence (Gilbert himself), belonged to a party of Austrian travellers who were returning to Europe. Leaving Fuad to purchase their equipment, Gilbert and Benet settled into the hotel. With only one afternoon before they left for Jerusalem, Gilbert was determined not to waste it in recovering from the voyage but insisted on their heading out to explore the town, which in addition to its Old Testament significance was central to the story of St Peter. Benet, in turn, demanded that they see the rock on which, according to Josephus, Perseus had rescued Andromeda from the sea monster.

'Fair's fair, Uncle! If I visit your place of devotion, you should visit mine.'

'You'll have to try harder than that to provoke me, Benet.'

'Don't worry, I shall.'

The veiled threat conspired with a colony of voracious mites to destroy Gilbert's sleep that night, but he was reinvigorated the next morning when Fuad introduced his rapidly assembled team. First was Bassem, a Damascene Christian, whom the dragoman described as 'skilfully in boiling eggs for many minutes, cooking fowls and breaking him with fingers, burning sheeps in four different ways, making coffee good as myself, and firing chibouks'. Alongside him were four ragged muleteers, Jadid, Amar, Mustafa and Mamluk, whom Gilbert could distinguish only by their clothing, although, given its air of permanence, that seemed to be relatively safe. Mamluk was the shabbiest of the quartet, dressed in what looked like a piece of sacking over a long grey shirt, his legs, feet and, for all Gilbert knew, everything else bare, yet he was the most esteemed, known as Hajji Mamluk, having made the pilgrimage to Mecca. They each had charge of a mule, loaded with equipment and supplies, as well as horses for Gilbert, Benet, Fuad and Bassem. Best of all, Fuad had obtained two European saddles from the departing Austrians to replace the narrow and unpadded Arab ones.

'Though Bishop not need one. He round and plumpy,' Fuad said, with an ingratiating smile.

'I've told you before, Fuad, I'm not a bishop,' Gilbert said, wishing that he could deny the rest of the description so emphatically.

From Jaffa to Jerusalem was about thirty miles and, by setting off at dawn, it was possible to arrive before the gates closed at dusk, but the last ten miles were a gruelling trek through three successive mountain ridges and, on the Austrians' advice, Fuad resolved to break the journey at the Latin convent in Ramlah. After threading their way through the Jaffa market, so crowded with importunate Arabs and obdurate camels that it was almost impassable, they found themselves surrounded by orange groves. The breeze was sweet and fresh and the azure sky flecked with clouds. Gilbert's heart soared as they crossed the Plain of Sharon: flat, fertile pasture dappled with wild flowers, among which must be King Solomon's legendary rose. After six hours riding through an increasingly barren landscape, they reached Ramlah, where the road was lined with beggars. Old men with withered limbs, young men with streaming eyes and women with screaming bundles competed for their pity and their piastres. Gilbert tossed them a handful of coins, fearing that it eased his conscience more than their plight.

With a grandiloquence that was growing tiresome, Fuad returned from the convent to announce that all of its rooms had been taken by the French pilgrims from the ship. On the hospitaller's recommendation, he would lead them to 'a very historic, very charmful caravanserai, run by honest Jew in Bab-el-Wady'. As they approached the crumbling fortress in which this was housed, its history was self-evident but its charms were harder to detect. The owner ushered them through a foetid courtyard in which a group of Arabs sat smoking chibouks, alongside their goats and mules, two camels and a clutch of chickens. After a flurry of *Assalamu Alaikums* and *Hayyak Allahs*, the muleteers joined their compatriots at the smouldering fire, while the owner escorted Gilbert and Benet up a set of precipitous steps to two interconnected cells, just large enough for Fuad to lay out their bedding. After a meal of indeterminate meat, which he trusted was not typical of Bassem's cooking, Gilbert stretched out on a mat crawling with lice.

The infestation in his bedding, together with the chatter in the courtyard, once again made sleep impossible. He was hard pressed to keep his temper the next morning when, with a grin as broad as his moustaches, Fuad asked whether he had 'had happy night, full of pleasuring dreams, yes?' He replied with a sardonic account of his verminous bed-mates, which Benet effortlessly capped with a description of a night spent hiding in the burning Customs Hedge at the height of the Mutiny. After an unpalatable breakfast of bitter coffee, rock-hard bread, and butter that tasted of sheep's tail, they left the caravanserai and headed into the Judean Mountains. The road was steep, strewn with rocks and tangled with roots and brambles. The journey took longer than anticipated and, at each twist and turn, Gilbert prepared for his first glimpse of the

Holy City, only to be disappointed. When at last it sprang into view, it brought a different kind of disappointment. Instead of the expected rush of emotion, he felt empty, perhaps because there was nothing remotely Christian in the vista. The high walls, surmounted by the impious excrescences of mosques and minarets, might as well have been those of Damascus or Beirut. For a brief, boyish moment, he pictured himself as a knight in the Lionheart's army come to liberate the city from Saladin, before making a sedate descent to the Jaffa Gate.

Having paid the requisite baksheesh to the Turkish sentinels, whose rapacity revealed their contempt for the city they were guarding, Gilbert and his companions entered the gate to find themselves beset by agents brandishing business cards, jabbering in English, French, Italian and a speculative mixture of the three.

'I had no idea there were so many hotels in Jerusalem,' Gilbert said.

'Is no hotel. Is room in his own filthy houses. Is pushing out wife, sister, father, mother, small crying baby. Filthy, filthy. But he think you too tired to make protest.'

With the horrors of the caravanserai fresh in his mind, Gilbert had little faith in Fuad's judgement, but his fears of a similar ordeal in Jerusalem were allayed when the dragoman secured them excellent rooms at the Hotel Mediterranean, a few steps from the Jaffa Gate and convenient for both the Protestant church and the British consulate. Its owner was a friend of Bassem's, a fellow Damascene Christian, whose Scottish wife had come out to Palestine as a missionary. To Gilbert's delight, she had not lost touch with her roots, as witnessed by the excellent dinner of cock-a-leekie soup, mutton pie, roast potatoes and carrots.

At breakfast the next morning, he ran through their programme with Benet. With so many sites vying for their attention, the obvious place to start was the Church of the Holy Sepulchre, not least because it shut at ten thirty. 'I suppose we should be grateful to the Saracens for leaving it standing. Small mercies, as they say. But then Jesus is one of their prophets.' His grimace at the presumption was softened by a mouthful of the homemade marmalade.

With Fuad in attendance, they quit the hotel and entered a district so squalid that, for all Mayhew's researches, Gilbert could not imagine its equal in the foulest London slum. With no pavements to the narrow streets, they picked their way through piles of ordure and offal, the stench intensified by the stuffiness. The towering houses with protruding roofs, through which the sun's rays barely penetrated, created an air of darkness and danger. They emerged into the church courtyard but the relief was only temporary, for what should have been the holiest site in Christendom had been appropriated by pedlars hawking their handicrafts and beggars their afflictions. No market was ignored: olivewood crosses from Bethlehem, rose petals from the Garden of Gethsemane, asphalt earrings from the Dead Sea, even prayer rugs from Mecca, contended for the pilgrims' purses with the lame, the crippled, the blind, the paralysed and the palsied, leaving only the dead absent from the recipients of Jesus's miracles. Recoiling from the godless spectacle, Gilbert strode to the porch, where the four Turkish guards lolling on divans, smoking, drinking coffee and casting disdainful glances at the crowd, added to the sacrilege.

Gilbert stood at the church door, accustoming his eyes to the sombre grandeur. The vast interior was cast in gloom, relieved by the flicker of candles in sconces and oil lamps overhead. Hordes of pilgrims, their complexions as varied as their clothes, wandered around, stopping at the many vaults and columns, canopies and shrines, oratories and altars: some kneeling in prayer; some telling their beads; others prostrating themselves. A troop of elderly Russians, many groaning and wailing, crawled from chapel to chapel. Rival masses rent the air, reminding Gilbert of the cacophony of medieval chantries. Baffled by the geography of the building, he seized on the offer from a Greek monk to give them a guided tour. Starting at the stone of unction where Christ's body was anointed, they moved to the pillars beside which He was first scourged and then crowned with thorns, before ascending the hill of Calvary to the sockets of the crosses on which He and the two thieves were crucified, and the rock riven by an earthquake when He gave up the ghost.

Having struggled to follow the monk's commentary, Gilbert was glad of his poor English when Benet scoffed at the likelihood of finding so many momentous sites under a single roof. He reserved particular scorn for the column that marked the centre of the world and the birthplace of Adam.

'I'm surprised they haven't preserved the primeval mud.'

'No doubt you favour Mr Chambers's crazed theory that we share a common ancestor with the apes?'

'Is it so crazy? On my last furlough in England, I took Henrietta to the zoological gardens in Regent's Park. We watched Jenny, the orang-utan, drinking tea as daintily as if she were in Mother's drawing room. This was no horse drilled in basic arithmetic or dog trained to jump through a hoop. If you'd seen her using her napkin to dab her chin, pouting when she was refused a biscuit, and then sitting quietly when the keeper told her she might have one as long as she behaved, you'd be in no doubt that she understood the basic rules of social conduct.'

'Jiggery pokery!'

'And all this isn't?' Benet asked, throwing out his arms just as the Russians crawled back into view.

Whether from conviction or habit, Benet showed greater respect when, turning westward, they came to the sepulchre itself, a richly ornamented shrine of multicoloured stone, laden with lamps and exuding a cloying scent, strangely reminiscent of a sickroom. Four Roman priests in gold and silver robes, with borders so stiff that they might have been made of wood, processed past, pausing at each corner to recite a portion of the Passion. With the guide pushing him through a restive crowd, Gilbert stepped into the inner chambers, the first containing a fragment of the rock that the angel had rolled away from the entrance and the second the tomb itself. He strove in vain to reconcile the gilded vault, adorned with costly icons, a marble slab shielding the tombstone from predatory pilgrims, with the modesty of its sometime occupant, before escaping the crush and returning to the body of the church. As he walked to a small Coptic chapel behind the shrine, he felt a drop of moisture on his head, and craning his neck, glimpsed a patch of sky through a broken tile, testament to the invidious rivalry of the Latins and Greeks, each preferring to leave the Saviour's tomb exposed to the elements than to allow the other the honour of repairing the roof.

Christ, who protested that his father's house had been turned into a den of thieves, now had to watch while his own was turned into a nest of vipers. Gilbert had no objection to the rival sects fighting among themselves, provided that it was not in Jerusalem. Having long pondered why God had allowed Muhammad to spread his pernicious creed, he had his answer: it was to purge the perversions of these false priests. But the day of reckoning was at hand. The Ottoman Empire was in decline and the British Empire in the ascendant. A new breed of Bible Christians would be settling in the Holy Land, who would confront the infidel not with ritual and obfuscation but with truth.

'A piastre for them,' Benet said, as they returned to the courtyard.

'I was pondering how much of true value would have been lost if Saladin had destroyed this church.'

'You amaze me.'

'Druze, he say, that just as worst Islams in Mecca, so worst Christians in Jerusalem,' Fuad interjected.

'Thank you, Fuad. Druze – the Druze – may be right.'

After a simple lunch at the hotel, Gilbert and Benet paid a call on two Jerusalem Christians who disproved the Druze dictum: Consul and Mrs James Finn. Finn, whose corpulence defied euphemism, was one of the few European diplomats not to reside in the ports of Acre or Jaffa, putting the service of God above the interests of trade. He and his wife Elizabeth were leading lights of the London Society for Promoting Christianity amongst the Jews. They had devoted much time and energy and a not inconsiderable fortune to improving the lot of the Jews in Jerusalem and, as they took tea in the elegant drawing room, which, mildew aside, might have been that of a well-appointed Home Counties villa, Gilbert questioned them about their work.

'Why the Jews especially? What of their Ottoman overlords? And the Arabs?' Gilbert asked. 'In my few days in Egypt, I witnessed all manner of vice. Are they not in need of God's word?'

'We're strictly forbidden to proselytize the Muhammadans,' Finn replied. 'It's regarded as not just a sin against Allah but a crime against the sultan.'

'Whose vengeance is closer at hand,' Mrs Finn said, with a delicate cut-throat gesture.

'If we're lucky,' Finn said, laughing. 'More likely, I'd be impaled and you'd be sewn in a sack and flung from the city walls.'

'Still, not to worry,' Mrs Finn said briskly. 'The Bible teaches us that the conversion of the Jews must precede that of all heathen nations.'

'So the Muhammadans will surely follow,' Finn added.

'Yes, but when?' Gilbert asked. 'We dispatch missionaries around the globe: to Asia; to Africa; to the Pacific. Do we deem the Muhammadans alone to be unworthy of Christ's blood – and the blood of the martyrs who bring it to them?'

'Blood! Always blood,' Benet interposed. 'How much more must we squander?'

'How dare you, sir!' Gilbert said, forgetting himself for an instant. 'You know full well that Theo, the cousin whom you profess to have loved, gave his life for the faith in New Zealand … Please forgive me. Yes, just half a cup, thank you,' he said to Mrs Finn, who had tactfully raised the teapot. 'My son, Theo, was murdered last summer. He had gone out to assist one of my Trinity friends, William Matthews, at the mission in Poverty Bay. Matthews and his wife, Elizabeth' – he smiled at Mrs Finn – 'had been there for twenty-five years. They had two daughters, much the same age as Theo. I'd hoped … but it was not to be.'

'The good die first,' Finn said.

'He was barely there a year, but Bishop Selwyn ordained him priest in Auckland. He worked tirelessly, but the hardest thing was to persuade the Maoris of the one true God. They would free their slaves; they would send their children to the mission school; but they would not accept that their god could also be the god of their enemies. And to prove it, one tribe – whom I shall not dignify with a name – mounted a raid on another while Theo was giving them communion.'

'And they killed him?' Finn asked.

'They ate him,' Gilbert replied.

'They did what?' Benet said.

'You weren't to know. Until today no one did outside New Zealand, apart from myself.'

'They ate him?' Benet asked in disbelief.

'Yes. Matthews tried to conceal it, but I could tell from his letters that he was holding something back. And as Theo's father, I had a right to know the worst.'

'We shall pray for him,' Finn said.

'And for you,' Mrs Finn added.

'I'm very sorry, Uncle,' Benet said. 'I've no doubt that Theo died nobly. But that doesn't alter the obtuseness of the missionaries in India. I hold them personally to blame for the Mutiny.'

'Strange, when everyone else blames a quarrel over cow grease!'

'To coin a phrase – one which you of all people should appreciate – that was simply the straw that broke the camel's back. The real reason was the missionaries' meddling, denigrating the culture when they didn't even speak the language. I tried to explain that the only way to win the natives' hearts was to respect their customs.'

'Such as child marriage, female infanticide and the immolation of widows?' Gilbert asked.

For once Benet was speechless, and Gilbert wished that Mrs Finn had not felt it her feminine duty to mediate. 'What matters is that everything is back to normal,' she said. 'Is it not the case that, when the Crown took over sovereignty last year, there were celebrations across the country?'

'In part yes, but not out of humble devotion. They thought that the Queen would tax them less than the Company.'

Fearing sedition, Gilbert announced that it was time for them to leave, whereupon, with a fetching blush, Mrs Finn asked if he would perform an irksome task and sign her copy of *A Child's Bible in Verse*.

'With the greatest of pleasure,' he said, wondering whether they used it in their mission. As Mrs Finn handed him the gratifyingly well-thumbed copy, Benet recited in monotone:

'Young friends, if on these rhymes you gaze
With profit and with pleasure,
Not my skill, but the Lord's be praised
For giving them true measure.'

'They were written for children,' Gilbert said quietly, 'not disgraced Oxford scholars.'

They left the consulate, arranging to return the next morning when Finn would conduct them to an audience with the governor, which was part courtesy and part expedience, since he alone could provide them with the firman necessary to visit the Haram al-Sharif and enter the region of Hebron.

At the appointed hour and without Fuad who was busy organising supplies, they passed through the fruit and vegetable market outside the hotel to find Finn waiting for them, dressed in a silver-braided tailcoat and breeches, with a white lace collar and cuffs, a three-cornered hat and a sword. He was attended by two janissaries, equally sumptuously garbed in red-and-gold embroidered uniforms and carrying long silver staffs.

'They accompany Mrs Finn and myself wherever we go in the city,' Finn said, with a self-deprecating laugh.

They walked through streets so dusty that it seemed as if the carpets and rugs strung overhead had just been beaten, to the governor's palace on the north of the Haram, near the first Station of the Cross. Although Gilbert knew that, of all the sacred sites in Jerusalem, the Via Dolorosa was the most conjectural since the Romans had razed the city to the ground after the Jewish revolt, he was outraged that the ungodly mixture of residence, prison and seraglio should encroach on even the symbolic spot where Jesus had been condemned to death. They entered the heavily guarded door to find themselves in a sweet-smelling courtyard lined with trees. The guards ushered them across an inlaid marble floor, into the audience chamber and up to a curtained dais, where the governor sat cross-legged on a divan. Finn bowed his head at which, with a barely perceptible nod, the governor beckoned him forward, kissed him on both cheeks and stroked his beard, before directing him to a carved chair to his left. Still sitting, he greeted Gilbert and Benet with a formal salaam and motioned them to the place of honour on a low divan to his right.

With supreme assurance, he addressed Gilbert in Arabic.

'He's asking how you are,' Finn interpreted.

Gilbert smiled broadly in reply.

'Actually, he asked how's your perspiration,' Benet interposed.

'I beg your pardon!' Gilbert said, the smile fading.

'Don't feel insulted,' Finn said. 'It's a common form of address. I was hurt to be greeted with "May your shadow never grow smaller!"' He patted his stomach. 'Until it was explained that it was not a reference to my avoirdupois but rather a hope that I wouldn't walk outside in the searing midday sun, when our shadows are, indeed, at their smallest.'

Mollified, Gilbert observed the conversation between Finn, Benet and the governor, responding when either of the Englishmen translated a remark aimed at him and trying in vain to ignore the screams issuing from the cellar. In what he recognised as a mark of esteem, the governor handed him the chibouk he had been steadily smoking and, fearful of giving offence, he refrained from wiping the spittle off the mouthpiece. The tobacco was acrid and he was seized by a thirst that the treacly coffee would not slake. He returned the pipe, but the governor waved at him to draw on it again, which he did, before passing it to Benet. And so they continued in a succession of compliments and puffs, until Finn, knowing the form, rose to take his leave, followed by Gilbert and Benet. They waited in the courtyard for the governor's secretary to bring them the firmans. It was only when they were back in the street that Gilbert realised that not once during the interview had the governor so much as shuffled his feet.

'Of course not,' Benet said, 'he has servants to do that for him.'

'And what were those blood-chilling screams?'

'Prisoners,' Finn said.

'Are the conditions that bad?'

'They are when you're being tortured.'

'Why? Has there been another Arab uprising?'

'No, a Jew was found stabbed at the bottom of a well. They're trying to ascertain which of his brothers did it.'

'Must it have been one of his brothers?'

'Unfortunately yes, if you're a Turk and trying to keep the peace.'

They returned to the hotel, where Gilbert and Benet entertained Finn to lunch, while the janissaries stood at the side, eyeing the food. Finn, offering advice on the itinerary, sought to dissuade them from venturing to some of the more remote destinations. 'Go to the north shore of the Dead Sea if you must when you visit Mar Saba, but you go to the south at your peril.'

'Even with an armed escort?' Gilbert asked.

'I was thinking less of the bandit tribes, although they're dangerous enough, than of the terrain itself: the Sebka – the Valley of Salt in the Book of Kings. The paths across the mudflats are so treacherous that even the most experienced Bedouin avoids them. And it's not yet the end of April; the desert sun may be intense, but the marshes will still be heavy with winter rain.'

'We shall take every precaution,' Gilbert said. While not wishing to offend Finn, he had been deeply disappointed in Jerusalem. The combination of the sordid streets, venal inhabitants, brutal Ottomans and sectarian feuds had stiffened his resolve to seek out the true holiness of the land in the desert, including the remains of its most unholy city.

'I have high hopes of recovering Sodom,' he said. Finn looked startled. 'I've read the accounts of Dr Robinson, Lieutenant Lynch, the Frenchman Chateaubriand, and several others, but of all the visitors to the desolate sea, only a handful have travelled to the southern shore. Ergo, that's where the ruins will be found.'

'Won't you go first to Jericho and Galilee? Surely they are of more interest?'

'To me, of course. But think how much harder it will be for those who mock God's Word to deny the fate of the wicked Sodomites if we can locate the surviving stones.'

Avoiding Benet's eye, he plunged his spoon into his pudding.

'Fascinating,' Benet said. 'I had no idea that was your plan. But I shall be happy to accompany you to Sodom, Uncle.'

'Then of course, I shall do everything I can to facilitate the journey,' Finn said, filling the awkward silence. 'The first thing is to hire a Bedouin escort, or rather two since, although they're nomads, they maintain strict territorial boundaries. For the northern region you must go to the Thaamerah. They're rebels and brigands, but once you're under their protection they'll defend you with their lives, even against their own brothers. For the south you can use either the Djahalin or the Rashaida. Given the choice, I'd go for the former. I'll send word to Hamdan, the Thaamerah sheikh, through the Greek convent in Bethlehem. When the time comes, he'll put you in touch with Abu Dahuk of the Djahalin.'

'I much appreciate it,' Gilbert said.

After lunch, Finn took them to the Western Wall, the sole remnant of the Temple complex where, for a fee, Jews were permitted to lament the downfall of their nation. They walked through a maze of narrow streets, the heat and closeness of the morning relieved by a breeze blowing in from the coast, and entered a small square where clusters of men faced a high, rough-hewn wall. All wore the same threadbare gabardines, most with black skullcaps, but two had wide-brimmed hats trimmed with fur. Some bowed their heads to the wall, others touched it; some read prayers, others recited Scripture; some bobbed to and fro, others stood transfixed. At the far end, two elderly women, shrouded in white, put their lips to cracks in the masonry, turning away to reveal cheeks streaked with tears.

They returned to the hotel and prepared to visit the Haram the next morning. Busy at the consulate, Finn sent the janissaries to protect them from the many fanatical Muhammadans who, not sharing the sultan's gratitude for their recent military assistance in the Crimea, objected to his opening up the sanctuary to the Franks. The precaution proved unnecessary since, with the firman valid only between daybreak and the second hour of prayer, they set out so early that the streets were deserted. They arrived unimpeded at the Tranquillity Gate, where a rap of the janissary's staff summoned the guards and the customary baksheesh secured entry. As the guards brusquely ordered them to remove their shoes and don felt slippers, Gilbert gave thanks that Fuad, eager to curry favour, knelt to help.

'I have a problem with my back,' he said to Benet.

'Yes, too much front,' Benet said, irreverently prodding his belly.

Suitably shod, Gilbert found himself in a vast courtyard, dotted with olive trees and cypresses and filled with fountains, shrines, minarets, pulpits and prayer niches. At its heart was the majestic marble-clad Dome itself, enclosing the peak of Mount Moriah, where long before David founded his city or Jesus rode in on an ass, Abraham had prepared to sacrifice Isaac. They entered the building, which Benet explained was not a true mosque but rather a canopy over the rock. Nevertheless, it was the first Muhammadan place of worship that Gilbert had ever been inside, and its stately harmony gave him further reason to deplore the excesses of the Holy Sepulchre. He gazed in wonder at the vast golden dome above a band of mosaics, whose arabesques and curlicues were hard to make out in the watery morning light, and then crossed the carpeted floor to the rock itself behind a latticework screen. Summoning him to one side, a Muhammadan official pointed to a vague indentation, which he maintained was the Prophet's footprint as he ascended to heaven, and to three smaller marks, which were the Archangel Gabriel's fingerprints as he held back the rock that tried to follow him. Gilbert smiled as indulgently as he had at his daughters when they discovered a fairy ring.

He gazed at the craggy mound and reflected on Abraham's story. Truth to tell – and it was a truth to be told only to himself – there was much in it of which he disapproved.

Firstly, he had passed off Sarah as his sister to Pharaoh. Then, he had acceded to her request that he father a son on her concubine, Hagar, rather than wait for God to provide him with an heir, an act that would have grievous consequences for his legitimate descendants. Nevertheless, it was impossible not to respect – indeed, to revere – his obedience in offering up Isaac, the thing that he loved most in the world.

'Are you musing on the sacrifice of a son?' Benet asked, leaning over the screen beside him.

'How about the heartlessness of a nephew?'

'I'm not the one brandishing a knife.'

'If you must know, I'm contemplating Abraham's supreme act of devotion to his creator.'

'You have to admit it's odd that he made no attempt to intercede for his own son, when just a few years earlier he had pleaded with God – argued with Him, even – on behalf of Sodom, a city that as far as we know he never visited.'

'He humbled himself to God's will.'

'Or was it pride?'

'What?'

'Was he so eager to prove his piety that he welcomed Isaac's death?'

'Only you!' Gilbert said, curling his lip.

'Well no, actually. I've been reading some of the early rabbis who claim that Abraham was angry when God substituted the ram, as though He deemed him unworthy of making the greater sacrifice.'

'That's perverse!'

'I couldn't agree more. But my real concern is Isaac. How do you suppose he felt to know that his father was willing to slaughter him? I doubt he ever recovered. What other reason can there be for his shadowy presence in the Bible? He's by far the feeblest of the Patriarchs. His bride is chosen for him by his father – or worse, his father's steward. In old age, he's hoodwinked by his wife and younger son.'

'Do you have a point to this? If so, please tell me.'

'No, you put it better than I ever could:

Dear father, do not shed a tear
For my unworthy life.
My youthful breast I humbly bare
To thy most blessed knife.'

'I'm flattered that it has stayed with you all these years.'

'So has "Baa, Baa, Black Sheep". Though since I'm a black sheep myself, that's hardly surprising.'

'You are finding stone where Prophet Abraham is making to sacrifice Ishmael,' Fuad said, come to join them.

'Isaac,' Gilbert said.

'No, on this stone is Ishmael.'

'The fact that the Druze see God in everything,' Gilbert said, 'doesn't give them the right to distort the truth.'

'Is not only Druze, is Islams.'

'Why does that not surprise me? We say white; they say black.'

'In this case, they say grey,' Benet interposed. 'It's generally accepted that the intended victim was Ishmael, Abraham's elder son, although some scholars plump for Isaac.'

'So what? Why should I pay any heed to the ravings of an illiterate camel driver? Carlyle explained that, in his youth, Muhammad accompanied his uncle to the fairs of Syria, where he met many Christians. Years later, when he fasted and hallucinated alone in the mountains, it was their stories that came back to him in garbled form.'

'It's a theory, I admit.'

'Do you, Benet, or are you one of those recreant Oxonians who, when Oxford race Cambridge on the Tideway, cheer for the lighter blue?'

Benet's scoffing had turned the sacrificial stone into a butcher's slab. Gilbert left the Dome and crossed the courtyard to the al-Aqsa mosque, where he was no more convinced by the footprint of Christ than he had been by that of Muhammad. He rejoined his companions to return to the hotel. At

Fuad's insistence, they took the 'charmful' route by the city wall, the epithet once again called into question when they came to a leper encampment. Never before had Gilbert seen such a profusion of deformities. Some had faces as gnarled as tubers; others were covered with festering boils. Some had skin like fish scales; others had fissured hides. Some had truncated limbs; others were limbless trunks. They screeched and squawked, as if the disease that ravaged their bodies had choked their windpipes. Yet among them were several healthy, good-looking children.

'What are the children doing there?' Gilbert asked. 'Aren't they at risk of contagion?'

'Is his children,' Fuad said. 'Up to age of ten, eleven, twelve, these children are as fine as Bishop. Then when he become men and women—'

'Is he saying that the disease attacks them when they reach puberty?' Gilbert asked Benet.

'Apparently.'

'Then why on earth do they go on breeding? Are they such slaves to their bestial natures?'

'Perhaps. Or perhaps it's the triumph of faith over experience. Perhaps they believe, against all the evidence, that God will be just and not afflict their children.'

Chastened by the encounter, Gilbert made a melancholy return to the hotel, but his spirits rose on discovering a message from Finn that Sheikh Hamdan had arrived in Jerusalem. Pausing only to fetch Benet, he hurried to the consulate, to find the sheikh, his dun headdress and robe looking doubly dowdy among Elizabeth Finn's vibrant chintzes. Small, squat and bandy-legged, with a face like a parched riverbed, he was instantly familiar to Gilbert from the illustrations in his Children's Bible. Here were Abraham, Isaac and Jacob come to life, disconcertingly through a descendant of Ishmael – although what was lacking in those pages was the feral smell. The sheikh stood to greet them, placing his right hand on his heart and raising it to his brow before taking each of their hands in turn. He plied them with questions about the health of their fathers and grandfathers, which Benet answered solemnly. The proprieties observed and the coffee brought, they proceeded to business. Gilbert, excluded from the discussion, witnessed Hamdan's grimaces with growing alarm.

'What's he saying?'

'That the journey is far too dangerous to undertake at any cost,' Benet replied. 'It's an obvious bargaining ploy.'

'And one for which we shan't fall.'

'Now he says that for two such fine Englishmen he's prepared to take the risk,' Finn interjected. 'He counts his life cheap to help you.'

'How cheap?'

'Don't be cynical, Uncle,' Benet said sanctimoniously, before turning back to the sheikh, whose price was lower than Gilbert had feared: a flat fee of a thousand piastres for himself, plus twelve piastres a day for each of the three horsemen and eight for each of the five infantry who would escort them as far as Hebron. The terms agreed, Finn summoned his secretary to draw up the contract, which Hamdan ratified with a seal produced from a filthy pouch inside his robe. Illiterate himself, he evinced little faith in either Gilbert's or Benet's signatures, requiring them to validate the bond with the inky impression of their signet rings.

After a further round of compliments, Hamdan departed, promising to return at dawn on Monday, thus leaving them one last day in Jerusalem. Its being a Sunday, Gilbert attended morning service at the Protestant church, where the bishop preached a sermon that, even struggling to follow the German, he found unduly short. The congregation was equally meagre, consisting as it did of the bishop's dour wife and daughters, the Finns, three American missionaries and three Jewish converts. Benet refused to go and Gilbert, weary of his constant carping, did not press him. He found him back in the hotel, writing letters in the lounge.

'Do you have any plans for this afternoon, Uncle,' he asked, 'or as it's the Lord's Day, are we to spend it in reading improving books?'

'Why? Have you brought some?'

'No. I was remembering Theo's account of Sundays at the rectory, where the biggest excitement was inspecting Toby's beetle collection or listening to Aunt Celia read from *Pilgrim's Progress*.'

'Theo read too,' Gilbert said, hearing again his mournful narration of Christian's fall into the Slough of Despond.

'Heaven forfend that anyone's birthday should fall on a Sunday! He said he'd had more fun when gated by the "brushers" at Shrewsbury.'

'Now I know you're lying. He loved Whatcombe Sabbaths: teaching at the school—'

'Where the village children mocked his vowels.'

'Playing the fiddle in church.'

'Only because you wouldn't allow him to play at home. He was a fine musician.'

'He was passable at best,' Gilbert said, with a pang of disloyalty. 'I never took you for a sentimentalist.'

'He used to say that you were two quite different people: Jehovah at home; Jesus in the parish.'

'What?'

'I shouldn't have mentioned it.'

'"Jehovah at home; Jesus in the parish?"'

'He didn't mean it. He was angry after you'd punished him.'

'I don't need you to justify my son to me: you who did him such harm, destroying his respect for everything of value.'

'I gave him self-respect. That's the most valuable thing of all.'

Gilbert moved away. He did indeed have plans to walk up the Mount of Olives but, in his present mood, he had no desire for Benet's company. Just as he was leaving the hotel, Fuad appeared in the lobby and insisted on joining him. 'Is many dangers for Bishop to go alone among Islams,' he said. Reluctantly, Gilbert accepted the offer. They quit the city by the Dung Gate, crossed the arid Kidron Valley and climbed the opposite slope through the tumbledown Jewish cemetery, many of its graves lying flat and indistinguishable from the scree. In a further desecration, a man was exhorting a boy to pelt stones at one of the few tombs which, despite the foliage poking through its dome, remained upright. Horrified, Gilbert dispatched Fuad to warn him that he was being watched, only to be taken aback when, after a long exchange, he returned with a sheepish grin.

'He say he is Jew. Tomb is tomb of Prince Absalom, son of great King David—'

'All the more reason to treat it with respect.'

'Prince Absalom, very proud man. Very long hair. He disobey against his father, great King David, and sleep with his father's women. They have big battle and Prince Absalom killed when very long hair is catching in branch of tree. Now all Jews when he have sons who disobey him, he bring him here and tell him story of Prince Absalom and make him to throw rocks against tomb. Then sons, he be sorry and obey his father.'

'If only it were that easy.'

'Is very easy, see. Is rocks everywhere.'

Continuing their ascent, they reached the Garden of Gethsemane where, in a rare complaint from one who revered order, Gilbert would have preferred more wildness. The eight well-tended trees, neat beds of roses, pinks and daisies and tidy pathways were more redolent of a civic park than the site of Jesus's betrayal. Further dismayed by the price he was charged for a bottle of oil by a monk who had abandoned at least one of his vows, he led Fuad out through groves of figs, almonds and pomegranates, as well as the fruit that gave the mountain its name. They reached the Chapel of the Ascension, where a party of Russian pilgrims had recently concluded a service. The custodian was preparing to lock up but, for the usual consideration, he allowed them to look around, proudly pointing out another of Christ's footprints, this one marking the last spot touched by His physical body on earth.

Leaving the chapel, Gilbert gazed out over Jerusalem, the setting sun lending a roseate glow to the Dome of the Rock. The air was clear after the dust and haze of the city, affording him a glorious panorama of a landscape that was as rich in beauty as in associations. To the west was the Upper Kidron Valley and to the south Hebron and its environs, but the most inspiring vista lay to the east, where the gleaming blackness of the Dead Sea could be glimpsed between the cobalt peaks of the Judean Hills and the purple tops of the Moab Mountains. Never before had he realised quite how small was the land that had dominated human history. Never before had he felt such a hunger to explore.

3

'Are you proposing to give us a sermon in the desert?' Benet asked.

Gilbert made no reply. His nephew had poked fun at his clothes ever since their first day in Alexandria, but the swallowtail coat, waistcoat, cravat and preaching bands were no casual attire. They were a statement of his identity, even if the language were one that few in Palestine could understand. He would no more have dreamt of affecting Arab robes than of wearing a High Church frock coat or Roman cassock. He shuddered and mopped the perspiration that had pooled beneath his square-cap.

He seethed with indignation towards the muleteers. Finn had warned him of the quirks of Arab timekeeping, but he had not expected to suffer them so soon. As promised, Sheikh Hamdan arrived at the Jaffa Gate at dawn. Mounted on a dapple-grey steed, clasping a spear and attended by eight of his tribesmen, he looked far more imposing than he had in the Finns' drawing room. The muleteers, however, not only turned up ninety minutes late but did so with insufficient provender. After a string of curses so extravagant that they lost their sting, Fuad took Hakim and Halim, the two servants, as alike as their names, to buy oats and barley at the bazaar. Far from thanking them, the muleteers complained about the extra load.

'They wish more baksheesh,' Fuad said.

'Should we invoke the sheikh?' Gilbert asked Benet, with a glance at the spear.

'No point. The Bedouin disdain them. They'd no more

engage with them than exchange one of their horses for a mule.'

They finally set off, three hours later than planned, through the Valley of Hinnom. After little more than two hours in the saddle, Gilbert caught his first glimpse of Bethlehem, surrounded by golden-white wheat fields. Reining in his horse, he offered up a prayer of thanksgiving, which was answered by a burst of heavenly music that was no less wondrous when he realised it was the church bells pealing noon. For once he was grateful for the myriad sects that produced such rare harmony. On entering the town, Sheikh Hamden conducted them to the Church of the Nativity, but all hope of visiting it was dashed when a monk met them at the enclosure gate, explaining that an outbreak of plague in the Greek convent had led the brothers to quarantine themselves and close the church.

After lunch in the shade of the Shepherds' Field, they set off for the convent of Mar Saba, travelling for four hours along dusty, winding roads lined with arbutus and dwarf oaks and free from the rocks and brushwood that had hampered their journey from Jaffa to Jerusalem. As they made the tortuous ascent of the southern slopes of the Kidron Valley, Gilbert felt his horse's exhaustion as much as his own, but the view from the ridge repaid the effort. The convent loomed above them like a wasp's nest. Walls and towers and stairways and buttresses jutted from the rock in a feat of engineering to equal any of Stevenson's bridges. It was impossible to determine how much was masonry and how much mountainside or, rather, how much was man's work and how much God's.

In response to Fuad's knocks, the hospitaller lowered a basket from the top of the gate-tower in which the dragoman placed the testimonial from the Greek Patriarch in Jerusalem. Several minutes later, the iron door creaked open and Gilbert, Benet, Fuad and Bassem were invited inside. The rest of the company was left to camp in the valley, since the monks harboured an age-old mistrust of all Arabs, especially Bedouin against whom they had built the fortified walls. After conveying Fuad and Bassem to the refectory, the hospitaller led Gilbert and Benet through an inner courtyard, past chapels and cells projecting from clefts and crevices, to two spartan bedchambers hewn from the cliff. He left them to rest and refresh themselves – something of a challenge given the facilities – before returning to show them the convent's chief treasure: St Sabbas's cave.

After a meal as frugal as the furnishings, the hospitaller escorted them back to their rooms before joining his brothers in the chapel. The temperature having plummeted since nightfall, Gilbert huddled beneath the meagre bedding and lit his pipe more for warmth than for pleasure. A few minutes later, Benet entered and asked to borrow some tobacco.

'It's a good way to keep out the cold,' Gilbert said.

'And kill off the smell of that monk,' Benet said, wincing.

'Trust you,' Gilbert replied, guiltily recalling his own wish that the convent's privations had not included soap.

'Thirty years cooped up in a cloister on a mountain ledge: sleeping on a bare board; eating nothing but bread and broth; walking barefoot in all weathers. And all because some fourteen hundred years ago a hermit in a cave met a remarkably – one might say, preposterously – docile lion.'

'He has taken vows, Benet.' For all his misgivings about the monastic vocation, he felt a sneaking admiration for men whose everyday lives embodied the mystery of human existence: poised over a precipice, sustained only by the rock of their faith.

The next morning they set off at four, before the monks had risen for dawn prayer. The air, although bitter, was scented with balsam. Day broke at six and by the time that they stopped for breakfast two hours later, the heat was fierce. Gilbert felt the perspiration dripping from the rim of his cap, square in name only, and seeping through his unmentionables to the seat of his trousers. For all that the road to Hebron was largely clear, there were sections where they were forced to dismount and creep forward on foot. The mules took precipitous shortcuts and it was hard to say which were the more doltish, the beasts or their masters, who with minimal effort could have kept them on track. Two slipped and lost their packs, causing long delays while they were reloaded.

'What's he saying?' Gilbert asked Benet, as Fuad screamed at Amar.

'May a cunny swallow you,' Benet replied with relish.

Shortly before noon, they reached the brow of a hill and the village of Beni Naim, traditionally the spot from which Abraham watched the burning of Sodom, and now the final resting place of Lot (Gilbert had given up trying to correct the Muhammadan *Lut* and instead pretended that he was travelling in a group of guttural Germans). The village, while substantial, was deserted, as if it had been the victim either of plague or plunder. Fuad, however, ascertained from the Bedouin that the inhabitants lived there only in autumn and winter, spending the months of pasturage among their flocks. Their absence removed any threat of attack as Sheikh Hamdan led the company through the eerie streets to the mosque. Despite the lack of worshippers, the courtyard was open and Fuad proposed it as a suitable place for their meal. While Bassem boiled eggs, the servants laid rugs and the Bedouin and muleteers tethered their beasts, Gilbert entered the mosque where, despite the gloom, the tomb was instantly apparent, covered by a red silk cloth embroidered with Qur'anic verses. With no custodian to object, he slipped his hand over the low rail and touched it. A tremor ran through his bones and he feared that his knees might give way. Except for Hamdan's brother, El-Khatib, praying and prostrating himself in the aisle, he was alone with one of the giants of Genesis.

Having paid his respects to Lot, he returned outside. Once

his eyes had adjusted to the dazzle of the courtyard, he was delighted to spot a large pile of olives and a melon among the dishes that Hakim and Halim had laid out on the rugs. Benet explained that, while he had been 'communing with a person or persons unknown', a peasant from the neighbouring village had arrived to sell his produce.

'Had you been here five minutes ago, you'd have seen Fuad and Bassem on the brink of fisticuffs over who had the right to buy provisions.'

'What earthly difference does it make?'

'The commission, Uncle! Or as you might say, the tithe.'

Although he had never felt at ease eating either with his fingers or on the ground, Gilbert found the food surprisingly palatable.

'So, what's next on the programme?' Benet asked, with uncharacteristic cheer. 'How about the Maqam an-Nabi Yatin?'

'Very helpful, Benet,' Gilbert replied, more indulgently than he would have done before eating.

'That's the Shrine of the Truthful Servant. According to the sheikh, Lot prayed there, although he didn't say when or how often. You can even see one of his footprints.'

'Another footprint!'

'Isn't that why you came here? To follow in the footprints of the Patriarchs?'

'*Footsteps*, Benet, as I perceive by your smirk you know.'

'You're too quick for me.'

'I must confess I'm surprised by the reverence in which the Muhammadans hold Lot.'

'He's a far more significant figure in the Qur'an than the Bible. Mentioned in more suras than Jesus.'

'Which just goes to show their delusion.'

'In their book, he's a major prophet. He doesn't settle in Sodom simply to avert a rift with Abraham. He's sent there by Allah to persuade them to renounce their wicked ways.'

'With a marked lack of success.'

'Inevitably. The people ignore him just as they do all the prophets in the Qur'an before Muhammad. And, although it retains an element of carnality, the sin of Sodom in the Qur'an is primarily its disregard for Lot, which, if you think about it, reflects better on God, since it explains His punishment of the women and children who can have played no part in the assault on the angels.'

'The ways of the Almighty are beyond our comprehension.'

'Sorry, I forgot … Moreover, the same is true of Lot's wife, who remains in Sodom and is killed not for disobeying God but for disrespecting her husband – surely you approve of that? The angels foretell her death at the same time as they warn Abraham of the imminent destruction of the city.'

'And do the daughters feature in the Qur'an?'

'I fear so. But even then the story has a different – and less distasteful – tone.'

'You surprise me!'

'In the Bible, as I'm sure you remember, Lot offers his daughters to the men unconditionally: "Do to them as is good in your eyes."'

'I remember.'

'In the Qur'an, his intention is rather to bring home to the men the depth of their depravity. I forget the exact Arabic, but it's to the effect that "What you are doing to my guests is even more loathsome to me than if you were to violate my virgin daughters."'

'I had no idea that you were such a keen student of the Qur'an.'

'As I told you, I've been exploring the different Scriptures. You set me on the path all those years ago, when we compared the Greek and Hebrew gospels.'

'But then you veered off it. Of course Lot's offer is unconditional. He shows us how far we must go to serve the Lord and his agents.'

'It's too far for me.'

'Even to say that is a sin.'

'In your eyes aren't we all sinners, tainted by Adam?'

'And redeemed by Christ.'

'But to me, sin isn't an inevitable, involuntary condition of being human but a free expression of humanity. It's a blow struck against centuries of cant and oppression, not weighed down by Adam's transgression but proudly asserting our own.'

Praying that Benet's blasphemy was a provocation and not a creed, Gilbert told Fuad to prepare for departure. Hebron lay beyond the hill, although the precise distance was hard to gauge, given the Bedouin practice of calculating journeys by time rather than length. For once their approach proved to be valid when they were forced to make a long trek upstream of a river that was too deep to ford. After passing a clump of gnarled and cratered olive trees, they came upon a majestic oak. All Gilbert's resentment of the detour vanished when Fuad identified it, courtesy of Hamdan, as 'most holy old tree of Mamre', and he realised that he was standing in the very spot where Abraham had built his altar to the Lord. Although five thousand years old, the tree was little larger than the one that his great-great-great-grandfather had planted in his park to mark King Charles II's Restoration. The sheikh, noting his interest, sent four of his men to encircle it, and even with arms outstretched their fingertips barely touched.

Ignoring Benet's barb that the Bedouin would take him for a Druid, Gilbert made a circuit of the tree, elated to know that he was walking not just in the footsteps of the greatest of the Patriarchs but of God Himself, who had conversed here with Abraham. He looked for evidence of that earth-shaking encounter, but there was nothing to be seen apart from the tree, an ancient well and the withered scrub. His inspection was cut short by Fuad, conveying a message from Hamdan that they must press ahead if they were to present their firman to the governor of Hebron before nightfall. Gilbert reluctantly remounted and rode on to a ridge, where he caught his first glimpse of the walled city, which, provided one discounted the pagan legend that Jaffa predated the Flood, was the oldest in the world. Here Abraham, Isaac and Jacob had lived and were buried; here David had been crowned and written psalms. A wave of melancholy swept over him at the thought that it was now in the hands of the infidel, compelling Christians – in St Paul's words, Abraham's seed – to beg their permission to enter.

As he made his way through the city gate, it was clear at once that their firman granted them entry but not welcome. Two women, gathering water at a well, glared at them as though they were latter-day crusaders, their swords wet with their children's blood. A group of urchins playing in the dirt hissed at them through jagged teeth. One threw a stone, which grazed Gilbert's ear, causing his horse to rear up. Hamdan raised his lance; Benet cocked his rifle; Fuad clasped his scimitar. Gilbert himself fingered one of Sir William's pistols, wishing that he had paid more attention to its workings.

Despite the danger, he refused to leave Hebron without seeing the Haram and the Tomb of the Patriarchs. So, while Hamdan took Fuad to present the firman to the governor, the remaining Bedouin escorted Benet and himself through streets that were even narrower and more sordid than those of Jerusalem. The houses were so tightly packed that they arrived at the Haram without warning when they turned to face a huge wall, at a guess fifty feet high, surmounted by minarets at each corner. The courtyard was said to contain a church, but that was impossible to verify since none but Muhammadans were allowed to enter. Three white-clad women stood at the wall beside a spy-hole, the closest that Jews might come to the tombs of their ancestors. They scurried away like startled does at the strangers' approach.

Gilbert put his eye to the hole. 'What can you see?' Benet asked.

'The portico of the mosque ... a prayer niche,' Gilbert replied, squinting at the shadows.

'How odd,' said Benet, to whom he had ceded his place, 'that you should see all that when the screen is down.'

Denied even a glimpse of the interior, they wandered around walls as forbidding as any fortress, until Hamdan returned with Fuad to take them to Abu Dahuk's agent, Sheikh Hamza. He led them down roads that bore the imprint of centuries of laden camels to a small house on the outskirts of the city. After posting a guard at the door, he introduced them to Hamza, a skeletal old man with skin as yellow and creased as parchment. By his side was a handsome youth with glossy hair, sable skin, small teeth and dark, melting eyes. Although his presence went unacknowledged, Gilbert presumed him to be the sheikh's grandson or even, given his indeterminate age, great-grandson. Hamza greeted them with ritual salaams before, to Gilbert's dismay, kissing them both three times on the shoulder, to which the only suitable response was a dignified smile. The customary courtesies were exchanged, with Benet speaking for both of them, although Gilbert was now so familiar with the formula that he was confident he could contrive a reply. As Benet set out their requirements, Gilbert and Hamdan watched Hamza go through the same pantomime of frowns and grimaces that Hamdan himself had done in Jerusalem.

'He suspects that we're looking for hidden treasure,' Benet explained to Gilbert.

'Why?'

'The Bedouin cannot comprehend the European taste for travel. It only makes sense to them if it's in pursuit of profit.'

'Then please assure him that I am after treasure: the treasure of visiting the lands in which Abraham and Jacob pastured their flocks, David fled from Saul and God wreaked vengeance on Sodom.'

'I'm not sure that that would help. We'd do better to confirm his belief in our foibles.'

While willing to play the eccentric Englishman to obtain the sheikh's aid, Gilbert refused to pay the extortionate 2,500 piastres a day that he was demanding.

'He says that it's for twenty-five men,' Benet reported.

'Why so many?' Gilbert asked. 'Finn informed us that there were no tribal disputes in the area. The only protection we need is from grasping Bedouin. Offer him four hundred and not a piastre more.'

Benet did as instructed, whereupon Hamza stormed out of the room, followed by the young man, who blushed. Hamdan puffed impassively on his pipe.

'I do not trust this man,' Fuad said, 'like water in a sieve.'

'I fail to see why we cannot deal with Abu Dahuk directly,' Gilbert said, ignoring Fuad, whose own probity was open to doubt. 'Why must we use an agent who'll be taking a hefty commission?'

'You were there when Finn said that the Djahalin were at war with the government over their refusal to pay tax. It wouldn't be safe for him to come to the city.'

'Yes, but he also said that there were only a hundred and fifty Turkish soldiers in the whole of Palestine. And I've yet to spot a single one in Hebron. The Bedouin must outnumber them by a hundred, if not a thousand, to one.'

'There were only forty thousand British in the whole peninsula to rule over more than two hundred million Indians. I often wondered why they didn't rise up and slaughter us all in our beds. When they finally tried, they failed spectacularly.'

'The odds are immaterial when God is on your side.'

Ten minutes later, Sheikh Hamza came back and calmly agreed to all their terms as if the man who had just left were his hot-tempered twin. Fuad drew up a contract similar to the one that Gilbert had signed with Sheikh Hamdan and, indeed, with Fuad himself. On his client's behalf, Hamza pledged to escort the travellers on an eight-day journey across the plains of Ein Gedi and around the Dead Sea by way of Kerak, for which he would receive four hundred piastres a day, half to be paid beforehand and the other half to be lodged with the Governor of Hebron to await their return.

Hamza accepted the money with fulsome expressions of gratitude, in which Gilbert detected no fewer than eight references to Allah, a practice that, for all its extravagance, he would have been happy to see adopted in Whatcombe, where few of his parishioners ever invoked God except in an oath. Hamza departed for Abu Dahuk's camp, promising to return in the morning. As a surety, he left the youth, Jabir, who, it transpired, was no relation of his but rather Abu Dahuk's nephew.

'He is greatly beautiful, no?' Fuad said, as Jabir returned to the room, wreathed in smiles. 'Druze, he say body is robe for soul. And his is robe made from golden thread.'

'You should save such sentiments for your wife,' Gilbert said, suspicious of the analogy.

'Wife, she in Cairo,' Fuad replied dismissively.

Gilbert felt a distinct unease, seeing as if for the first time the fleshiness of Fuad's features: the ruddy cheeks; bulbous nose; sensual mouth. But his anxieties were forgotten when Benet, speaking to Jabir, called out.

'I was relating your dearest wish, Uncle. Jabir says he can take us to Sodom.'

They returned to the centre of town to deposit the rest of the fee with the governor, trusting to the gathering darkness to protect them from any further hostility. Hamdan led them out of the gate to a gravelly hill a mile or so to the west where, during their absence, Hakim and Halim had pitched three tents: one large one for Gilbert and Benet, and two smaller ones, for Fuad and Bassem, and the servants and equipment. It was the first time that Gilbert had entered the tent and he was pleasantly surprised by its furnishings: two trundle beds with fresh linen and wool mattresses; a trestle table for eating and writing; two folding chairs; a china dinner service; ewers and basins; a Persian carpet. The only drawback was the thin layer of dust on everything, which, as he discovered from Fuad, had been blown in by the sirocco that had risen while they were with the sheikh.

'I speak to Halim, who say it is Simoom, which sweep in from nowhere, pull pins from ground and cut rope. I say he is lazy and lying and worthy of beating.'

'Nonsense,' Gilbert said, increasingly disturbed by the dragoman's readiness to resort to the whip. 'Even if the dust were inches thicker, the tent would be more commodious than the lodgings in Ramlah and Mar Saba.'

The Bedouin and muleteers would sleep in their cloaks as was their wont, the former taking it in turn to keep watch in case the men of Hebron launched an attack. Jabir, however, announced that he would lie outside the entrance to Gilbert and Benet's tent. Despite Benet's recognition of the honour paid them by the sheikh's nephew, Gilbert was uneasy with both the suggestion that they were unable to defend themselves and the almost canine servility, which did not accord with either Jabir's stature or status.

Wearied by the day's exertions Gilbert fell asleep almost at once, only to be woken by a series of cracks, which convinced him that the threatened raid had occurred. Rousing Benet from a sottish stupor, he grabbed his pistol, more to bolster his confidence than to use. He peered out of the tent, to find that the cracks were caused by the largest hailstones he had ever seen, more like shards of glass than ice. Black clouds scuttled across the leaden sky. The wind ripped the ropes from the ground but, despite Fuad's misgivings, the pegs held fast. The Bedouin were tending their terrified horses, but both the muleteers and their mules were preternaturally calm. Despite the tumult, Gilbert felt a rush of excitement. A few hours earlier the sun had been beating down on them and now the wind roaring through the tent was as bitter as a Whatcombe winter. Even the climate in this extraordinary land was unique.

Shivering, he was about to return to his bed when he caught

sight of Jabir, or rather the glint of his smile in the shadows. 'Come inside!' he called, trusting that his tone would ensure comprehension. 'Fetch a towel,' he added to Benet, who had stirred himself sufficiently to light a lamp.

'Don't fret, Uncle. He'll be fine.'

Gilbert looked at Jabir, so wet that he seemed to be deliquescing. 'He'll catch his death.'

'He's a Bedouin, made of stronger stuff.'

As if to prove the point, Jabir shook himself so violently that the spray hit Gilbert, who saw with dismay that his own legs were naked.

'Do something,' he said to Benet, as he grabbed his trousers. 'Why are you laughing?'

'Can't you hear? The rain has stopped.' Benet walked to the entrance and stared out. 'In a few hours the ground will be as dry as a bone.'

'And in the meantime?' Gilbert asked. 'He can't sleep in the wet. He's the sheikh's nephew.'

'Then he can bunk with us.'

'Don't be idiotic!' Gilbert said. 'He'll have to go in with Fuad and Bassem. It might help to keep the peace.'

'You might find they fight over Jabir.'

'What on earth for? He's not a servant.'

Benet took Jabir to the adjacent tent, lingering so long that Gilbert fell asleep before his return. The next morning the sky was clear and the air fresh and the only evidence of the storm was the sodden path to the latrine tent. Despite a double dose of Rochelle salts before bed, Gilbert spent longer at stool than he deemed proper, so he was relieved to step outside and find the muleteers, servants and even some of the Bedouin at prayer. Among the recusants were Fuad and Jabir huddled together, sharing a pipe. Fuad greeted his curt nod with a broad grin, as though aware of his travails.

'Is good tent Fuad is buying for Bishop to make ease with himself, yes?'

'Ask Jabir why he isn't praying with the others,' Gilbert said peremptorily.

'He no pray. He bad Islam.'

'Can he read like Sheikh Hamza or is he illiterate like Sheikh Hamdan?'

'He no literary,' Fuad replied, after a few words with the youth. 'He say read and writing just for fellahin. He very ignorant. Wait!' he added, as Jabir continued to speak. 'He say Prophet Muhammad, blesseds be upon him, do not read or write, so why must he?'

'The prophet had Gabriel – Jibril – to guide him,' Gilbert said, his reverence for learning outweighing his mistrust of the faith. 'Without books, how will Jabir know the history of his own people, let alone the rest of the world?'

'Bedouin, he have teacher who tell him stories of tribe to last forever in his head. Bedouin, he have hundreds of stories in head.'

'But there are other stories – greater stories – that he'd learn. Our Saviour, Jesus Christ, wasn't raised in one of the rich scribal families in Jerusalem but in a poor carpenter's shop. Yet He could read and write – and not only with a pen and paper, but with His finger on the ground when He was challenged by His enemies. As a boy, far younger than Jabir is now, He was able to debate with the wisest scholars in the Temple. Ask him if he'd like to know the true story of Jesus, who's much more than just the Prophet Isa. Ask.'

Despite the heavy penalty for proselytising a Muhammadan, there was a spark in Jabir that made it worth the risk.

Fuad conveyed his request to Jabir. 'He say "Yes, please. Bishop must tell him this truth about Isa. But Fuad, he must always be there to translate."'

Gilbert walked back to his tent with a sense of achievement. Bassem brought his breakfast with a face as black as the previous night's sky. Gilbert was packing his effects when he was startled by an agonised scream. He was about to investigate when Benet came in to report that, while striking the equipment tent, Mustafa had been stung by a scorpion that had sheltered from the storm. Accustomed to treating mild disorders in the village and warned that, in the desert, every Westerner was regarded as a practised physician, Gilbert had brought along a well-stocked medicine chest, but he had no remedy for a sting unknown at home. The best he could offer was the oil of hartshorn for snake bites and, after consulting Benet, he hurried to the half-dismantled tent where Mustafa lay, sweating and shaking, while Jadid and Amar shouted exhortations in his ear and Hajji Mamluk raised his eyes to heaven. Hakim and Halim cowered at a safe distance, as though the sting were contagious, and the Bedouin went about their business, their customary indifference to the muleteers now bordering on callousness. Taking charge, Gilbert instructed Benet, who was dosing himself with brandy that elsewhere would be given to the patient, to hold Mustafa's head, while he cut the sting from a calf that was already dangerously swollen. Mustafa's screams were silenced by Fuad. 'I tell him not to disturb Bishop,' he vouchsafed, unbidden. The screams recommenced when Gilbert liberally applied the hartshorn to the wound, before bandaging it with one of his own handkerchiefs.

'Is wasting on this fellow.'

Putting little faith in the treatment, Gilbert asked Fuad to tell Mustafa that there was nothing to do but wait (which Benet informed him he had rendered as 'whether you live or die is a matter of no importance') and instruct the other muleteers to assist the servants in striking the tents, packing the equipment and loading it on to the beasts. 'You would do well to remember that the hours of departure are clearly specified in the contract. If you continue to fall behind, we might have to review your fee.'

'What must I do?' Fuad said. 'Their ropes are long.'

'Then tell them to shorten them.'

'No, Uncle,' Benet interjected. 'It's local parlance. It means that they work slowly.'

'Is true,' Fuad said. 'What will you wish me to do? Beat them?'

'No,' Gilbert replied wearily. 'I don't want you to beat anyone. Just see to it that they make haste.'

By the time Sheikh Hamza arrived with the news that Abu Dahuk was expecting them, the mules had all been loaded and Mustafa was starting to rally. He had stopped gulping, regained colour in his cheeks and recovered the use of his leg. He was even able to hobble alongside his mule, although Gilbert insisted on his comrades redistributing their loads so that he could ride for the day. One by one, the muleteers walked solemnly up to Gilbert and pressed their foreheads to his hand.

'Careful, Uncle,' Benet said. 'Next, they'll be hailing you as a prophet.'

They headed down the rough track from Hebron to Kurmul through vast fields of ripening wheat, the surest sign yet of God's promise to Moses. They travelled all day, not even stopping for lunch, a simple meal of hard-boiled eggs and unleavened bread that Gilbert ate in the saddle. To his considerable satisfaction, he had mastered the art of removing the shells with one hand while the other held fast to the reins. The greatest hardship was not the blistering sun, jolting path or biting saddle but the swarm of horseflies that pursued him across the plain and, notwithstanding their name, appeared to find the rider more appetising than his mount.

'Never mind,' Benet quipped, his own flesh preserved by alcohol. 'There's always a fly in the ointment.'

It was dusk when they reached the Djahalin encampment. The view was spectacular as they descended a gentle slope to a field scattered with forty or fifty black goatskin tents. Scores of Bedouin were hard at work and, as they approached, it grew clear that all of them were women: churning milk; grinding flour; fetching water and firewood. At the sight of the strangers they scuttled into their tents.

'Are all the men out on a foray?' Gilbert asked Fuad.

'What is this *foray*? Is not good English word,' Fuad replied, as ever refusing to admit ignorance.

'Reconnoitring. Hunting for food or enemies.'

'Oh no, is inside tents. This is Bedouin way: man look after weapons and horses and listen to stories of tribe; woman must work for all else.'

On entering the camp, they were thronged by Djahalin men and boys. Some greeted acquaintances among the Thaamerah. Others held out their hands and pipes with demands for baksheesh and *tunbak*. Gradually they gravitated towards Gilbert.

'What do they want from me?' he asked Benet, struggling to conceal his anxiety.

'They're fascinated by the paleness of your skin. Mine's baked through after India.'

'Really?' said Gilbert, under the impression that he had turned lobster pink. Emboldened, he stared back at the Djahalin, who were darker than the Thaamerah. All of them, young and old, had sinewy bodies and gaunt cheeks, which, with their deep-set eyes and aquiline noses, gave them the look of Gothic carvings. Dressed in simple, shapeless robes with camel's hair belts, they fixed their attention on his clothes. He was grateful that Jabir, his self-appointed protector, continued to discharge his duties, loudly chiding a man who grasped his waistcoat.

'Have they never seen an English gentleman before?'

'It's your buttons,' Benet said.

'What of them?' Automatically, Gilbert pressed his hand over the six jet buttons that Celia had sewn on in memory of Theo.

'They take them for talismen.'

'Then please disabuse them!' Gilbert said, for the first time wishing that Fuad's prelation of him was real and he was entitled to wear an episcopal cross.

The two sheikhs, Hamza and Hamdan, escorted them to Abu Dahuk's tent, instantly identifiable by the large lance plumed with ostrich feathers at the entrance and the magnificent bay charger with arched neck and high-flung tail picketed at the side. Gilbert entered to find it unexpectedly cramped, divided by a central curtain that screened off the women's quarters. It was sparsely furnished but stuffed with carpets and cushions as if at a parish rummage sale. The air reeked of burning palm oil and foetid bodies, to which the Bedouin appeared insensible. Jabir, who walked with a more marked swagger now that he was back among his own people, rubbed noses with his uncle, who was seated on a divan. Sheikh Hamdan followed suit. Gilbert, so shy of unfamiliar flesh that he dreaded Maundy Thursday, shrank from the prospect of such intimacy, not least with a man whose nose was so pronounced, but, to his relief, Abu Dahuk welcomed Benet and him with salaams.

Jabir led them to the divan on Abu Dahuk's right, which, unlike the punishing one in the governor's palace, had a rudimentary back formed from two camel saddles. A large black slave in a meagre loincloth knelt at their feet, which he raised on to a small rug. A second slave served coffee with a consistency more like tar than treacle, from a pot with a spout as elongated as the stem of a chibouk. Abu Dahuk plied them with the standard questions about their fathers' and grandfathers' health, to which Benet responded with customary eloquence. The two men conversed freely, with Benet translating the more pertinent of the sheikh's comments, such as his pledge that from then on he and his tribe were the Englishmen's to command. Gilbert nodded his thanks, although one glance at Abu Dahuk shattered any semblance of servility. He was tall and tawny-faced, with a heavy beard and a high brow above the hawk nose. He was dressed more sumptuously than any Bedouin they had yet encountered, in a red fez and a gold-and-white embroidered jacket over a scarlet robe. He had huge equine teeth, which he lost no opportunity to display, grinning immoderately at Benet's remarks, which were evidently more amusing in Arabic.

The preliminaries dispatched, Abu Dahuk announced that they had killed a kid in honour of their guests. 'And at our expense, I'll be bound,' Benet whispered to Gilbert, who was less exercised by the cost than by its being served by slaves. He longed to explain to his hosts, as he had once done to abolitionist groups across East Anglia, that the fact that the different races comprised different links in the Great Chain of Being did not mean that they stemmed from different roots or that the lower races were any less precious to God. Just as a spaniel was an inferior breed to a greyhound but both issued from the pair of dogs that Noah transported on the Ark, so the Arab and the Chinaman and the Ethiopian all descended from the same parents as the European. Their disparate characteristics – moral, intellectual and physical – were easily explained since, although Adam and Eve were Caucasian, the harsh climate, inimical habitat and poor diet in the southern and eastern hemispheres (of which he now had personal experience) had led to a degeneracy in both the characters and complexions of the natives.

In a show of sympathy, he scratched the slave's head when he held out a dish of olives. Noting Benet's frown, he kept his hands in his lap when a second slave brought a dish of grey, greasy bread. 'What's this?' he asked Benet, who shrugged.

'*Semen*,' Sheikh Hamza replied.

'What?'

'Don't worry,' Benet said, thumping his chest to hide his laughter. 'You're not back in the Shrewsbury dormitory. *Semen* is Arabic for melted butter.'

Gilbert's relief was short-lived since the two slaves carried in the largest platter he had ever seen, with an entire goat laid out on a carpet of rice and gravy, its severed head staring at its tail from atop its belly. He knew to expect neither plates nor cutlery since Benet had warned him of the Bedouin belief that a communal dish was more sociable and that, when Allah had given them fingers, it was an affront to Him to use forks. After a slave brought a basin of water for them to wash their hands, Abu Dahuk afforded Gilbert the honour of taking the first piece and he braced himself to tear a strip from the belly. He had raised his arm when Benet called 'No, the right hand, Uncle! You use the left in the privy.'

His appetite lost, Gilbert tore off a chunk with the prescribed hand, strenuously chewing the stringy meat, while the others took their fill. His misery increased as he watched each of the Bedouin in turn scoop up a mound of rice and gravy, toss it into a perfect sphere and pop it in his mouth without dropping a grain. Even Benet produced something vaguely oval, whereas no matter how hard he tried, his rice remained an amorphous mass and the gravy dribbled on to his clothes.

The food and fug having made him sluggish, Gilbert found himself communicating with Abu Dahuk directly, laying his hands under his cheek and closing his eyes to simulate exhaustion. Benet intervened, needlessly worried that the sheikh would take offence. While no doubt planning to carouse through the night, he deputed Jabir to conduct his guests back to their tent. Barely had they stepped outside than they were confronted by a determined crowd. News of his cure of Mustafa having spread, Gilbert was called on to treat a variety of ailments. He felt the same sense of fraudulence and insecurity as on the occasional Sunday when he mounted the pulpit unprepared. Nevertheless, he trusted that the Lord who healed all those who had faith in Him would guide his hand. He charged Benet to fetch his medicine chest and Fuad to marshal people into line. Then, with the aid of their translation and the patients' mime, he dispensed the remedies. Brandy and salt, his Whatcombe cure-all, would be unacceptable here, so he applied navelwort and rosewater to the ubiquitous eye infections; valerian and quinine to any internal complaint; and Sanders Golden Ointment to wounds that by rights should have been cauterised. His confidence deserted him only when he was confronted with a man in the throes of an epileptic fit.

'I tell him you say he is penetrated by djinns,' Fuad said.

'Well ...'

'Absolutely not,' Benet interposed. 'This man is not possessed by devils. He suffers from fits, like Alexander the Great, Julius Caesar and, indeed, the Prophet Muhammad.'

'Still, is best for ignorant people. Druze, when he have man or woman with djinn, he chain him to wall with iron collar. Djinn, he soon grow weary of living in so small space, so he jump out. But this people, he never think of that. He never think of nothing.'

A veiled woman and two young boys dragged the epileptic away, since none of the men would touch him. Gilbert and Benet returned to the tent, where three Thaamerah stood guard, and Jabir once again squatted at the entrance. Gilbert gave him a chary smile and went inside, where Benet promptly made up for the alcohol that he had been denied during the meal. To Gilbert's regret, it rendered him neither affable nor even maudlin but belligerent.

'Such excellent people, wouldn't you say, Uncle? We could learn a lot from them.'

'Surely we've already learnt it from the French philosophers with their *noble savagery*?' Gilbert replied coldly.

'You see savages; I see a highly principled people, living clean lives in the desert, untainted by thousands of years of so-called civilisation.'

'Clean! I've just dispensed vast quantities of quinine and camphor for wounds that have festered for lack of simple hygiene.'

'Trust you to take the word literally!'

'You should remember that, however principled they may appear, they are infidels and inherently wicked.'

'What would you have me do: creep out in the dead of night and massacre them in their tents?'

'I'd have you start by laying aside the Arab and Indian scriptures and returning to your own.'

'What if they are my own? What if I don't make such arbitrary distinctions?'

'Nothing in God's world is arbitrary. And if it is not too great a leap, I suggest you recall the passage in Numbers where God ordered Moses to kill the entire population of Midian. Or the First Book of Samuel where He commanded Saul to destroy all the Amalekites. They mightn't have been guilty as individuals, any more than the women and children of Sodom whose fate exercised you yesterday, but they were guilty collectively, as nations that had offended the Lord.'

'I feel sorry for you, Uncle. You worry about the challenge to faith from geology, from biology, from the higher criticism and from every kind of logical thought, but what about the challenge from basic morality?'

'What morality can ever equal God's? We can no more conceive of His goodness than we can fashion the mountains and frame the stars.'

'That's a metaphor, not an argument.'

'Can a worm understand a bird? Can a bird understand a fox? Can a fox understand a man? Can a man understand God?'

'How telling that you should choose your examples from creatures that kill one another!'

'You're drunk!'

'Then what a pity that I don't have my virgin daughters here to debauch!'

'Did you come on this journey purely to torment me?'

'Not purely, Uncle,' Benet said softly, 'never purely.'

Fearful that he would be unable to sleep, Gilbert took a large dose of chlorodyne and was woken the next morning by a hullaballoo in the camp. For once Benet was not sunk in torpor, and, setting aside their differences, both men hurried out to see a group of six Djahalin pelting one of their fellows with stones. The victim stumbled forward, his arms shielding his head, which was dripping blood. As if judging the distance to be safe, he turned back and raised his hands, only to be assailed by another volley, which fell short save for one stone that hit him in the stomach. He dropped to the ground, clambered up and darted down the path, whereupon the men abandoned the pursuit, relinquishing their missiles and returning to their tents.

'Would you try to find out what happened?' Gilbert asked Benet.

'Summary justice, I suspect.'

'But why?'

Benet approached the three Thaamerah sentries, who had watched the assault with the same indifference that they had done Mustafa's agony.

'Some of the Djahalin caught him pilfering our supplies,' Benet explained on his return.

'Did they tell no one? Where's Abu Dahuk?'

'They considered him unworthy of the sheikh's regard. He shamed the whole tribe by stealing from us while we're under their protection. Any greater acknowledgement of the crime would have shamed them even more.'

'But is it a stoning offence?'

'The stones were symbolic.'

'He was bleeding.'

'I meant that it wasn't the martyrdom of St Stephen. They were drumming him out of the tribe.'

'How will he survive alone in the desert? Will he join another tribe?'

'I doubt it. He's become a pariah. He'll either die of hunger or be killed by a predator, man or beast.'

'It's barbaric.'

'Tell that to my father who sentenced a sixteen-year-old boy to seven years' transportation for poaching a hare.'

'He was a habitual offender, tried with due process of law. Not everything is ammunition for your private battle with your family: your country: your God.'

'Still, if we fail to find the ruins of Sodom beside the Dead Sea, we can always discover it newly restored in the colonies. I read that the city's sin is rampant among the convicts.'

'Theo did not go to Australia; he went to New Zealand.'

'What?'

'I … I'm sorry.'

'What does it have to do with Theo? Who mentioned him?'

'I'm sorry. I was confused. I have not yet said my prayers.'

Gilbert retreated into the tent and, rather than trust to his own devices, read the Order for Morning Prayer, until Hakim and Halim came to pack up the furnishings. He had assumed that the Thaamerah would leave now that they had safely delivered them to the Djahalin but, to his surprise, Sheikh Hamdan and his men gave every indication of accompanying them.

'Think of it as double the protection,' Benet said.

'And doubtless double the payment.'

Unlike the Thaamerah, the Djahalin had not been officially disarmed. With their swords tucked in their belts and matchlocks slung across their shoulders, Abu Dahuk and his eight horsemen resembled nothing so much as the brigands in the tale of Ali Baba, although their faces were suited to a less fanciful entertainment. They made their way out of the camp, up the path that the visitors had taken the day before and across a rocky plain that, within a mile, had become utterly barren, with neither shrubs and grasses nor any of the broken walls and displaced boulders that had stippled the landscape from Jerusalem to Hebron. This was the true Judean desert, where John had lived on locusts and wild honey and Jesus had fasted for forty days and forty nights. Gilbert had pictured it as a bleak and craggy English moorland; now he saw the utter desolation, the 'waste howling wilderness' of Scripture. The only signs of life were a colony of vultures and a panther dining off a dead ibex in predatory harmony. Four of the horsemen, matchlocks raised, rode towards the panther, which padded off, seemingly unconcerned. Then, just when the hunters were close enough to fire, it eluded them in one mighty, mocking leap.

The heat was torrid. Gilbert's throat was parched, his neck and ears were burning and the spittle with which he wet his blistered lips was sour. He had not undressed fully since Mar Saba and the lice he had caught from the convent bedding showed no sign of satiety. As they scaled arduous slopes, only to descend vertiginous drops, he felt like a counter in a game of *Errand Boy*, moved one step forward for every two steps back. Moreover, it was the unscrupulous Bedouin who spun the top and controlled the board. Such were the twists and turns of the route, with teasing glimpses of sunlit water followed by protracted stretches of bare rock, that he began to suspect the Dead Sea itself of being a mirage.

Just when his dejection was at its height, he found himself on the brow of a hill with a bird's eye view of the sea hundreds of feet below. The Mountains of Moab, now a bleached blue, rose up on the opposite shore and the Caves of Ein Gedi lay beneath him. Beckoning Fuad to translate, Abu Dahuk drew Gilbert's attention to the dark towers of Kerak castle, perched on the distant peak. Gilbert's heart quickened when the sheikh pointed to a large greyish rock in the foreground, which he identified as 'Jebel Usdum'. He could scarcely contain his euphoria when Fuad added 'Is Mountain of Salt, Bedouin name for Sodom.'

The mountain was too far away to reach by nightfall and Abu Dahuk announced that they would pitch camp at Ein Gedi. The route was as circuitous as ever and at one point Gilbert was convinced that they would have to turn back.

Having come to a ravine where the path had crumbled, they were forced to descend a near perpendicular scarp. Horsemen and muleteers edged their beasts down a zigzagging track, little more than a fault line in the rock, which, had it been an inch or so steeper, would have been impassable. Miraculously, they all survived with only a sack of barley lost in the gorge. Hajji Mamluk and El-Khatib prayed; the muleteers embraced; even the sheikhs looked relieved as they continued along a narrow ledge, before resuming the descent over mounds of powdery rubble. Finally they arrived at the foot of a cliff, still several hundred feet above the sea where, in stark contrast to the aridity all around, a torrent of water cascaded into a large pool, amid a lush vegetation of mimosa, sorrel, reeds and rushes.

'*Fih maieh!*' El-Khatib shouted in one of the few Arabic phrases for which Gilbert required no translation, since the joy of finding water in the desert rendered it unequivocal. Bedouin, muleteers and servants alike rushed towards it, throwing themselves on their bellies to drink. Worried that Benet was set to follow suit, Gilbert put a restraining hand on his arm and led him there sedately, although once at the edge, he himself cupped the water and lapped it up with a relish that would have been unthinkable elsewhere. Eager to protect his privacy, he deputed Fuad to keep watch while he immersed himself behind the natural curtain of the falls. Never had a simple bathe brought him so much pleasure, as he splashed the ice-cold water on his skin and scratched the lousy infestation with a makeshift sorrel brush. Benet soon joined him, showing no more concern about stripping naked than a schoolboy in the Severn. Whether from a general aversion or local prohibition, the Bedouin shunned the pool, preferring to scrub themselves with handfuls of gravel.

As darkness fell, Hakim and Halim gathered thorns to build a fire, which burned fitfully but took the chill off the evening air. Bassem cooked a meal of cauliflower soup and chicken stew, which Gilbert unrepentantly ate with his own cutlery off his own dishes, while Benet dipped his fingers in the communal pot. Then, as moonlight silvered the pool and shrouded the cliff in shadow, the entire company sat around the fire to hear Abu Dahuk tell stories of his heroic past. With Benet loath to miss a word, Gilbert was dependent on Fuad for what he surmised was a highly coloured translation. After various tales of raids, in which stealing his enemies' sheep appeared to be as laudable as stealing his guests' provisions was base, Abu Dahuk described how he had once driven a host of his foes over this very precipice. All had been killed except for the sheikh's son who returned to his father, entreating him to sue for peace. The father consented, provided that Abu Dahuk paid blood money for the number of the dead Thaamerah exceeding that of the dead Djahalin.

'Are you saying these were the warring tribes?' Gilbert asked Fuad.

'This is surely so. And Sheikh Hamdan, he is son.'

After the sheikh had finished speaking, one of the Djahalin horsemen strummed a triangular, lyre-like instrument and the rest of the Bedouin began a chant, which, to Gilbert's untrained ear, was strangely reminiscent of the call to prayer. With so little variation in tune and tone, he felt sympathy for the frog that set up an antiphonal croak. No sooner had the song ended than, brandishing a sword, Jabir strode into the centre of the circle, from which the rest of the company drew back. They clapped and stamped as he marched on the spot, first holding the sword aloft, then slicing the air above his head, and finally sweeping it in a figure of eight as he leapt over the fire. He repeated the sequence several times, with the leaps growing ever higher and the sweeps ever broader.

'He is very pleasing to see,' Fuad said to Gilbert.

'I think you mean "exciting to watch".'

'Why is this? Prophet Muhammad, he say there is three

things most refreshing to the eye: green leaves and trees; flowing water; and beautiful face. Here, I have leaves on bushes and water in springs, and beautiful face on boy.'

'Take care,' Benet said, turning away from the fire. 'The Prophet also warned us against gazing at beardless boys with eyes more tempting than houris'.'

'But he is not without beard. He has hairs on chin.'

'That makes it all the more improper,' Gilbert said.

'We plough field and scatter seed. Shall we abandon field when seed has sprouted?'

'Men are not crops!'

'I have written poem about Jabir. As Bishop is most noble English poet, shall he wish to listen to it?'

'Now may not be the best time,' Benet said.

'Why not?' Gilbert said grimly. 'I have yet to hear any of Fuad's work.'

'Lord Benet, you will put it in good English, yes?'

'Plain English will be enough,' Gilbert said.

'Don't you trust me, Uncle?'

Fuad began to recite and Benet to translate almost concurrently, stopping once or twice to question a phrase or ask him to repeat a line.

'*My love is a youth as pure as jasmine,*

His face glows like the sun by day and the moon by night,

All other faces are eclipsed when I am by his side … no, *in his presence,*

The locks of his hair are like palm trees surrounding a spring … rather apt, wouldn't you say?

His breath is as fragrant as roses,

His tongue is as sweet as honey,

His legs are as lithe as a gazelle's,

His buttocks are like the golden sand dunes.

He weakens my eyes but strengthens my limbs,

He makes my penis (you did ask!) *stretch like the neck of a camel,*

Surely, if the prophet Lut saw this youth, he would not condemn me for loving him?

Fuad, you've excelled yourself.'

'It's an obscenity,' Gilbert said.

'What?' Fuad asked.

'Pay no attention. My uncle is of the dum-de-dum-de-dum school of versifiers.'

'I'm more concerned with the words than the rhythm. *Stretch like the neck of a camel*? That great furry thing …'

'It's poetry, Uncle, not to be taken literally. Any more than *Pilgrim's Progress*.'

'Of course! To you, nothing is to be taken literally.'

'Please keep your voice down! The Bedouin are watching.'

'Let them! Perhaps Sheikh Abu Dahuk would care to know the kind of attention his nephew attracts?'

'No, he chooses to look the other way. They don't subscribe to your Anglo-Saxon Protestant morality.'

'You might remember that, while he's in our employ, your friend is subject to Anglo-Saxon Protestant authority. We can indict him to Finn on our return.'

'You're overexcited. Fuad, please leave us now.' The dragoman hovered. 'We'll talk in the morning.'

'He has a wife and children in Cairo.'

'Oh Uncle!'

Mortified, Gilbert retired to the tent, the only one to have been pitched at Ein Gedi, since Fuad, Bassem, Hakim and Halim were sleeping alongside the Bedouin in the caves that surrounded the falls, the same caves in which David and his followers had hidden from King Saul, a precedent that would once have thrilled him. He lay awake, as first Benet entered and then the Arabs dispersed, until nothing could be heard but the occasional hoot of an owl and cry of a jackal. They made a fitting counterpart to his self-reproach. How could he have failed to grasp Reedy's warning about Fuad's inclinations?

The next morning both Fuad and Jabir were unusually subdued, convincing Gilbert that he could postpone confronting them until they reached Sodom. The servants and muleteers, as though sensing his mood, loaded the equipment without complaint, and, after breakfast and prayers (Gilbert's being both perfunctory and distracted), they made the final descent to the shore. Scanning the landscape, Gilbert caught a glimpse of fortifications on the crest of a nearby mountain. Loath to consult either of his translators, he drew his horse up to Abu Dahuk's and pointed enquiringly at them. 'Sebbah,' was the sheikh's terse reply, but it was sufficient to identify them as the ruins of Masada, the once impregnable citadel of Herod the Great. Like so much else in the Holy Land, the mountain bore witness to its own history, the blood-red rock evoking the mass suicide of the Jewish rebels, helpless against the Roman legion mustered below.

Shortly afterwards, they reached the shore. Gilbert gazed in awe at the translucent waves gently breaking on the sand. Just as his first sight of Jerusalem had been disappointing, so his first sight of the Dead Sea was an unexpected delight. The noxious fumes reported by Pliny the Elder were natural evaporation. The mephitic odour that led the Crusaders to dub it the Devil's Sea issued from underwater deposits of bitumen. Nevertheless, the Bedouin appeared deeply reluctant to approach it. Even the dauntless Abu Dahuk squatted several yards from the water's edge, watching it with a guarded expression. Gilbert wondered whether, as desert dwellers, they felt an innate antipathy to the sea, alien to islanders such as himself. But on questioning Abu Dahuk, Benet discovered that the antipathy was unique to this one. They believed that no one ever drowned in what they called the Sea of Lut but rather endured everlasting torment, their flesh rotting and bones cracking, on the seabed. Resolved to put paid to such credulity, Gilbert removed his shoes, coat and trousers and, with both skin and modesty protected, stepped into the water.

It was deliciously warm but thick with salt and he struggled to wade the twenty or so yards until it reached his waist. Clamping his jaws tight against any rogue ripple, he rolled on to his back. With the water so dense that he barely had to push to keep afloat, he felt doubly buoyant.

4

'Water!' Gilbert croaked as he stepped on to the sand, desperate to wash away the acrid, oily taste of the mouthful of sea he had swallowed. Grabbing the *girba* that Halim held out to him, he threw back his head, putting his lips to its rim as though he were drinking from the goat's udder rather than its skin.

The Bedouin appeared to regard his swim as an even greater folly than the trip itself. Not one of them would touch the nut-shaped piece of bitumen he had picked off the surface, as if its very provenance were a curse. His clothes dried swiftly in the baking sun, leaving briny patches on the cap and stockings, like a ploughman's sweat marks. With all eyes on him, he dressed hastily, struggling to maintain his poise as he stepped into both trouser legs at once. As soon as he was ready, Abu Dahuk announced another detour, since dense clumps of tamarisks and reeds made it impossible to proceed along the shore. Instead, they were obliged to scale a sheer slope, down a narrow track with such sharp bends that Gilbert's horse was not only nose to tail with Benet's but brushed the hooves of a Djahalin horse on the ridge above. To add to his discomfort, he was beset by mosquitoes, which, not content with biting his face and hands, insinuated themselves into his underwear, attacking his private flesh with impunity. Yet he made no complaint since, after the warring sects in Jerusalem and the closed shrines in Bethlehem and Hebron, the bites were a minor blight on the journey.

Before he knew it, they were standing on the top of Jebel Usdum. As though sensing his disappointment, Abu Dahuk explained that the salt was covered by a layer of limestone (in Fuad's phrase, a 'rug of chalk') and that its full magnitude was only visible from below. With the sun shining in their eyes and the path crumbling beneath their feet, the descent was the most gruelling yet. The riders dismounted and led their beasts gingerly down the dizzying track, stumbling over boulders and sinking into mounds of dust. Jadid's mule, ignoring his gentle prods, lost its footing and plunged hundreds of feet down an escarpment. The Bedouin as ever disdained the muleteer's disaster, while Fuad risked provoking another when, with no regard for anyone's safety, he stood in the middle of the track and berated Jadid for negligence, forcing Gilbert to intervene. To his surprise, he had become, if not fond of, then, accustomed to the muleteers and he pledged to compensate Jadid for the loss.

They arrived on the shore to be greeted by the mangled mule, its wounds already thick with flies. Jadid flung his arms around its neck and kissed it as tenderly as if it were his dead wife. Unnerved by the grisly spectacle, Gilbert wandered off to explore the mountain, a vast near-perpendicular precipice of greyish-white salt, standing about a hundred yards from the water's edge and stretching as far as the eye could see.

'Bishop please, sheikh is wishing you to look up high.' Fuad approached, flanked by Abu Dahuk and Benet, as though trusting that their presence would protect him from any further remonstrance about the poem. 'This is column of wife of Lut when she is made into salt.' Gilbert stared in amazement at the huge pillar protruding from a shelf halfway up the rock face, which he had attributed to erosion. Now that he examined it more closely, it had a distinctly human, possibly even female, shape. 'For one day in every month this white salt is becoming red when she is having her stain.'

'Nonsense!' Benet said. 'Next, you'll be telling us that the wind whistling though the cleft is the sound of her lamentation.'

'Druze, he say all things is possible for Allah.'

'True,' Gilbert replied uneasily.

'You're not saying you believe this twaddle?' Benet asked.

'Maybe not, but surely the tradition is of value?'

'It's not even part of their tradition. They hold that Lot's wife perished in the conflagration of the city.'

'So they have nothing to gain by lying.'

'They're telling you what you – and all the other Frankish travellers – want to hear.'

'Surely not your saintly Bedouin, untainted by civilisation or whatever?' Gilbert asked, averting his eyes from Abu Dahuk, who stood with a deferential grin like a porter waiting for a tip. 'They could never be so cynical!'

'They're not. It's in the nature of Arabs to wish to please. They know what you want and try to give it to you. It's courtesy, not cynicism.'

'How convenient!'

They followed the cliff for a mile or so until monotony overcame them and they made their way back along the shore and up a craggy trail to a hillock crowned by a pile of boulders of a similar shape, although in a far worse condition, to those of the Temple in Jerusalem and the Haram in Hebron. 'Redjom-el-Mezzorrhel,' Abu Dahuk said, as emphatically as if he had quarried them himself.

'Heap of fallen stones,' Fuad translated.

'Thank you, Fuad. I suspect even my uncle could have worked that one out.'

'But this fallen stones is Kharbet Usdum.'

'These are the actual ruins of Sodom?' Gilbert asked.

'Yes, is where Bishop wishes to be, no?'

The answer was an unqualified 'yes', although it sounded odd to say so when he was standing in the rubble of what, with the possible exception of Babylon, was the most iniquitous city of all time.

'Is more, look!' Fuad said, after a further exchange with

Abu Dahuk. 'Is more stones and walls on this hill and next one.'

Gilbert gazed across the cracked riverbed to the neighbouring hill, strewn with boulders, some upright, some overturned, some half-buried in marl. Embarrassed by his own whimsy, he pictured the city, divided in two, with the palace, temples and public buildings on one side and the private houses on the other. Looking around, he even conjectured that one of the coping stones might have been Lot's.

Only the two sheikhs, Abu Dahuk and Hamdan, joined them on the hillside. The other Arabs remained at the bottom, watching even more warily than when Gilbert had ventured into the sea.

'What new superstition is this?' Gilbert asked Fuad.

'Is no superstition; is Prophet. El-Khatib, he speak words of Prophet Muhammad, who say not to enter sites of Allah's punishment unless you are wishing to have same punishment falling on you. This people are not wishing to have same punishment as people of Lut.'

Despite the injustice of Lot's having lent his name to the sin he so roundly denounced, Gilbert was delighted by the further evidence of the city's location.

'You don't really believe that this is Sodom?' Benet asked.

'When Scripture, topography and tradition all combine, who am I to disagree?'

'But there are so many other explanations for the stones. A landslide or primitive grave markers or the limestone that was removed when they mined the salt.'

'Other explanations perhaps, but why must you let your own prejudice – some might say, your own need – blind you to the most obvious one? See, they're even charred!'

'Or else blackened by age or sulphur.'

'Lest you hope to add the city to your list of biblical fables, it might interest you to know that as late as the Council of Nicea, there was a bishop of Sodom. His name was Severus. But then the see disappeared.'

'I'm not surprised; his card would have caused a stir. But I'm less concerned with whether or not the city existed than with the way that its fate has been misappropriated.'

'Which is how, pray?'

'Look at the story in both traditions: the Bible first, which tells how twenty-five years before it was destroyed, Sodom was attacked by a powerful alliance of five neighbouring states.'

'Because they stopped paying tribute to the King of Elam: money that was plainly a bribe to persuade him to overlook their sins.'

'It's not so plain from my reading, especially when one of the states was Shinar or, as we now know it, Babylon, which must have had plenty of sins of its own to overlook. But we'll let that pass.'

'And who was it who came to their rescue? Abraham.'

'Quite. So you'd think that they'd have been even more grateful to his nephew, Lot. But the people of Sodom – I say people because the women are too often ignored – were notoriously inhospitable. In the Qur'an, they remind Lot that they have forbidden him to entertain strangers without permission.'

'You scour the infidel texts like a mudlark in a sewer.'

'Very well then, back to the Bible! Ezekiel, a prophet whom, as I recall, you held in the highest regard, claimed that the sin of Sodom was pride.'

'I esteem him for his lack of sentimentality. He didn't indulge the Jews simply because they were exiled and enslaved.'

'Later rabbinic tradition went further, depicting the city as uniquely cruel and unwelcoming. It's no surprise that they were so hostile to Lot's guests, whom they took to be spies. Lot, for his part, concealed their identities. So in the familiar way of primitive societies, the men undertook to rape their enemies. It was punishment, not lust.'

'Was that the reasoning you used on Theo?'

'You talk as though I'd tried to corrupt him, not console him.'

'Didn't you?'

'Even if Sodom did exist – even in this very spot – and some memory of its cruelty found its way into both the Hebrew and Arabic scriptures, that's no excuse for invoking it, however many thousands of years later, to condemn conduct that bears no more resemblance to it than a fencing foil does to an assassin's knife.'

'Who's the one arguing from a metaphor now?'

'When you caught Theo with the farrier—'

'So he told you! I suspected as much.'

'You not only persuaded my father to revoke the man's tenancy, throwing his wife and children on to the streets—'

'His presence polluted the parish.'

'But you dispatched Theo halfway across the world in an attempt to hide your shame.'

'Not my shame, his! How could he look his mother and sisters in the eye? I feared that he would give way to an even greater sin – a sin for which there can be no remission – the sin of despair.'

'And how opportune that, within a year, his mission was attacked and he was murdered: no longer an outcast but a martyr!'

'When did you become so callous? You've never known what it is to love a child – the flesh of your flesh – and it's painfully clear that you never shall. I swear on this ancient stone, sanctified by the Lord's wrath, that my sole concern was to shield Theo from further temptation. But his letters home were so formal, confined to his work at the mission and the beauty of the countryside, nothing of what was in his heart. What if he found the Maoris as degenerate a race as we've found the Arabs? What if far from repenting of his sin, he succumbed to it, and the tribe killed him for reasons other than his faith? What if – I can hardly whisper the words – he is not in heaven but damned eternally to hell?'

Gilbert's anguish was so intense that he longed for even

Benet's reassurance, but it was withheld. 'That's something you'll just have to live with.'

Fuad, beaming as if the stones held no more terrors for him than a twisted ankle, announced that Abu Dahuk was eager to press ahead and pitch camp at Zouera-el-Tahtah, a name from which very few Arabic excrescences had to be removed to arrive at the biblical Zoar. Excited by the evidence of this second ancient city, Gilbert strode along a track, which, for all he knew, was the very one taken by Lot and his family when they fled Sodom.

The short trek took about twenty minutes, confirming the biblical account in which the fugitives made their way there between the first blush of dawn and the full sunrise. After a cursory examination of the fallen stones, Gilbert asked Fuad to find out from Abu Dahuk whether there were any sign of the cave in which Lot and his daughters sought refuge when they in turn fled Zoar. Fuad returned to say that there were – or rather, 'was' in his singular locution – many caves beneath the surrounding cliffs. Without a word to Benet who sat, hip flask in hand, in what passed for contemplation, Gilbert followed the two sheikhs and three of their men into a subterranean labyrinth. His eyes took several minutes to adjust to the dark, the Bedouin oil lamps no brighter than fire-flies. The air was dank and the floor slippery and he grabbed hold of a well-placed stalactite to keep from stumbling into a hole. It was impossible to know whether this particular cave had any biblical heritage, but he felt confident that, having guided his steps this far, the Lord would not desert him. As the Bedouin led him deeper into the murk, he reflected on the relationship between Lot and his daughters after their incestuous coupling, which Moses, for reasons of either space or propriety, had omitted to describe. Did Lot recollect what had transpired or did he dismiss it as delirium? Did his daughters inform him that they were with child? Did their children ever discover their true parentage and make the acquaintance of their father-grandfather? So many questions! Not even the Qur'an could assist him since, according to Fuad: 'For Islams, Lut did not eat fruit of his daughters' orchards.'

The sun was setting as they left the cave. Gazing at the multicoloured cliffs, the yellow limestone bases rising to the oxblood sandstone peaks, he wished that Hugh were there to sketch them. Walking back to the tent that had been pitched in his absence, he wished more generally that the travel arrangements had never been altered and it was Hugh, not Benet, whom he would find inside.

Supper was subdued, in part because with no stream or spring for miles around, Bassem had been obliged to boil stagnant water for the soup and coffee, which tasted indistinguishably foul, and in part because everyone, Bedouin, muleteer and servant alike, was brooding on the perils ahead. Abu Dahuk, inspecting the brimming rock pools, declared that the winter rains had been exceptionally heavy and the Sebka, which they had to cross to reach Kerak, would be a swamp. He urged them to turn back, but Gilbert, buoyed by his success with Sodom, was doubly determined to reach Gomorrah. Sensing the sheikh's displeasure, the Arabs dispersed at the end of the meal, foregoing the revelry of the previous night. Gilbert, likewise, retired to his tent, where the loyal Jabir had already taken up position, even if the only dangers on such a remote shore were scorpions and snakes.

Gilbert undressed in haste and longed to fall asleep before Benet's return, but his chlorodyne had been one of the casualties of the mule's fall, so he was wide awake when Benet marched in and, rather than making for his own bed, hovered over Gilbert's, spoiling for a fight.

'You think that I debauched him, don't you?'

'I am doing my utmost not to think about it.'

'Well, for your information I didn't. It would have been like debauching myself.' Doubting that his nephew was a stranger to onanism, Gilbert was not reassured. 'Theo confided in me how desperate he was; you were right to fear that he was contemplating suicide. I convinced him that there was a world outside England where people lived by different rules.'

'And indulged in unmentionable practices.'

'Believe me, there are far worse on your own doorstep. I could take you to a brothel in Gray's Inn, where for a few pence the men who rule the land and make the laws and yes, preach the sermons, can stick pins in a ten-year-old girl's cunny or watch her eat their wastes.'

'The Lord will punish them.'

'That's as may be. In the meantime it was you who punished Theo and his farrier.'

'I had no choice. They were discovered in the old tithe barn.'

'Yes, by two of the spies you sent to seek out Sabbath-breakers.'

'They thought they were wrestling. They ran to warn me that Hewitt was strangling Theo.'

'Ah, the innocence of children! That's one thing to be said for recruiting them young. Savonarola would be proud.'

'Thank God that they weren't led astray – and by my own son! How could I condone his sin? Unlike you, I don't make my own rules. I live by the Bible.'

'Then you should read it more closely.'

'It's my constant study.'

'You're very quick to quote Moses, but what of Samuel, who wrote of David's love for Jonathan?'

'A love so pure that it passed the love of women.'

'Or so passionate! Why do you suppose Saul hated David so violently? Was it simply because he saw him as a threat to his throne? Or was it because of his son's devotion to him, a devotion that had been publicly – and for Saul, shamefully – expressed when Jonathan, a prince, stripped off his robe, his tunic, his belt and even his sword, and gave them to David, a peasant? This was indeed a love "passing the love of women".'

'Enough! I'd rather sleep outside with the Arabs than spend another night in here with you.'

'Surely that's going too far? The wild beasts perhaps, but not the Arabs!'

After pulling on his jacket, trousers and shoes, Gilbert grabbed an oil lamp and stepped outside, where Jabir's desertion of his post at least ensured that he had not overheard the quarrel. The temperature having scarcely dropped since sundown, he was tempted to emulate the Arabs and sleep on the ground but decided that his dignity would be better served by a cave. He picked his way to the cliff, where the plumed lance lodged in the rock identified the first cave as Abu Dahuk's, and the plain lance propped against a boulder identified the second as Hamdan's. He walked past two more caves, whose mouths were choked with rubble, and entered the fifth. The floor was reassuringly firm and there was no tell-tale drip. With his lamp casting as much shadow as light, he proceeded hesitantly until he found himself treading on something soft. Shuddering, he aimed the lamp downwards to discover Fuad and Jabir intertwined, the man's clothes rumpled and the youth naked.

Revulsion was followed first by rage and then by panic, as he shook and kicked the bodies, inducing no response. He spotted a small pipe by Fuad's shoulder and caught a hint of mint and burnt rubber in the musty air. It was clear that, fearful of discovery, they had made a suicide pact and he wondered whether it would be kinder to let the poison take effect. Instantly contrite, he ran for help, trusting that his yells needed no translation. He reached the mouth of Hamdan's cave and, heedless of protocol, seized the lance, striking it against the boulder. Bedouin came towards him from all directions and, stumbling over the rocks, he led them back to the cave where Abu Dahuk snatched his lamp and rushed inside, followed by Hamdan and a dozen men, several with daggers drawn. Gilbert hovered at the entrance, unsure whether the ensuing cries were those of horror or grief. Moments later, Abu Dahuk strode out, hauling a naked Jabir by the hair. The youth struggled to escape his uncle's grip while scrambling to maintain his footing. As Abu Dahuk dragged him into his cave, his men returned to the body of the camp. Gilbert, afraid for Fuad, stared into the yawning gloom but, bereft of his lamp, he dared not enter.

'Fuad, Fuad!' he called, his voice echoing in the void. Not knowing what else to say, he repeated the name with increasing urgency until the dragoman slowly emerged.

'Is no good, Bishop,' he said softly, holding up the snapped pipe as if that were the cause of his misery. One look at his face, its fleshiness still pronounced despite the downcast expression, was enough to erase all trace of Gilbert's sympathy.

'You disgust me, Fuad. You've broken the laws of God and nature. You've brought Sodom back to life in the very place where it was wiped out.'

'Is no good, Bishop.'

'Trust me, the British consul shall hear of this.'

Shunning the profaned cave, he returned to his tent to find Benet deep in conversation with two Thaamerah. At Gilbert's approach, he broke away and hissed in his face. 'You've excelled yourself this time! Wasn't it enough that you destroyed two lives in England without doing the same here?'

Outraged at the injustice, Gilbert brushed past him and entered the tent.

Benet followed, repeating the charge. 'Do you have any idea what you've done?'

'They were coiled together like snakes.'

'And no doubt there was an apple core beside them!'

'No, some kind of pipe that they'd been smoking. I was afraid they were trying to poison themselves.'

'What would be the point, when they have you to do it for them? God knows what punishment they'll be dealt.'

'Why, if the Muhammadans are as indulgent of the vice as you profess?'

'Indulgent, as long as it's not exposed. Shame, not guilt, is what drives them. When I was in Muttra, I heard a case of a boy raped by bandits. Everyone in his village knew what had occurred. He'd crawled home with blood dripping from his anus. But his parents insisted that he had been butted by a goat. They refused to let him testify. Their one concern was to avoid humiliation.'

'No doubt they trusted to a higher justice.'

'Oh no doubt! I have a friend … let's call him Benedict.'

'No, Benet, spare me!'

'Benedict is a man who … how can I put this politely? Oh what the hell, there are no ladies present and you've taken off your bands! He enjoys being ridden by Arabs.'

'I shall pray for him.'

'Bully for you! At first he was perplexed – horrified even – that his partners wouldn't look him in the eye after congress. It was as if they were revolted by what they had done.'

'Then they had more decency than … your friend.'

'But he came to understand that it was consideration, not contempt. They wanted to spare him the evidence of his shame: the shame of playing the woman's part.'

'My one solace in this sordid affair is that the offender is Fuad, not you.'

'You needn't have worried. You have to respect yourself far more than I do to entertain desire for someone so beautiful … so noble in body and spirit as Jabir.'

'Then I thank God for your self-disgust.'

'Let me tell you a story.'

'Now?'

'I was widely commended for leading the convoy to Agra at the start of the Rebellion.' Gilbert mouthed *Mutiny*. 'And I trust that I proved worthy of my charge. But there were others whose courage went way beyond the call of duty. I owe my life to the love and loyalty of one of my clerks.'

'I dare say he was well rewarded,' Gilbert replied, uneasy at Benet's mention of love.

'Oh yes, he received his due reward. Tajdar, the clerk in question, was with me when we foiled the ambush by the sepoys at the Muttra treasury. What's more, he devised our escape, exhorting us to disguise ourselves in the sepoys' turbans, tunics and cavalry boots. Even so, my voice and complexion might have betrayed me and, as ill luck would have it, the night sky was brighter than usual since the streets were lit up for the festival of Dussehra. Tajdar took command of our small group and, when we were questioned, explained that we were troops from Bhurtpore on our way to bathe in the Ganges and that I was practising *mauna* – that's a vow of silence – in thanksgiving for having defeated the enemy. Although he was a Muhammadan, he ended each exchange with the Hindu cry of "Glory to the Holy Ganges!"'

'All very admirable, but I fail to see how it pertains to the matter in hand.'

'Really? I called him my clerk, which is what he was to the world at large, but in private he was my friend, my particular friend.'

'Please don't tell me anything that you'll regret.'

'I regret a great deal, but for Tajdar's sake, not mine. When I was with him – and I mean *with him* – I attained a state of ecstasy that I can only suppose is what's felt by a yogi, an Indian mystic, who buries himself in the earth, taking in air and food and water through a reed.'

'You've made the earth your element, Benet. It's not something to be proud of.'

'Nearing the end of our flight, the pain in my shoulder grew so acute that I could barely walk. Afraid of holding the others back, I told – no, ordered – them to abandon me. They all did, except for Tajdar. It was the only order of mine he ever disobeyed. When marauding rebels set fire to the customs hedge – the hated barrier the Company had erected to prevent the smuggling of salt and opium – he dragged me into its roots until they'd moved on, despite the danger that the wind would change, sending the flames shooting towards us. Eventually, half-cajoling, half-carrying me, he got me to Agra. By then I was delirious and unable to remonstrate with the guards who, distrusting every native, refused him entry to the fort. Telling me not to worry, he left to find lodgings in the town. All was well until Greathed's troops arrived. Finding Tajdar outside the gate, waiting for news of me, they took him for a rebel seeking the opportunity to strike. So they shot him. That, if you want to know, is the real reason I resigned from the service: not the transfer from the Company to the Crown, not even because I no longer believed that we had any right to impose our will, our values and our laws on the Indians, but because I owed it to Tajdar not to side with his murderers.'

'I don't know what you expect me to say.'

'How about "God moves in a mysterious way" or "The wages of sin is death". No, that won't work, will it, since I'm still alive?'

'Benet, please—'

'I'm tired, Uncle. We have a busy day tomorrow. I'm going back to bed.'

The next morning, Fuad was nowhere to be found. Gilbert and Benet sought out Bassem, who was surprisingly distressed by his adversary's misfortune. He described how, swearing him to secrecy, Fuad had left the camp in the dead of night. He told Bassem that he was afraid of retribution, although whether that were the rough justice meted out by the Bedouin or a judicial process instituted by Gilbert was unclear.

'He's on horseback and Bassem gave him food,' Gilbert said, eager to dissociate Fuad from the Djahalin thief driven defenceless into the desert. 'He can be back in Hebron in two days – less, if he rides fast.'

'And negotiates the ravines and passes and paths that fall away or come to dead ends,' Benet replied.

Fuad's own doubts about his chances were revealed when

Bassem handed Benet a sachet containing a dozen poems that he had written over the past two days.

'His final testament,' Benet said.

'Or just for safe keeping,' Gilbert replied.

Benet leafed through them as they breakfasted on brackish coffee and hardboiled eggs with green shells.

'What sort of poems are they?' Gilbert asked tentatively.

'Love poems. And at first glance very good ones. He seems to have found his muse in Jabir.'

'Then you must burn them.'

'I'll do no such thing! I shall publish them here. And I shall translate them.'

'Into English?'

'No, Chinese!'

'There's no call for sarcasm.' Gilbert remembered the lyric that Benet had recited at Ein Gedi. If its stream of epithets were typical of Fuad's work (which, given his indolence, seemed likely), then by a few judicious amendments his lover could be legitimised. But when he suggested it, Benet replied that he would rather burn them, demonstrating that he was more intent on causing a scandal than honouring his friend.

'No reputable publisher will take them.'

'So, I'll distribute them among a small but distinguished circle.'

'It's not hard to guess what distinguishes them.'

'Not every poet's ambition is to have a copy of his doggerel on every schoolchild's desk.'

With Fuad's flight, Gilbert left Benet to deal with Abu Dahuk. Although the Sebka remained waterlogged, the sheikh waived his objections to their crossing it and, indeed, was so eager to set off that he deigned to chivvy the muleteers and servants himself. After searching the camp, Gilbert caught a glimpse of Jabir, surrounded by a phalanx of Djahalin. He felt a rush of pity for the youth who had been seduced by a gross and unprincipled poet. He longed to teach him the doctrine of atonement but, in Fuad's absence, he would be obliged to speak through Benet, like a fairground ventriloquist with a wayward doll. Never had he felt his lack of Arabic more acutely and, composing his features into a sympathetic smile, he walked towards him, but the Djahalin closed ranks in what now looked more like an armed guard than a random grouping, and Jabir refused to turn his way.

Trusting that they would have a chance to talk later, Gilbert mounted his horse and waited for the signal to depart. Abu Dahuk led them across the spur of a hill and down a rugged scarp to a thicket of reeds and thorns that marked the beginnings of the Sebka. They continued along a barely visible track, with spiked boughs jutting out to tear the men's faces and the beasts' flanks. Once on the other side, they found themselves in a landscape unlike any other: vast mudflats covered by a thin crust of salt that glinted silver in the sun, interspersed with darker patches of bog. Here and there, a branch, deposited by the winter floods, protruded from the ground like the arm of a luckless traveller swallowed by the mire.

Abu Dahuk in the van issued strict instructions that they were to follow in a single file, each man and beast keeping to the foot- and hoof-prints of the one in front. For once, not even the most headstrong mule made off on its own but stuck to the thin line of grasswort, the clearest indication that the ground beneath was solid. Nevertheless, it shook and cracked, which Gilbert trusted was due to the fragility of the crust and not the network of caverns that was reputed to run below the marsh. He found himself reciting childhood prayers and suspected that the murmurings all around attested to the Muhammadans doing the same.

All at once Jabir's horse careered off the path and into the quagmire. Within seconds its hind legs disappeared and it reared up, throwing its rider back at an angle of forty-five degrees, like the statue of a general killed in battle. The horse slowly but perceptibly sank, pitching and flailing, yet Jabir made no attempt to break free. All around, the Arabs stood stock still, which Gilbert took first for horror and then for fear, until it dawned on him that it was approval. They were watching not an accident but an execution. The glimpse of Abu Dahuk whipping the horse had been no trick of the light. The sheikh had cold-bloodedly sent his nephew to his death.

'Somebody do something!' Gilbert cried, as the horse sank to its nostrils, its desperate scream stifled by mud. Jabir, buried up to his shoulders, submitted like a saint to martyrdom. 'For God's sake, help him!' Gilbert added. With no one responding, he spurred his horse forward, only to find the reins snatched by one Bedouin while another came up from behind to hold him steady. 'Do something, Benet!' he cried again, although it was evident that all hope was lost. As the mud reached Jabir's neck, his jaw gaped, but there was no way of knowing if he were trying to shout since the mud constricted his windpipe.

Suddenly there was an eerie gurgle and a resonant plop, as if the earth itself had sounded a farcical note to undercut the horror. As the mud engulfed Jabir's turban, its surface evened out until it became one with the surrounding flats, lacking even the singularity of a grave.

Benet walked his horse gingerly along the track to Gilbert. He held out his hip flask. 'Drink!'

'I can't,' Gilbert said, trembling too violently to clasp it.

'Lean forward!' Benet pressed the flask to his lips. Gilbert, unsure if he were seeking strength or oblivion, took a long gulp.

'They murdered him,' he said at last.

'Yes.'

'Why didn't he struggle?'

'He wanted to redeem himself.'

'There are other ways.'

'Not in the eyes of the tribe.'

'And you let it happen.'

'The time for heroic gestures is past. I should have made mine in Agra.'

'Is there nothing we can do?'

'We can tell the story – suitably expurgated – in Hebron or Jerusalem. But do you suppose that the Ottoman authorities, who were afraid to move against the Djahalin when they withheld their taxes, will pursue them for this?'

'So we carry on, as if nothing has happened?'

'We have no choice. We can't make our way alone and I doubt that God will dispatch Gabriel to our aid as He did to Hagar's. Just a minute!'

A grim-faced Abu Dahuk rode up to speak to him. He resolutely refused to meet Gilbert's eye.

'What did he say?' Gilbert asked, as the sheikh returned to the head of the column. 'Did he offer any explanation?'

'Of course not. He sees no more need to explain himself to us than to his horse. He insists that we turn back. The accident – his word, not mine – proves that the Sebka is treacherous and his men are refusing to go a step further. He gave his word to return us safely to Hebron and he intends to keep it.'

'So we abandon the attempt to circle the sea and find Gomorrah?'

'You found Sodom, didn't you? Isn't that enough?'

FIVE

City of Angels

'If God doesn't punish America, He'll have
to apologise to Sodom and Gomorrah.'

Ruth (Mrs Billy) Graham, 1965

As my story draws to a close, it is fitting that it should do so in the self-styled City of Angels. Here, where the most enduring myths of the past hundred years have been fashioned, I have been granted a new lease of life. Just as I am the first angel to have been named in the Bible and the first to have been depicted in paint, so I am the first to have appeared on screen. The occasion was the 1903 film, La vie et la passion de Jésus Christ, *which, as its title suggests, was made not here but in France. In it, I played my traditional part at the Nativity, as I did again after crossing the Atlantic to New York for the 1912 one-reeler,* The Star of Bethlehem. *When the studios relocated to the West Coast, I was quick to follow, making my Hollywood debut in the 1936 film,* The Green Pastures, *in which, in a rare – almost unique – nod to my universality, I was embodied by a black actor. Although the folksy narrative has since been condemned, it contained my favourite line of dialogue to date, when I heralded the divine presence, calling 'Gangway! Gangway for de Lawd God Jehovah!'*

Biblical subjects rapidly became cinematic staples, on account both of the strength of the stories and their exceptional license to circumvent the censorship code and provide a hint of eroticism (think of Herod and Salome, Samson and Delilah, David and Bathsheba, even Adam and Eve). My fellows and I played our canonical roles but, as time passed and the filmmakers grew in confidence, they transported us from the sacred world into the secular. We were recast as guardian angels, fallible but well-disposed, tailored to an age of spiritual laxity. Gone were the days when my presence struck terror in even those called by God, with Daniel falling flat on his face, Muhammad ready to throw himself off the mountaintop and Mary herself recoiling. Instead, we were comforting, cosy figures, as was evidenced by our names: no longer Gabriel, Raphael, Ramiel, Raguel and Michael, but Dudley, Clarence, Arthur, Charles and Mike.

Our portrayal in these films owes more to folklore than to Scripture – unless you view the psalmist's claim that 'He shall give his angels charge over you' as a profession of our perpetual vigilance. Curiously, there is a surer theological basis for my most recent incarnation as a warrior angel in a spate of apocalyptic films. It was St Paul – never a favourite of mine after his pledge to the Corinthians that 'we will judge angels' – who maintained that we would come into our own in the cosmic battle between good and evil at the end of time. Poets and painters have long depicted that cataclysm but none has had recourse to the resources of the cinema. I suspect that my prominence in these films owes more to an easy recognition factor than to any character traits I may have acquired over the years. And while I grant the right of each new era to put its own stamp on us, I must admit that, listening to wigmakers and costume designers debate the length of our hair and shape of our wings, I feel a pang of nostalgia for the days when St Thomas Aquinas brooded on how we might have bodies but not bodily functions and Maimonides mulled over the extent of our free will.

I have travelled far since the Israelite scribes first represented me as God's messenger, an impersonal agent of divine providence. So in the 2005 film, Constantine, *in which my androgynous nature is underlined by the casting of a woman, I take it upon myself to make mankind worthy of God's love by unleashing hell on earth, in the hope that the survivors will redeem themselves through suffering and repentance. But my plan fails; my wings are burnt; I become mortal and subject to pain. In 2010's* Legion, *the premise is reversed. It is God who has lost faith in mankind and orders His angels to effect its extinction. Michael disobeys and descends to earth, cutting off his wings: a wound as much spiritual as physical. Setting sentiment aside, I lead the fight against him and stab him to death with my mace. But my victory is short-lived for, even as I am engineering universal destruction, Michael returns, life and wings restored, to explain that God has resurrected him since it is he, rather than I, who is executing His will, doing not what He asked but what He needed. Michael flies back to heaven and I am left alone.*

While I have been spared the indignity suffered by Michael, who saw himself portrayed in the film to which he lent his name as a messy, malodorous, overweight slob, who slurped his food and scratched his crotch (so much for Aquinas!), I am fastidious enough to prefer my depiction on panel and canvas to my impersonation by actors, however skilful, on film. There can be no denying that the medium has disseminated my and my fellows' images to a global audience of which previous generations of artists and writers could only dream. Yet the very prevalence of the images gives them authority, while their permanence runs the risk that the actors who create them will be credited with an immortality that was hitherto unique to us.

Flesh and Brimstone (Film)

From Wikipedia, the free encyclopedia

Flesh and Brimstone (German: *Fleisch und Schwefel*, French: *La Chair et le Souffre*) is a 1986 American epic drama film directed by Hugh Davenport and scripted by Howard Edelman from his National Book Award-winning novel of the same name. The film was condemned by religious groups for its revisionist interpretation of the biblical stories of Abraham, Lot and Sodom.

Despite the controversy, *Flesh and Brimstone* was widely praised by critics on its release. It was nominated for five Academy Awards, including one for Frank Archer in his last screen appearance. It won for Best Visual Effects (Lyle Perkins, Isabella Testorini & Paolo Grandi) and Best Original Score (Chymical Warfare). It was also notable for marking the screen debut of Daniel Stirling.

In 2015, the film was selected for preservation in the National Film Registry by the United States Library of Congress, as being 'culturally, historically, or aesthetically significant.'

Directed by	Hugh Davenport
Produced by	Bela Zipser
Written by	Howard Edelman (based on his novel)
Starring	Frank Archer Laura Bennett Porter Wright Dorothy Hillard Dana Adams

Music by	Chymical Warfare
Cinematography	Arturo Nobile
Edited by	Anne Greenwood Wendell B Holmes
Production company	Cornerstone Productions
Distributed by	Columbia Pictures
Release dates	November 11, 1986 (New York City premiere) November 14, 1986 (United States) March 20, 1987 (United Kingdom)
Country	United States
Language	English
Running Time	110 minutes
Budget	$10.8 million
Box Office	$5.75 million domestically $22.8 million worldwide

Contents

Plot

Abraham, a semi-nomadic sheep- and cattle-herder, prostrates himself before the image of his god, Yahweh, a bearded figure in a horned helmet, his left hand brandishing a spear and his right hand raised in blessing. He sacrifices a goat, ram, turtle-dove and pigeon in thanks for his safe return from Egypt. Prominent among the watching tribesmen is his nephew, Lot.

Lot asks Abraham why Sarah has kept to her tent since their return. He replies that she is suffering from women's troubles. Lot sends his wife, Idrith, to nurse her and Sarah reveals how, having denied their marriage to Pharaoh, leaving him free to take her as his concubine, Abraham can no longer look at her without picturing her in Pharaoh's embrace.

Estranged from Sarah, Abraham lusts after Idrith, embarrassing her with his attentions. Afraid to tell Lot, Idrith confides in Sarah. To protect her niece and give Abraham the son that she herself has lost hope of bearing him, she offers him her Egyptian handmaid, Hagar.

Hagar gives birth to Ishmael. Abraham, delighted with his newborn son, names him as his heir and orders Lot and the entire tribe to swear allegiance to him, in token of which they must have themselves circumcised, as he did with Pharaoh. Lot refuses and, to avert further hostility, uncle and nephew agree to part company, with Lot settling in the Jordan Valley and Abraham in the plain of Mamre.

Lot finds that the land he has chosen is too arid to sustain his family and bondsmen. At Idrith's suggestion they move to the Canaanite city of Sodom, where Lot's industry and integrity earn him widespread respect. The king appoints him as his chief magistrate, a post that, to prevent corruption, is reserved for foreigners.

After his initial revulsion, Lot comes to accept the city's same-sex practices. He explains the Israelite taboo to the king, who replies that desert people are hidebound and their high infant mortality rate leads them to favour procreation over pleasure. When Lot asks if the men have no wish for sons to carry on the line, he replies 'Of course, but we also wish for friends to carry on the community.' He urges Lot not to restrict his desires and offers to select a suitable companion for him. When Lot counters that he is happily married, the king replies 'So am I.'

Sarah flees to Sodom. She tells Idrith how Abraham burst into her tent, claiming that Yahweh told him that she would bear his child. Her mocking laughter provoked him and he forced himself on her, returning nightly until she was unsure whether her blood had dried up forever or he had achieved his aim. Now that her pregnancy is confirmed, she is torn between wanting the child for its own sake and hating it for Abraham's. She prays daily to Asherah for a girl.

Idrith seeks to comfort her by showing her the sights of the city. She takes her to the temples of the moon god, Yarikh, and the storm god, Baal. She introduces her to mixed gatherings where Sarah finds herself talking to men with a freedom that she has never enjoyed among her own people.

Abraham is outraged by Sarah's flight and the threat of losing his child. Questioning how he can retain the respect of his men if he cannot control his wife, he sends his steward, Eliezer, to Sodom to fetch her back. Lot welcomes him into his home, but Eliezer is horrified by the household shrine, where an idol of Yahweh stands among a host of Canaanite gods. He berates Lot for abandoning the faith of his tribe.

Sarah accompanies Eliezer back to Abraham. When Lot and Idrith urge her to stay, she declares her dread of being the cause of bloodshed since, with his authority challenged, Abraham would be bound to attack the city. On her return, Abraham shuns her, putting her in the charge of Hagar, who treats her with ill-concealed contempt. Sarah ruefully remarks that her handmaid has become her jailer.

Eliezer describes the horrors of Sodom to Abraham: its luxury, laxity and, worst of all, its perversity. Claiming that Lot and the Israelites have been induced to honour idols, he urges his master to take up arms against the city to prevent its influence spreading. Abraham fears that with only thirty men at his command he has little chance of success, since, while the Sodomites may be weak, their fortifications are strong. So, making a further sacrifice to Yahweh, he exhorts him to wipe out a city that flouts his decrees, asking 'Did you not charge our forefather, Noah, to go forth and multiply?'

In heaven, Yahweh is losing patience with the incessant demands of a small tribe that takes up a disproportionate amount of his time. Knowing that he will enjoy no peace until he responds to Abraham's request, he summons Gabriel and Raphael and dispatches them to Sodom, giving them full authority to determine its fate. Transformed into handsome young men, they arrive at the city gates where they encounter Lot, who, hearing that they have travelled far, invites them home to dine. He apologises for the hostile glances they are attracting and explains that, ever since Eliezer's visit, the Sodomites suspect all strangers of being Abraham's spies.

Oblivious of their true identity, Lot introduces the angels to Idrith and his daughters. Adinah, the younger, swoons over them, but Dinah, the elder, mocks her, maintaining that men of such beauty are never interested in girls. Leaving them to prepare the food, Lot escorts the angels to the baths to recuperate from their journey. They enter the steam room and glimpse men making love in the haze. Gabriel is shocked by the deviance, but Raphael rejoices in the intimacy. They return to the changing room where Lot sees that they lack genitals. Gabriel explains that they are angels sent by Yahweh but that their fleshly form is incomplete. 'The lower organs are reserved for humans,' Raphael says sadly.

Idrith has cooked a lavish meal and is affronted when the angels decline it. Lot, keeping their secret, tells her that they are fasting. As the family eat and Dinah and Adinah chatter, a band of men appear at the door, inviting the newcomers to join them in the fields to worship Baal. Lot refuses on their behalf, whereupon the men accuse him of wanting to keep his handsome visitors to himself. He swears that his motives are pure, explaining that, to the Israelites, hospitality is a sacred trust. As the men grow restive, he asserts that he would rather they took his daughters to venerate Yarikh, offering them up to copulate with his priests, than shame him by laying hands on his guests.

Dinah and Adinah are outraged that their father should treat them as no better than temple prostitutes. Lot is caught between defusing their resentment and deflecting the men's aggression, when Gabriel comes to his aid. Drawing himself to his full height, his eyes blazing and the shadow of his wings covering the wall, he berates the men for their effrontery before blinding them. He dismisses Raphael's protests, declaring that Abraham was right and Sodom must be destroyed.

Gabriel deputes Raphael to lead Lot and his family out of Sodom. He orders them not to look back on pain of death but, as her husband and daughters press on, Idrith accuses them of betraying the very people who made them welcome when their own tribe rejected them. Proclaiming that she would rather die in Sodom than submit to Abraham, she turns back in defiance. All at once she is engulfed in a fireball, which recedes as swiftly as it appeared, leaving no trace of her other than an imprint on a nearby rock. Lot gazes at it in horror, and Dinah and Adinah fling themselves on it weeping. As their tears melt its surface, they realise that it is salt.

Raphael leaves them to continue their journey alone. They reach Zoar but are recognised as fugitives from Sodom and cast out. They head into the mountains, where, huddled together, Dinah and Adinah blame Lot for all that has happened, from his bartering their virginity to their mother's death. They plot revenge, drugging and seducing him. He wakes the next morning to find them naked beside him, their arms and legs entwined with his. He listens aghast as they explain what they have done and ask if they now deserve to die like their friends in Sodom. 'I feel my baby growing inside me,' Dinah says. 'To which god will you dedicate it, Father? Yahweh or Yarikh? Tell me!' Lot stumbles out of the cave, gazes into the vast, empty landscape and weeps.

Cast

Frank Archer as Lot
Laura Bennett as Idrith
Porter Wright as Abraham
Dorothy Hillard as Sarah
Dana Adams as Bera, King of Sodom
Daniel Stirling as Raphael
Alan Jameson as Gabriel
Blake Gillette as Yahweh (voice)
Jason Dawkins as Yahweh (body)
Juliet Clark as Dinah
Glynis Opie as Adinah
Lee Outerbridge as Eliezer
Barbara Sokolsky as Hagar

Production

Background

Veteran producer Bela Zipser acquired the rights to Howard Edelman's *Flesh and Brimstone*, which, in the author's words, 'examines the founding myth of homophobia from a feminist and gay perspective,' on its publication in 1983. Edelman wrote that he had been brooding on the novel for thirty years and, while the burgeoning gay movement of the 1970s gave him the impetus to write, the advent of AIDS added the urgency.

Zipser, who hailed the novel as a masterpiece, persuaded Columbia Pictures, for whom he had produced several of its biggest hits in the 1950s, to back the film. He presented it as a corrective to Hollywood's best-known venture into Sodom, Robert Aldrich's *The Last Days of Sodom and Gomorrah*, where sexual perversity was personified by Anouk Aimée's Sapphic queen, a figure so generic that she was not even afforded a name.

Zipser hired Edelman, a veteran screenwriter for *Kraft Television Theatre* and the NBC soap opera, *Another World*, to adapt his own novel. Both Fred Zinnemann and Joseph L. Mankiewicz are reputed to have turned down the chance to direct, but Zipser insisted that his first choice was always British film and theatre director, Hugh Davenport, whose 1980 *Tristram Shandy*, with its celebrated combination of period interiors and contemporary exteriors, he described as a 'dry run' for *Flesh and Brimstone*, in which biblical settings and customs were coupled with twentieth-century attitudes and language.

Many Hollywood insiders claimed that Zipser's legendary instinct had finally deserted him. Biblical epics had long been out of fashion. In March 1985, while *Flesh and Brimstone* was in pre-production, Bruce Beresford's *King David*, the first in the genre for two decades, was released. It was a critical and commercial disaster. Meanwhile, the box-office failure of Arthur Hiller's *Making Love*, touted as the first mainstream gay love story, proved the appeal of gay-themed films to be equally limited.

Zipser was undeterred, and he and Davenport set about casting. For the central role of Lot they chose Frank Archer, who had starred in Zipser's 1972 drama, *Tree House*. By a neat coincidence, Archer had been offered the part of the evil prince Astaroth, subsequently taken by Stanley Baker, in *The Last Days of Sodom and Gomorrah*, when Henry Koster was slated to direct and Stephen Boyd to play Lot. Davenport wanted Stewart Granger, Lot in the Aldrich film, to play Abraham, but he was unavailable, and the part went to two-time Oscar winner, Porter Wright. Laura Bennett, Archer's sparring partner in the celebrated series of 1950s Warner Brothers comedies, now played his wife, Idrith. Former silent-screen star Dorothy Hillard brought her six decades of experience to the part of Sarah. For the roles of Lot's daughters, Dinah and Adinah, and the angels, Gabriel and Raphael, the director chose young British stage actors, Juliet Clark, Glynis Opie, Daniel Stirling and Alan Jameson. The most controversial casting was that of eight-year-old Jason Dawkins as Yahweh, his voice dubbed by Blake Gillette, seventy years his senior.

Filming

Principal photography began on 1 October 1985 and ended on 10 December 1985, with five days of pick-ups from 13–17 January 1986.

Apart from the Yahweh scenes, shot at Pinewood studios, England, the film was shot entirely on location in and around Ouarzazate, Morocco.

The senior technical crew, headed by legendary cinematographer Arturo Nobile, was Italian, and the junior crew was Moroccan.

Location conditions were gruelling, with several members of the cast and crew succumbing to stomach upsets and skin complaints. Two of the grips caught malaria and were evacuated to Casablanca.

Filming was delayed for ten days when the mock-up of Sodom, constructed from a traditional mixture of earth and straw, was reduced to sludge by a freak storm.

Music

Davenport entrusted the score to the upcoming folk-rock group, Chymical Warfare. Their compositions contributed greatly to the film's success. The integration of ancient – if not wholly authentic – instruments, including an oud, harp, sarrusophone, rhaita and lute, with electric guitars and synthesisers, perfectly captured the film's tone.

The soundtrack was released by Arista records in November 1986 and reached number one in the charts for four non-consecutive weeks in the spring of 1987. It was reissued in a Deluxe edition to mark its thirtieth anniversary in November 2016.

Reception

Box Office

Flesh and Brimstone opened in 42 theatres on 14 November 1986, where it grossed $763,308 ($18,174 per screen) in its opening weekend. By the end of its run it had grossed $5,746,880 in North America. It was also released in West Germany, France, United Kingdom, Hong Kong and Japan, where it was a surprise hit, grossing almost $23,000,000 worldwide.

Controversy

Edelman's novel had divided opinion on its publication. Lavish praise in the mainstream media was offset by bitter denunciation in the religious press. Father Padraic Quinn SJ, writing in *America*, described it as 'morally abhorrent, historically inaccurate and theologically illiterate.' Dr Daniel Teller, writing in the *Jewish Press*, condemned it as an 'unfounded and unforgivable slur on the father of our faith.'

The attacks grew in both ferocity and number after the announcement of the screen version. The controversy reached its height during the months prior to the film's release, with groups as diverse as the Christian Broadcasting Network and the Anti-Defamation League of the B'nai B'rith putting pressure on Columbia Pictures not to release it and cinema chains not to exhibit it. Bailey Cooper of the Southern Baptist Convention extended the campaign to Columbia's parent company, Coca-Cola, calling on the Convention's fourteen million members to boycott its products, an appeal that had minimal impact.

Both the East Coast premiere at the Ziegfeld Theatre, New York, and the West Coast premiere at the National, Los Angeles, were accompanied by rowdy demonstrations. The former was led by Edelman's 89-year-old father, Mendel, who had publicly disowned his son on the novel's publication, sitting shiva, the seven days of Jewish ritual mourning.

Interviewed while dedicating a hospice for AIDS victims in Washington three days before the New York premiere, Mother Teresa of Calcutta urged Catholics across the country to 'pray to the Blessed Virgin to prevent this evil film being shown.'

The studio, citing the First Amendment, refused to be swayed. It did, however, agree to insert a disclaimer at the end of the titles, stating that 'the film you are about to see departs from the widely accepted truths of the bible story,' despite Davenport and Edelman's preference for the phrase: 'a modern reworking of an ancient myth.'

It also agreed to minor modifications to the opening sequence of animal sacrifice and a subsequent sequence in a steam bath, after representations from Jewish and Christian religious groups prompted the MPAA to change its initial rating from an R to an X. Davenport, claiming to be unaware that his contract did not grant him the final cut, refused to supervise the re-editing, which was undertaken by Zipser, enabling the original rating to be restored.

News of the cuts has long fuelled speculation about explicit homosexual scenes locked in the studio vaults. Several Internet chat rooms contain accounts from members who purport to have seen them. Despite repeated denials by Davenport, who has insisted that he was hard pressed to bring in the film on time without producing extraneous pornographic footage, the speculation persists.

Critical Response

Flesh and Brimstone received generally positive reviews from American and European critics, with reviews aggregator, Rotten Tomatoes, giving it a 'fresh' 93% rating and an average score of 8.2, based on the reviews of 45 critics. Metacritic gave it a weighted average of 84 out of 100, which translates as universal acclaim. Siskel and Ebert gave it 'two thumbs up'.

Vincent Canby of the *New York Times* declared that '*Flesh and Brimstone* breathes new life into the biblical epic. British director Davenport has crafted a film of beauty and subtlety. In his hands a theme that could have been sententious or sensational or both is sharp and invigorating.' Richard Corliss in *Time* wrote that 'it confounds its critics and proves that a film with an overt political message can be popular, moving and entertaining.' Marjorie Bilbow in *Screen International* praised the originality of both the film's conception and execution, offering particular plaudits for the bipartite portrayal of God, 'his form that of an innocent child, his voice that of the Ancient of Days.' In the *Advocate*, Vito Russo described it as 'a rare Hollywood film that neither patronises, trivialises, nor vilifies gays. A beacon of hope in these troubled times.'

Accolades

Academy Awards

Best Actor – Frank Archer (nominated)
Best Actress in a Supporting Role – Dorothy Hillard (nominated)
Best Adapted Screenplay – Howard Edelman (nominated)
Best Original Score – Chymical Warfare (won)
Best Visual Effects – Lyle Perkins, Isabella Testorini, Paolo Grandi (won)

BAFTA Film Awards

Best Actor – Frank Archer (nominated)
Best Actress in a Supporting Role – Dorothy Hillard (nominated)
Best Direction – Hugh Davenport (won)
Best Adapted Screenplay – Howard Edelman (nominated)
Best Cinematography – Arturo Nobile (won)

Best Special Visual Effects – Lyle Perkins, Isabella Testorini, Paolo Grandi (won)
Best Score – Chymical Warfare (won)

Golden Globe Awards

Best Motion Picture, Drama – *Flesh and Brimstone* (nominated)
Best Director – Hugh Davenport (nominated)
Best Actor in a Motion Picture, Drama – Frank Archer (won)
Best Actress in a Supporting Role – Dorothy Hillard (nominated)
Best Screenplay – Howard Edelman (won)
Best Original Score – Chymical Warfare (won)

David di Donatello Awards

Best Cinematography – Arturo Nobile
Best Foreign Film – *Flesh and Brimstone*

Frank Archer was named Best Actor at the Valladolid International Film Festival for his performance as Lot.

Home Video

When *Flesh and Brimstone* was released on VHS and Laserdisc, many video rental stores, including the market leaders, Blockbuster, refused to stock it, claiming a responsibility to protect their staff and a reluctance to offend their customers. It was first released on DVD in the United States in 2000. For its 30th anniversary in 2016, Sony issued a 4k digitally restored edition. Special features included a featurette on the 2016 restoration, interviews with director, Hugh Davenport, and actor, Daniel Stirling, and the original theatrical trailer.

See Also

The Bible in film
List of films based on the Bible

List of religious films
List of LGBT-related films

External Links

Flesh and Brimstone at the Internet Movie Database
Flesh and Brimstone at Box Office Mojo
Flesh and Brimstone at Rotten Tomatoes
Flesh and Brimstone at Metacritic
Film Trailer at YouTube
Film Study Lecture on *Flesh and Brimstone*

1

As they drew up outside the Holy Transfiguration Church, Frank scanned the streets for reporters. The funeral of his long-time manager was unlikely to attract the attention of Hollywood's press corps, but his regular visits to Cedars-Sinai in recent weeks had not passed unnoticed and there was no way of knowing whether a legman for the *Globe* or the *National Enquirer* might be snooping around. Crossing behind the car, he offered his arm to the Countess as she stepped out. Chief mourner at her son's funeral was not a role that she would ever have chosen but, now it had been thrust upon her, she was playing it to the hilt. He was struck by the elegant propriety of the black-and-grey silk suit perfectly tailored to her slight frame. A diamond-and-sapphire dragonfly sparkled on her lapel, a sixtieth birthday present from Gene and himself that she liked to hint had been a fifteenth one from the Tsarina. Its true provenance was the least of the secrets that he was keeping from her friends. He fixed his eyes ahead as he escorted her up to the door, where they were greeted by the priest who, with his bushy beard and beetle brows, was straight out of central casting. Indeed, during one of their first encounters at Gene's bedside, he had proudly confided to Frank that he had been an extra in the recent NBC mini-series, *Rasputin*.

The church bells rang in a slow peal from the smallest to the largest, symbolising, as the priest explained, Gene's journey from youth to maturity, and ended with a single chime, symbolising his permanent departure from life. Frank, dazed by that permanence, led the Countess up the aisle to the solea steps, where the pallbearers laid the coffin in front of the glittering iconostasis. Regardless of his misgivings, she had been adamant that the coffin should be open and all the traditional rituals be observed. So, while the bottom half was covered in a green velvet cloth embroidered with the Orthodox cross, the top displayed Gene's embalmed body, a wreath with a prayer of absolution on his forehead, a cross beside him on the pillow and an icon of his patron saint, Eugenios of Trebizond, in his hands. As the congregation gathered at the steps, a server distributed candles, which the priest lit from a taper. Listening to the impenetrable litany of psalms and prayers, Frank was consumed by the fear that, even in the airless church, his flame would blow out in a final betrayal of Gene.

He distracted himself by surveying the congregation. Forty years of dissimulation had left him with few intimates. Chief among them was Howard, looking furtive, as though wanting to take back all the doubts he had ever expressed about Frank and Gene's relationship. It was typical of his oldest friend that he should be standing, not with the luminaries among whom he could finally claim a place, but beside Frank's former housekeeper, Marybeth, holding her candle aloft as if at a Baptist service. He had often longed to ask her how she reconciled the doctrine of her Church with her unswerving devotion to her employers, but he had been afraid of the answer. A few feet behind them stood Audrey, who had flown in from Virginia. Gene, who had resented Frank's most fleeting encounters with other men, had been far more indulgent of his four-year marriage. Not only did he recognise the value of deflecting gossip and placating the studio, but he genuinely liked Audrey. Moreover, he formed a deep attachment to her son, Tommy, becoming the one stable influence in that troubled boy's life. No parent or step-parent attended as many of his Little League games or school concerts or even helped so assiduously with his assignments. Indeed, Frank suspected that the two of them had been more distressed by the divorce than either of the principals. He was touched that, despite having vowed never again to set foot in the same room as his mother, Tommy had put aside his grievance to honour Gene.

From the corner of his eye, he spotted a sprinkling of familiar faces, among them Laura Bennett, Diane Jenner, Meg Graham and Edith Sutton. Howard had often mocked his particular affinity with his female co-stars but, even if he had made his name as a swashbuckler or a cowboy, it would have been the same. Men in Hollywood were as ruthless off screen as on. And gay men, with the added fear of exposure, were the worst. Those behind the camera could afford to be less guarded, hence David McKinley's standing closer to his partner, Byron, than Frank and Gene would ever have allowed themselves, or rather than he would ever have allowed Gene. David, who had directed him in three of his early Warner pictures, accepted that the open secret of his relationship with Byron confined him to the realm of women's weepies and light comedies, whereas his former assistant, Brandon O'Brien, who had escaped the Hedda Hopper slur of eternal bachelordom in four wretched and increasingly violent marriages, took his pick of crime stories, action movies and thrillers. Yet, as the years passed and Brandon grew more bitter than his most hard-bitten hero, Frank was in no doubt as to which of them had struck the better bargain.

Several of the congregation, while not as typecast as the priest, were noticeably Slavic. They were fellow members of the church who had come to support the Countess. He had met many of them over the years when she had inveigled him into fundraising appearances and, more recently, when she had invited them to Gene's hospital room, to join in the liturgy for the dying. He longed to know if they had believed her story of his heart failure, or had their suspicions been aroused by the warning sign on the door and the protective masks that muffled their prayers? And what of the priest himself? Had he feared to sit too close to Gene as he gasped the words of his final confession? Banished to the corridor, Frank had mused on what he might be saying. Was he reverting to a childhood faith and repenting a lifetime of sin? Or was he simply spouting a comforting formula? Either way, the priest would have to take it on trust. If Frank, familiar with every timbre of his voice, could only make out the odd syllable, how would a stranger understand anything at all?

Whether the confession had freed him as his mother claimed or exhausted him as Frank suspected, the priest had no sooner left than Gene entered his final agony. Every breath tormented him, and he paused so long between them that Frank held his own in trepidation. Finally the nurses withdrew, leaving Frank and the Countess alone with the wasted figure. She babbled to her son in Russian and mopped his brow, while he clutched his lover's hand, trying to convey the emotions of a lifetime in a single touch. 'I'm telling Eugeny how kind it is that you're here,' she said, filling Frank with a murderous fury that to the very last she should seek to belittle their relationship. But even as his fury seethed, he knew that he should direct it equally against himself. What Gene had wanted more than anything else was for his love – the essence of his being – to be acknowledged openly and this, for their different reasons, the two people closest to him had refused to do.

He was brought back to the present by an acrid smell as the congregation snuffed out their candles. After a further Slavonic prayer, the priest invited them, in English, to come up and pay their final respects. The Russians, knowing the form, led the way. Frank's stomach constricted as the first man leant over the coffin, but the morticians had been so skilful at covering Gene's lesions that his cheeks barely looked blotched. They had charged an extortionate fee but, given Howard's stories of hospital porters in San Francisco leaving men, often sick themselves, to carry out their dead in body bags, Frank had been happy to pay. Despite Howard's righteous indignation, he could not blame them. No one knew how the disease was spread, whether by blood, semen, sweat, saliva or mere touch. If the last, he trusted as he watched the Russians kiss Gene's forehead either that it did not survive death or else that the make-up created a barrier. While all his friends, including Howard, took the safer option of kissing the icon or the cross, he planted a kiss squarely on his lover's lips, only to realise with a pang that it was the first time he had ever kissed him in public.

After the Countess gave Gene a last kiss, stroking his cheeks as if in search of their former softness, the priest anointed his forehead with the sign of the cross. The pallbearers closed the coffin and carried it down the aisle. Returning outside, Frank found that news of the Hollywood visitors had spread through Little Armenia, causing a crush in the forecourt. Bemused by the smattering of applause, the Countess paused before waving a black-gloved hand at the crowd who, Frank suspected, were equally bemused by the greeting, racking their brains for the name of this long-forgotten star. He ushered her into the car and the funeral cortège set off on its final journey along Fernwood and North Western and on to the Freeway. Midway down Barham, they passed the Warner lot, triggering Frank's memories of the studio where he began his career. Its proximity to Forest Lawn no longer seemed a joke, as they followed the hearse through the gates and across rolling meadows, in which the scattered graves and plaques looked as picturesque as the sculptures in a formal garden.

The pallbearers led the procession to the grave. The Countess, showing no sign of fatigue, stood as the priest sang the short service of entombment. She then followed him in tossing first a clod and then a handful of coins on to the coffin. Frank, watching as pockets and purses all around him were hastily emptied, confined himself to an earthy adieu. After the previous night's vigil, there would at least be no funeral breakfast. He could not face another well-meaning friend sharing his memories of Gene, let alone extolling his gentle spirit, as though it had been a prerequisite of living with Frank. He had his own memories of Gene – thirty-four years of them – that he wanted to contemplate undisturbed.

First, he had to accompany the Countess back to Brentwood. Sitting beside her in the back seat of the sedan, he pointedly shut his eyes, but it was a hint that she either did not or would not take.

'Now I will die alone,' she said, suddenly looking every one of her ninety years.

'Nonsense,' Frank said, clasping a satiny hand. 'You have all your friends … you have me.'

'You know how I have always seen you as my second son. Eugeny's brother.'

Frank wrested his hand away and clenched it in his lap. After years of alternately denying and decrying his relationship with Gene, necessity had forced her to acknowledge it. Yet, despite the petty point-scoring, despite the veiled animosity that had hurt Gene far more than it had him, he could not help admiring her. She was a survivor. Unlike his own mother who had manufactured drama (although she would have deplored the utilitarian verb), be it a hairdresser's treachery or a dressmaker's defection, the Countess had known tragedy. Born Olga Babunin, youngest daughter of a provincial landowner, she had married Edmond de Tréfile, a French engineer at the Imperial Court, giving birth to her only child, Eugeny, in May 1917, three weeks after Lenin's train reached Russia. After Edmond's death at the hands of the Bolsheviks, the Countess took the well-travelled route from Moscow to Paris, the gruelling conditions later inspiring one of her most colourful anecdotes: 'There was no food on the train, so we had to eat the pet parrot.' Spurned by her in-laws, she profited from her former pastime and became an embroideress for Chanel. She lavished all her affection on Gene, who flourished at school, passing his *baccalauréat* with the highest honours, gratifying his mother by his proposal to study engineering at the *École Polytechnique*. He never took up his place since, with the rise of Hitler and the risk of war, the Countess no longer regarded France as a safe haven and, in 1937, she sailed with him to New York. Her conviction that, in a country with no aristocracy of its own, she would be doubly valued proved to be false, and she had to content herself with a job as a saleswoman at Bergdorf Goodman. She stayed there for thirty years, selling jewellery and perfume to women she despised until, despite her unconcealed disappointment in her only son, she moved to Los Angeles to be near him in retirement.

'A man like you cannot begin to know the pain of losing a child,' she said, the old resentment resurfacing as Frank saw her to the door of her condominium.

'No,' he muttered under his breath, 'I'll have to settle for losing the love of my life.'

Frank was more anxious to return home than after three months on location. The traffic on Sunset was light but, either because it was a funeral car or simply a hired one, the driver took the roads up to Kew Drive at a snail's pace. Entering the hall, he felt like an intruder. The house was Gene's domain and, although they had resolved not to fall into fixed roles, it was inevitable that with so much more time on his hands, Gene should take charge of domestic matters. Besides, as he himself had said, whereas Frank grew up in a mansion on North Shore, Lake Michigan, he grew up in a sixth-floor walk-up in Les Halles, so that furnishing a house was a new experience for him. Yet even in the sitting room that he had made his own, there were few mementoes of their joint life. Rather, it was a veritable museum to Frank: photographs and posters and awards – even the *Harvard Lampoon* Worst Actor of 1965 trophy that, eager to show himself a good sport, he had been the first recipient to accept in person.

Hisato, their – no, his – butler, knocked and entered, his

funeral suit exchanged for the familiar apron and striped trousers.

'I thought you will wish a tray, Mr Frank,' he said.

'Thank you,' Frank said. 'Please leave it on the table. I may want something later.'

Hisato was followed by Popeye, Gene's dog, who trotted into the room, looked about and growled at Frank.

'You stop this now,' Hisato said, ineffectually tapping the dog's muzzle.

'He misses Gene,' Frank said, 'it's understandable.' Although they had chosen the golden retriever together, he had quickly made his loyalties clear, since when they had never wavered.

'Does that dog have no self-respect?' Frank had asked, only half in jest. 'It's nauseating to watch him fawn on you.'

'It's a good thing someone does,' Gene replied, his tone equally equivocal.

Popeye's intuition put Frank to shame. He had recognised that Gene was sick long before he showed any symptoms, sniffing him disconsolately and playing dead when he called.

'I take him away, Mr Frank,' Hisato said. 'Bad dog to disturb Mr Frank! Come here with Hisato.'

'No, it's fine. I'd like him to stay. Thank you, Hisato. I'll ring if I need anything.'

Hisato walked out, leaving Frank and Popeye alone. Having long made fun of Gene for treating the dog like a character from *Aesop's Fables*, Frank was convinced that he was talking to him.

'It's just you and me now, bud,' he replied. 'I know you think I took him for granted and you're right – God, you're right! – but I did love him. You have to believe me.'

The dog continued his low growl before padding across the room and laying his head on Frank's lap. That simple gesture of affection, even forgiveness, touched him more deeply than all of his friends' condolences, and he choked back his tears.

'How pathetic am I? You're a dog, a bloody dog! And I still can't bring myself to cry in front of you. If it had been the other way round – it should have been the other way round – Gene would have turned this room into Niagara Falls. I didn't deserve him. But then I don't need to tell you that. Thirty-four years! How long is that in dog years? My head's too muzzy to do the math. We met way back in 1950. You work it out!'

Frank had first encountered Gene in Long Beach. He had been drinking at Schwab's with a bunch of bit-players, who were snickering about the Gothic apartment block on Ocean Boulevard where the 'fruitcakes' and the 'jelly beans' hung out. He had not caught the name and would not have dreamt of asking, even though he suspected that some of the guys knew it better than they were willing to admit. So one Sunday he drove down there, scouring the Boulevard until, glimpsing a churchlike spire, he parked and walked round to the forecourt where, amid the panoply of preening muscle men was Gene, his silver-blond hair glinting in the sun, his sleek Slavic body standing out from all the nut-cracking biceps and washboard stomachs. Their attraction was instant, although neither was looking for anything more than a fling, especially not Frank, who still intended to marry and settle down, and not solely for the sake of his career. That career would have been in ruins had he been spotted by one of the scandal rags, since he was starting to make a name for himself, albeit one still several rungs below the title. Gene, as he soon discovered, had less to lose.

He had not found the move to New York easy. Grappling with English, he had been unable to continue his studies or even to obtain a steady job. At twenty, to his shame, he was still dependant on his mother. But with the outbreak of war he came into his own, first as a French-language announcer on the Voice of America, and then, after Pearl Harbour, as a private in the US army. For eighteen months he fought in the Italian Campaign until he was arrested in a barn with a local farmer, who for the rest of his life he was convinced had been a decoy, and shipped back to military prison at Camp Lee. He was subjected to a battery of psychiatric tests, during one of which a tongue depressor was thrust down his throat. He struggled not to gag in the belief that it would prove his virility, whereas his tormentors saw it as confirming his mastery of fellatio. He was given a blue discharge, denying him not only all veterans' benefits but the college place offered under the GI Bill. Desperate to hide the truth from the Countess, who expected him to complete his education, he told her that he was heading to California to break into films.

Convincing himself that it was a genuine dream and not just a serviceable lie, he hitchhiked across the country. Arriving in LA, he took various odd jobs, tending bars, waiting tables and painting the house of a small-time agent, who found him occasional work as an extra. Eventually, he was given a line: 'How ya doin, Jim?' which in years to come became known as *The Line* among his friends, who would regularly greet him with it, and, if the joke ever palled, he was too sweet-natured to show it. When they had known each other a few months, Frank begged his agent to put him on his books but, with an excruciating lecture about not mixing business and pleasure, Lenny refused. He had more luck with the casting department at Warner who, after his pitch about the great-looking newcomer he had met at a rodeo, agreed to give Gene a test. But the camera, which Frank was coming to acknowledge as his truest friend, was less indulgent to Gene. On screen, his beauty seemed bland and the accent that sent a tingle down Frank's spine sounded coarse. Gene took the rejection far more equably than Frank but, ultimately, even he had to accept that *The Line* would be *The Only Line*.

Frank's own journey westward was far smoother. After Yale, he spent a miserable year writing copy for Benton and Bowles, from which he was rescued by Thorley, his mother's 'musical' younger brother: an epithet that, until embarrassingly late, he attributed to his trusteeship of the Chicago Symphony Orchestra. His uncle never visited him in New Haven, but he saw him perform in the Dramat's charity gala at the Waldorf. Convinced of his nephew's talent (and, Frank suspected, not averse to making mischief for his sister and brother-in-law), he introduced him to a friend at the William Morris agency in New York, who in turn recommended him to Lenny Glass at their Hollywood office. Unlike Gene who thumbed lifts and slept in cheap motels, Frank took the Twentieth Century and rented a bungalow at the Chateau Marmont, where good fortune pursued him. Lenny knew that Jack Warner was worried about the studio losing out on the sophisticated comedies that were proving so successful at Paramount and MGM. None of its male stars – Cagney and Bogart and Flynn and Edward G. Robinson – exuded the debonair charm of Grant or Gable or Stewart. Together with Max Arno, Head of Casting, Lenny persuaded Warner that in Frank he had found his man.

After a series of kid-brother/best-buddy roles, he landed the big one: Sergeant Bobby Wheelan in *Release*. Bert Colquhoun may have ended up with Susan Brett, but it was the letter Frank wrote to her from the field hospital at Monte Cassino, freeing her to fall in love again if he didn't pull through that won him the hearts of millions of women across America, along with the Golden Globe for Most Promising Newcomer of 1951. The studio capitalised on his success by casting him not in another weepie but in *The Prodigal Son*, the first of the hit comedies that he was to make over the next decade. He played a string of peppy, preppy young men, rescued from a life of starchy privilege by confident young women such as Lois Bridges, Laura Bennett and Deborah Lane. Since his natural tendency was to stroll through life with the wry smile and insouciant shrug that had so incensed his father, it was no great acting stretch. He fretted about his lack of technique, but David McKinley, the most supportive of his early directors, assured him that the key to acting on screen was sincerity. As long as he believed in what he did, the rest would follow.

Since he was congenitally lazy, he had been happy to concur. It was the same reason that he had never defied the studio's wishes. He felt a huge debt of gratitude to the Warner machine for finding him a house and housekeeper, clothes and car, and even starlets to date. Howard, two thousand miles away in New York, clipped the pictures of Frank and his latest sweetheart from the fan magazines and sent them west with captions ranging from the wittily lewd to the downright filthy. What he failed to realise was that a movie actor didn't stop being a movie actor once the final credits rolled. Gene, although more understanding, was offended by the personal questions Frank was asked by *Silver Screen*, *Film Land* or *Whisper* on the colour of his shorts ('White'), whether he wore pajamas or slept in the nude ('It depends on the sheets'), and whether he preferred blondes or brunettes ('Blondes, provided they're natural'). The question he had to field most often, at least until he met Audrey, was why he was still single. His stock answer, catching his trademark brand of breezy non-chalance, was 'Sure I want to marry, just as long as there's a clause in the contract enabling me to be loaned out if a more attractive property comes along.'

The true answer, of course, was that he was already committed. Three months after they met, Frank asked Gene to move in with him – *in* being the operative word since they could never be seen out together. Even in a dimly lit movie theatre they sat apart. Frank felt an illicit – almost erotic – thrill to know that an invisible thread connected him to the lover two rows in front of him, but Gene was wretched, longing for his place in Frank's life to be recognised. In the early days of their relationship, before the Frank Archer on the movie posters forever eclipsed the Franklin Archer Fairchild on his birth certificate, Andover diploma and Yale sheepskin, Frank offered to give up acting if it would make Gene happy, but Gene dismissed it as another line. What would he do instead? He had no wish to return to advertising, let alone to follow his brother into their father's grain empire. He would lead an idle, unproductive life, dependent on his mother's handouts, which, as Frank realised too late, was precisely the life he had offered Gene.

Looking back, he recognised what had lain behind that thrill in the anonymity of the cinema. He loved Gene and he never stopped loving him but, whether from his own need for novelty or, as he preferred to think, the male need to scatter his seed, he was increasingly drawn to other men. After growing up watching his mother take tea with his father's mistresses, he held deceit to be a greater vice than infidelity. He assured Gene that, far from posing a threat to their relationship, his dalliances strengthened it, since the surest route to a break-up was for them to invest all their desires, sexual as well as emotional, in one another.

'Jizzing's like sneezing: just a pleasurable reflex.'

'Oh really?' Gene replied. 'Most of us try to suppress our sneezes. We don't sneeze in other peoples' faces. And we're certainly not proud of the snot in our Kleenex.' By the time Frank switched to a culinary metaphor, Gene had annexed the moral high ground.

Gene left him three times during their first decade, forfeiting a little more autonomy each time that he yielded to Frank's entreaties to return. Eager to prove to him that his jealousy was unwarranted, Frank sought to include him in his affairs, whether by inviting a third party into their bed or taking him to a private bacchanal but, even in a sea of beautiful young men, he stuck close to Frank, who, despite knowing that he should feel flattered, felt ridiculous. 'What kind of man sticks to his own partner at an orgy?' he asked Howard, his closest confidant in matters of the heart.

'You've institutionalised him,' Howard said. 'He's spent too long in the Franklin Fairchild facility for the criminally in love.'

When, either from pent-up lust or wounded pride, Gene embarked on affairs of his own, he made such an unconvincing philanderer, appearing to derive so little pleasure from the encounters that, far from assuaging Frank's guilt, he compounded it. But his guilt at Gene's discomfiture was nothing compared to his guilt when he contracted AIDS.

Two years earlier, the acronym had signified nothing more sinister than an Aircraft Integrated Data System. Then Howard, who had moved to San Francisco, told him of a lethal cancer that was attacking gay men. Frank derided his paranoia, not least when he cited a government conspiracy to pump out poison through the ionisers in nightclubs. Nevertheless, the cancer continued to spread. Howard reported more and more deaths, not only of friends but of shopkeepers, workmen and members of his gay AA group. That, as Frank told him, was the price of living in a subculture (if the news had been less sombre, he would have said *ghetto*). He, who for all its constraints preferred to be part of the mainstream, did not know of a single casualty. Then Gene fell sick.

At first he was just tired, and Frank, seven years his junior, joked that he was showing his age. Then he developed a rash on his back, chest, arms and face. Blissfully unsuspecting, they attributed it to the new brand of chlorine tablets Dennis had used in the pool, and Gene, true to form, was more concerned with sparing his feelings than treating his own painful and unsightly rash. After three weeks during which he obdurately refused to see a doctor, the rash disappeared and his only persistent symptoms were mild fever and acute fatigue. Frank was due to fly to Thailand to play Bert Lyons, a Wall Street banker searching for his son missing after an undercover CIA operation. He offered to pull out but Gene would not hear of it and, in ten weeks of daily phone calls, neither he nor the well-briefed staff admitted that anything was wrong.

No sooner had Frank returned home than he discovered how much they had been hiding. Stepping through the front door, he was hit by a stench of rotten eggs, rotten fish and compost, which Hisato, who hurried out to greet him, explained came from the Chinese herbs he was boiling in the kitchen.

'For seasoning?' Frank asked, disoriented.

'No, for Mr Gene, his tea.'

'Where is Mr Gene?' Frank asked, his unease growing. 'What sort of tea?'

'You must be calm when you see him, Mr Frank.'

'Where is he?'

'He is in the pool house being rolfed.'

For a moment Frank wondered if this were a euphemism, the equivalent of being *Ralphed* or *Richarded* or even a non-native speaker's version of *being rogered* but, when Gene shuffled on to the terrace, his face unshaven and blistered, his body emaciated, any suspicion of sex vanished into the dark recesses of his mind, from where he knew it would emerge to shame him later. The therapist, who with consummate tact, showed no sign of recognising him, even though his polished smile, flawless tan and muscular torso all screamed 'aspiring actor', left, promising to return on Friday. Frank, struggling to reconcile this new Gene with the one he had seen only ten weeks before, realised that he must make the first move, although when he did, Gene shrank from the pressure of his embrace. They moved indoors where, after Frank had poured himself some bourbon and Hisato brought Gene his tea, Gene listed the three diseases he had contracted during his absence: Kaposi's sarcoma; toxoplasmosis; cryptosporidium.

'I've never heard of any of them.'

'No wonder since you're not an elderly Jew, a cat or a sheep.'

Gene's flippancy highlighted the preposterousness of his plight. It was as if someone had played a sick joke, picking out the three most obscure conditions in the medical dictionary and inflicting them on him.

'Why didn't you tell me?'

'You were working.'

'So? I'd have caught the first flight back.'

'There was nothing you could do.'

'I'd have been here with you. I'd have looked after you.'

'I had Hisato and Sheila. My friends have been great.'

'And you told them all to say nothing?'

'I know what the movie meant to you.'

'And do you know what you mean to me?'

'This isn't about you, Frank.'

'And what if you'd … been taken to hospital?'

'I'd have told you then.'

'Have you had a second opinion … a third? Have you spoken to Debra?'

'Sure. They can find nothing … well, nothing they can make sense of. There's some anomaly in my white blood cells. They did a test where they infected me with germs—'

'What?' Frank asked, reminded of Camp Lee.

'Wrong word. Injected! And the germs were benign. But my system didn't fight back. I'm a medical mystery. I suppose that's something after being predictable all my life.'

'Don't laugh about it!'

'I wasn't.'

'We'll beat this thing together, I promise.'

Numbed by the news, Frank visited Gene's physicians, whom he suspected of withholding information as blatantly as the CIA bosses had done from Bert Lyons in Bangkok. Since they could offer nothing but palliative care, he swallowed his cynicism and fostered Gene's faith in alternative therapies. He joined him every morning in his affirmations, finding no difficulty in loving 'my eyes, my nose, my lips, my chin' (which, after all, were loved worldwide), but floundering when it came to loving 'my liver, my kidneys, my intestines, my spleen'. He accompanied him on an exhaustive quest for the perfect piece of crystal to focus his energies, just as they had previously scoured the city for a rare piece of Meissen. His composure snapped only once, when Gene consulted a Native American healer who laid hands on him, prayed with him, instructed him to find the warrior within himself and then told him that his disease had disappeared. As Gene relayed the good news, all Frank's frustrations flooded out. 'Really?' he shouted. 'Have you looked at yourself in a mirror lately instead of through the eyes of your spirit guide? Your back looks like something out of *101 Dalmatians*!'

Gene became sicker and sicker and weaker and weaker. The simplest tasks became ends in themselves. He was unable to stand unaided and either Frank or a nurse had to help him to wash and shave. He developed shingles down the left side of his face, lumps behind his ears and herpes in his anus. He sweated so heavily at night that it concealed his incontinence. He grew hypersensitive to noise, especially the telephone, complaining that it pounded in his head like a dentist's drill. The irony was that he needed dental treatment to extract an infected molar but, as he would never have borne it, he was left in pain.

He travelled back and forth to hospital but, after a failed operation on a brain tumour, he remained there permanently. Frank gave up the role of Joe Kennedy, which would have required his spending a month in London. He and the Countess watched over a disintegration so rapid that it appeared to have been filmed with time-lapse photography. Gene lay propped up on the pillows like an affront to life: reduced to skin and bones, or skin and pathogens. One tube poked out of his mottled chest to help him breathe and another to drain the accumulated fluid. His thin hair was so slick with sweat that it looked as if it had been plastered down to hide his peeling scalp. His terrified eyes rolled round in their sockets. The decline was not merely physical. Having once humbled Frank with his gentleness, he now horrified him with his aggression. He accused the nurses who were emptying his catheter of raping him. With no strength left in his hands, he threatened to bite them if they changed his sheets. Not even the kindest nurse was willing to take the risk, so he was left soiled. His favourite target was Frank, who began to dread his moments of lucidity more than his delirium.

'I don't want to die and leave you.'

'You're not dying.'

'I don't want to die and leave you to live it up.'

'That's the illness talking, not you.'

'I am my illness. What else is there?'

The gravest crisis came when his mother arrived with her icons. Unable to see the images, he weighed the wood in his hands and traced the shape of the crucifix. While the Countess prayed that he would return to the bosom of the Church, Frank trusted that the childhood relics would comfort him. Instead, he was plunged into anguish, moaning that he had led a wicked life and was destined to spend eternity in hell. Frank, doomed to burn alongside him, could say nothing to help. The priest's offer to hear his confession brought some relief, but it was a visit from his Reiki therapist that finally calmed him. Sweeping her hands over his body, unblocking and balancing his chakras, she broke off and told him in hushed tones that there was an angel on his shoulder. 'He's there to protect you because you can no longer protect yourself. You see?' she added to Frank, who bit his tongue. What he did see was Gene's joyous smile and a milky radiance in his eyes, which reappeared several times over the following days. When asked if there were anything he wanted, his only reply was 'Angel.'

There would be no angel when Frank died. Nor would he renounce the pleasures of the flesh. It was the sight, touch, taste and smell of another man that made him feel most alive and, after spending the afternoon among ghosts, he felt impelled to indulge his senses again. He dismissed the flicker of guilt as irrational. Having never believed that he was betraying Gene when he was alive, he refused to do so now that he was dead.

He rang Teri, the Hollywood madam who had shocked him a few months earlier by describing him as her most longstanding client. They had met when she was a make-up artist at Warner and bonded over Robert Colbert. 'Nice ass!' she said as the studio's latest signing strode through the wardrobe department, no doubt in search of a pair of weathered chaps.

'What do you mean?' he asked, terrified that he might have let his eyes wander.

'Honey,' she said, 'you got nothing to fear from your Aunt Teri. There ain't no secrets in this chair. I'm like a priest, 'cept I don't give you no penance.' She emitted a laugh worthy of Barbara Stanwyck in *Walk on the Wild Side*, a role in which, as he was soon to discover, she would have been well cast. Sitting drowsily in her chair at six in the morning, actors opened their hearts to her as to no one else, even their wives – especially their wives. 'Sure as shooting, with men the problem boils down to one thing,' she said, and she had taken it upon herself to address it, building up a stable of attractive, accommodating and practical girls. But when one legendary action star repeatedly failed to live up to his image, she decided to change tactics. The Tracy that she sent to his room at the Beverley Wilshire was a six-foot-three cowboy and, after his initial protests, proved to be exactly what was required. From then on, she dealt primarily in men, whom she found more reliable and compliant, less demanding, and (that laugh again) more lucrative.

She retired from the studio in the sixties but kept up her sideline. Frank had called on her services at least once a week for the past thirty years. Howard, who regarded his own antics on the Hudson River piers as acts of liberation, condemned Frank's use of hustlers as exploitative, maintaining that he could attract any man he wanted and only paid them to fulfil his need for control. Frank retorted that it was kinder both to Gene, who knew that it was a purely commercial transaction, and to the hustlers themselves, for whom there would be no pretence of emotional engagement or professional gain.

As Teri offered him her condolences, he realised that, although they had never met, she knew more about Gene than many of his oldest friends. If she saw anything unseemly in his request for 'valet service' – her preferred euphemism, especially on the phone – she kept it to herself, but then he could hardly set his moral compass by a woman whose only allusion to AIDS had been that all the hysteria was bad for business.

He dismissed Hisato and Sheila for the night and waited for Clay, who drove up to the gate on the dot of nine. He buzzed him in and directed him up to the house. For all his claims not to be prescriptive, Clay was exactly his type: a clean-cut farm boy with a down-home manner and just a whiff of dirt on his boots. He had no idea if he were the genuine article or if the closest he had been to the Midwest was eating a jello salad, but no one knew better than he the power of the image. He offered him a beer for form's sake and led him upstairs. For once he left the light off, so that the room was lit solely by the moon. He shuddered as Clay put his hand beneath his shirt.

'I didn't have you down as the nervous sort.'

'I'm sorry. Someone must have walked over my grave.'

'What's that?'

'Just an expression.' But it was an expression that led him straight back to Forest Lawn. He was overwhelmed by the conviction that the disease that had robbed him of Gene had infected him and no amount of firm young flesh – and Clay's was certainly that – could cure it. The thought of death was so pervasive that he was unable to respond to Clay's expert fellatio. Was it just the morning's burial that put him in mind of a bird pulling a resistant worm from the ground? Refusing to risk further humiliation, he shook his head and pushed Clay away. That moment, a watery moonbeam hit the photograph of Gene beside the bed, illuminating his most winning smile.

2

The flight attendant, handing him his drink, leant a little too close and lingered a little too long. The faint aroma of sandalwood, spearmint and sweat gave Frank, as ever lowering his guard on leaving American soil (if not yet American airspace), a momentary tingle. But for all the attendant's fresh-faced appeal, he dismissed the prospect of a furtive fumble on a crew bunk as beneath the dignity – and, on current form, beyond the capacity – of a sixty-three-year-old actor. So with a regretful smile, which would have been more potent projected on a seventy-foot screen, he sat back to gather his thoughts.

Who would have imagined, back in 1949, when he made his screen debut as a prom king in *Goodnight Ladies* that thirty-six years later he would be flying to Morocco to play Lot in the film of his friend Howard Edelman's *Flesh and Brimstone*? Having no more planned his career than anything else in his life, he was constantly surprised by its longevity. He had made a natural progression from comedies of love and marriage to comedies of adultery and parenthood along with a less predictable move into the world of crime and espionage, in large part thanks to Brandon O'Brien, who steered him to his one Oscar-winning role in *Undiscovered Country*. The thrillers gained him new fans without alienating the old ones. Even in the early sixties, when the only audience seemed to be teenagers petting in the back rows, he remained in demand. And when the Hollywood offers dried up, he packed his bags and headed to Europe. Not for him a two-scene cameo in a bloated disaster movie. Instead, he worked with Italian and French directors, who knew his old movies better than he did and treated him with true respect.

In the year since Gene's death he had turned down all offers other than a spot hosting *Saturday Night Live*, but he realised that it was time to return to work, if only to prevent himself obsessing about every spot and sneeze. He had chosen Lot over a comic mobster in New Jersey and a Jesuit missionary in Paraguay, less on account of the role than as a favour to Howard. He knew that for all the novel's success the movie was a gamble. Biblical epics were widely regarded as box-office poison. The recent failure of Bruce Beresford's *King David* would have given any producer pause for thought. Bela Zipser, however, remained defiant, insisting that *Flesh and Brimstone* transcended genres. Nevertheless, and despite Howard's condescending claim that he was the one who had lobbied for him, Frank was aware that if the project were to go ahead, it needed bankable names.

Bela wooed him with his customary assiduity, insisting that he would only make the film if Frank played Lot, a line that they both knew he had employed many times before, not least when he inveigled Frank into playing opposite Sandy Lewis in the inchoate *Tree House*. But Bela's chicanery was so shameless that it was part of his charm. Nothing about him – not even his scar – could be taken at face value. His origins were clouded in mystery, which, to be fair, was not wholly of his making, since the Central European province where he was born had changed hands so often that a more forthright man than Bela would have been hard-pressed to say whether he were a Hungarian, a Ukrainian or a Pole. In the late 1920s, his widowed mother brought her large family to New York where, according to an early profile, Bela worked for a gang of bootleggers. In the late 1930s, he moved to LA to sell cinema advertising. Even in a city where reinvention was the norm, his was remarkable. Having contrived to become Publicity Director at Columbia, he was given his own production division and contracted to make six films a year. But while the actresses on his arm and Impressionists on his walls might be some measure of success, he longed above all for intellectual prestige. Nothing would have pleased him more than to make a biopic of Albert Einstein with a script by Arthur Miller, a score by Stravinsky and art direction by Picasso. Until then, he had to be content with the adaptation of a prize-winning novel, which, in the words of one critic, 'takes the Bible into the world of Alfred Kinsey and Margaret Mead'.

That comment alone had been enough to attract Hollywood interest, and Howard was swamped with offers from producers whom he suspected of wanting a sex-and-scandals version of the old swords-and-sandals epics. He sought advice from Frank, who urged him to go with the highest bidder, since, if the film were ever made, it would bear so little resemblance to the book that the cash would provide much-needed consolation. In the event, he took a smaller fee from Cornerstone in return for the chance to write the screenplay. Frank, who found it almost as hard to adjust to Howard's late-life success as he did himself, was amused when, after years of decrying Hollywood and all its works, he began to adopt its jargon, reporting that he was 'flying down to LA for a confab with the execs'.

Howard was his oldest friend and living proof of the adage that opposites attract. They had met in the fall of 1945 when Frank returned to Yale for his junior year. His military service had been short and inglorious. After graduating from the Navy's R12 programme, he had been assigned to an aircraft carrier that was en route to be decommissioned, followed by a decoding job in Washington. Howard, however, did not serve, wearing his 4F status like a badge of honour. Their friendship had blossomed when they were both tapped for membership of the Scroll and Key. With a father who was president of the Chicago Board of Trade and a mother who traced her lineage back to Huguenot nobility, not to mention his own leading roles with the Dramat, Frank was an obvious choice for one of Yale's senior societies, but Howard was more controversial. In the first place he was a Jew, a word spoken in polite circles in much the same whisper as *cancer* or *bankrupt* and, in the second, he was a homosexual, a word that was barely even breathed. But he had made a name for himself in the Yale Lit and the Lizzie, and the society was keen to extend its reach in the egalitarian aftermath of the War.

With his curly hair, thick pebble glasses, day-long five o'clock shadow and a nose that might have featured in a Nazi caricature, Howard did not fit Frank's image of a homosexual. True, he dressed differently from everyone else he knew, rejecting the button-down shirt, striped tie, Brooks Brothers suit and Daisy Bucks, which were the unofficial uniform on campus, for a T-shirt and cords, although the reasons for that appeared to be thrift rather than fashion. His background was equally incongruous, as Frank discovered one evening in the spring of his senior year when, like the fourteen other Keys Men, Howard took his turn to tell his life story. He could still hear his voice, alternately pained and defiant, as he described his childhood in the Bronx, where his dentist father presided over a strictly Orthodox household. 'We kept Shabbat; we kept kosher; we kept the holidays. I wore a yarmulke and *davened* three times a day.' Frank was certain that he was not alone in failing to pick up all the references, but he was loath either to betray his ignorance or to interrupt the flow as Howard explained how, at fifteen, he was arrested in a gay bar in Greenwich Village with fake ID. 'By some fluke, the cop who picked me up was one of my father's patients. As a favour to him, he agreed to let me off so long as I saw a shrink. Though to be honest, his picture of what I could expect if I were sent to the state penitentiary sounded kind of appealing.' He laughed, as if daring his listeners to demur. 'The shrink sucked his pen, which I found telling. He asked me to put a rubber band on my wrist and flick it every time I saw a man I found attractive.

By the end of three months my wrist was so numb that it was futile; I could lust after as many men as I liked. When my father saw that the treatment wasn't working, he sent me to the rabbi, in whom he had much more faith. The rabbi told me that God gave us the inclination to sin but he also gave us the cure – not the rubber band but the Torah. So I read it – every word – but when I pointed out some of the more egregious inconsistencies, not to mention the transgressions of most of the patriarchs, he reviled me as a blasphemer.

'The moment of truth came one Friday night when I skipped Shabbat dinner. Much as I relished my mother's cooking, I refused to join my brothers and sisters and line up to receive my father's blessing. He was waiting for me when I returned home. I told him I'd been receiving my own blessing – several, in fact – in Central Park. He smacked me across the head and threw me out. I went back to the Park and slept on a bench, bang in the middle of the cruising ground. Sometimes I slept in a bed if one of the men who came on to me took my fancy. Then I lucked out and met Wendell, a curator at the Met. He adopted me (unofficially), sending me to school and teaching me about a culture beyond a few square miles of cultivated desert in the Middle East. When my wild ways and, more to the point, my wilder gentlemen callers, proved too much for him, he sent me packing. But by then I had the confidence and the savings to apply to college, and a professor I met through Wendell, who shall remain nameless, persuaded me to try for Yale. Hence my presence in this august company.'

His fourteen listeners sat silently, each assessing the uneventfulness of his own life with differing degrees of relief and regret. Howard's unabashed sexuality presented a greater challenge to Frank than to any of the others. He had had sex for the first time the previous year on Induction Training – popularly known as Seduction Training – with an auto mechanic from Denver, thereby either confirming or establishing a lifelong predilection for blue-collar men. Racked with guilt, he had vowed to a God in whom his belief was rapidly waning never to repeat the lapse. He squired eligible girls from the Social Register to parties and balls, grateful that their code of propriety prevented their permitting any familiarities below the waist. Returning from active service, he devoted himself to the theatre, both as an outlet and a purge for his desires. When he came to tell his story, he boasted that the romantic opportunities he had enjoyed in summer stock were as rich as if he had broken into Bryn Mawr. Thirteen faces looked at him with envy; the fourteenth with suspicion, a suspicion that was put into words when he called on him later that evening in his dorm.

'I want you to write a piece for the magazine.'

'I can't write to save my life.'

'You're too modest! That story you told about dating the actresses at the Barn Theatre was pure fiction.'

'I'm heterosexual!'

'Now I know you're a fag. If you were straight, you'd simply have said you were normal.'

Frank gazed at Howard in alarm as his legs gave way and he found himself slumped on the bed. In a movement that was smoother in retrospect than it had been at the time, Howard sat beside him and his reassuring hug turned into a kiss. Frank was too stunned to know whether he enjoyed it. Moreover, he was conscious that at any moment his roommate might return.

'Do you want the evening to end here?' Howard asked.

'I don't know. No. That is I don't think so,' Frank replied wretchedly. 'But where can we go? Back to the hall?'

'And defile the hallowed memory of generations of Keys Men? I think not. Never fret, I know the perfect place.'

It turned out to be the Taft Hotel. Frank, whose ardour had dwindled with every step they took off campus, felt it vanish completely as he stared at the forbidding red-and-white facade. 'How can you afford this?'

'Relax! I don't expend my charms exclusively on WASPS. Come on!' He led Frank round to the staff entrance, telling him to wait while he went inside to find his friend, Joey, one of the bellboys. Frank, struggling to maintain his composure in the face of two giggling chambermaids, was plotting his escape when Howard returned with Joey who, belying his name and function, looked to be at least sixty. He blushed as Joey appraised him approvingly before leading them up four flights of almost ostentatious bleakness to his bedroom, which would have been cramped even on board ship.

'Enjoy!' he said, as he left to resume his shift. Frank did his best to obey, even though there was enough of his father in him to resent the obligation to a menial and enough of his mother to worry about the clutter of the room. As for himself, the thrill of holding another man in his arms was enough to offset the fact that, in an ideal world, Howard with his hairy, bony body was not the one he would have chosen. As he lay back after climaxing, he attributed his vague sense of disappointment to a combination of inexperience and nerves. It was a disappointment that Howard seemed to share since, with his Lucky Strike adding to the fug, he leapt up and pulled on his shorts, saying 'Right! Now we've got that out of the way, we can be real friends.'

Friends they had remained ever since, despite all that life had thrown in their paths. Howard had cast himself, unbidden, in the role of Frank's conscience: the uncompromised artist as against the Hollywood sell-out, the proud gay man as against the closet case. He had disapproved of both Frank's partners. While cordial to Gene, he never appreciated his qualities, insisting that Frank needed a lover who would challenge him. He was openly hostile to Audrey, refusing to accept that Frank's feelings for her were genuine and dismissing their marriage as a studio stunt. His own affairs were short-lived, as he struggled to reconcile his desire for a soulmate with his commitment to free love. Then, in his mid-fifties and long resigned to solitude, he met Max, a dour San Franciscan correctional counsellor. After a taxing bicoastal affair, he moved west to be with him. Five years later, he published his third novel to widespread acclaim.

'So coupledom has its rewards,' Frank said.

Irony apart, he knew that Howard's achievement was attributable to far more than a supportive relationship. For thirty years he had eked out a modest living writing television scripts, while being too contemptuous of the medium to possess a set. He had published two novels, which appeared without fanfare and vanished without trace. Finally he had written the book that he was born to write, a radical reworking of the myth of Sodom, which he identified as the cornerstone of gay oppression. If it were possible for a novel set thousands of years in the past to be autobiographical, then *Flesh and Brimstone* was it. Not only was Sodom a thinly veiled version of the gay communities in Greenwich Village and the Castro, with fertility rites in the fields replacing phallic worship in the clubs, but Abraham, the tyrannical patriarch and villain of the piece, was based, from all Frank knew of him, on Howard's father. Moreover, by his very public rejection of both the novel and its author, Lev Edelman had stoked the controversy that confirmed the book's success. Nothing, however, had done more to give it pertinence than the arrival of AIDS. By the time of its publication in September 1983, over 1,500 Americans had died of the disease. Now, a little more than two years later, the figure had risen to over 10,000, with 15,000 others known to be infected. Frank suspected that one reason for the book's acclaim was the guilt of the liberal intelligentsia at its impotence in the face of the crisis. If so, he could think of no worthier beneficiary than Howard.

As he stepped off the plane in Marrakech, Frank was determined that his performance would reflect his commitment to both subject and author. With the heat melting the tarmac and the air as muggy as a boiler room, he wished that he had allowed himself more than a day and a half to acclimatise before he was due at the studio. Trusting that Bela had sent an assistant to cut through the red tape, he walked down the long airport corridors where the loud whirr was the only evidence of the air conditioning, past billboards on which the Arabic script promoting American products looked like graffiti. As he entered the immigration hall, a tall young man wearing a flat blue-and-white hat and an oversized *Coke Is It* T-shirt, which was either a gift from the company or else shameless sycophancy, held up a handwritten sign, WELCOME MR FRANK ARCHER, in which the 'R's were inverted. After waving like an overzealous extra, he scurried over and led Frank out of the queue, to the consternation of two elderly Spaniards who had just put a name to the face. 'No, no need for this. You are Mr Frank Archer. Everyone in Morocco is grateful that you have come to this country. His Majesty the King is grateful that you have come to this country.' The two scowling soldiers patrolling the hall suggested otherwise, nevertheless the officials had been well briefed and Frank was whisked through passport control, customs and baggage reclamation, into a waiting car.

'It is good for me now to introduce my name. I am Abdo al-Jaidi. I have the honour of welcoming you to Marrakech. I have been sent from Ouarzazate to accompany you, although I am a very busy man on this film. I am second assistant director on this film.'

'I'm delighted to meet you,' Frank said, enjoying the benign self-importance with which Abdo gave the impression that he would be behind the camera, rather than simply ensuring that the actors arrived on set on time. 'Is this your first experience of filming?'

'My first, yes. But Mr Bela Zipser, who is the producer, he has told me that he can see that I "have what it take". Those were his very own words.'

'I bet they were.'

Abdo's chatter not only enlivened the half-hour drive through a disconcertingly drab landscape, but offered Frank a timely reminder of what it was to be twenty and full of hope. They entered the ornate lobby of the Mamounia hotel, where the hastily summoned manager informed him, with a mixture of bashfulness and pride, that he had been allocated the Churchill suite, the rooms that had been occupied by the former prime minister when he came to Morocco to paint. The manager led him up to a plush sitting room furnished with a roll-top desk and one of the worn leather sofas whose scratches and scuffs the British regarded as marks of distinction, but it was only when he moved to the window that he understood why Churchill had described it as the most exquisite place on earth. In the foreground were the hotel gardens, aisles of olive trees, lemon trees, palm trees and cacti, interspersed with roses, gardenias, jasmine and flowers of every sort, and in the background, the snow-capped peaks of the Atlas mountains, fleecy as clouds in the turquoise sky. For all his fears about the heat and the hygiene, he felt a surge of joy at the prospect of spending two months amid such beauty.

The following morning they left Marrakech at ten for the five-hour journey to Ouarzazate. With its forests of pine and cedar, terraces of maize and barley, and villages of mud-brick houses, the countryside was spectacular; but the roads were so winding, the air conditioning so weak and the dust so pervasive, even inside the car, that by the time they arrived, he felt sicker than during the turbulence over the Azores. They drove down a tree-lined boulevard, whose wrought-iron lampposts and stone fountains recalled the French Moroccan stamps in his boyhood album. Stiff and sore, he stepped out of the car at the Grand Hotel du Sud, the Grand at first glance appearing to be an honorific. He had not realised how painfully his head was pounding until he entered the lobby, to be accosted by Howard.

'God, you look rough!'

'I've just spent five hours on a road that makes the bends in the Hollywood Hills look like a crosswalk.'

'Have you lost weight?'

'What is this?' Knowing full well what it was, Frank broke away. Howard was concerned about him. Ever since spring when a test for the AIDS virus – or, as he must now call it, the HIV virus – had been licensed for use in blood banks, Howard had been urging him to take it, largely, Frank suspected, because he believed that he had infected Gene. But with no cure in sight, the only effect of a positive result would be to confirm his place on Death Row. He preferred to rely on his own test, inspecting his skin for spots more assiduously than at any time since he was twelve.

Loath to face further scrutiny, he spent the evening in his suite, two plain white rooms filled with wooden fretwork furniture and hung with daguerreotypes of the Sahara. He went to bed at nine, sleeping fitfully on account of the din from the patio. At midnight, he took a second Restoril and, whether because of the drug or the noise or the heat or the journey, he plunged into a nightmare in which he was being inducted into the Hollywood Walk of Fame. As he knelt to immortalise his prints in cement, the plaques around him opened like graves and hands shot up to grab his legs. The hands were followed by the heads and bodies of scores of movie stars. He kicked and punched, but he was unable to break free as they dragged him down into the cold, dank darkness, from which he emerged sweating in swampy sheets.

He had breakfast with Howard who, after apologising for his brusqueness the previous afternoon, enthusiastically detailed the preparations for the shoot. Frank was the last of the principals to arrive, but any hope of a rundown on his fellow actors was dashed when, one by one, they entered the dining room. First was Porter Wright who, with his usual disdain for any emotion for which he was not being paid, nodded casually to Frank and made his way to the buffet, before turning as if on a whim to greet him.

'Good flight?'

'Unremarkable,' Frank replied. 'We touched down in Madrid.'

'Hate the place. More dog crap per square mile than anywhere else on the planet. Good to have you on board!' Duty done, he returned to the food.

'Short and sweet,' Howard said.

'Sweeter than he used to be. We've made three pictures together. He hasn't changed.'

'He must be at least eighty.'

'He's never forgiven me for beating him to the make-up chair one morning thirty years ago. I was afraid I'd committed some fearful faux pas, offended an older actor, even though I had higher billing. But the make-up girl—'

'Not—'

'No – another one – told me that he needed fifteen minutes every day with a teabag on his eyes to repair the previous night's damage.'

'No change there then! From what I've seen, he drinks the younger actors under the table. It's a wonder anyone'll insure him.'

'Darling!' Laura Bennett hailed Frank as distinctly as if her passport to Hollywood had been a decade on Broadway rather than a year as Miss Ohio. She swept through the room to the delight of the tourists, before catching her heel on an uneven tile. 'The old team back together again!'

'Not so much of the old!' Frank said, as he kissed her and pulled out the chair beside him. No one could awaken memories of his carefree youth as readily as Laura. In four films in the early fifties, they had made such a sparkling pair of sparring lovers that fans all over the world had urged him to propose to her. But life could never imitate art since she was not only married to Aubrey Lancaster, the English composer, whose first love was his German Shepherd ('That's a dog,' she helpfully pointed out), but a lesbian. Frank had slept with her once on the set of *The Prince of Fifth Avenue*, when she claimed that it would help them to bring out the truth of their romance: an episode that had left him with a lifelong mistrust of method acting. The studio, robbed of a happy ending for its celluloid sweethearts, fashioned a tragic one, with Laura asserting her loyalty to Aubrey and Frank left to nurse a broken heart.

'Now whatever dirt you two have been dishing, I want you to dish it all up again for me.' The waiter came to take her order. 'Black coffee, please. And be a pet and fetch me some honey. All you have on the buffet is that lethal tomato jam.' She turned to Frank. 'Montezuma's Revenge.'

'Wrong continent,' Howard said.

'Same effect.'

Laura had little chance to enjoy either the gossip or the meal before Abdo summoned them to the studio. Howard, more nervous than either of the actors, bustled them out to the hotel forecourt where a fleet of beaten-up Peugeots and Mercedes was waiting. Ushering Frank and Laura into the first, he explained that the cars had been brought there from Spain by hippies who sold them to buy drugs. 'Driving any distance in this, they'd need them,' Frank said, as they juddered down five miles of unpaved road and turned into the newly built Atlas Studios, its crenellated towers and ornamental gateway resembling a film set itself. They drew up beside the sole sound stage where Frank spotted Bela, short, bullet-headed, barrel-chested and dressed in a powder-blue safari suit.

Bela greeted him with a hug that, to a casual observer, might have seemed paternal before handing him over to Ilyass, the first AD, who led him inside. As his eyes adjusted to the gentler light, he made out four long tables arranged in a square, beside one of which Hugh Davenport was standing with an elegant young woman. Hugh was forty-five but, with his short, sandy hair, wire-frame glasses and smooth pink cheeks, he looked as though he should still be in high school. Spotting Frank, he gave a friendly wave and continued talking to the woman, whom Howard, confirming his insider status, identified as Lucia de Fiore, the make-up supervisor. Frank had an uneasy first-day-at-school feeling as the room filled up with actors. He recognised Dana Adams who, as one of Hollywood's best-known Lotharios, was bold casting as the King of Sodom. He was chatting animatedly to Barbara Sokolsky, an actress whom Frank had discovered when, seeking mindless distraction after Gene's death, he took himself to see *Liberty Bodice*, a campy spy thriller in which she played the title role. He was heading towards them when Howard introduced the young English actresses, Glynis Opie and Juliet Clark, who were playing his daughters. They in turn brought over Alan Jameson and Daniel Stirling, who were playing the angels, all four of them veterans of Hugh's stage productions in London. After shaking hands, he looked more closely at Daniel, whose high cheekbones, soft brown hair and piercing green eyes had, according to Howard, ensnared Hugh.

'I can see the attraction,' Frank whispered to him, 'but surely he's straight?'

'That is the attraction,' Howard replied. 'For Hugh, rejection is the root of passion.'

As befitted her age and eminence, the last to arrive was Dorothy Hillard, who had been a star of the silent screen before Frank was born. The epitome of ingénue innocence, she had survived a scandal when a lip-reader in Boston claimed that during her love scene with Ramon Novarro in *The Maid of All Work*, she mouthed every swear word in the dictionary. She had not only made the transition to talkies but had rarely been out of work since. When asked the secret of her survival, she replied 'Always saying "yes".' And, while there must have been times when, with hindsight, she wished that she had said 'no', her presence, however low down the cast list, dignified even the dullest material.

'Franklin!' she exclaimed, as though they shared a familial intimacy. 'I shall cry. Don't you love this business of ours? You don't see one of your favourite people for years and then you do and it's as if you were never apart.' She threw her arms around his neck and kissed him full on the lips.

'Right. May we have you all now, please?' Bela asked, sitting down at one of the tables. 'You'll find your names by your chairs.'

The actors searched for their places with the giggling apprehension of five-year-olds. After a momentary confusion between Laura Bennett and Leora Bertiti, the costume designer, for which Laura blamed her bad eyesight and Abdo his bad writing, everyone was seated. Frank was gratified to find himself on Bela's left, with Laura on his left and Porter on hers. Hugh was on Bela's right and Howard on his, with Arturo Nobile, the brilliant director of photography, with whom Frank had worked on Felice Graffiano's *Risorgimento*, on Howard's right, and so forth, down to the location and production assistants on what must now be considered the bottom table. Starting with Bela, everyone stated his or her name and role, with varying degrees of self-consciousness.

'Right,' Bela said, 'let me begin by welcoming you all as we embark on this new adventure. I think I can say without fear of contradiction I've made one or two pictures that will stand the test of time. Some of you here have worked on them. The rest of you, I'm sure, will have seen them. But I'll stake both my Oscars – even my Renoirs – that when they come to write my obituary (not for a good twenty years, I hope), *Flesh and Brimstone* will get top billing. Howard has written a great book but, more than that, he's written a great screenplay. Hugh, I know, will make a great film. But it hasn't all been plain sailing. I'm aware that some of your agents warned you not to get involved.' Frank worried that Lenny had said nothing to him. 'This isn't the first film on the subject to be made here. That honour goes to Robert Aldrich's sixties epic, *The Last Days of Sodom and Gomorrah*. But the country was much freer then. It's now in the grip of a religious revival and we have to tread carefully. King Hassan has given this project his personal blessing. He's ordered his chief ministers and the governor of Ouarzazate to provide us with every assistance.' He nodded at Souheil ben Sail, the location manager, and Karim Tabbal, the second unit manager, the two senior Moroccans on the team. 'But – and it's a big *but* – they're under the impression that the film we're making is *The Fall of Babylon*.' Frank sensed a stir around the table. '"Why?" I hear you ask. Simple! Last year, Bruce Beresford planned to shoot *King David* here (and I promise that's the last time you'll hear me mention that wretched film), but the local imams and what have you raised a hoo-ha about the insult to the prophet. Who knew that David was a prophet in Islam? I thought he was one they'd left to us! As it turns out, Lot stands even higher in their pantheon. So we daren't risk any trouble. Unlike Beresford, we can't afford to up sticks at a moment's notice. I only wish we had a twenty million dollar budget. I'd be a happy man.'

With that familiar plea of penury, Bela ceded the floor to Hugh, who expressed his excitement to be working on the film, praising the originality and daring of the script, the talents of the cast and crew and, in what seemed like an afterthought, the energy and dedication of the producer. 'The key thing to remember,' he said, 'is that this is not a biblical epic.' Frank felt Bela tense. 'It's a human drama that happens to be set in biblical times. So I don't want anything highfalutin. Fabrizio and his team have created some magnificent sets here in the studio.' Hugh nodded at Fabrizio Magri, the production designer. 'And God or Yahweh or Yarikh has done his best for us outdoors.' Laura tittered politely, but Hugh's manner was so dry that Frank could not be certain of his tone. 'They will provide the element of grandeur. You must just be true to your characters and the story they have to tell.'

Declaring that it was a rare privilege to have the writer on hand, he asked Howard to say a few words. Frank prayed that he would stick to the brief and be brief, rather than milking the opportunity for which he had waited so long.

'Bela spoke of *The Last Days of Sodom and Gomorrah*, which was made when Morocco was a far more tolerant society. Still, I doubt that even the most fanatical Muslim could have objected to it, unless on the grounds that God's wrath and all those expensive special effects were wasted on destroying a Sodom without sodomites, where the only hint of lust was the queen ogling the slave girls performing a cooch dance.'

'I could live with that,' Dana called out.

'Sorry, but on this film, you're batting for the other side,' Howard replied. 'And our depiction of Sodom will be very different. Bear with me while I give you some background. I've been accused of perverting the pristine truths of the Bible. Which is a contradiction in terms, but never mind. As a boy, I studied the Torah and read the Sodom story in its "purest" form (that's *pure* in inverted commas). I saw the hoops that rabbis and scholars had to jump through to prove that Moses was its author. I was beaten – and that's not in inverted commas – by my father for asking how Moses could have described his own death at the end of Deuteronomy. But I wear my welts with pride. The Jewish Bible, like the Christian with which I'm less familiar, was compiled for political as much as for spiritual purposes. The ancient myths of Israel and Judah were combined when the two kingdoms were united under King Hezekiah. But they, along with so much else in the Bible, only assumed their final form when the Jews were exiled to Babylon. I know that Bela has cited the fall of Babylon as our cover story and, down the ages, the city has become a byword for decadence – the Great Whore and all that – but actually the ancient Israelites took far more from their stay there than they cared to admit. Many of their laws were founded on the ancient Hammurabi code. Popular stories, such as the Flood and the Tower of Babel, show direct Babylonian influence. But of far more significance was their need to atone for the sins that were the cause of their exile. In the past, they would have done so through sacrifice in the Temple. But there was no Temple in Babylon so, instead, they laid fresh emphasis on the Bible, writing it as an act of atonement and reading in it the chronicle of that atonement.'

'So did the Jews bring the story of Sodom into Babylon or take it out?' Bela asked impatiently.

'Both. The myths of Abraham, Lot and their families are among the earliest in the traditions of both Israel and Judah and the many inconsistencies in the existing account attest to the problem of combining them. But the scribes who revised them would have had access to the archives in Nebuchadrezzar's palace.'

'It's Nebuchadnezzar. With an "n",' Porter interjected. 'I played him in *The Fiery Furnace*.'

'I'm sorry, but it's an "r". We've got it wrong all these years.'

'Oh well, another performance bites the dust,' Porter said darkly, as though Howard had shredded the negative himself.

'Let's just call it the king's palace,' Howard said, eager to appease him. 'From the cuneiform tablets in the archives they took the fire and brimstone that feature in the ancient Akkadian creation myth and applied them to the destruction of Sodom. Most decisively – not to say, disastrously – they added the element of homophobia in an attempt to distance themselves from the same-sex practice in Babylonian temples.'

'It's not even consistent,' Daniel Stirling said. 'If you approach the story logically, the punishment should apply only to people who have sex with angels.'

'I'm game, sweetheart,' Dorothy replied, aware that he was playing Raphael.

'Be careful what you wish for,' Daniel said archly.

'She's old enough to be his grandmother,' Frank whispered to Laura.

'And so it starts,' she replied.

After a short refreshment break, they began the table read. With the scenes in heaven to be shot in England, Yahweh was the only principal character unrepresented so, either shrewdly or ironically, Hugh asked Bela to stand in for him, or rather them since, by a process that was left unexplained, the part was to be played by two actors. At the end of the day, Bela departed for Casablanca en route to Rome, where he was to make his headquarters during the shoot. 'You are like my children,' he said expansively. 'No child wants Poppa looking over their shoulders or breathing down their necks—'

'Or rummaging in their drawers,' Laura said to Frank, as Bela eyed Juliet.

'While they are hanging out with their friends. But I'll only be a few hours away, ready to hop on a plane at a moment's notice. Now go on, make the film; make history; make me proud!'

Buoyed by Bela's enthusiasm, they set to work. After three days of rehearsal, the unit moved into the desert to shoot the scenes in the Israelite camp, starting with Abraham's sacrifice to Yahweh on his safe return from Egypt. Souheil had assembled three hundred extras from Christian villages, since no Muslim woman would contemplate showing her face on screen. They were noticeably darker than the locals whom Frank had seen in Marrakech, and far more so than Dorothy, Porter and himself, even in bronze make-up, but no one commented on the discrepancy. They rehearsed all morning with Hugh directing the extras through Ilyass who, despite speaking several Arab dialects, relied largely on gesture. They broke for lunch, but no sooner had they returned to the set than a dust storm of biblical proportions blew up, rendering filming impossible. The actors were ferried back to the hotel, while the extras were billeted in huts once occupied by the French Foreign Legion.

The next morning they returned to shoot the scene. Porter, whose grasp of his lines had been tenuous during the rehearsal, fluffed take after take, even confusing the animals that he was sacrificing. First, he imputed his lapses to dehydration and it took a while for the crew, unversed in his ways, to realise that the regular swigs from his hip flask were not helping. Then he laid the blame on the clouds of insect repellent that Abdo sprayed to scatter the flies before each take. With the scene finally in the can, Hugh tried to make up for lost time by moving straight on to the scene where Abraham presents his newborn son, Ishmael, to his tribesmen, but once again a dust storm erupted to thwart him. The actors and crew headed back to the hotel, tetchy, burnt and bitten. Only the extras welcomed the prospect of an extended engagement, during which they could enjoy the lavish meals produced by Youness, the permanently harassed catering manager; the unlimited supply of Coca-Cola, Sprite and Fanta, which, in deference to the parent company, were the only drinks allowed on set; and, most importantly, the attentions of the unit doctor and nurses.

Despite the purity of the light, filming in the desert was a trial. The sun was so intense that, by the middle of each morning, Arturo had placed both a parasol and a damp towel over the camera to prevent its overheating. 'It's a pity he can't do as much for the actors,' Laura remarked to Frank. Porter's failing memory was a permanent source of tension. Dorothy, sensitive to the frailties of age, painstakingly tested his lines, which he nonetheless mangled the moment that the camera rolled. His relations with the director sank even lower when, after eight abandoned takes of Abraham's farewell to Lot, Hugh asked him with icy calm to do it again. 'This time we might even go for the odd word of the script.'

'You should have hired Sir Laurence Olivier!' Porter retorted, with a sneer on the *Sir*.

'Don't think we didn't try.'

Porter stormed off the set. Frank was not privy to the stratagems that were used to entice him back, but he returned half an hour later, word perfect, and Hugh called for the scene to be printed after the second take. As on every evening, the footage was flown to Casablanca in a single-engine plane that looked so like the *Spirit of the St Louis* that Frank half expected Lindbergh or, at the very least, Jimmy Stewart, to wave from the cockpit. From there it was put on a commercial flight to Rome. With no projection facilities yet in place at the studio, the best news of the day came when Hugh relayed the message from Bela, curt as ever in a cable: 'Rushes OK. Best.'

Given all the delays, Frank was grateful that, unlike many directors he had known, Hugh did not shoot acres of superfluous footage, trusting to make sense of it in the cutting room, but had a clear vision of the finished picture in his head. Five days behind schedule, they filmed the last of the desert scenes: the fight between Lot's men and Abraham's men that precipitated Lot's departure for Sodom. The following morning, the unit itself departed for Sodom, or rather the Kasbah at Ait Benhaddou, which was to stand in for its walls. They were not the first to recognise the cinematic potential of the fortified cluster of towers and houses; indeed, the ancient buildings (which, to Frank's astonishment, were made not of stone but of a mixture of earth and straw) had been restored ten years earlier for Franco Zeffirelli's *Jesus of Nazareth*. 'For once the Christians have paved the way for the Jews,' Howard said. Over two days, they were to shoot three arrivals at the city gates: Sarah's, Eliezer's, and the two angels'. Frank was surprised by how flustered the normally unflappable Hugh became around Daniel Stirling, spending longer running his scenes than any of the others, giving him reams of notes and making minute adjustments to his dress and posture before springing back as though he had been burnt. As the day drew on and the blazing sunlight turned the walls an ever deeper red, he grew increasingly excited by the match with Daniel's 'russet' (to Frank's eye, rust-coloured) hair, ecstatic when a particular pattern produced an effect 'like a Botticelli halo'.

Frank was not called for the next three days, the first in the studio, while they filmed scenes between Abraham, Sarah and Hagar. He politely declined Souheil's offer to drive him to Casablanca, much to the location manager's chagrin. Howard, rarely mistaken in such matters, had identified him as gay even before he dolefully described how he had been trapped into marriage: 'My wife, she drugged me with drink made from scorpions and woman's blood.' He had no doubt hoped for a few days of licence in the city but, with the heat and broken sleep having sapped his energy and the bumpy rides in cramped jeeps having cricked his back, Frank preferred to rest in his room or beside the pool, chatting to the French and German tourists who made Ouarzazate their base for trekking in the Sahara.

Tiredness shielded him from the tensions on set, which were relayed to him by Howard and Laura, with whom he dined every evening at the hotel. The chief culprit was Porter, who grabbed Dorothy too roughly in the scene where Sarah returns to Abraham, twisting her arm. She stormed out, demanding to see the doctor, who diagnosed a strained tendon and signed her off work for three days. Hugh insisted that he could film around her, but Ryan Ledger, the production manager and Bela's eyes and ears in Ouarzazate, fretted about further delays. Porter then offended Glynis Opie, whose chirpy 'good mornings' were a universal irritant, by repeating the greeting to her twenty times in as many voices and trusting that that would satisfy her for the rest of the shoot, whereupon the British actors closed ranks and cut him dead. Most damagingly, his relationship with Hugh hit rock-bottom, the director addressing him only through intermediaries, after Porter publicly called him a 'Limey cocksucker'.

Elsewhere, location fever was mounting. Dana Adams lived up to his reputation by sleeping with Juliet Clark, and

Dorothy Hillard, doctor's note notwithstanding, bedded her angel. Despite describing the episode as 'about as much fun as catching your dick in the zipper', Daniel broadcast it widely, claiming that not many twenty-six-year-olds got the chance to sleep with a silent-screen legend. Howard, less sympathetic than Frank to brash young actors, accused him of playing fast and loose with Hugh. Frank, however, suspected that, in textbook fashion, Hugh welcomed his protégé's cruelty as an opportunity for self-abasement. He appeared to savour his misery, eating alone in the dining room where, with the exception of Porter who drank his meal at the bar, the rest of the cast and crew had split into groups. Frank twice invited him to join Howard, Laura and Dorothy at his table but he refused, pleading the need to prepare the next day's scenes. Howard, who had spent a month with him working on the script, maintained that the real reason was his lack of small talk.

Unrequited passion was not Hugh's only problem. Daily missives were arriving from Bela, installed in his Roman palazzo and increasingly alarmed by the overruns. As ever, he implied that the pressure came from above, instancing the spate of personnel changes at Columbia since the project had been given the green light. The new Head of Production was horrified to find that they were making a 'fag film'. They had too much invested in it to pull out, but he was adamant that they would not spend another cent. It was left to the hapless Ryan to convey the news to Hugh who replied, with a little too much relish, that he had been trained at a school where big boys beat little boys with impunity, so he had learnt to stand up to bullies. If Bela were unhappy with his methods, he should call a halt to filming and replace him. The producer graciously backed down. The next day, with unwonted extravagance, he added a word to his cable: 'Rushes OK. Very best.'

With the domestic scenes in both city and camp in the can, it was time to introduce the Sodomites. Given the reluctance of the Christian extras, otherwise so amenable, to enact the brawl between Lot's men and Abraham's men for fear of losing face, it was evident that no villagers, whatever their religion, would portray the Sodomites, even in the guise of Babylonians. So Souheil bussed in two hundred men and twenty-five women from Marrakech. Most were expatriates, who had come from Europe either on the hippie trail or in quest of what Teri, in a euphemism more offensive than plain speech, once described as 'mahogany merchandise'. The rest were Moroccans who, unable to live as freely as in the days of colonial rule, were obliged to pursue clandestine pleasures. Souheil, betraying a more intimate knowledge of the cruising grounds than might have been wise, trawled the hammams and the souk and the gardens of the Koutoubia mosque to find men who were willing to express on screen a love that was forbidden off it.

The extras entered into their scenes with more gusto than the actors. Dana, having declared that he would have no problem kissing and fondling his slave boy ('I'm an actor – whatever Miss Kael might say'), was reluctant to nuzzle his nipple.

'Don't you guys miss titties?' he asked Hugh.

'Not since I was two,' Hugh replied, telling him gruffly to think of it as sucking out a sting.

Daniel, true to form, was more histrionic. After two of the Italian grips came down with malaria while rigging the scene in the baths, he bared his chest in the hotel bar and called on any passing mosquito to take a bite. He was particularly exercised about the effect on his reputation of Raphael's missing genitals. 'I know it's the character, but these things stick,' he said to Frank. 'It's why your agent tells you not to play gay.' Frank wondered if he were being deliberately offensive or simply obtuse. 'I don't want to be known as Daniel no-balls.'

'There's not much danger of that,' he replied. 'You've left none of us in any doubt of their potency.' As well as his night with Dorothy, who had maintained a judicious distance from him ever since, Daniel had conducted simultaneous affairs with Isabella, the special-effects supervisor, and Graziana, the continuity girl, the latter losing no opportunity to cry on Hugh's already sodden shoulder.

Frank, ever more aching and feverish, was as impatient with the delays on set as Bela, only to provoke one himself in the climactic scene where the Sodomites call at the house to invite the angels to worship Baal. Over the two-month shoot, he had grown impatient with the younger actors' persistent questions about their motivation. Scorning such self-regard, he held that everything they needed was in the script. He had the greatest respect for Howard's creation of a more rounded and credible Lot than the original. Reading the Bible story, he could never understand why a righteous man should stay so long in such a wicked city, let alone why he offered his daughters to the Sodomites when, in the first place, they were clamouring for men and, in the second, those men were angels and therefore inviolate. By portraying Lot as rebelling against Abraham's despotism and emphasising his friendship with the king, Howard had accounted for his residence in Sodom. By turning his direct offer of his daughters to the assailants into a conditional one to the priests, he had alleviated the horror. Nevertheless, it was hard to credit that, however desperate, any father would envisage his daughters becoming temple prostitutes. Every time Frank tried to say the line he dried. Embarrassed by his failure (not least in front of the extras), he explained his difficulties.

'May I make a suggestion?' Howard asked Hugh.

'Be my guest,' Hugh replied wearily.

'Lot knows that the angels have come in response to Abraham's request. This makes him all the more determined to do things by the book, so that they can find no fault with his practice. It's possible to feel a residual respect – loyalty even – for the customs of a tribe long after you've abandoned its beliefs.' He broke off. 'You're smiling.'

'Thank you.' Frank remembered how Howard still fasted on Yom Kippur, and he spoke the line without a slip.

With the angelic vengeance unleashed, the last week in the studio was devoted to the destruction of the city and Lot's family's escape. The construction crew had built a remarkable warren of temples, towers and houses, all from the same earth and straw as the Kasbah at Ait Benhaddou, with which it had to blend. Bela returned to oversee the shooting of his most spectacular – and costly – sequence. That night Frank was roused from a drug-induced sleep by what sounded like the rattle of gunfire. Having heard about the food riots in Rabat and Fez, he feared that they must have spread to the smaller towns. He rushed to the window, but his relief on finding that the sound was that of torrential rain vanished when he entered the dining room the next morning to be greeted by Dorothy's doom-laden pronouncement that 'Sodom is no more.' The earth-and-straw city on the outdoor lot had been reduced to sludge. Although similar buildings had lasted for hundreds of years at Ait Benhaddou, these new ones had been rapidly and flimsily assembled, leaving them vulnerable to the elements: not the fire and brimstone that Isabella and her team had prepared, but a freak storm.

'You can't legislate for an act of God,' Laura said.

'Please don't say that,' Glynis said, clutching her crucifix.

Although the sun was dazzling and the hotel staff had tidied the garden, it felt disrespectful to sit by the pool. Frank joined his fellow actors in the lounge, where they swapped possible scenarios, ranging from the absurd: 'Couldn't we burn the Kasbah?' (Barbara) to the apocalyptic: 'Typical! My first film and they'll have to abandon it' (Daniel). At noon, Ryan returned from the governor's office with weather records showing that it had been the first October storm in the province since 1972. These were duly cabled to Lloyd's, who replied four hours later with an assurance that both the reconstruction and postponement would be covered. Bela immediately gave orders for the set to be rebuilt indoors. While sharing the general euphoria, not least for Howard's sake, Frank dreaded the prospect of the shoot, already two weeks behind schedule, being prolonged. He was suffering from the heat; his eyes, inflamed by dust, oozed pus every morning; his stomach was so upset that his urine was the colour of his diarrhoea. After consulting the doctor, who diagnosed acute enteritis, he presented his certificate to Bela, adding that, unless his scenes were wrapped within four days, he would have to fly out to recuperate.

'You hold a gun to my head,' said Bela, his centipede-shaped scar throbbing as ever when he felt threatened. Frank was more worried about the gun he was holding to Hugh's. The director, looking like a prisoner reprieved from execution only to learn that he has terminal cancer, agreed to shoot the scenes of the family fleeing the city in the Taourirt Kasbah, trusting that the showers of sparks and odd burning beam would become a full-scale conflagration in the edit.

For his final scenes Frank had to return to Ait Benhaddou, where a cave in the nearby cliffs was to serve as the mountain refuge for Lot and his daughters after they fled Zoar. Until recently it had housed a Berber family who lit it with oil lamps, rather than the 1,000-watt lights that the grips were struggling to rig within its narrow and irregular walls. While it would have been easier to build a replica in the studio, Hugh, having compromised on so much else, insisted on this measure of authenticity.

Frank drove out at dawn with Howard, refusing any other companion in case he required the commode. The severity of his enteritis was now evident to everyone, and Bela and Hugh were determined to complete his scenes before he collapsed. With the grips still hard at work, Hugh struggled to find space in the cave to rehearse. Frank prayed that, seeing his discomfort, Glynis and Juliet would forego their usual questions but, instead, they embarked on a lengthy discussion as to whether they were more disgusted at having sex with their father or proud of taking revenge. It was an obvious delaying tactic. Six months ago, their nudity waivers must have seemed a small price to pay for roles in a major feature; now the reality hit them, and Glynis, in particular, was desperate to retain her shift. Hugh, however, was adamant that nakedness was necessary to bring home the horror of the incest. Frank was relieved that, in true Hollywood fashion, his self-exposure was restricted to glimpses of thigh when his robe rode up to his hips. For the first time that he could remember, an opportunity had been missed for him to bare his chest. He wondered if Howard had spoken to Hugh.

They shot the scene, starting with the girls picking leaves from a clump of wild rue that had been hastily planted outside the cave, Howard's intoxicating herb striking Frank as more widespread in the wilderness than the Genesis writer's wine. With Lot sound asleep, the daughters stripped and took turns to arouse him. Frank was unsure how far he should respond, given that the biblical Lot appeared to be oblivious of his seduction. Hugh suggested that he give way to a growing passion that blinded him to everything but itself, adding that 'the "God was I drunk last night!" line isn't always a lie.' He directed him to take gradual command of the situation, kissing and fondling the girls as they sat astride him, before pulling them down and mounting them.

After breaking for lunch, they returned to film the scene where Dinah and Adinah confess to their father that they have slept with him. Frank wished that Howard had given Lot a moment of tragic self-awareness in which, like Oedipus, he tore out his eyes, or even a speech in which he confronted his daughters with the reality of what they had done and the likelihood that any children they bore would be damaged. But, instead, he had favoured the girls, with Dinah explaining how, to punish Lot, they had sacrificed the very virginity that he had been ready to sacrifice to the priests, sending him reeling from the cave in wordless despair.

As he waited for the crew to set up his final scene at the cave mouth, Frank hobbled across to a nearby stone, sitting to remove a shoe from the foot that had pained him all day. 'You've been bitten,' Glynis said, pointing to the small purple lump on his sole.

'It was only a matter of time,' he replied quietly, before replacing his sock and shoe and heading to the catering tent. He felt oddly elated, knowing that, with his worst fear realised, he had nothing left to fear. The arc of his life had been drawn and all that remained was to follow its course.

He sat chatting with Glynis and Juliet, as they waited for dusk to fall or, for cinematic purposes, dawn to rise. Then, with Hugh marvelling at the effect of the sunset on the uterine cleft in the rock, they were called to their marks. Putting his arms around both daughters, Frank delivered his last lines in the film and, as he now suspected, in his career: 'I lay the blame for my fate on Abraham. I am his kinsman and must pay for my part in the deaths of the good men and women of Sodom.'

'Print it!' Hugh shouted, at which Ilyass stepped forward.

'A round of applause please, everyone,' he said. 'That completes Mr Archer's final scene.'

3

The day after he returned from Morocco, Frank made an appointment with his internist, Debra, showed her his lesion and asked for an HIV test. Struggling to hide her concern, she took his blood and referred him to a dermatologist. He in turn took a biopsy and, explaining that the lesion (there was no euphemistic *spot*) was too large for him to remove, sent him to a plastic surgeon in Beverley Hills. A week later he received the results of both tests, the dermatologist telling him that he had Kaposi's Sarcoma and Debra that he had antibodies to the HIV virus.

'That's good, isn't it?' he asked disingenuously. 'It means that my body is resisting infection.'

'Not in this case.'

Much to his indignation, Debra seemed more worried about his mental than his physical state. She urged him to confide in one or two trusted friends, insisting that he 'mustn't try to fight this thing alone', although they were both aware of the futility of trying to fight it at all. He listened courteously to the platitudes she dispensed in the absence of pills, booked the first of the regular appointments that would come to form the framework of his life, and headed home. Hurtling round the hillside bends (although he was thirty years too old for any 'live fast, die young' legend), he contemplated whom he might tell. His closest relative was his older brother, with whom he had never been intimate. Mason, who coupled envy of his celebrity with disapproval of his lifestyle, would be dutiful but cold. And, while he could rely on his friends' loyalty, he was less convinced of their discretion. He considered telling

Lenny, who had just sent him two scripts. Secrecy was in his interest since, if the news broke, his most lucrative client would be shunned even in Europe, where they were blaming Americans for the spread of AIDS. But in the end, his dread of sympathy outweighed his need of support.

Having spent the past forty years concealing the truth of his sexuality, he was confident that he could do the same for his illness. In all that time he had had only three close calls. The first was during his second year at Warner, when he attended a party hosted by an art director in Malibu, which was raided by the police. He rang Lenny, who sent a hotshot attorney, Harry Weissman, who paid off the cops and had the evidence against him buried. The second was a decade later when he was cast opposite Jimmy Stewart in *The FBI Story*. He failed to foresee that, in addition to vetting the script, the Bureau would investigate the actors, informing the studio that they were employing a known homosexual. Jack Warner, as ever a law unto himself, dropped him from the picture but renewed his contract. The third was in the mid-seventies when one of Teri's hustlers tried to blackmail him. Outraged as much on her own behalf as his, she appealed to another client, a veteran character actor with contacts in the Mob. Their 'friendly' visit left the once handsome young man looking like WC Fields, as Frank could vouch from the Polaroid obligingly slipped into the packet of retrieved negatives. From time to time (but never too often), the Mob called in the favour, flying him out to Las Vegas to be wined, dined and photographed at one of their clubs. There, he and the character actor exchanged wary greetings, and Frank despaired at the depths to which he had sunk.

With his health uncertain, Frank turned down both roles now on offer: the foul-mouthed grandfather to Hollywood's latest tow-headed urchin and the fifty-year-old Leonardo da Vinci losing his heart to Lisa del Giocondo while painting her portrait. To appease Lenny, he agreed to make a guest appearance on *Hollywood Squares* in February and film an episode of the hit crime series, *The Equaliser*, in May. Otherwise, his only commitment was to the publicity campaign for *Flesh and Brimstone*, which was slated for a November premiere. 'Just in time for the kiddies' Christmas outing,' Howard said wryly. With the opening announced, the opposition mobilised. Not since *Baby Doll* thirty years earlier had a film been subject to such a concerted attack. Catholic presenters on cable networks prophesied eternal damnation, not only for the filmmakers, whose fate was already sealed, but for anyone who bought a ticket. Baptist pastors, on first-name terms with their Saviour, held nationwide rallies that convinced the General Cinema chain not to exhibit it, thereby restricting its release to a handful of independent movie houses in major cities. Not to be left out, Jewish groups denounced it as anti-Semitic.

The studio kept its nerve (and protected its investment), refusing to withdraw the film. Its support, however, was qualified. On the one hand, it cited the First Amendment; on the other, it invited selected religious leaders to view a rough cut, agreeing to insert a disclaimer after the opening credits and even to consider making changes, a prospect that Hugh refused to countenance. Howard, accustomed to his publishers' unalloyed commitment, berated Columbia's pusillanimity, not least given its 1953 version of *Salome*, in which, in a total inversion of the Gospel story, Rita Hayworth performed the dance of the seven veils to seduce Herod into sparing John the Baptist.

Frank, who had renounced Christianity at Yale in favour of what, when pressed, he described as ethical hedonism, distanced himself from the religious controversy. He felt directly implicated, however, when the American Family Association and Focus on Family, neither of whose members had seen the film, accused it of propagating AIDS. In a series of interviews with the *New York Times*, *Vanity Fair* and *Harper's*, he was asked whether, by its sympathetic portrayal of the Sodomites and rejection of the principle of divine vengeance, *Flesh and Brimstone* was encouraging the acceptance of homosexuality and therefore the spread of infection. Charily, he replied that he was no expert on epidemiology but, from what he had read, HIV was a virus transmitted through bodily fluids, irrespective of orientation. He added that, when preparing for the film, he had learnt that it was not until 1973 that the American Psychiatric Association stopped classifying homosexuality as a mental illness. 'I know people who have lived most of their lives under that classification. Having so recently dissociated them from one disease,' he asked, heedful of his pronouns, 'are we now to identify them with another?'

'But as I understand it, what the AFA is saying,' the *Vanity Fair* interviewer replied, twisting her pen in her hair, 'is that AIDS isn't just God's vengeance on homosexuals, it's His vengeance on every one of us for our tolerance of homosexuality. He's turned against liberal America. Our doubts about the truth of the Bible and even His own existence have driven Him to punish us.'

Aware that she was playing devil's advocate, Frank could do little more than condemn an attitude redolent of the Middle Ages, when Jews and other outsiders had been blamed for the Black Death. Howard, meanwhile, was equally exercised by the bigoted protesters and the closeted studio executives ('Uncle Toms, or should that be Aunt Dorothys?'), who refused to give the film their wholehearted backing. Bela, on the other hand, was thrilled with publicity that money couldn't buy. He was planning a premiere at the Ziegfeld Theatre in New York to outdo that of the Aldrich film in London, where slave girls leading panthers and cheetahs had paraded among the guests.

'You will be there?' Howard asked

'As long as I'm up to it,' Frank replied, letting his guard slip.

'You would tell me if something were wrong, Frank?'

'Of course. It's still those bloody amoebas.'

'Why don't you come and stay for a few days? I'd fly down to LA but I'm up to my eyes in stuff here.'

'Maybe next month or September.'

'Next week, or I'll make the *Enquirer* an offer it can't refuse!'

'Well in that case ...'

Frank wondered if it were a side-effect of his illness that he needed to be cajoled into taking the smallest decision. The following weekend he flew to San Francisco, hired a car and drove into the city, enchanted as ever by the delicacy of both the buildings and the light. Howard and Max lived in Russian Hill, a neighbourhood that had been an outpost of bohemianism when Max first moved there but, since the real estate boom, was being colonised by yuppies. Frank, who had resolved to be conciliatory, knew that the easiest way to goad Max was to congratulate him on his sound investment.

He arrived to find Howard, shirtless, mowing the pocket-size lawn.

'I should have brought my camera.'

'Look at you!' Howard said, giving him a pungent hug. 'Even on a sweltering July day, you turn up like something out of the Sears catalogue.'

'What about you, with your hippy hair?' Howard had let his curls tumble down his neck as though to offset his receding hairline. 'And that belt ... is it a skull?'

'It's Navajo Indian.'

'Sorry, scalp.'

Citrus, Max's marmalade cat, slunk through the garden with her back arched and tail bristled, ignoring both Howard and Frank. 'Bitch!' Howard said. 'All the effort I've made with that cat and it still resents my place in Max's life.'

'Much like Max with me.'

'What effort have you ever made? Let's go inside. You must be bushed.' He moved to pick up Frank's case.

'I'm a year younger than you,' Frank said, grabbing the case from him.

'Sorry, force of habit. I'm a Jew, programmed to be hospitable. Remember Lot?' He led Frank into the house. 'Max, come on out! Our honoured guest has arrived.'

'Yeah yeah!'

Max emerged from the kitchen, with the ominous announcement that he had been cooking and grazed Frank's cheek. For all Frank's misgivings about him, he could not deny that Max had his own unique style. Capon-plump with a face like a child's drawing of the Man in the Moon, he wore a harlequin velvet waistcoat, knee-length cheesecloth shirt, and decade-old tie dye jeans.

'You look well,' he said, as if coached.

'I am well,' Frank replied. Only the two lesions on my feet and the fungus underneath my toenails and the yeast infection in my mouth; not bad, all things considered, he said to himself.

They adjourned to the sombre sitting room. The house was the only one on the street to have survived the 1906 Fire when, according to Max, its mistress and her maids drenched their petticoats in vinegar to douse the flames. In keeping with the original décor, he had furnished the room as a nineteenth-century parlour, with heavy swag curtains, burgundy fabric wallpaper, floral hooked rug, maroon velvet fainting couch, fringed lamps and a collection of cow creamers, which he stressed that he had bought before they became fashionable. It was a sign of his devotion that Howard, who had less interest in possessions than anyone Frank had ever known, should not only respect Max's collection but dust it.

As Max perched on the arm of Howard's chair, carefully smoothing the antimacassar, they made a touchingly improbable couple. Howard had confided in Frank that, for the first time in his life, he was monogamous, apologising as much for betraying his principles as for having a lover who was twenty years his junior. Both had tested negative for HIV. Frank knew too little about Max's past to be surprised by his result but he knew enough about Howard's to share his incredulity at his. While others asked 'Why me?', he asked 'Why not me?', presenting himself as living proof that the virus did not discriminate. He seemed almost offended by his negative status, as though it diminished him as a gay man. To compensate, he and Max had thrown themselves headlong into the fight against AIDS, Max delivering food to housebound patients and volunteering as a counsellor, and Howard as part of a grassroots group that lobbied City Hall. They were heavily involved in the campaign against Proposition 64, the initiative to be put to the November state ballot that AIDS be declared a communicable disease and those infected quarantined.

Frank wondered whether Howard and Max realised that a prime candidate for quarantine was sitting opposite them. He listened uneasily as Howard explained that, while their immediate target was state legislation, the true villain was the federal government, which spent billions of dollars on less virulent epidemics, ignoring AIDS because it was perceived to be a gay problem. As a proud patriot, Frank had always voted Republican. Moreover, he had raised funds for Reagan's 1980 presidential campaign. They had known each other at Warner in the early fifties and their paths had crossed many times since. He might have expected that a man, notorious at the studio as a womaniser, would have shown more humanity. The charitable explanation was that he was afraid of antagonising his Moral Majority supporters; the uncharitable one was that he was an arch-hypocrite.

Howard and Max were united in their resolve to defend what they called 'our liberties' but differed over what those liberties were. Like many couples of Frank's acquaintance, they required an audience before whom they could rehearse their arguments. Although exhausted from the flight and eager to rest before dinner, he was thrust into the role. To his amazement, he found himself siding with Max, whom Howard was berating for puritanism, in the dispute over shutting down sex clubs.

'They give us an identity,' Howard said.

'How, when you rarely know one another's names?' Frank asked.

'A communal identity that's greater than any individual. Not everyone needs his name above the title.'

Try as he might, Frank found it hard to discern any communal spirit in the anonymous encounters that Howard had enjoyed in New York. His own experience with hustlers might have been cynical, but at least he had not felt the need to empty his pockets in case he was robbed or secrete his name and address in his sock in case he was murdered, before calling one up. There were some liberties that it was a blessing to surrender.

He finally escaped to his room, directly above Howard and Max's, in the old attic. He took a shower and lay down for a five-minute doze, only to wake two hours later when Howard summoned him to dinner. He feigned enthusiasm for the aduki bean, sweet potato and squash stew, not even protesting when Howard attributed his recent burst of creativity to Max's macrobiotics. After the meal, he returned upstairs, his sleep disturbed by a dream in which the men from the Malibu party harangued him at a premiere, berating his perfidy in abandoning them all those years before. Somehow they contrived to be behind both bars and barriers, young and old, healthy and diseased. 'Help us!' they cried, as he saw to his horror that his date for the night was Harry Weissman. 'Get us out of here too!' He woke to find his sheets damper than on any morning since his return from Morocco. He made a listless attempt to wring them dry, trusting that the moisture would evaporate in the heat.

With Max heading off to San Quentin and Howard working on a sketch for a benefit at Theatre Rhino, Frank was left to himself. Whether it were from witnessing his hosts' easy affection or simply breathing the San Francisco air, he felt the first flicker of desire in months. He skimmed the *Bay Area Reporter*, lingering over the hustler ads, picturing the services they offered, at once excited and frustrated by the elusive abbreviations (ABC, CBT, FOBU). But, with his body as lethal as when the Soviet scientists packed it with anthrax in *The Time Bomb*, he had no intention of hiring anyone. Instead, enticed by another advert, he decided to try out the all-male movies at the Tea Room Theatre. He rarely enjoyed pornography; the routine action, hackneyed dialogue, cheap sets and wooden performances offended both his sensibilities and his craft. Nevertheless, having embraced celibacy, he had no choice but to seek second-hand stimulation or else to rely on his imagination, which was fashioning scenarios he preferred to suppress.

He took the Powell-Hyde cable car downtown, his peaked cap and sunglasses guarding his anonymity, until he stepped off at Union Square, where two young Texans asked if he would take a photograph. Sighing, he removed his glasses and pushed a strand of hair under the cap. He was about to ask where they wanted him to stand when the man handed him the camera, pointing out the viewfinder and shutter release. He returned to his girlfriend, threw his arm around her shoulders, grinned and gave a thumbs up. After a moment of bemusement, Frank burst out laughing so loudly that he started to shake, at which the man snatched back the camera and bustled his girlfriend away, leaving Frank to reflect on his misapprehension. What might once have been a salutary lesson in humility was now a painful reminder that his glory days were over. Why wear the cap and glasses when the disease was sufficient disguise?

He walked down Market and McAllister and up to Eddy, past a huddle of vagrants, a pair of scarred and scabbed addicts and a floridly dressed pimp. He pressed his watch face to the inside of his wrist and clasped his right hand firmly on his pocketbook. Hostile glances followed him to the theatre marquee where, with mixed feelings of anticipation and dread, he entered the foyer. Scanning the placards, he was surprised to find that, between films, the Tea Room offered live performances from a troupe of young men whose naked chest-shots adorned a grimy wall. Personal appearances were evidently as valued here as in Hollywood, since the headliner was Mike Hardwood, fresh from his starring role in *Flashing Gordon*. Frank recalled the beauty pageants he had judged and state fairs he had opened during his years at Warner. The association was galling, even without the double-edged 'In the Flesh'.

He bought his ticket from a morbidly obese man who appeared to have assumed the dimensions of his kiosk and stepped through a twin set of curtains into a tiny auditorium, where he was stifled by a heavy aroma of sweat, mildew and disinfectant. Apart from a faint red light above the exit, the only illumination came from the flickering images on the screen. It took a moment for his eyes to adjust to the gloom, enabling him to make out the ten or so rows of seats, three on either side of a narrow aisle, with a scattering of patrons, some staring straight ahead, others slumped as if sleeping. Frank took his place, a discreet distance from his nearest neighbour, and attempted to pick up the plot, although, given that the first scene featured two men wearing nothing but boots in a woodland clearing and the second four men wearing nothing at all in a log cabin, there were few clues.

The film ended, and for several minutes the audience sat silent in semi-darkness. Then, to a blast of disco music on the scratchy sound system, the minuscule stage was flooded with pink light, a mirror ball began to revolve and Mike Hardwood, clad head to toe in leather, stepped out of the tangled tinsel curtain to the left of the screen and started to dance. First, he removed his jacket to reveal a rigid torso beneath a studded harness and then, his chaps to reveal a snake-print jockstrap. He stroked his chest, stomach, arms and thighs and fondled himself inside the jockstrap, never once glancing at his audience, as though afraid of contagion. Once again, the patrons remained passive and Frank wondered whether they were mimicking his gestures beneath newspapers and jackets. Suddenly, the music changed. Hardwood jumped off the stage with far more vigour than he had displayed on it and strode into the auditorium, visiting each of the men in turn, clambering on to their seats, gyrating above their heads or rotating his crotch in their faces. The men also came to life, caressing whichever part of him was closest, before asserting the one power they had over him by thrusting tips deep into his jockstrap. Frank fumbled in his pocketbook, hoping that in the half-light he had not taken out a fifty or a hundred. But when Hardwood approached him, he felt unusually squeamish and slipped the bill into his hand.

Hardwood departed to a smattering of applause. Five minutes later *Flashing Gordon* began, but the settings were so rudimentary, the performances so risible and the foreplay so mechanical that Frank felt cheated. Intrigued by the toing and froing through the exit door, he went to investigate, finding himself in a murky corridor suffused by the familiar rock-pool tang of sex. At the far end, Hardwood, naked apart from his socks, was spread-eagled against the wall, while two older men devoured him. None of the three objected to an audience and Frank stood transfixed until, unnerved by the rawness of their passion after the posturing on screen, he returned to his seat. He sat through two more films, punctuated by a performance from a heavily tattooed Latino, who posed precariously on the rattling arms of his seat, rubbing his chest and thighs and exuding a sharp odour. Neither the films nor the man attracted him, yet he did not feel bored. It was as if time were moving at a new pace, which had nothing to do with either distraction or fulfilment.

After the second film, a third performer of a very different stamp from his predecessors took to the stage. He was rangy, with a blaze of red hair and a cluster of freckles on his chest, which he revealed when he whipped off his undershirt and shorts far too fast, leaving himself totally exposed. Where the others had rubbed and stroked, he masturbated with a mixture of desperation and defiance. With spectacular timing, he ejaculated just as the main theme from *2001* reached its climax. Tucking his penis into his saggy jockstrap, he made the customary lap of the audience, accepting their tributes, both manual and monetary. Banishing his earlier scruples, Frank pressed a twenty dollar bill into his jockstrap, trusting that his fellow patrons would be equally generous since, having given his all, he would be too drained for a repeat performance. But to his surprise, when he ventured into the corridor, he found the youth on his knees, circled by three men, who passed him impassively between them. He walked towards them, not knowing whether he wanted to drag them off or join in. Just as he reached them, the young man looked up and, with a faraway smile, beckoned him forward.

'It's thirty bucks for a private show.'

'Not my thing,' Frank said, wondering how he defined *private*.

'No sweat,' he replied with a shrug and resumed the task in hand.

Desperate for air, Frank made his way through the auditorium and into the street. He headed up to Geary in search of a drink. Sprawled on the sidewalk was a skeletal man with a spidery sign reading *Homeless and HIV, Please Help*. Shocked, he folded a hundred dollar bill into his hands and hurried on before he was forced to assess his motives. He found a diner and ordered coffee. The waitress stared at him so intently that he hid behind the menu, forgetting for a moment that anyone could look at him without disgust.

'Did no one tell you you're the spit of Frank Archer?' she asked.

'They did once,' he said.

The image of the redhead whirled through his brain. Unlike

his two colleagues who had calculated every thrust and pout, he had been all too natural. It was as if he had stripped off his clothes so quickly in order to bare his soul. Torn between regret at having refused the private show and dismay that the youth should have invited his own degradation, Frank was consumed by the desire to see him again. Mindful of the danger – and not just on the street – he returned to the theatre and asked the cashier if the afternoon's performers would be appearing in the evening.

'Give 'em a break. All new boys. Half-price for same day re-entry.'

'There was a red-haired dancer. Freckled.'

'That'd be Buck.'

'Buck?'

'You don't want to waste your time with him. He's trouble. Some real hot boys on tonight.'

'There's no picture of him on the display board,' Frank said. 'Is he casual?'

'Casual, yep, you said it. Too fucking casual! He brought in a lousy little snapshot from the booth in Uncle Maime's. Jeez!'

'What about tomorrow? Will he be back here tomorrow?'

'Sure,' the cashier said, turning back to his puzzle. 'He'll be back here tomorrow. You come back tomorrow. Very busy all weekend. No movies, just boys.'

Although it was Saturday, Frank was able to return without arousing suspicion. After a leisurely brunch, Max left to see clients at Project Shanti and Howard continued to work on his long overdue sketch. Trusting that he knew enough about landscape architecture to parry any questions at dinner, Frank told him that he was off to the Lawrence Halprin exhibit at the Modern Art Museum, and made his way to the Tea Room. Standing at the back of the packed auditorium, he brushed off a string of wandering hands until the steady drift backstage enabled him to secure a seat. After four lacklustre performers, he was impatient for Buck. He stepped into the corridor where two naked youths were receiving the homage of their devotees. He asked one, who was pressing a bald head to his groin, if he knew when Buck would appear, only to be told to 'Get lost!' before he had a chance to elaborate. With the other unable to answer, he went outside to quiz the cashier, when he spotted the tattooed Latino, named on his photograph as Sebastiano Blaze, entering the foyer.

'May I ask you something?' he said.

'Depends.'

'Would this help?' Frank held out a twenty dollar bill.

'What d'you think, dude?' Sebastiano replied, pocketing it.

'I'm looking for a guy who was on stage with you yesterday. Buck.'

'Who?'

'Red hair. Pale skin. Freckles.'

'Oh, you mean Jonah?'

'He called him Buck,' Frank said, pointing to the cashier.

'Over here!' Sebastiano led Frank into the street. 'Fat Pete sacked him because he was on rock.'

'Rock?'

'You know, crack … dice … cookies.'

Frank had little experience of drugs, preferring to see the world through his own eyes than in a haze, however colourful – although Gene claimed that the real reason was his fear of losing control. This further evidence of Jonah's frailty steeled his resolve to help him.

'Do you know where I might find him?'

'You're not a cop? Or a PO?'

'Neither. I just want to talk to him.'

'I get it,' Sebastiano said grinning, and Frank chose not to disabuse him. 'He's crashing here in the Loin. I been there. Let me see now … where was it?' Frank took out a twenty-dollar aide-memoire. 'I know. Just two blocks down the street. First house on the corner of Turk and Larkin. Tell him Seb says "hi".'

Having left his watch and pocketbook at home and tucked all but a few bills in his sock, Frank, who would never have dreamt of walking alone in downtown LA, strode boldly through the Tenderloin. Arriving at the designated house, its windows boarded up and daubed with graffiti, he feared that Sebastiano had tricked him, but the open front door gave him hope and, with no thought for his own safety, he stepped into the dimly lit vestibule. The three gashed doors behind heavily padlocked grates smacked of drug dens or gang hide-outs and so, braving the broken banisters and missing stairs, he climbed up to the second floor. Here, there were no grates or padlocks and one of the doors was ajar. Peering inside, he found Jonah lying face down on a mattress that looked and smelt as if it had been salvaged from a dump.

'Hi,' he said, unsure whether Jonah were sleeping. 'I saw you at the theatre.'

Jonah sat bolt upright, revealing the number nine on his blue-and-yellow T-shirt. 'What the fuck?' he asked.

'At the theatre where you were dancing,' Frank said, as neutrally as possible. 'I gave you fifty dollars.'

'Man, you must have needed it real bad.'

'I didn't ask you for anything.'

'You some kind of wacko?'

'Some might say so.'

'Good on you, man.' Jonah's face relaxed into a snaggle-toothed smile. 'I'm out of it.' He lay back on the mattress.

'I went to see you again there today.'

'Fat Pete sacked me on account of how I missed my shift. But he'll take me back. The johns like me.'

'I'm not a john.'

'Whatever.' Jonah's eyes drifted shut.

'Jonah!'

'You still here?' he asked, sitting up blearily.

'More to the point, are you?'

'Where else would I be? This is my place. Oh sure, I see

what you mean. I'm just kind of spaced out. I need the rock to dance and I need to dance to pay for the rock. Wackadoo!'

'The answer might be to give up both.'

'It's no big deal. Me, I just smoke; I don't ever shoot,' Jonah said, as though the distinction were a moral one. 'Man, it's awesome. No one should be allowed to feel that good. But then it's bad, real bad, like if someone's holding you down in the bath, pressing you under real hard so as you can't breathe. Until you come up again. You always come up. Do you want to play?'

'No.'

'Then give me some bread. Just a few bucks. It's only fair, man. You're in my crib. You're breathing my air.'

Frank, who had been struggling to hold his breath in the foetid atmosphere, took a generous gulp, inadvertently justifying Jonah's claim. He stared at the heap of pizza boxes, Coke cans and Hershey wrappers littering the room. 'I'd like to buy you a meal.'

'No, it's Friday.'

'Saturday.'

'I can't eat every day. Not food. I'm like all cramped up inside.' He started to take off his T-shirt.

'I told you, I'm not here to sleep with you.'

'Not for you, man. For me. I'm burning up here. Come on,' Jonah said, with a daunting come-hither smile. 'Just twenty bucks. Ain't I worth twenty bucks?'

'You're worth a great deal more. You shouldn't sell yourself so cheap,' he replied, to the echo of Teri's laughter.

'I knew it,' Jonah said, reaching out and grabbing his crotch. 'You're hard!'

'I have AIDS,' Frank said, acutely conscious that the first person in whom he confided, far from being one of Debra's 'trusted friends', was a stranger, ignorant of his identity, who would have no credibility in court.

'So? We all have to die of something.'

'With that attitude, you'll die far too young.'

'You threatening me?' Jonah jumped up, his eyes at once ablaze and unfocussed.

'Of course not. I'm trying to protect you.'

'I got all the protection I need. I got friends, see, downstairs, with guns. I just have to bang on the floor and they'll come running. Pow, pow!' He put his hands together and shot onomatopoeic bullets at Frank. 'Come on, man. I know you're loaded. Just ten bucks.'

'Not for you to buy drugs.'

'Then get the fuck out of here! Go on, fuck off out of it!' He pushed Frank out of the room, leaving a ghostly handprint on his shirt.

The dispiriting encounter made him all the more grateful to be leaving San Francisco in the morning. He returned home, where he spent August and September fighting a lingering bout of bronchitis. Apart from occasional visits to the Countess and regular Sunday lunches with David and Byron, he saw no one. His closest companion was Popeye, whose affection he had painstakingly won. One evening when he was reading in bed with the dog beside him, a liberty he had never permitted him in Gene's day, a distraught Audrey rang with the news that Tommy had died of an overdose. Although shocked, he was not surprised since, if ever anyone had been destined for an early grave, it was his former stepson. At once so privileged and so deprived, he had been the victim first of a rancorous divorce and then of a rootless adolescence. In his twenties, he had failed as a competitive yachtsman, rock band manager, butterfly farmer, and finally husband, having married a country singer even more troubled than himself. The last time that Frank had seen him was at Gene's funeral, shortly after which he had been convicted of battery and spent a year in a Montana jail.

Frank flew to Newport, where the funeral was to be held in the summer cottage Audrey shared with her senile mother,

Loelia, and slow brother, Quinn. It was a house in which he had never felt welcome. Audrey's parents had disapproved of her marriage to an actor, even one with a more illustrious pedigree than their own. But then they had disapproved of her divorce from Austen. Despite the tangible evidence of his cruelty, her mother exhorted forbearance, assuring her that scars fade with time. Choking back his resentment, he entered the drawing room, where he found both women, together with a sharp-featured nurse in a starched uniform whom he trusted was there for Loelia. Offering his condolences, he hugged Audrey, who felt more birdlike than ever, breaking away when her mother began to scream.

'Are you one of his men?'

'Whose, Loelia?'

'Buonaparte's? He came here last night on his way to Bunker Hill. He wanted shelter for his troops. I refused when they told me he was a Bolshevist.'

'Hush, Mother. It's Frank. You remember Frank? Tommy's stepfather.'

Her eyes filled with tears yet, notwithstanding her loss, she treated her mother with the tenderness that had captivated him when they first met aboard the *Queen Mary*. He had told Gene then and there that, were he ever to marry, she would be the one, even though to the best of his knowledge she was the devoted Mrs Austen Pellingham III. He invited her to stay should she visit LA and, to his surprise, she called him four years later when she came to California for the Santa Anita handicap, having survived a divorce whose prurient details had been trumpeted across the globe.

As their friendship deepened, Audrey felt it only right to tell him that, on doctor's advice as well as her own inclination, she had foresworn sex. Frank responded by admitting that, despite his temporary exile to the pool house, Gene was far more to him than just a manager. Audrey was delighted to find that the last barrier to their intimacy had been removed, while Frank was thrilled to think that for the first time his image might become a reality. Having resolved to propose, he sought permission not from her father but from Gene who, to his relief, was all in favour. Not only did he like Audrey, but he regarded her as less of a threat than any of Frank's 'flings' and expressed the hope that marriage would put paid to his philandering. Audrey, for her part, appeared to be equally attracted by the prospect of being a movie star's wife, living in a clement climate and hoodwinking a public that had hounded her.

The first two years of marriage were an extended honeymoon. Everyone, including the newlyweds themselves, agreed that they made a charming couple. They were a genuine, if unconventional, family, with Gene keeping Audrey company while Frank was filming, and all of them looking after Tommy. But Audrey's nerves grew increasingly brittle. Her protracted custody battle with Austen took its toll and her ultimate victory brought little joy, since Tommy blamed her for separating him from the father he both loved and feared. Desperate for distraction, she accepted every invitation and, when none was forthcoming, threw impromptu parties of her own. Frank regularly returned from the studio to find the house filled with strangers, until he took to slipping in at the back door, asking Marybeth to fix him a sandwich and creeping up to bed. Reluctantly, they decided to separate and, for once, the press statement citing mutual affection and respect was true. Audrey returned east to resume life among the Upper Ten, squired by a stream of socially prominent, financially embarrassed men, an arrangement that suited everyone except Tommy, who lost the only stable home he ever knew.

Frank had promised to visit him in jail, but Morocco and AIDS intervened. As he sat in the hushed church, listening to the priest's hollow sermon, he bitterly reproached himself for his neglect. Determined not to make the same mistake with

Jonah, he bade farewell to Audrey and her family, carefully avoiding Austen, left paralysed and speechless by a series of strokes, and drove to the airport where he switched his flight from LA to San Francisco. On arrival, he checked into the Fairmont without contacting Howard, and the next morning returned to the Tenderloin, only to find Jonah's house even more ramshackle than before: the front door smashed, two of the grates in the vestibule torn down and the doors kicked in – although whether by a rival gang or the police was impossible to tell. The upper floors were equally derelict, the only sign of life an intrusion of roaches. Despondent, he made his way to the Tea Room, the one other place that might hold clues to Jonah's whereabouts. The cashier was in his booth, still hunched over a puzzle book.

'May I ask you something?' Frank asked.

'Free country.'

'Do you remember a red-haired performer who was here when I came in July? Jonah. Although he went under the name of Buck.'

'Sure. I'll tell you now what I told you then. That kid ain't no good. A guy like you should know better.'

'Like me?'

'Please! Those shades ain't fooling no one.'

At any other time, the cashier's words would have sent him running, but Frank was possessed by the need to find Jonah. Seeing Sebastiano's photograph still up in the foyer, he felt fresh hope.

'May I buy a ticket?' he asked.

'What do you think?'

The cashier tore off a faded ticket and handed it to Frank, who felt that he was returning to the scene of a crime. The patrons looked as if, apart from venturing backstage, they too had not left their seats since his last visit. He sat through three films and two performances in increasing gloom, until Sebastiano emerged from the tinselly curtain and embarked on a routine that, to the best of his recollection, was identical to that of two months before. The moment it was over, he rushed through the exit door, where Sebastiano was waiting to greet his fans.

'What are you after?' he asked, as Frank brandished a twenty-dollar bill.

'Information.'

'Oh yeah? What sort?'

'About Jonah, who used to dance here. I spoke to you once before. You told me where to find him, in a house on the corner of Turk and Larkin. Do you remember?'

'May do.'

'Do you know where he is now?' He pressed the twenty in Sebastiano's clammy palm.

'He came back. He and Fat Pete had some kind of thing going.'

'The cashier?'

'The boss man, sure. But he was more spaced out than ever. I heard he was hanging at the Meat Rack, outside the Peter Pan bar at Market and Mason.'

'What time?'

'Any time, dude. Take your pick.'

Afraid that the cashier might not be alone in recognising him, Frank waited until dark to investigate. Even so, he asked the cab driver to drop him two blocks from the bar, inadvertently picking the Chez Paree, a strip joint with a neon sign of a fishnet-clad leg about to do a high kick.

He walked towards the bar, where three men were standing a studied distance from each other, their nonchalant poses belied by their hungry stares. One of them, instantly identifiable by his hair, was Jonah.

'How much?' he asked, eager to escape as quickly as possible.

'Thirty,' Jonah replied.

'Come on then.'

'You got a place?'

'No, don't you?'

'I know a hotel where you can rent a room for an hour. Real cheap.'

'That'll do fine.'

They walked in silence to the Alder hotel, two blocks south of Market. Had Frank been driven by lust, the drab, dusty foyer with the single chipped vase of plastic roses and the yellowing sign reading 'No prostitution, drugs, drug-dealers, weapons, loitering, trespassing, drinking of alcohol' would have killed it. Although to all appearances they were breaking the first of these rules, the desk clerk handed Frank a key. He followed Jonah up the stairs, shocked when he switched on the light in the dingy bedroom to see that his face was pustular, his cheeks raw, and his nose and right eyelid swollen.

'What happened to your skin?'

'No sweat, man, I'm clean. I don't have AIDS or nothing. It's impetigo – man, what kind of a name is that? I thought it was like when you were afraid of heights. But I got it from picking up bills from the johns at the Tea Room and then touching my face. Because money is dirty. There's nothing dirtier than money. Now they won't let me dance there and they're why I got it. Dickheads!'

'Do you remember me?'

'I can't rightly say, but then half the time I don't remember myself. I wake up and think "what the fuck?". Then it comes back to me. Did we trick? Wait! No, now I remember you. You're the movie star.'

'How did you know that?'

'I didn't. It was Fat Pete. He told me some bigshot movie star had come looking for me. I thought he was fucking with me, man. He said he hadn't recognised you till later. He said you used to be real good-looking.'

'I'm sorry to disappoint you.'

'I don't know zip about the movies. My pa would never

let any of us go. The first time I saw one I was thirteen and hitched into Medford.'

'Did you enjoy it?'

'I can't rightly say. I enjoyed the old-timer who gave me a blowjob in the restroom. So what do you like me to do?'

'Can't we just talk?'

'You're weird.'

'Really?' Frank asked, wondering what could be more weird than an old man fellating a teenager in a cinema lavatory.

'I ain't got nothing to say.'

'Where will you sleep tonight?'

'Depends who's paying.'

'And if no one does?'

'There are places. A guy I know in a movie house lets me sack out in his booth. And, if he's not working, there's the park. But you have to watch out for the freaks.'

'What if I pay for you to sleep here?' Frank asked, dismissing the thought of taking him back to the Fairmont.

'And you'll sleep here with me?'

'No.'

'Why'd you do that?'

'Because I can.'

'Gimme the money instead.'

'No way.'

'You can't blame a guy for trying,' Jonah said, flashing his broken smile.

'Will you do that? Then I can come by in the morning and drive you along the coast.'

'Why?'

'What's with all the "whys"? Because we both need to get out of the city … because I want to help you.'

'Gimme some bread. That'll help me.'

'I'll give you two hundred dollars – no strings – at the end of the day.'

'You really are weird!'

'Promise me you'll be here.'

'Maybe.'

To Frank's surprise, Jonah was waiting in the foyer when he drove up the next morning. 'I'm only here because I want to,' he said.

'What better reason? I'm taking you up to Russian River.'

'You'll bring me back, right?'

'You'll just have to trust me.'

After stopping to buy Jonah a milkshake and some doughnuts, they drove along the freeway to Bodega Bay, retracing a journey that Frank had made with Gene four years earlier.

'Tell me about your life,' he asked, as Jonah slurped his drink.

'Don't you have your own life? Why do you want mine?'

'I don't. I want to know about it so I can help you.'

'No, you don't. You say you do but that's just to make you feel good about yourself. Dick, dick, dick, that's all johns think about! It's inside your heads all day long. Where can I get some dick? Where can I get some more dick? If I go out at lunch, will I get some dick? If I stop by the restroom, will I get some dick? Have I got time for some dick before I go home?'

'That's a pretty bleak view of human nature.'

'So? When a john asks me what do you like, what he means is what do you like that I like. He doesn't give a shit about me. Just wants to be sure that we'll click well enough so as he can drop his load.'

'Not everyone's the same.'

'No? You get your kicks by listening to me talk. So, you want me to talk dirty?'

'Not at all. I want you to tell me about yourself.'

'That's not worth two hundred bucks. It's not worth twenty.'

'Let me be the judge of that. Where did you grow up?'

'Applegate Valley, Oregon. Next question.'

'What was your father?'

'A bastard. My three brothers were bastards. I quit school at fourteen, jacked my eldest brother's bike and hightailed it out of there. And I ain't never going back. That do you?'

'Not at all. That's two dollars' worth. You'll have to do better than that.'

'My folks are God-fearing Methodists. I was always the odd one out. When I was born, I had all this red hair. My grand-pappy told my ma I had the devil inside me. Nothing I did over the next fourteen years made him change his mind.'

'Another two dollars' worth.'

'We'll be here all day!' Jonah said, snuggling in his seat and, for the first time, appearing to enjoy himself.

'We've got all day.'

'You want to hear when I first did it? That must be worth at least ten bucks.'

'Possibly.'

'Bible camp. He was a deacon of our church and one of the camp counsellors. He called me into his cabin and told me there'd been complaints. Some of the other boys had told him I was a girl. He needed to check me out. So he made me take off my clothes. He said my skin was too soft for a boy. Then he started stroking my dick – though the word we used was tallywacker. It got hard, so he said it showed how I wanted it. And he pulled down his shorts and fucked me. He shot his scum inside me. When he pulled out, there was blood and he went ape. He blamed me for the blood on his dick.'

'He raped you?'

'That's just a word.'

'Was there no one you could tell? What about your father?'

'You kidding me? My father, elder of the Free Methodist Church. Leader of the local chapter of the John Birch society – you know, against your rights, my rights, any rights but their own.'

'That's sad.'

'No shit? Was that worth ten bucks?'

'Let's stop the calculations. I'm giving you the money. You tell me what you think is important.'

'No way! There has to be a price. There's always a price. You say you don't want my butt or my dick. You want my thoughts … my story, as if that makes you better than the rest. Well, it don't. No way, man!'

They arrived in Guerneville and went for a pizza at Stumptown Annie's, where Frank had unfinished business. On his visit with Gene, they had been introduced to the owner, Leonard Matlovich, the gay air force sergeant who had taken on the US military. Gene, who had never fully recovered from his blue discharge, was excited to meet a man who had risked his career for his principles. Matlovich was equally excited to meet one of his favourite movie stars. Only Frank was uneasy. Feeling cornered, he refused to be photographed, faked a headache and left. Although he apologised later to Gene, he had long regretted his rudeness to Matlovich and hoped for a chance to make amends. But the restaurant had changed hands, so he sat and watched while Jonah ate an eighteen-inch pizza with every topping except mushrooms, which reminded him of home. In-between bites he related the rest of his story, which he seemed as anxious to complete for his own sake as for Frank's.

'I met this Cuban guy in Union Square. He told me how I could dance at the Tea Room. He showed me the ropes: how to get by and how to do the johns on the side. At first it was gross, but you sort of get used to it.'

'I'm sorry.'

'Why? It's not your fault. The third day I was there, one of the guys snuffed himself. OD'd on Quaaludes and sleeping pills. What a waste!'

'Was he your age?'

'Shit man, not that sort of waste! He should have done it in front of a cop car. Left them to clean up the mess.'

Frank leant across the table and clasped Jonah's arm. To his relief, he did not recoil. 'Have you given any thought to what you want to do next? You can't stand on street corners forever.'

'Course I have. I'm going to LA.'

'I live in LA.'

'Big deal! Are you asking me to move in?'

'No,' Frank said, his rational mind to the fore.

'Why say it then?'

'I might be able to help you find a job … somewhere to live.'

'Oh yeah, I get it. And you'd come by nights to collect the rent?'

'No, I really want to help you.' He thought of Howard and how different his life would have been without his curator. 'Put you through college.'

'No way! College is for wooses. I got a job lined up. See!' He took a grubby, crumpled card from his pocket, with the name and address of Hunter Coburn, Courvelle Studios, San Fernando. 'He's a talent scout. He saw me at the Tea Room. He said there was a market for redheads.'

'In porn?'

'I just got to get my shit together and my face clear and then I'm heading out to LA. I'm going to grow me a little beard. One of those goat things, you know. And I'm going to bulk up. And then I'll call him. See, you're not the only one who'll be in the movies. He said he can make me a star.'

4

Ever since his appearance at the Golden Globes, rumours had been circulating about Frank's health. The camera that had once been his friend had betrayed him. It was not until he saw himself in the footage that he realised how haggard he looked. Felix Butler, his press spokesman, put out a statement that he was suffering from amoebas contracted fourteen months earlier in Morocco. Nevertheless, the rumours persisted, and friends coupled their concern with veiled hints about alternative diagnoses. A spate of opportunistic infections racked him, body and spirit. Was it shallow of him to be most anxious about his lesions? They had spread from his feet to his chest, until he no longer used the pool for fear of being seen by the staff. Then a week after collecting his statuette at the Beverley Hilton, he developed shingles, first on his ribs and shoulders and later on his neck, leaving his skin itching, burning and scabbed.

The announcement of his fifth Oscar nomination on the eleventh of February should have thrilled him but, although he was grateful for the accolade, which, given the timing, felt more like a valediction than a validation, he feared that the ensuing media spotlight would increase the risk of exposure. To his delight, *Flesh and Brimstone* featured in four other categories: best original score; best visual effects; best supporting actress for Dorothy; and, especially welcome, best adapted screenplay for Howard. The studio, rewriting history as flagrantly off screen as on, claimed credit for its staunch support of the film in the face of exceptional pressure; Bela, with greater justification, declared that his faith had been vindicated. Although no one could have been happier than Frank at the reversal in the film's fortunes, he balked at the campaign of interviews, talk shows, private screenings and meet-and-greets that Columbia and Cornerstone were launching to woo the Academy's voters. How could he commit to any public appearances when days of bowel-wrenching constipation were followed by chronic diarrhoea?

After fifteen months of concealing his condition, a bout of pneumonia forced him to seek help. Debra insisted on his admission to Cedars-Sinai and, with practicalities to be addressed, he turned to his agent. Despite a professional relationship of nearly forty years, they had never been intimate and he was touched by Lenny's unwavering loyalty. He hurried to the house with a huge spray of lilies for which he immediately apologised – 'Goddammit, I told the girl, I didn't want a wreath' – before kissing Frank's forehead in a mixture of sentimentality and bravado. Given the stories the previous spring that Burt Reynolds was being treated for AIDS in San Francisco, Lenny insisted on blanket secrecy. He arranged for the hospital to register him under an assumed name and, feeling wistful, Frank chose Bobby Wheelan. Then, after hiring a private nurse and a guard and seeing him installed in a room that was the twin of the one in which Gene had died, Lenny left, promising that 'we're going to lick this bitch of a disease.'

Frank wished that his physicians showed similar confidence. They pumped him full of Pentamidine, an experimental drug that cleared the pneumocystis from his lungs, but they were unable to predict how long it would last or, indeed, where the next breakdown in his immune system would occur. The worst thing, at least for one accustomed to controlling his own fate, was the uncertainty. He asked doctors, nurses, even orderlies how much time he had left: 'Days, months, years?' Their only answer was 'Not days.' He tried to recall the various stages of Gene's illness, but they merged into a sickly blur. Moreover, he realised that he had failed him by focussing on his physical decline. The damage to his brain had been all too tangible but, until it began its rampage through his own system, he had not appreciated how the virus blighted the mind. He lost control of his emotions more distressingly than of his bladder. The pain was so relentless that a momentary respite left him terrified that his senses were failing and yearning for the reassurance of the next stab or spasm.

Days drifted into nights. The hospital routine, at first a source of fascination, soon palled. He was contemplating whether to relax the No Visitors rule when the guard asked if he wanted to see a Father Willard Maddox. 'Show him in,' he said, animated by the prospect of a conversation with anyone who was not a medic – even a priest.

'You're not wearing a collar,' he said, as Father Willard entered in shirtsleeves and chinos.

'I'm not here in a pastoral capacity, although I'm happy to help in any way I can. I'm your patients' representative.'

'Have we been unionised?'

'If you've any comments – complaints or even praise – about the staff and conditions, I'm your man. If you want any shopping or letters written or—'

'Aren't you on the wrong floor? Shouldn't you be with the guys on Medicaid?'

'I am. But movie stars are also entitled to representation.'

'So word is out?' Frank asked in dismay.

'Not at all. But the guarded door and the name gave it away. My favourite film as a kid was *Release*.'

'You'll be discreet?'

'As the confessional. But remember, you can hide from the staff; you can hide from the world; you can't hide from God.'

'I wondered when we'd get round to Him.'

'We don't have to.'

'No, I'd like to. My brain's atrophied – and not just from the virus. You'd think that this would be my opportunity to read Proust, but I can barely flick through *Harper's*. Though I ought to warn you that I'm not religious. I've always regarded faith, which presents itself as humility, as a kind of arrogance, with its claim that I'm so special … so important, that only an all-knowing, all-powerful being could have created me. And what's more, a being who endorses all the prejudices of my tribe.'

'Some might say it's more arrogant to suggest that we're the products of blind chance, that no intelligence greater than our own created this extraordinary universe.'

'It doesn't look so extraordinary from where I'm lying, but we'll let that pass; I know that credulity is part of your job description.' Seeing the priest's pained expression, Frank invited him to sit down. 'Tell me honestly, are you the patients' representative or God's?'

'Can't I be both? I was at St John's Seminary, teaching, when I became more and more disturbed by the reports of discrimination suffered by AIDS patients, not least from within the Church. All the sermons about God wiping out a second Sodom! I asked myself what Christ would do if He were alive today.'

'I thought that Christians believed He was.'

'I meant in His physical person. Would He condemn the victims and instruct His followers to do the same, or would He express solidarity with the outcasts?'

'Ouch! That's telling me. One day one of the most desired and envied men on the planet, the next a pariah.'

'Everything happens for a reason, even if we can't see it. Maybe you needed to eat crow?'

'Wasn't there an easier way to show me?'

'God's ways aren't the easy ways but the right ways.'

'Sorry, I forgot.'

'So whenever someone says that AIDS has been sent by God, I agree, then explain that it isn't as a punishment but as a spur for our love and compassion.'

'I can see you have all the answers.'

'Quite the opposite. But I stand by the ones I have. So I resigned from the seminary and applied for the job here, working with AIDS patients, many of whom are rejected even within the hospital system itself.'

'I know all about the body bags.'

'I help men who want me to contact their families and others who want me to keep them away. Perhaps the hardest thing is to tell parents who've wished their son dead that he's actually dying.'

'Bravo! Forgive me if you detect a note of cynicism, but isn't this in the best tradition of your Church? I'm not hot on names but I remember saints who kissed beggars' feet and lepers' sores. Would you like to kiss my lesions?' He unbuttoned his pyjama jacket.

'It's understandable that you should be angry.'

'I'm not angry; I'm disgusted. You claim to be here to help us, when you need us to be helpless so that you can parade your goodwill. Just as you need us to sin so that you can forgive. And, even more deviously, you need the Church to be callous so that you can be humane. Not just holier than thou but holier than the pope!' A shooting pain from his ribcage drove him down on the pillows. 'I'm not sure if any of that made sense.'

'It made perfect sense, I'm afraid.'

'Don't look so hurt! You don't have the right. Try having an iron band pressing into your chest; a herd of elephants stampeding through your head; bonfires blazing in your guts and feet. You get the picture?'

'Is there anything I can do? Should I call a nurse?'

'You can listen. Just listen. Isn't that what you're supposed to do in those little boxes of yours? The truth is you're a fraud. You're here earning gratitude from all these terrified (what was the word? Oh yes) outcasts—'

'I assure you the last thing I want is gratitude.'

'Bet you still get it though – when the whole time you share their sin.'

'Of course. We're all of us sinners.'

'No, I don't mean in a bland, human condition way. But that you're gay yourself.'

'So?'

'So all this is self-interest. There but for the grace of God …'

'If you wish. And I'm glad that you acknowledge His grace. But in my case it touched me when I was very young, long before I hit puberty. I was ten when I was called to the priesthood and that calling was much stronger than any sexual urge. I took a vow, and I believe in keeping vows, whether to a husband or wife or lover, or God.'

'You've dedicated your life to God, who you say created this extraordinary world, and yet you renounce one of the greatest joys it has to offer.'

'Oh that old chestnut! It's like the claim that Christ's chastity made Him less of a man. Wrong! It made Him a different kind of a man. I maintain that God gave me both my sexuality and my priesthood, and He gave me the conflict between them. I haven't rejected my sexuality but, through my work here, I've found a way to express it that fulfils my calling.'

Frank wanted to argue, if only to challenge a man who, unlike himself, had found a way to reconcile his contradictions, but he could think of nothing to say. Engulfed by fatigue, he fell into a deep sleep in which he was swimming upstream with a shoal of salmon, who transformed themselves into eagles and carried him up to the sky. He opened his eyes to find Father Willard sitting by his bedside.

'I'm sorry. I must have dropped off for a minute.'

'Two days.'

'Don't play games with me!'

'I'm not. I've just come in. I'm sorry if I startled you. It's Thursday.'

'I feel as if I'm living in *The Lost Weekend*.' Yet, to his surprise, the sense of stepping outside the normal parameters of time was not sinister but exhilarating. 'I've been thinking of you.'

'I'm honoured.'

'And how much I despise you.'

'That's your privilege. I'm not after admiration any more than gratitude.'

'Fight back, damn you! You don't have to humour a dying man.'

'You're not dying. Your PCP's clearing up neatly. You'll be going home soon.'

'Of course, positive thinking! I shan't ever die. I'm immortal, forever flickering on a TV screen near you.'

'That's a pretty tawdry sort of immortality, compared to the joys of eternal life.'

'Who says I'll get to taste them? Given my record, surely I'm destined for hell?'

'I don't believe in hell.'

'Which is the reason I despise you. I've more respect for the bishops and pastors who condemn us. At least they uphold the truth of the Bible.'

'Which they pluck from its pages like a withered flower.'

'What?'

'When I was a boy, my mother used to press wildflowers in books. Years later, she'd retrieve them. Preserved, sure, but shrivelled and brown. Some had even crumbled to dust.'

'And your point is?'

'I believe that the truth of the Bible is alive – that is alive to interpretation … recreation. Which is what you did.'

'Me?'

'I saw *Flesh and Brimstone* last winter.'

'How come? Your Church rated it O for Morally Offensive.'

'I'm not that easily offended. Besides, I'm granted some leeway. I used to teach a module on religion and cinema.'

'Of course you did!'

'It's a remarkable film. And a textbook example of what I used to tell my students.'

'Don't keep me in suspense!'

'That the Bible is a human document. It wasn't dictated by the Holy Spirit any more than the Koran was dictated by Gabriel. It's an attempt by generations of scribes and prophets, evangelists and preachers, to understand the divine plan, first for the land of Israel and then for the whole world.'

'Try telling that to the Southern Baptist Convention!'

'I do. I shall.'

The question of biblical authority was not one that exercised Frank, but as ever he responded to the show of passion. After his initial hesitation, he came to welcome Father Willard's visits, teasing him that he was neglecting his needier patients in the glow of Hollywood glamour. 'Glamour! Have you seen yourself lately?' the priest asked, a retort that brought tears of gratitude to Frank's eyes. When the doctors gave him, if not a clean bill of health then a decent enough one to allow him to go home, he considered inviting him to visit, before conceding wryly that it would not be long before he returned. So, after sneaking through the bowels of the hospital, they said goodbye at the delivery entrance.

'I feel as if I'm about to be exchanged for a Soviet agent,' Frank said.

'Just handed to your Hollywood one,' Father Willard replied, as Lenny arrived to collect him. They drove straight to Kew Drive, where Hisato, Sheila and Dennis were waiting for him. Lenny had hired two Ecuadorian nurses, Edison and Graciela, who escorted him to the den where a hospital bed had been set up. The moment he saw it, a wave of exhaustion swept over him and he crawled beneath the sheet. Later that afternoon, unable to put it off any longer, he set about ringing his few close friends to break the news of his illness. The first was Howard, whose semblance of shock was no more convincing than Hisato's of normality. He offered to catch the next flight out but Frank, assuring him that he was not yet on his deathbed, deferred the visit until he had regained his strength. He next told Audrey, fearful that, having barely recovered from the press intrusion after Tommy's death, she would be faced with a fresh onslaught after his own. She also offered to come and stay, and he was tempted to agree, if only to alleviate her bereavement, but prudence prevailed, and they settled for daily phone calls.

The Countess, whose suspicions had been aroused by his silence, arrived unannounced one afternoon, took one look at him and declared 'You will soon be together with Eugeny.' She offered to bring a healer from her church but, even if he had been disposed to accept, her mournful tone would have dissuaded him. He refused to follow any spiritual or remedial practice from an alien tradition. So, while willing to dose himself with Vitamin C and submit to lymphatic drainage, he would no more try Indian or Chinese medicine than he would bathe in the Ganges or brandish the *Little Red Book*.

Lenny remained a rock. Echoing the pundits' view that it was Paul Newman's year, he prevented Bela's bullying Frank into Oscar campaigning. At the same time he insisted that he was vetting projects for his return to work. Frank, not to be outdone, proposed that they look for a prisoner-of-war story, which for once would not be let down by the star's robust health, or else a melodrama in which one of his former screen wives returned to nurse him through cancer (there could be no suggestion of a less palatable disease). Then, overnight, a lesion appeared on his cheek. His face had been his fortune, and his fortune was spent. From now on, the only roles open to him were Frankenstein's Monster and the Man in the Iron Mask.

Two days later, he had his first fit and was readmitted to hospital. He was given a room sufficiently like the previous one to be disorientating. On the first night he got up to go to the bathroom and found himself tugging a wardrobe handle.

His legs gave way and, not knowing whether to laugh or cry, he peed. Feeling strangely liberated, he began to chart his body's frailties with the same fascination that he had once done its strengths. Having lifted his veto on visitors, he took a perverse delight in their discomfiture at the sight of his wasted cheeks and oozing eyes and the dandruff like synthetic snow on his pillow. He was amused when to a man – and woman, in the case of Laura and Marybeth – they recoiled from the musty smell of his lesions and stationed themselves by the window, which, though welded shut, afforded the illusion of fresh air. He struggled to show an interest when, from a misplaced belief in their efficacy, they issued bulletins from the world of health. As with Gene, the most selfless of men, life had shrunk to his own concerns. All others were not merely an intrusion but an affront.

Lenny monitored his progress as closely as the doctors, in the hope that he would be fit enough to attend the Oscars on the thirtieth of March. When it became clear that he was too ill, Felix put out a statement that the amoebas had spread to his liver and he was being treated at Cedars-Sinai for hepatic abscesses and anaemia. Howard, who had flown to LA with Max for the ceremony, reported that the hospital had roped off part of the car park for outside-broadcast vans in the event of his victory but, with the ballot having closed two days before Felix's announcement, Frank could not even count on the sympathy vote and, as predicted, Newman won. Howard also lost to Ruth Prawer Jhabvala for *A Room with a View*, but he did not seem unduly disappointed. Even the illness of his oldest friend could not dispel the euphoria he had been feeling since November when, in the same week, Proposition 64 was defeated by a two-thirds majority and *Flesh and Brimstone* received its premiere in New York. Despite his promise to return to fiction, he was discussing further screen projects, the most intriguing being *Love for Sale*, a candid Cole Porter biopic that would be a corrective to the sanitised

Cary Grant vehicle, *Night and Day*. Frank, who had attended several of Cole's all-male pool parties in his youth, smiled at the memory, before wondering whether his own life might be similarly reappraised.

Three days after the Oscar ceremony and the day before he was due to fly home, Howard was visiting Frank when Father Willard arrived. Eager that the two men should meet, Frank declined his offer to come back later, only to realise his error when Howard, incapable as ever of distinguishing the individual from the institution, took the priest to task for the actions of nuns at a San Francisco hospice, who had urged their patients to refuse medication and offer up their pain to God.

'That's not only a disgrace but a denial of the Incarnation,' Father Willard said. 'Christ – God – has offered up His pain so that we don't have to.'

'You forget,' Howard said. 'I'm a Jew; I killed Christ.'

'We all killed Christ. And we kill Him again every time we reject the truth of His sacrifice.'

For all his fury with the nuns, Frank sensed that there was a part of Howard that wanted him to suffer, as if he were the hero of one of his early unpublished (and unpublishable) novels. Chastened, he would admit his HIV status to the world in solidarity with thousands of less privileged patients.

'So it's out of the closet and into the infectious diseases ward?' Frank asked when, after Father Willard's abrupt departure, Howard once again broached the subject of such an admission. 'I've thought of it. Of course I have. Keeping up a front is so exhausting. I suppose I might have been infected by the blood transfusions for my anaemia.'

'What anaemia?'

'Don't be a jerk! Whatever you may say, I refuse to betray my legacy. I've made seventy-four films: a few clinkers; some watchable on a late night or a dull afternoon; but a good half that have stood the test of time. I don't want people to dismiss them as fake.'

'Of course they're fake. You're an actor.'

'And what about all the kids who write to me, wanting to grow up and be Frank Archer? Don't I have a responsibility to them?'

'What about all the kids who grow up thinking they can never be Frank Archer because they're not the sort to get the girl in the final reel? Don't you have a responsibility to them too? And to Gene? Shouldn't you write him back into the story? You were together for more than thirty years: how many Tinseltown marriages last that long?'

'It wasn't a marriage.'

'Whose fault is that? Don't you see the fallacy in professing loyalty not to your lover, not to your friends, not even to your family, but to your public? And if the truth comes out once you're dead, you'll just be another hypocritical movie star, another cheating corpse.'

'No doubt you'll make sure of that.'

Having been healthy all his life, Frank had not appreciated the power that the sick could exert simply by closing their eyes. What would be unpardonable discourtesy in any other context was here quite legitimate. And when he looked up again, Howard had left.

He remained in hospital a further week until the doctors had brought his seizures under control. David and Byron drove him home and he asked them to give him a few minutes alone on the terrace. As he breathed the air, as pure as any in Los Angeles, and took in the view, from the evergreen glades through the smog-capped skyscrapers to the snaking freeways, he felt at peace. Then Edison summoned him inside for a dose of Pentamidine, jabbing it into his buttocks with retributive relish, and reality set in.

The days passed with so little variation that he began to wish that the climate were more extreme. Then one morning as he sat gazing aimlessly at the pool, he was interrupted by Dennis, who said that, driving in, he had spotted a man slumped against the gatepost. 'I thought he must be a bum. He looked real dirty. But then, when I called to him, I could see that he's sick. Real sick.'

'What sort of sick?' Frank asked.

'I think he's sick like you, boss,' Dennis said haltingly. 'He looked at me and said "922 Kew Drive". He kept on saying "922 Kew Drive". Like he knew you or something. Should I call 911?'

'No,' Frank said, banishing his fears of undercover reporters and psychotic fans. 'Fetch Edison and bring the guy up here.'

Frank was waiting when Dennis and Edison drove up from the gate and the nurse lifted the sick man gently off the back seat of the car. His body was wizened, his skin sallow and flaky, his eyes twitching and festering, and the thick red hair of which he had been so proud was matted and drab, but he remained unmistakably Jonah. Frank reached out and took his hand, pressing it to the hollow of his chest.

'Jonah, is it you?'

Jonah half-opened an eye. 'Hey, Mr Bigshot Movie Star, I found you.' His face creased into a smile, immediately followed by a grimace as if at the effort that the smile had cost. Frank told Edison to carry him inside and put him to bed in the den. Shooting him a reproachful glance, the nurse obeyed. It was not until Jonah was propped up on the pillows, the topmost coating of grime removed, that Frank realised what lay behind the glance. In Edison's world, men like Frank and Jonah were so insatiable that, even though the only bodily fluid they might exchange was pus, they must instantly surrender to lust. Frank would have sacked him on the spot had he not been such a proficient nurse, as shown by his gently coaxing the stick-like Jonah into drinking one of Frank's high-protein shakes.

'How did you find me?' Frank asked, when Jonah could bear no more of the wet-sawdust taste.

'I bought a map of movie stars' home from a man on Santa Monica. On the map it's all flat, but you're so high up.'

'You walked here?' Frank asked incredulously.

'I think so,' Jonah replied, before vomiting over the bed. 'Shit, man, I'm sorry. Shit, I'll clear it up.' He made a vain attempt to stand.

'It's not a problem,' Frank said, as Edison deftly removed the sheet. 'We're here for you. But we need to get you to hospital.'

'No way!'

'Don't worry. I promise it won't be for long. Just so the doctors can take a look at you.'

'I don't have any bread.'

'But I do, so stop worrying. You don't need to worry about a thing. I promise.'

Frank kept the second of his promises, taking Jonah to Cedars-Sinai and ensuring that he was seen by his own physician. It soon became clear, however, that the first promise was not in his gift. Jonah was seriously ill. The freckles on his chest and shoulders were subsumed by lesions. His mouth was so riddled with herpes that he was unable to swallow and had to be fed intravenously, although the doctor said that there were similar sores on his digestive tract. He spent most of the day asleep, waking for just a few minutes at a stretch. Frank arrived early each morning to sit by his bedside, gripping his hand in the hope of infusing him with his own depleted strength. Having never supposed that life was fair, he had never brooded on its inequity, until he compared his own imminent demise after a lifetime of fulfilment with Jonah's after one of misery and abuse.

'Am I going to die?' Jonah asked, startling Frank, who was dozing.

'Yes,' he replied softly.

'Good.'

'Do you mean that?'

'Course. Any case, what does it matter? That nuclear plant that exploded in Russia last spring …'

'Chernobyl?'

'The particles are in the air. The whole world's fucked. What will my pa say then?'

'Would you like to see your parents?'

'They won't come.'

'Even if I send them the tickets?'

'Why are you doing this? We never even tricked.'

'Perhaps that's why,' Frank said, grateful that the welter of emotions he had felt on first seeing Jonah had settled into compassion. 'I wish you'd picked up that bloody map sooner. I wish you'd been at the hotel as you promised the day after our drive. Where did you go?'

'Guess! No, San Fernando. That two hundred you gave me paid for the trip.'

'To see the talent scout?'

'Not just him,' Jonah said bitterly. 'Directors. Producers. Cameramen. I don't know the names for what some of them do. But they all wanted to test me. They even brought me here.'

'To the hospital?'

'Shit no, man! To LA, Beverley Hills. Guys who live in places bigger than courthouses. They said they were the backers and the distributors. And I thought, what the fuck? It's only fucking. It's not like I've never been fucked before. One guy even wanted to sniff coke off my butthole. What's that about, man? Gross!'

'Who knows?' Jonah was rubbing a tooth that had been irritating him for days. 'I'd leave that for the doctor.'

'No need. Look!' Jonah showed him the tooth, which had fallen out in his hand. 'And I didn't even pull it.'

'No,' Frank said, unable to share his relief.

'One less to clean!'

Jonah lay torpid on the pillows, not rallying until after the nurse came to monitor his vital signs. 'I started to wonder if

I'd ever make a film at all,' he said, harking back to his days in San Fernando.

'You wouldn't be the first kid in this town to wonder that.'

'But I made two. Three scenes but two films. One's called *A Fistful of Douglas*. I can't remember the other. I looked in Blockbuster, but I expect it's not out yet. Are your films in Blockbuster?'

'Most of them. Not the latest one. They've banned it in case it offends their customers.'

'Then I took sick. Woke up one morning with this thing on my leg like I was swimming in the creek and a leech had stuck to it. But it wouldn't come off, not even with a knife. So I showed it to one of the guys on set and he freaked out. Said I had AIDS and no one would work with me. Two-faced fuck! They all got it. It just doesn't show yet.' He sat up and flung back the covers.

Frank pressed his arm in reassurance and restraint. 'Hush now, save your strength.'

'Why? Who wants it? What's it good for?'

Struggling to keep pace with his symptoms, the doctors told Frank that Jonah had at most two days to live. His temperature soared to 106 degrees, but his remaining teeth chattered and he complained of feeling cold. His eyelids were so swollen that they no longer opened, but the eyes behind them were blind. His body seemed to shrivel like an apple core in the bed. Despite the cologne that Frank rubbed on his temples, he smelt as rank as a broken-down freezer. He rasped and wheezed and spluttered and hacked. Sometimes he murmured the odd word, but Frank quickly learnt neither to query it nor to reply. After a few hours when his breathing was so faint that Frank sat stock-still for fear of disturbing him, he whispered quite distinctly 'My grandpappy said I was the Devil and here I am in the City of Angels.' Then he died.

Frank offered to pay to transport his body home. From the name on his patient admission form, an intern at William

Morris tracked down the Voight family in Applegate Valley, explaining that, having befriended Jonah after he collapsed at his gate, Frank wished to do him this final service. When his family showed no more interest in him dead than alive, Frank bought him a plot at Forest Lawn. A fresh attack of PCP prevented his attending the funeral, but a group of his friends, led by Hisato and Dennis, followed the coffin to the grave. Against Lenny's advice, Frank chose to put both his given and his porn star names on the headstone. 'Who knows,' he said, 'maybe his dreams of immortality will come true? The three scenes he filmed will turn out to be classics of the genre, and men who fulfilled their secret fantasises watching Buck Fillmore on screen will seek out his grave.'

'You kidding me?' Lenny asked. 'Who knows if those scenes were printable? Who knows if those jerks even had film in their cameras?'

'Maybe not,' Frank replied, 'but the two names together convey a truth about Jonah that neither does alone. One day someone strolling through the cemetery may chance on them and figure it out.'

Meanwhile, it was the truth about himself that preoccupied Frank. Refusing to die of liver failure and anaemia while men like Jonah bore the stigma of AIDS, he resolved to disclose his condition. He confided in no one but Lenny and Felix and, when neither tried to dissuade him, he realised that the end was near. However stressful it might be, he preferred to talk on television, where his words would be heard unmediated, than to a newspaper or magazine. Felix was confident that every news programme in the country would be eager to host him, but the only serious contenders were *20/20* and *Sixty Minutes*. Lenny favoured the former, not least because Mike Wallace of *Sixty Minutes* was notorious for his hostile comments in the 1967 documentary, *The Homosexuals*. But Felix claimed that Wallace had recanted and it was precisely because of his reputation that an interview with him would carry weight. Frank agreed and authorised Felix to negotiate with the producers in New York.

He was too weak to travel to the studio, so the producers agreed to film him at home without the familiar backdrop. On the day of the recording, the crew arrived early to set up, but the interview was delayed while the production manager searched for a replacement cameraman. She informed Frank that their regular one had missed the flight from New York, but one of the runners, inadequately briefed, let slip that to maintain secrecy no one had been told the subject of the interview until they arrived in LA. The cameraman, invoking his wife and young children, refused to take part. Frank was appalled. He could have understood – if not forgiven – such an attitude three years earlier, when Gene was dying and no one could be sure how the disease was spread. But now, when the modes of transmission were well-established, the crew had nothing to fear unless they were expecting him to slit his wrists in a gory climax.

If Frank had any doubts about the wisdom of speaking out, the cameraman's attitude dispelled them. He lay on his bed in the den, chatting fitfully with Father Willard, whom he had invited for support, when without warning he vomited.

'Nerves?' the production manager asked.

'AIDS,' he replied.

Wallace proved to be a tough interviewer. He began with some general questions about Frank's career, before asking why he had left it so long to own up to his sexuality. 'Critics might say that it's too little too late.'

'And they'd be right. But I hope that kinder souls will agree that "better late than never".'

'Don't you feel that you were duping the public all those years?'

'Not on screen. I tried to be true to every character I played, whether he were a womaniser or a monk. You may remember Ambrosio?'

'Fondly. You never played a homosexual?'

'No, but who did, except in a coded or caricatured way? That's why my last film, *Flesh and Brimstone*, is so important. Although I play the strictly heterosexual Lot, the film offers a rounded picture of homosexuals, as well as exposing the wellspring of homophobia.'

'What about off-screen?'

'What about it?'

'Weren't you "playing straight", as they say, off-screen as well? For a time you were even married.'

'Yes, and let's make one thing clear, I loved my wife. It was an attempt to be something I was not – or, more accurately, something more than I was – but it was an honest one. The pressures on us all, even someone as cocooned as me, were so intense. You saw it for yourself when you presented the first network documentary on homosexuals.'

'That was twenty years ago,' Wallace said sharply. 'I'm surprised anyone remembers.'

'Oh I remember. I watched it with Gene, my partner of thirty-four years. You said that homosexuals were incapable of forming lasting relationships, that all we were interested in were one-night stands and casual pick-ups.'

'Are you saying that those didn't interest you?'

'No.'

'No, you weren't interested or no, you're not saying it?'

'No, the latter.' Frank's head reeled. He could see where the questions were leading, but he had not come this far in order to turn back. He refused to hide behind his perfect relationship with Gene any more than his marriage to Audrey. 'Gene and I had an understanding. It might not have suited everyone, but it did us. It wasn't either/or; we had our long-term commitment and our passing flings.'

'Many men would envy you your freedom.'

'There's a price to be paid for it, just as for everything else.'

'And we can all see what that is,' Wallace said. 'I salute your courage in choosing to appear tonight without make-up, but the damage those passing flings has done is written all over your face. You have AIDS.'

Frank struggled to keep calm. Felix had secured a guarantee that he himself should be the one to break the news, so as not to seem to be caught off guard, but either the producers had not told Wallace or else he had ignored them. 'That's correct,' he replied. 'But it isn't a simple case of cause and effect. AIDS is a virus. Unlike our current administration, it doesn't discriminate. You and I are old enough to remember the polio epidemic of the 1950s, which disproportionately affected children. Did we stigmatise them or did we redouble our efforts to find a vaccine?'

'Is that why you're speaking out today?'

'I'd be delighted if anything I said accelerated the quest for a vaccine, but the reason I'm speaking out is that I can … I should … I must. My life is drawing to a close. In the Middle Ages, a man made his will on his deathbed, immediately before his final confession.' He glanced across the room at Father Willard, to whom he owed the information. 'These days, the camera has taken the place of the confessional so I'm opening my heart to you. And I hope what I've said will be remembered, not only for my own sake but for the sake of the many others who have died and will continue to die, ignored and unlamented, except by a handful of friends who may be dying themselves.'

The interview left him so depleted that he was too tired to watch it when it aired at seven that evening. But even with his head as heavy on his pillow as an effigy on a tomb, he could not fail to be galvanised by the news the next morning. The programme's impact had been greater than he had dared hope. Reports of his illness featured on the front pages of papers across the nation. Phone calls of support and approval were interspersed with requests for statements. Flowers arrived by the van load until, running out of vases, Sheila took to propping them on the steps of the pool. Nor did it end there. Over the next few weeks he received more than twenty thousand letters, some with gifts: good luck charms; remedies; teddy bears; bibles; hand-knitted sweaters and socks. Some were addressed simply to Frank Archer, Hollywood, like the childhood letters he had sent to Father Christmas, Lapland. Even his admission of infidelity did not appear to have shocked his fans. No doubt there was the usual quota of abuse, but it was kept from him. The only example he saw came from Jonah's father, Ezekiel Voight, who claimed that he had infected his son and demanded a million dollars in damages. He was horrified, but Lenny assured him that the claim would be laughed out of court. 'There's no evidence that you ever met Jonah before he collapsed at your gate. The only hold his father had on you was the threat of bad publicity. Now that your life's an open book, you've nothing to fear.'

In the aftermath of the interview, his once proud body, now shrunk to a skeletal 122 pounds, began to give up. The drugs he was taking to control his seizures were suppressing his white blood cell count, which had to be over 750 if he were to tolerate the treatment for his latest opportunistic infection, CMV. His doctors were obliged to balance the risk of blindness from the CMV with that of permanent damage to his nervous system if he reduced his anticonvulsants and suffered another fit. They chose to maintain the drugs, which suppressed his white blood cell count still further. In the course of one morning, the world slowly drained of colour as in a cinematic fade. By the early afternoon, he was blind.

He resisted returning to hospital, begging the doctors to allow him to die at home and, with the medical and support staff in place, they agreed. Friends came to say their farewells: Audrey and the Countess, now most easily recognisable by their perfume, Audrey wearing her trademark Acqua di Palma, and the Countess ever faithful to her Parisian patroness; Howard and Max; Laura and Diane; David and Byron;

Father Willard. Mason and his wife Sybil flew in from Chicago, with their sons, Julian and James. Frank was so moved when his brother, who had kept him at arm's length all his life, leant over the bed and hugged him that he burst into tears. Mason, who had not wept at either of their parents' funerals, followed suit, and six decades of rivalry were washed away. At one point Frank found himself talking to Teri, although he knew that he might be hallucinating, just as when he heard photographers setting up tripods on the terrace. He screamed at the nurses to draw the curtains, accusing them of conspiring to sell pictures of his deathbed. They protested and he sputtered an apology but, in his darkness, he fancied that the cameras were still there.

Visitors came and went, but Gene was a constant presence. He had been dead for three years, although such distinctions no longer had any meaning. Frank felt his head beside him on the pillow as it had been so often in the past, and his energy spreading like sunlight on his chest. He was unable to touch him, but that signified nothing since his hands were numb. Suddenly he disappeared, to be replaced by an all-pervading glow. Frank was instantly aware that it was Gabriel: not the avenging angel of *Flesh and Brimstone*, but the exquisite youth of a Botticelli *Annunciation*.

'You are Gabriel?' he asked.

'Yes.'

'Can I get you something?' Howard asked.

'I laughed when Gene's therapist said that she saw an angel, but here you are for me.'

'I've always been here for you; it's only now that you're ready to see me.'

'Of course we're here for you. We're all here for you,' Lenny said.

'You have nothing to fear. I will guide you through the transition.'

'Do you mean the gates?'

'There are no gates to heaven. Heaven is unconfined.'

'His face is so pale,' Audrey said.

'Shall I call the doctor?' Howard asked.

'They can't hear you.'

'Not yet. But when their time comes, they will.'

'He's babbling,' Howard said.

'Why did he say that? My voice has never been so clear.'

'Not to them. They hear only its echo. It's time to take flight.'

'How? You don't have any wings.'

'No, but you do.'

Frank gazed in bemusement at his bare shoulders but, on turning to the wall, he saw a pattern of plumage much like the one that Arturo had created for the film. Then as his wings unfurled behind him, he realised that the shadow was real.

'Are you ready?' Gabriel asked, as Frank giggled helplessly.

'Forgive me,' he said. 'I've played my fair share of death scenes. I know I should be terrified or angry or bitter or contrite or at the very least resigned, not behaving like a schoolgirl.'

'He's choking!' Audrey said.

'No,' Father Willard said, 'it's his death rattle. It won't be long now.'

'How can they get it so wrong?'

'Didn't you? All those scenes you played full of terror and bitterness and the rest when, as you see now, you should have been full of joy. This is your chance to make amends.'

Frank looked up into a radiance a thousand times more brilliant than the brightest key light. He had no script, no costume and no make-up; there were no fellow actors to support him and he suspected that he would be required to do his own stunts. But he had never felt so confident of his rightness for a role. So when a voice more resonant than the angel's shouted 'Action!', he moved to his mark, took a leap of faith and soared.

ACKNOWLEDGEMENTS

For help and advice on matters great and small, I should like to thank Luke Brown, Rupert Christiansen, Sarah Dunant, Martin Fletcher, Andrew Gordon, Joe Harper, Selina Hastings, Clive Hirschhorn, Bruce Hunter, James Kent, Ruth Leon, Bernard Lynch, Diarmaid MacCulloch, Angeline Rothermundt, Piers Russell-Cobb, Mark Solomon and Katherine Stroud.

As ever, Hilary Sage has been my first and most assiduous reader.

Many books have informed my research. While listing only those of direct import, I am indebted to all the works that have illuminated the worlds which my characters inhabit.

Robert Aldrich, *Colonialism and Homosexuality*

Y. Ben Arieh, *The Rediscovery of the Holy Land in the Nineteenth Century*

Karl Baedeker, *Palestine and Syria, Handbook for Travellers 1876*

Jean Bottero, *Everyday Life in Ancient Mesopotamia*

Gene A. Brucker, *The Society of Renaissance Florence*

Vern L. Bullough & James Brundage, *Sexual Practices and the Medieval Church*

J. L. Burckhardt, *Travels in Arabia*

Steven Collins & Latayne C. Scott, *Discovering the City of Sodom*

David W. Daniels, *Babylon Religion*

R. B. Dobson, *Church and Society in the Medieval North of England*

C. B. Elliot, *Travels in the Three Great Empires of Austria, Russia and Turkey*
John D'Emilio, *Sexual Politics, Sexual Communities: The Making of a Homosexual Minority in the United States*
John Gray, *The Canaanites*
Samar Habib, *Islam and Homosexuality*
Judith M. Hadley, *The Cult of Asherah in Ancient Israel and Judah*
O. B. Hardison Jr, *Christian Rite and Christian Drama in the Middle Ages*
John Wesley Harris, *Medieval Theatre in Context*
S. H. Hooke, *Babylonian and Assyrian Religion*
Herbert P. Horne, *Alessandro Filipepi, Commonly Called Sandro Botticelli, Painter of Florence*
Arthur Frederick Ide, *The City of Sodom and Homosexuality in Western Religious Thought to 630 CE*
Arthur Frederick Ide, *Yahweh's Wife: Sex in the Evolution of Monotheism*
Mark Jordan, *The Invention of Sodomy in Christian Theology*
P. M. King, *The York Mystery Cycle and the Worship of the City*
V. A. Kolve, *The Play Called Corpus Christi*
Scott Siraj Al-Haqq Kugle, *Homosexuality in Islam*
E. W. Lane, *The Manner and Customs of Modern Egyptians*
Ronald Lightbown, *Sandro Botticelli: his life and work*
J. A. Loader, *A Tale of Two Cities: Sodom and Gomorrah in the Old Testament*
William Muir, *The Life of Mahomet*
Saul M. Olyan, *Asherah and the cult of Yahweh in Israel*
D. M. Palliser, *Medieval York 600–1540*
Pierre J. Payer, *The Bridling of Desire: Views of Sex in the Later Middle Ages*
Frederik Pedersen, *Marriage Disputes in Medieval England*
Michael Rocke, *Forbidden Friendships*
David Rosenberg, *Abraham: The First Historical Biography*

Jacques Rossiaud, *Medieval Prostitution*

Louis Félicien de Saulcy, *Narrative of a journey round the Dead Sea, and in the Bible lands, in 1850 and 1851*

Naomi Shepherd, *The Zealous Intruders: The Western Rediscovery of Palestine*

Randy Shilts, *And the Band Played On*

Mark S. Smith, *The Early History of God*

Paul Strathern, *Death in Florence: the Medici, Savonarola and the battle for the soul of the Renaissance City*

Anabel Thomas, *The Painter's Practice in Renaissance Tuscany*

William M. Thomson, *The Land and the Book*

Lucy Toulmin-Smith, *English Gilds*

Richard C. Trexler, *Public Life in Renaissance Florence*

Roland de Vaux, *Ancient Israel*

Martin Wackernagel, *The World of the Florentine Renaissance Artist*

Julius Wellhausen, *The Babylonian Exile*

D. J. Wiseman, *Nebuchadrezzar and Babylon*

K. L. Wood-Legh, *Perpetual Chantries in Britain*

Ron Zadok, *The Jews in Babylonia*